Michael J Mc Glynn grew up in County Clare among the crags and wild places of the West of Ireland. His interest in writing was held in abeyance while he pursued his career as an antiques dealer. He now lives at Lough Derg between the heather-strewn, wooded hills of Clare and North Tipperary. This is his first novel.

Veiled Summer

Michael J Mc Glynn

A NOVEL

Rushwater

First published in Ireland 2012

British Library Cataloguing in Publication Data. A CIP record
for this book is available from the British Library

ISBN 978-0-957275713

Copyright © 2012 Michael J Mc Glynn

The moral right of this author has been asserted.

Rushwater Publishing
Inis Cealtra, Ballina, Killaloe, County Tipperary, Ireland

www.rushwaterpublishing.com

To
Eabha and Stuart
and
the memory of Dee & Andrew

Veiled Summer

There was a door to which I found no key:
There was a veil past which I could not see.
- *E. Fitzgerald,* The Rubáiyát of Omar Khayyám

The Child

Midlands, Ireland
1944 -1952

Echo surrounds me. Sound reaches out, caressing me. Warmth presses against me with an enveloping softness; and sweet-scented breath is gentle over me.

I have my own sound. I hear it now, somewhere above me:
Seánie!
I hear it again, closer now:
Seánie!
I am floating safe and warm in the echo that makes my sound.

I am one with the light and the shadows and everything that is about me.

Echo is the breath and warmth of mama; *sound* is mama's voice; the sweet-scented air, gentle over me, is the pale, round, hunger-appeasing softness near to mama's heart. She is always there, surrounding me, enclosing me.

There are other voices now, high above me and far away, but mama's is the voice I know. She has a voice that calls to me: "Seánie!" and a voice that is everywhere inside me and around me when she sings:

> *I know where I'm going*
> *And I know who's going with me*
> *I know who I love*
> *But the dear knows who I'll marry…*

Mama is a long way off when she stretches out her arms: "Come, Scánie! Come to mama!" She smiles and reaches out; and my legs and arms move and I fall into the softness of her warmth.

Where I am always, I can see to another place that is great light and has no beginning and no end and I want to go there. When mama carries me outside it is so big that I hold on tight to her and I am silent.

I know when she is gone and I am so happy when she is back and her lips are soft against me.

I am standing and I am walking now, and I can go alone outside into the big place of light and trees and big black birds and small birds that hop and whistle. I can feel the wind but I cannot see it. I can see the sun and the clouds that sometimes hide it and sometimes move in the sky, like the ships that sail in the ocean that mama tells me about when I go to bed.

I am a boy.

"We're going to the seaside," mama says.

I have a red bucket with yellow seashells on it and a wooden spade for digging in the sand. I am sitting beside mama in a bus, looking out the window all the time. The world is passing by so fast it hurts my eyes and I have to look away.

"When will the sea be here?"

"Soon, Seánie…put your head in my lap and have a little rest."

I want to keep watching the world passing by, but I put my head into mama's lap. Her hand is soft and warm on my hair.

"We're here, Seánie!"

The noise of the sea frightens me and I am holding tight to mama's hand. A huge roll of white, roaring water rushes towards me and I turn to run away but mama's hand holds me.

She laughs: "Don't be afraid. You'll be alright."

I turn back. The great, rolling water has grown very small and slaps against my ankles, cold and sharp. In a moment, the sea is again rushing towards me and I wrap my arms around mama's leg and watch as the tumbling, foaming water grows smaller and smaller and ripples over my feet.

I am no longer afraid and I am not holding mama's hand. I am running towards the sea and then away from it, like the other children. Mama is sitting on the sand watching me and smiling.

"We'll build a sandcastle."

I am digging and digging, filling my bucket with sand, the noise of the sea all around me. I am using my two hands to carry it to mama. She piles the sand into a mountain and flattens the top with her feet and hands. She turns the bucket upside down, gives the bottom a slap and a castle is sitting on the mountain. She makes a ring of castles, with more in the centre. Seashells cling to the walls and sit on top of the towers. Soon it is just one big, wonderful castle.

We eat from the basket, sitting on the pink blanket. The sand is soft and warm and is like the colour of mama's hair. My bread tastes of sand, and sand is on my lips and on my teeth and in my mouth. The lemonade takes it away but it comes back again.

Children are burying a daddy. They are shrieking and laughing and covering him with heaps and heaps of sand. Only his head is sticking out. The daddy is shouting: "Help! Help! I can't get up!"

They grab his arms and try to pull him out.

"More! More! Pull harder! Pull!" the daddy shouts.

He comes up out of the sand and they all fall down laughing and shouting. Sand is on his back and on his legs. He rolls on the sand and they jump on top up him. He stands up and runs away. They all run after him.

I have no daddy.

The sea is coming nearer now.

"We'll dig a moat," mama says.

She makes a channel to the sea. The water comes in, slowly at first, then faster and faster and soon there is a river round the castle. I am so excited and I have to mind it when other children come to look.

The river around the castle is getting bigger now and the sea is bashing against it. The castle is falling down in small pieces and is melting into the water. I try to keep the sea away, but it is too strong and too fast.

I run to mama. She is laugh-talking with a man.

"The castle is breaking!"

She lifts me in her arms: "We will build another one the next time."

I stay with her and watch, until my castle melts into the sea and the white rolling water covers it over.

The man is still here.

"It's time to go home," Mama says.

The man holds mama's hand and she is smiling.

"Saturday, then…two o'clock?"

"Yes," mama says.

Auntie Claire tells mama to take me with her.

"I just wanted to go for a little cycle on my own…that's all," mama says, but she gets my coat and puts me on the carrier of her bicycle.

"Where are we going?" I ask her, as she walks with the bicycle down the path to the gate, but she doesn't answer.

"Where are we going?" I ask her again.

"We're going to the river."

"Where is it?"

She tightens the strap around me and cycles away without saying anything.

The man from the seaside is waiting on the bridge and lifts me down off the carrier. Mama is smiling now: "You remember Jim, Seánie?"

I am sitting on Jim's shoulders. We are walking down by the river. My hands are around his head and I am holding on tight. The grass is far away and I can see over the river to the trees and the fields.

"Be careful," mama says.

"He's as safe as a house." Jim's arms are around my legs and mama is walking behind. She is touching my back with her hand.

Jim's hands are under my armpits and he lifts me very high: "Down we go."

I come down through the air and I am standing on the grass.

"Here!" Jim gives me a bag of sweets from his pocket.

"Don't eat them all, Seánie, or you'll be sick," mama says.

We are sitting on the grass, and mama and Jim are laughing and talking all the time.

There is a big bird, with a long neck and long legs, standing in the water at the other side of the river.

"A heron," Jim says.

I am watching it. It is walking and standing, and walking and standing.

"What is the bird doing?" I ask mama.

Mama doesn't answer. She has her arms around Jim and they are saying nothing. I pull at her arm:

"Mama?"

"Eat your sweets, Seánie."

The heron waves its wings up and down, and flies over the water.

"Look mama!"

Mama won't look. She is lying on the grass with Jim and they are pushing their heads together.

I am looking everywhere on the river, but the heron is gone.

"No!"

Mama is pushing Jim's hand away.

"No!"

"Come on, Annie."

"No! No!"

Mama is pushing hard now and Jim's mouth is making funny sounds. He is lying on top of her and I am frightened.

"You bitch!"

Jim pulls his head away from mama and there is blood on his lip.

He hits mama on the head and mama is screaming; and then a man comes running and he is shouting. He has a fishing rod in his hand and he throws it on the ground.

Jim is running away and the man is running after him and shouting all the time.

Mama stands up and fixes her skirt. There is blood on her mouth.

"Are you all right?"

The man is back. He looks at Mama's face.

"It's just my lip", mama says.

"The bastard…do you know him?"

"Yes." Mama says.

I am shaking and shaking and holding on to mama's skirt.

The man goes away and comes back with his fishing rod. He walks with us to the road and lifts me up on the bicycle:

"Stay far away from him."

"I will", mama says.

We are nearly home when I remember I left my sweets at the river. At the gate mama says: "You are not to tell Auntie Claire about the man at the river."

I have a schoolbag with a lunch in it and I am at the school with mama. There are children everywhere and there is a lot of noise. I want to go home again, but mama kisses me and goes away. The teacher, Miss Doyle tells me to sit beside a boy on a long seat. I put my head down on the wood and I cry.

"Seánie…Seánie Luhan!"

Miss Doyle has a ball in her hand. It is green and blue and red. She takes a piece from it and rolls it up and then takes another piece and another and in a minute she has a made a cat. She squashes up the cat and makes a man.

She gives me the ball. It is soft and feels nice but I put my head down on the wood again and cry.

When we go out to play the other children scream and run and push and shove. I don't want to play. I want to go home.

A long time after I have eaten the bread and jam and drunk the milk in the bottle, Auntie Claire comes to the school to take me home.

"Where's mama?"

"She's at work…she'll be home soon."

I don't want to go to the school anymore.

"You're a big boy now. Big boys go to school."

"I don't want to go, mama."

"If you don't go to school you won't be able to do to all the great things you dream about doing when you grow up."

"What things?"

"Oh…maybe being the captain of a great ship, sailing on the sea or…"

"I want to stay with you."

Mama buttons my coat: "You can stay with me…but you still have to go to school."

Francy is my friend and we play tig and running and jumping with the other children. When we get sticks and hit ourselves on the backside we play horses and jockeys.

I can make a cat and a dog and a house with the marla. The teacher, Miss Doyle says: "Good boy!"

She has a loud voice for shouting: "Be quiet, children!" but her voice is soft like mama's when she sings.

I am coming home from school with Francy. I am nearly six now. There is a big branch near the bank of the river. There was a storm last night. It must have broken off the tree. It is a hard job getting it near enough so we can throw it in the water. Maybe it will sail down the river. I drag it by the branches and Francy lifts the heavy end. We push and push and finally it falls into the river. I cannot see Francy for a minute and I am frightened. Then he stands up and he is soaking wet. When he climbs out of the river we laugh and laugh.

Auntie Claire is waiting for me at the gate and she gives out to me for being late home from school and for getting my clothes wet.

She is always giving out. She never plays, not like mama. I have to sit in the kitchen and do my lessons. I am learning my seven times tables: "Seven and one is eight. Seven and two are nine. Seven and three are ten…"

"Be quiet and learn them to yourself," Auntie Claire says. This is very hard. It is easier when I learn them out loud.

Mama is home from work. Auntie Claire is still angry.

"He's your responsibility, Annie."

"I'm doing the best I can."

"Well…I can't be sitting here worrying."

"I can't stay at home all the time. I have to go to work."

"If the child had a proper…"

"Don't start that again."

"It's the child that suffers in the end no matter what…"

Mama grabs me and she pulls me outside along the path and we walk down the road very fast.

"Are we going away, mama?"

Mama stops and sits on the wall. After a long time we go home to Auntie Claire.

We have the summer holidays now. Francy is very excited when he comes running in after supper. There is a badger on the heath. The men are hunting him. His daddy is there. Mama says I can go, but stay with Francy and his daddy.

The heath is a great big up and down place with furze bushes growing in clumps all over it. I am holding the daddy's hand and we are running with the shouting men and barking dogs.

"Look…see him! There he goes!"

I cannot see anything.

We are running again and I am very excited.

We are standing near one of the clumps of furze. The badger is in there. The dogs are rushing in and out and I can hear snarling and barking. The men are standing all around the furze. They are shouting at each other and calling to the dogs.

There is a scream.

Through the men's legs I see a dog walking very slowly. Blood is falling from his head.

"He got him in the throat."

"Poor old Brandy."

The dog makes a funny noise. He walks sideways and falls down. Blood is on the grass.

"He's done for."

A man lifts the dog in his arms and takes him away.

The other dogs are still barking and running in and out of the furze.

Someone shouts: "Hold the dogs! We'll burn him out!"

"Get the dogs out…now!"

"Patch…come here…Patch!"

"Here boy…come…good dog!"

The men are holding the dogs' necks. The dogs are barking loudly and their heads are going up and down trying to pull away, but the men hold on.

"Stand back!"

I smell smoke. I hear a crackling sound, like the breaking of dry sticks for the fire at home. The crackling grows louder and the smoke is hurting my eyes. When I wipe them with the sleeve of my jumper I see the fire rising into the darkening sky. I am afraid.

I hear crying.

"Mind the children…"

"Stay back! Stay back!"

Sparks are shooting into the sky and flying everywhere. Small pieces of burning wood are falling near my feet and the air around my face is burning on my cheeks.

"Keep back! Keep the children back!"

The flames are getting smaller and smaller now. I can see a dark huddled shape running up and down inside the black-red branches and flying sparks. I am really frightened when the badger runs to the edge…

"Get ready!"

…and runs back in again. He runs out and back, out and back. Each time there is a shout: "Get ready!" but the badger runs back into the burning place again.

"Here he comes!"

The badger runs out towards the men. I squeeze beside Francy into the daddy's front and hold on to his arms. The men are shouting and hitting the badger with sticks and shovels. The badger keeps on running but he is not able to run fast.

The men stand away. One man has a big iron bar.

"Aim for the nose!"

The man swings the bar. There is a loud '*thumk*' and the badger is not moving any more.

I come nearer.

"He's an ugly lookin' brute," a man says.

Another man presses him with his foot: "He put up a good fight."

The badger doesn't look so big. I see dark scorched yellow-brown fur. His head is on its side; his tongue sticking out from the side of his mouth.

"I want to go home now," I tell Francy's daddy.

Mama is in the kitchen making an apple-tart. I tell her all about the badger and she shakes her head: "The poor animal."

"Francy was afraid, but his daddy was there."

"I don't know why Francy's daddy didn't…"

"Why have I no daddy, mama?"

She stops rolling out the dough.

"Because…because he's very far away."

"But why can't he come?"

"He…just can't."

"Is he dead?"

"No…I don't know…" she rubs her hands on her apron and

bends down and hugs me "…all that excitement is just too much for a little…"

"But why doesn't my daddy come and see me?"

Mama stands up: "Here…I have a special job for you to do." She pulls a chair over beside her.

"But…"

"Up we go!" She lifts me up on the chair: "Now…watch!"

She catches the rolling pin by the handles and rolls it up and down until the dough gets very thin. She picks it up and covers the apples in the dish and cuts off the bits that are sticking out around the edges.

She takes a fork from the drawer: "I want you to very carefully stick the fork into here…that's it…good boy…and here…and here…"

"Why does the fork have to stick into it?"

"So the apple-tart can breathe while it's baking."

I don't understand.

"How…?"

"One more…good boy. Now…we'll make it very special." She starts making letters from little bits of the dough and putting them on top of the apple-tart "…here's S…and now E…and Á…and N…and I…and E…SEÁNIE! Now…we'll have a lovely tart with your name on it."

I never had apple-tart before with my name on it.

Auntie Claire says she will send mama and me away. I am standing in the yard. I can't go into the house. Auntie Claire took off all my clothes and I am cold. When I put my hand in the tar in the big barrel the men left at the crossroads it was very soft and smelled nice, like the liquorice in Brady's shop. Francy put his hand in as well. Some of the tar fell on my clothes when I tried to take it away from my hands and it stuck on my hair. Francy's mother said his daddy will murder him when he gets home. She told Francy to stay there and don't move and she brought me home to Auntie Claire.

"My God! That child will be the death of me."

"Butter is the only thing, Claire."

Auntie Claire is putting butter on my hair and in my eyes and on my arms and everywhere. I am crying because she is doing it so hard.

Mama comes home and Auntie Claire is shouting and mama is shouting and mama slaps me and I am very sore and I am crying. She cuts my hair off with the scissors and puts soap on it and it hurts my eyes. She keeps washing me in the tin bath until I am hurting everywhere.

"In to bed and stay there!"

"I'm hungry, mama."

"Be quiet!

"Mama! I'm hungry."

"Be quiet! You'll remember not to go near the tar ever again."

I am seven and I am going to make my First Holy Communion. I have new clothes and a medal with a white ribbon and a white prayer book with a picture of Jesus on the cover.

I am kneeling in the church with the other children, waiting to go to confession to tell my sins to the priest and I am very nervous. Miss Doyle said I have to stand up on the kneeling step in the confession box or else the priest won't see me.

It is dark inside and smells like the cupboard under the stairs. I can hear the sound of the priest through the wood.

A small door slides open in front of my face with a rattling sound. The side of the priest's face is close to a wire window with light inside it.

"Bless…me…father…for…I…have…sinned…this…is…my first…confession."

"Yes, child?"

I can't remember anything.

"What sins do you want to confess, child?"

I remember suddenly: "I told lies I said a bad word I was disobedient I hit Francy in the stomach…and…and…" Before I can tell him about sticking my hands in the tar barrel, and about the chalk I stole when no one was looking, the priest says: "Good child…say three Hail Marys for your penance. Now say an act of perfect contrition for all your sins."

"Oh my God… I am heartily sorry…"

While I am saying it the priest bends his chin down to his chest and says words I don't understand and waves his hand around: "God bless you child" and closes the small door. I trip coming out of the confession box because the daylight blinds my eyes for a second.

When I am kneeling down saying my penance, I can hear Francy telling his confession in a very loud voice.

"Corpus Christi."

I stick out my tongue as far as I can and the priest puts the white circle of Jesus's body on it. I close my mouth and wait until I am kneeling down before I try to swallow it. It's not supposed to stick to the roof of my mouth but it does and I am frightened because I ate a piece of bread when I got up and I wasn't supposed to. But I was very hungry and it was only a small piece. The priest said that there was a boy of seven already in hell because he did bad things. I have to keep on swallowing and swallowing until it goes down and I am glad.

Francy's mother is waiting outside her gate. She gives me a shilling and a slice of bread and blackcurrant jam. Auntie Claire gives me two and six before I go with mama in the bus to the city.

We are in Woolworth's and it is huge. There are millions of toys and things in it, and a lot of people. The toys are high up on the counters and mama lifts me up so I can see them.

There is one thing I love: a man in red clothes on a silver motor bike. The man behind the counter winds it up and comes out to the front. He puts it on the floor and the motor bike goes whizzing along. I am so excited. It is the most wonderful thing I have ever seen.

I look up at mama.

She smiles: "All right. You can buy it."

I give the man all my money and he gives me back sixpence. He puts the man on the motor bike in a box and wraps it in paper.

"I'll mind it," mama says. "Now…we must have something to eat."

The smell inside the cafe makes me hungrier. I have a plate of chips and ice cream. Everything tastes lovely. I want to look at my motorbike man again, but mama says: "Wait until we go home. We're going to the pictures."

I am very frightened and holding on tight to mama's arm. There is a dark, stormy place and a boy is running. His name is Pip. I scream as a bad man jumps up and grabs him and I am glad because he doesn't kill the boy. An old, old lady is in a white dress in a great big dark and dusty house. She screams and screams when her clothes go on fire but a man puts out the flames with his coat.

I am glad when I come out into the daylight again.

I wake up screaming. The man in the storm is after me, trying to kill me. Mama says: "Hush, it's only a bad dream. You'll be all right now. Go back to sleep."

"Telegram", the man says.

Mama tears it open and looks at the paper inside. She keeps looking at it, and then she turns and leans her head against the wall and I can hear her crying.

"Mama!" I put my arms around her. Auntie Claire comes into the hall and takes the paper from mama's hand and looks at it. She pulls me away: "Leave your mama be," and brings me into the kitchen.

"Your granddad is dead", she says.

"I never saw my granddad."

"You did…when you were a baby."

"Did I?"

"Yes…you were too small to remember him."

Auntie Claire keeps holding me because she knows mama is crying very loudly and I want to go to her.

"Don't be upset. Your mama will be alright."

Mama doesn't go to work. She lies in the bed, every day, staring at the wall. Her eyes are red all the time and her face is white and looks old like Auntie Claire's.

"Are you going to get up, mama?"

"Go outside and play, Seánie."

It is a long time before Mama goes to work again.

I am eight today. Mama brings me a present when she comes home from work.

She smiles: "*Peter Pan in Kensington Gardens.*"

It is a big book with a lot of beautiful pictures. In the front there is a little boy with no clothes on and he is sailing in the sea in a boat made from branches and ropes and white cloth.

"*There now arose a mighty storm and he was tossed this way and that*" mama smiles again, as she reads aloud the words underneath the picture.

The postman gives me the letter in the big brown envelope to take into mama. She reads it, then holds it in her hands and walks to the window, just staring out. After a long time she turns and puts her arms around me: "We're going home, Seánie…we're going home."

The Man

1

West of Ireland
Early Summer 2001

Four weeks ago, under the canopy of a pale blue sky, seagulls gliding lazily across my vision, my head angled backwards, I lay on the warm sands of Praia da Senhora da Rocha in the Algarve, staring up at the ochre cliffs towering above me. I was at peace, feeling the heat of the sun reach deep into my bones. Adding to my feeling of contentment was the thought that, later on, I would walk on the well-worn cliff-path among the vivid blue pimpernels, the clumps of thrift and the yellows and pinks of so many other wild flowers I could not name.

I turned my head sideways and looked away to where the curious little fishermens' church of Nossa Senhora da Rocha stood high on a boat-shaped promontory: a beacon of hope and consolation for those who wrestled their livelihood from the sea. My gaze moved slowly along the cliff-top and then downwards to the dark opening of the low, narrow tunnel that linked the cove I lay in with the next. I had made my way through it in an awkward crouch, on the previous day, feeling a sense of adventure I had known only in childhood.

Looking upwards again, at the rough, irregular cliff face, I had a fleeting image of the quarry where I played with Tommy, Mikey and Billy Sullivan the summer I came back with my mother to live in Ballycrag when I was eight or nine years old. I thought then that the steep sides of the disused quarry were gigantic cliffs and that the pool of water in the centre was a lake.

The memory of that time led to another and this road that I am walking on here, today, loomed startlingly clear in my consciousness. I sat up, clasping my knees to my chest, a comfort against unsettling thoughts. Mixed in with the rumble of the surf, I imagined I could hear the ringing sound of my nail-shod boots as I made my way to school, on what was then, the rough and stony surface of this country road.

I stood up and walked to the sea's edge, barely conscious of the slap of the restless sea against my legs. I stood there for a long time, lost somewhere in an horizon infinitely less clear than the horizon that lay before me across the green-blue and heaving white of the Atlantic ocean.

Walking back to where my clothes were, I unconsciously dragged my feet in the sand, much in the same way as I had sometimes reluctantly dragged them to the schoolroom at Lisbeg all those years ago. Fear gnawed at my insides then, at the prospect of being in the presence of the master who caused me to tremble whenever I was conscious of his eyes on me, or whenever I was at the receiving end of the searing words on his tongue.

My hotel room did not seem as welcoming that night as it had been previously; nor did the consoling, ceaseless murmuring of the sea lull me to sleep as it had done before. I drifted in and out of a waking-dream, coming alert each time as the recollection of that summer in Ballycrag pressed in on me. The old, troubling thought re-entered my head then, the thought that has haunted me so often over the years, the thought that I have never known who my father was.

Over the next two days, I succeeded in pushing it to the back of my mind and by the time I boarded my flight at Faro it was temporarily locked away again.

On my return to London, an invitation to the *Centenary Celebrations of Lisbeg National School* awaited me. It was the last item of mail I opened and the most unexpected, and yet, I was not as surprised as I might have been to have received it. It was as if the recollection I had experienced while on holiday had in some way prepared me for it. What I was not prepared for was the resurgence of memory and the unlocking of the same old nagging thought that preyed on my mind more than ever.

Yesterday evening, only minutes before I left for the airport, I phoned my mother to tell her that I was going to Ireland on business for a few days. I did not correct the impression she had that it was Dublin I was setting out for. She has grown quite used to my absences over the years. My search for paintings for my gallery and for the private collections of particular clients has taken me abroad to cities all over Europe and further afield, so a brief trip to Ireland did not excite any curiosity in her. I said nothing about the invitation. I did not want her to know.

I left my hotel early this morning and parked the car I had hired at the airport in a gateway, about four miles from the school. The centenary celebrations do not take place until tomorrow but I want to walk this road alone, unimpeded and undisturbed. I have no feeling of pleasure, no sense of excitement only a vague sense of hope that I can at last come to terms with a part of my life that is like a recurring shadow across my heart. If there is any joy at all in it, it is in being here in the restful abundance of the Irish countryside in summer.

For less than two months, I walked to and from school along this road, almost always in the company of the three Sullivan brothers. Mikey Sullivan was the one I grew closest to, especially during the three or four weeks of the school holidays I spent with him before we left Ballycrag. He is the only one who could have been responsible for the issuing of the invitation to me. No one else would have known where to send it to, or would have thought it worthwhile to do so my time spent at the school was for such a short period.

Mikey was the first person I saw when I arrived that summer in Ballycrag after what seemed to me to be the longest journey anyone could ever make.

Seated on a cushion and wedged between boxes of belongings, in the back seat of the car my mother had hired, I eagerly watched the strange, new countryside floating by. As the miles of twisting, endless road unfolded, I fell asleep.

My mother's voice woke me: "What, Johnny?"

She must not have heard what our driver, Johnny Reilly, was saying to her over the noise of the engine.

He raised his voice: "I was just sayin' we should stop for a bite to eat."

We were approaching the outskirts of a town. I caught a glimpse of a church spire, a veil of tremulous light from the May sun blurring its outline. I wondered how we could pass through the town itself, that afternoon, there seemed to be so many people, so many pony traps, carts, motor cars and lorries blocking up the main street.

"Jaysus!"

Johnny's swear, coinciding with a cry of alarm from my mother, sent a stab of fear through me, as the forelegs of a rearing pony almost crashed down on the bonnet of the car. I shouted: "Mama!"

She twisted her head around: "It's all right, Seánie! It's all right."

Leaving the car parked in a side street, we walked back into the noise and bustle of the town centre, the warm air heavy with the smell of horse dung and petrol fumes, and entered a hotel.

I had never before seen so many people eating together in one place and I was fascinated by the sounds of knives and forks striking off plates and the loud hum of conversation. My mother sat, picking at her food, while Johnny relished a steaming plate of bacon and cabbage, piled high with mashed potatoes. He washed down great forkfuls with intermittent gulps from the pint of stout he had ordered, the moment we had sat down. I had a bowl of soup and a sandwich, and stewed apple and custard.

"That was badly needed." Johnny wiped his mouth with the back of his hand and sat back.

"How long more, before we're there?" I asked him

"Not too long now, Seánie. As soon as you finish up your apple and custard we'll be off."

"Just how long, is not too long, Johnny?" my mother looked concerned.

"Barrin' a breakdown or somethin' else, we'll be there in an hour or so...but don't be worryin', ma'am, the old car is goin' fine so far."

I fell asleep again and woke once more at the sound of my

mother's voice: "Turn right at the next cross, Johnny. Ballycrag is only a mile from there."

A little while later I stood up, excitement stripping away the fatigue and the drowsiness as the hill, on which I would now live, loomed before us.

2

On the other side of the hill, Mikey Sullivan stood completely still for a moment, listening intently for the call he had heard away in the distance. Climbing up on the gate and looking out over the expanse of meadow that swept upwards to the gable of my grandfather's cottage, he heard the call again, louder and closer this time, a shiver of excitement rippling through him. Holding on tightly, his eyes trying to focus in all directions at once, he held his body completely still, until the strain was too great and his disappointed breath broke the silence. *It must have landed somewhere.* Climbing higher, he pressed his stomach into the top bar of the gate and leant forward, cupping his hands around his mouth:

"Cuck-coo! Cuck-coo!"

Silence.

"Cuck-coo…cuck-coo."

Nothing.

His eyes searched the line of trees between the meadow and the cottage. *Maybe the cuckoo's found a nest there.*

He ran up by the side of the thickening grass, pausing briefly, his heart missing a beat at the shrill cry of a startled blackbird. He covered the last few yards stealthily, the way he had seen an Indian brave stalk a deer in the pictures. He moved cautiously from tree to tree, his eyes straining upwards for a sight of the bird of summer he had only ever seen flying in the distance, but never close at hand. It was no use: the cuckoo must have passed by him undetected or else it had flown away in the opposite direction.

He moved away from the trees and climbed over the wall into the yard of the cottage, feeling free to wander around at will. He made his way to the front and peered through a window. *Paddy Luhan's bedroom!* He had been in it for a few minutes, the day after the old man's funeral. His mother had been stripping the bed, folding the blankets, and putting them in the wardrobe. The sheets were in a pile on the floor.

"I'm taking them away for washing" Mollie Sullivan had answered in reply to his idle curiosity.

"Why? Paddy's dead. He won't need them anymore."

"Go outside and play and stop bothering me with your questions."

He stared through the window now, at the iron bed with its brass knobs and the striped horsehair mattress.

A dead man's bed!

The hairs prickled just a little on the back of his neck.

I'm looking at a bed a man died on. A stone-cold, dead, old man. His ghost might even…

He turned abruptly away from the window, the unexpected sight of a wandering black tomcat, directly behind him, causing him to cry out in fear. The cat paused for a brief moment, the hairs on its arching back beginning to rise, before it shot off the ground and beat a hasty retreat out over the back wall.

Mikey followed the cat with all speed for a short distance and then stopped, feeling foolish: "Anyone would get a fright if a cat sneaked up behind him like that." He spoke aloud in the quiet, finding comfort in the sound of his own voice.

Returning to the front of the cottage he paused, hearing the laboured noise of an engine as the car, carrying my mother and me, began its slow climb at the other side of the hill. When he was certain that it wasn't the engine sound of any of the cars that regularly used the road through Ballycrag, he walked along the path to the gate and leaning on it, waited.

Travelling up the final stretch of the hill, the engine protested loudly and painfully.

"Will the car be able to make it to the top, Johnny?" My mother sounded doubtful.

"She'll make it. The old engine's as strong as a horse."

She held her breath then, until the car, struggling in first gear, and at a snail's pace, finally made it over the crest.

31

The road ran downwards between hedges of hawthorn laden with the white of the May blossom; with here and there ash and sycamore rising high from banks of fern and briar, and leveled out before the piers of the entrance gates to the Sullivan home. Away in the distance, the winding road was lost between hedgerows abundant with the heavy growth of late spring.

Just below the brow of the hill, at the entrance to our cottage, the figure of Mikey, leaning on the gate, was dark and indistinguishable against the evening sun. My mother leant forward, drew a sharp breath and put her hand to her mouth: "For a moment I imagined it was my father."

As the car slowed and came to a halt at the gate, Mikey's first instinct was to run away, but curiosity held him back. My mother opened the passenger door.

"What's your name?"

"Mikey…Mikey Sullivan."

"Are you Mollie Sullivan's son?"

He nodded.

"Would you please run down home and ask your mother to give you the key to the cottage? Tell her Annie Luhan sent you."

After a quick glance at me, Mikey sped down the hill. It is almost fifty years ago, since his bright, appraising eyes looked into mine for the very first time.

This road, stretching five miles from our cottage at Ballycrag to the school, is unchanged, except that it is tarred now. It is still narrow and still hedged on either side by the wild unruly growth of grasses, thistles, thorn trees, briars, honeysuckle and the odd clump of gorse. Here and there rises a birch, a sycamore or an ash whose smooth grey bark we sometimes studied with an eye to cutting a suitably shaped branch from which a hurley could be made. The landscape is much the same as I remember it, with only a few new houses to disturb it. Through gaps in the hedge I can see the browns and mossy greens of the marshes, and further away, the rising dry ground and cattle grazing.

Here, at this point on the road, is the turnoff for the boreen that led to Hungry Jack Maran's cottage. I had feared for my young life during the hours he had held me there, the sickening smell and the gloom that had pervaded the place adding to my dread. I had not been able to summon enough courage to make my escape until Jack had slumped across the table and the growling in his throat had changed to drunken snores. Panic-stricken, I had run out into the pallid light of dawn and down the boreen, expecting at any moment to hear his roars and the thud of his boots behind me.

That was later on. The story of that summer begins, if there really is ever a beginning to any story rather than just another chapter in the course of a life, on the morning that Mikey Sullivan told me about the plan that had been made for that afternoon after school.

3

"Why are you doing it?" I asked Mikey.

"Cause we have to. You can come if you like. Me and Tommy are in charge…Billy's helpin' us."

"I'm in charge!"

Mikey turned his head and looked back at his brother, opened his mouth and closed it again. It never did him any good arguing against Tommy, who was at least half a head taller than him and about twelve or thirteen then. Mikey was a couple of years younger and Billy was the same age as me.

Mikey caught my arm: "D'you want to come?"

I felt uneasy: "I don't know."

"He's too scared to come," Billy said.

"No I'm not, Billy," I said smartly. "I'll go alright."

I was fearful that afternoon, struggling to keep up with the others, the weight of the rope I had volunteered to carry hurting my shoulder, the thin material of my shirt providing no protection against the chafing of the rough coils. The rope slid to the ground.

Tommy looked back at me: "Do you want Mikey to carry the rope?"

We were crossing by the edge of the back meadow of the Sullivan farm, trousers ends already soaking wet, knees red from the swishing of the long wet grass.

"No!"

I hooked both arms under the coils and awkwardly lifted it up to my chest and struggled on. I wanted to do my part, but now I began to feel more and more uneasy and uncertain.

"How deep is it?" I asked.

"It's very deep, Seánie", Tommy said, over his shoulder.

"It's desperate deep," Mikey said. "There's no bottom to it at all."

We carried on in silence for a while.

"If it had no bottom, wouldn't the water fall out at the other side of the world?" Billy voiced the question that had been forming in my mind.

Tommy stopped short and brought the rest of us to an abrupt, fearful halt behind him. Even Bouncer, the puppy, who had been straining against the makeshift lead of white ribbon and binding twine in Tommy's grip, stopped struggling and peered up at him from the long grass. Tommy stared into the distance for a moment or two: "It's not bottomless," he said, and moved on again.

"Mikey, why did you say it has no bottom?" Billy lifted the sack he had been trailing behind him and hugged it close to his stomach.

"Well, it mightn't be bottomless, Billy, but I can tell you one thing for sure," Mikey paused, "I wouldn't like to fall into it."

We climbed over the rusting, iron gate that led into the crag, quiet and solemn now, the grim task ahead stifling conversation. Tommy, the last to climb, hoisted Bouncer in his arms and handed him over the gate to Mikey, the wriggling, steaming puppy, smelling of ripe summer grasses. Brown flakes of wet rust from the neglected gate clung to our hands and we rubbed them hard against jumper fronts and trousers legs. Streaks of rust lay on our clothes like traces of ancient armour and the acrid smell of iron tickled our nostrils.

Tommy continued to lead the way, dragging a playful, resisting Bouncer behind him. The last remaining raindrops, from the morning rains, clinging to rocks and clumps of rushes, sparkled fitfully as the sun came and went from behind an armada of clouds sailing across the sky in a light, warm wind. Pools of water had formed here and there in the soft marshy ground and we were careful to avoid them: there was no pleasure to be derived from wet feet squelching in wellington boots.

We reached the big crooked rock that Mikey, only the week before, had solemnly told me had once been part of the arsenal of a rampaging giant. Tufts of grass, sprouting here and there from the pitted and gouged surface, were the handholds I had used to climb to the top with him. Perched nervously on what I thought was a great height, he had explained how, for him and his brothers, it was at various times a pirate stronghold overlooking raging seas, or a beleaguered Fort Apache, or simply a vantage point from which they could survey the limits of their world. Here Tommy paused and turned to look at Billy and me, making sure we had the sack and the rope. Without a word, he moved on once more. We were almost there.

A snipe rose suddenly, its sharp, grating cry startling all four of us and flew its fast, weaving arc of escape out and away over the pond. At the water's edge, Tommy, with Mikey beside him, tightened his hold on Bouncer and stared at the green-slimed, peat-black surface.

Billy poked his head between his brothers: "It doesn't look that deep to me" he said, a tremor in his voice.

"It's deep all right." Mikey stroked his chin: "Very, very deep."

I moved cautiously forward. After a quick glance into the murky depths, I moved back into the rushes, well away from the pond.

"Bring over the sack, Billy." Tommy had a look of grim determination.

"Open it up now."

Bouncer began yelping and squirming, refusing to allow even a paw to be thrust into the sack.

"Will you hold it open, Billy!"

"I can't!"

"Mikey! Come over and give us a hand. "

Billy and Mikey held the sack open while Tommy pushed the resisting, whining puppy into it, quickly twisting the neck of the sack and denying Bouncer any chance of escape.

"Bring over the rope, Seánie."

I didn't move.

"Seánie! Bring over the rope!"

"No!" I wanted no more part in this.

"Seánie…!"

I threw the rope. It fell out of Tommy's reach. He turned to the other two: "Hold on to the sack. Don't let go of it."

Bouncer howled and struggled all the harder now.

Tommy picked up the rope: "Let go of the sack. I'll take it now."

He wedged the sack between his knees with difficulty, the squirming and howling of Bouncer not making it easy. He wound a few feet of the rope round the neck of the sack and tied a knot in it, leaving plenty to spare. He handed the sack, with its trailing rope, to Mikey: "Hold on to that. I'll be back in a minute."

The clouds had all but disappeared and the sun was hot now. Sweat broke out on Mikey's forehead, misting his glasses. The unrelenting howling of Bouncer, and the unceasing straining of the sack, began to unnerve him.

"Help me!"

Mikey looked over at Billy, who had moved away to stand beside me. Billy made no effort to answer his call for help.

"Hurry up, Tommy!" Mikey shouted

Tommy came back slowly, chest heaving, arms straining, and dropped a big rock beside Mikey

"Gimme the rope."

Tommy stood the rock on end. Balancing it upright, he wound part of the trailing rope around it and tied a double knot. He let the rock fall back on the ground and placing his right foot on it, he pulled on the slack rope as hard as he could. Satisfied, he dropped the rope.

"Mikey, you lift up the sack as soon as I pick up the rock. I'll count one, two, three. When I get to three, I'll throw in the rock and you throw in the sack at the same time."

Tommy bent down, working his hands under the rock. The veins at his temples stood out and his face was scarlet as he manoeuvred it up over his knees, then to his waist and finally, his whole body quivering, he held the rock chest high.

"Now…Mikey…lift…up…the sack."

Mikey hesitated.

"Mi…key!"

Mikey grappled with the howling, jumping sack, barely lifting it off the ground.

"One…two…" Tommy was searching for breath, "three…now!"

"Wait! Wait!" Mikey dropped the sack.

It was too late. Bouncer emitted a final blood-curdling howl, as the sack flew off the ground in the wake of the rock. Slimy, muddy water splattered Tommy and Mikey as the rock hit the surface with a resounding splash and sank instantly, taking Bouncer with it.

Billy and I, faces stricken, moved hesitantly to the edge of the pond. The water was still swirling, bubbles rising and popping.

"He's sinking now." Tommy's voice was shaking, the sweat running down his face, salting his eyes.

We stood in silence, until the bubbles stopped rising and the surface of the pond was smooth again.

"I'm going," I said and after a few reluctant steps, I began running towards home.

One by one the others followed me across the crag. Tommy was the last to leave.

4

"Seánie! Wait for me!" Mikey called out.

One part of me kept me running on, but another part of me - the part that wanted so much to belong in the world of the Sullivan brothers, to look up to them, to be one with them - slowed my feet. Since I had come to live close to the Sullivan family, I had sensed that my life was changing, changing from a feeling of isolation to a more comfortable feeling of belonging. I did not want to lose that.

I stopped running now and waited for Mikey to catch up.

By the time we trudged into the yard, the four of us were together again. Mollie Sullivan was hanging out the washing, her apron pocket bulging with clothes pegs, a few in her mouth. The smell of wet clothes and washing soap drifted towards us.

"Bouncer's drownded," Billy said.

Mollie took the pegs out of her mouth.

"There's bread and jam on the table…you go in too, Seánie."

We sat around the kitchen table, bleached almost white from Mollie's constant scrubbing, the dark-brown knots like pieces of polished marble pressed into the surface. A heaped plate of freshly baked bread, smeared with butter and jam, began to disappear rapidly, the sweet taste of the blackcurrants and the smooth feel of the milk, offering some measure of comfort.

"It was horrible…" Billy shivered "…really horrible."

Mikey shook his head: "It was deadly."

"It had to be done", Tommy said, chewing slowly on his bread. "It was Bouncer's own fault. He should've stopped chasing and scattering the hens and the chickens all over the place. He wouldn't be dead now if he had."

Billy wiped his mouth with the sleeve of his jumper: "Because he's a dog, maybe he didn't think there was any harm in it."

"I don't think dogs know whether something is right or not," Mikey said, "I don't think they think at all. I think they only do things, Billy."

"He shouldn't have killed the chicken." Tommy finished eating and sat back in his chair his arms clasped around his stomach: "Daddy said we'd have nothin' left to put on the table if Bouncer carried on the way he was."

"He wasn't really a dog," Billy looked across the table at me "he was only a puppy, Seánie."

"He was still a dog, Billy", Mikey said. "He was only young, that's all". He turned to Tommy: "Do you remember the picture we went to with daddy? It…"

"What picture?"

"The one about Lassie, the sheepdog."

"Lassie Come Home?"

"Yeh, that one. It was…"

"I never saw that picture, Mikey." Billy was offended: "Why didn't daddy…?"

"You were too young, Billy."

"No, I wasn't."

"Yes, you were."

"Shut up!" Tommy said crossly.

We ate in silence for a while.

"Just think," Mikey said. "While we're sitting here, Bouncer could still be sinking all the time, deeper and deeper in that…"

"Shut up, Mikey." Tommy glared at him: "If you don't shut up I'll…"

"All I was going to say was…"

"I said shut up!" Tommy was angry now.

Billy wiped his sticky mouth on the sleeve of his jumper again: "Do dogs go to heaven when they die, Mikey?"

"I don't know. Maybe they do."

Silence again.

"Is there a rat's heaven?"

"Don't be stupid, Billy."

"I'm not stupid, Tommy." He looked across at me: "Will we go over to the quarry?"

"No", I said, "I'm going home."

"I'll go," Mikey finished his milk. "I might find more of the stones that look like curled up snails…are you comin' Tommy?"

"No. I've a pain in my stomach."

Mikey jumped up from the table: "Come on Billy". He turned towards the doorway and stopped: "Bouncer!"

His cry was half-way between a scream and a shout as the puppy, his wet, chocolate-coloured body trailing green slime, his short tail wagging as fast as dragonfly wings, came in over the doorstep.

I knocked over my chair and ran around the table to where Tommy was standing, grabbing his arm.

Bouncer came warily into the kitchen, trailing muddy water, his tail still wagging at propeller speed.

"Mammy! Mammy!" Billy rushed out into the yard: "Bouncer was drownded, but be came back."

I held on to Tommy who was staring at the apparition, his hands clenched, his chest rising and falling.

Mikey stood nearest the puppy, eyeing him suspiciously.

"The poor creature…" Mollie said, coming in, Billy holding on to her skirt, "…take him outside and wash all that stuff off him. And give him something to eat," she called after us.

I don't remember how much later it was when Bouncer, his coat dry and gleaming in the sun, his belly swollen from the extra large bowl of food Tommy had given him, regarded us with an indifferent air as we stood around him, still marvelling at his return.

The big, heavy rock had dragged him down into the murky depths of the pond, with no hope of escape. Of that we were certain. God, or a Guardian Angel or some form of supernatural power had intervened on his behalf. Of that too we were also certain.

"We'll go to the quarry." There was still more than an hour left before supper and Tommy was feeling good. "Bouncer can come with us."

The four of us set off, running and jumping, shouting and laughing, pausing now and then to wait for an overfed, relaxed, waddling Bouncer to catch up with us.

In the quarry that late afternoon we played cowboys and Indians. Bouncer was ordered to stand guard over a trail, a role he carried out by falling fast asleep in the sun. It was one of those wonderful summer evenings filled with a wealth of promise. The kind of evening when the ups and downs of life, especially for a child, are suspended, it would seem, forever more. Despite the hunger pangs that told us that it was time to go home for supper, we delayed longer than usual, not wanting to let go of the pleasure that was ours.

On our way back, we talked again about Bouncer's miraculous return from the depths of his watery grave, relieved that the event had ended so happily. We could not have known then, that there were other events set in motion that same day, events that would end not in happiness but in despair and tragedy.

5

About the time that the Sullivan brothers and I were making our way to the quarry, my mother, Annie Luhan, weighed down with shopping bags, got off the bus at the crossroads, a mile from our home. Minutes later she passed Hungry Jack Maran and Willie Cray, the council workers responsible for filling the potholes in the road. They leant on their shovels, intently watching her, nodding their heads in return to the smiling greeting she gave them.

She was a beautiful woman of twenty six years old then, with long fair hair, blue eyes and skin that had the glow of ripe corn in the light of an evening sun. Taller than average, with full breasts and a slender waist, she carried herself with grace and elegance. She bore a strong resemblance to her own mother, Alice Jennings, who had been adopted when she was a baby and who might easily have been thought to be Scandinavian.

Alice Jennings was an accomplished dressmaker and my mother had naturally learned the art from her, even though Alice had died when my mother was thirteen years old. It was income from this trade she hoped to use later on, to support us, along with the rent from the land she leased to Andy Dolan.

As Annie passed out of earshot, Willie Cray slowly removed the butt end of a Woodbine from behind his ear: "Lord, but that's one fine lookin' woman."

Hungry Jack lifted his cap and ran a calloused hand over his flat greasy hair: "She's that all right, Willie."

Willie struck a match and held the flame in his cupped hands to the cigarette butt: "She'd make the hairs rise on a gooseberry."

Hungry Jack made no reply.

"Fancy her now, would you?" Willie ran a beefy arm across his sweating forehead, bending his head to conceal his grin.

Hungry Jack scratched at his scalp and continued to gaze after Annie.

"Well, Jack! Would you fancy her or not?"

Hungry Jack put his cap back on and pulled down hard on the peak: "Arra…what would I be doin' fancyin' someone like her?"

"Ah now, Jack…she'd be a lot aisier than you'd think."

"How so?" Hungry Jack turned his attention to Willie his nicotine stained tongue resting on the lower lip of his open mouth.

Willie sucked at the Woodbine: "Ah…you'd have no trouble gettin' in there…" he threw the butt on the road and stamped on it "…a one like her would be desperate for a man."

Hungry Jack took a pack of Sweet Afton from his trousers and lit a cigarette, drawing the smoke deep into his lungs and blew it out his nostrils: "She's a fine lookin' woman…she could have anyone she wants."

Willie rested the shovel against his shoulder and spat on his hands. Wiping them on his sagging belly, he grasped the shovel and thrust it into a pile of chips: "No…'tisn't like that at all"

"I don't folley you."

Willie looked sideways at Hungry Jack from under half-closed eyelids: "All a man has to do with a woman like her is walk in an' as soon as he gets the chance grab her…sets her off straight away. She'd be on top of him in a flash."

"You're jokin'!"

Willie withdrew the half-filled shovel and threw the chips into a pothole "No…I'm not…anyone with any bit of experience 'ill tell you that." The shovel clanged against slivers of stone as he patted the barely filled pothole: "No decent man would be bothered wid her though…couldn't afford to be seen with her nayther." He stood back and surveyed the pothole: "Mind you, if a man didn't care one way or the other, he could be in there an' havin' the time of his life." He patted the pothole again: "To tell the truth I'd be in there myself only I'm a married man."

Hungry Jack lived alone and was still a bachelor at thirty-five. He had never been in bed with a woman. He had once tried it on with a travelling woman that had called to the cottage begging, but she had grabbed a frying pan from the ashes and had nearly split his head open.

Willie Cray's bulky frame shook with silent laughter now as a tense Hungry Jack stared after the receding figure of Annie.

Further along the road Annie heard the sound of a motor car travelling in her direction. She did not turn her head until she was aware of the nearness of it, moving slowly behind her. She stood aside on the narrow dusty road and smiled as she recognised Joe Sullivan at the wheel. The car stopped as it drew level with her.

"'Tis too hot to be dragging all those bags around, Annie," Joe said, as he got out of the car. He took the bags from her and put them on the back seat.

"Thanks, Joe."

Annie settled herself in the passenger seat, glad of the lift. Her feet felt as though they were burning in the high heel shoes.

"Hot in town today, I'd say, Annie?"

"Yes, it was."

The dust swirled up behind them as they drove towards Ballycrag.

"I told you before, if you'd let me know, I could give you a lift into town."

"Thanks, Joe."

Joe looked across at her, his eyes sweeping downwards from the soft rounded profile, and the unblemished skin, to the swell of the breasts under the cream blouse. His gaze lingered, his hands tightening on the wheel.

Annie's heart missed a beat as the car swerved: "Mind the road!"

Joe swore, grappling with the wheel, narrowly avoiding a collision with a stone wall. He heaved a sigh of relief.

"Sorry Annie. That was a bit too close for comfort."

Annie welcomed the distraction, feeling the tension rising inside her.

"The hill field looks like it's ready for cutting, Joe."

"I was thinking about that. I must say it to Andy."

Andy Dolan rented the small farm from Annie, including the hill field, as he had done from her father before her. Joe Sullivan, who had moved with his family to the thirty acre farm in Ballycrag, a year after Annie had left the area, kept a few cows, did a little bit of tillage but survived mainly from the income derived from his factory work in the town. He also did odd jobs for other farmers whenever he could. This year he would help Andy Dolan with the saving of the hay.

"Will the grass be dry enough?" Annie asked. They were travelling up the hill at Ballycrag.

"This weather would dry anything…you're settled in all right now, Annie?"

"Yes, Joe."

"If there's anything you need," Joe reached over and touched her hand, resting against her thigh, "anything at all, don't be shy about asking."

Annie shifted in her seat: "Everything's fine at the moment. Thanks all the same." Her voice had a slight edge to it. Joe withdrew his hand and drove on in silence.

The sun was burning through the roof of the car and the smell from the engine and the old and worn interior was stifling. The passenger and driver's windows were open to the last, but the warm air passing through them did little to stop the sweat that oozed everywhere from Joe's body. He squirmed in his seat, feeling his trousers cutting into his sweating groin.

Annie turned in the doorway of the cottage, taking the bags from Joe: "That's far enough, thanks, Joe. I won't keep you any longer."

"No trouble, Annie. Anytime."

As he opened the driver's door, Joe glanced over the roof of the car, but she had already disappeared into the cottage.

He allowed the car to freewheel down the hill and parked near the bottom. He walked a few yards into the meadow, feeling the thickness of the damp grass push against his legs. It was ready for cutting all right and was drying out fast. He would suggest to Andy Dolan to do it on Saturday.

He bent down and grasped a bunch of the long ripe growth in his hand. A good rich harvest, ready for the mower blade! His gaze swept upwards over the meadow and came to rest on the chimney of the cottage barely visible over the trees. He shook his head and lowered his eyes, twisting the grass in his sweating hand. He pulled hard, the effort straining his shoulder muscle. He threw the broken strands away and stood massaging his shoulder, his eyes finding the chimney of the cottage again.

"Holy Jesus!"

He jumped back at the rasping cry of a corncrake, a few feet from where he stood, the sound unnaturally loud in the quiet. The ungainly, chestnut-grey body rose out of the grass before him, legs dangling, awkward in its flight, the wings a flash of bright orange against the afternoon sun.

He walked back out to the car and sat in. Sticking his head out the window, he twisted it so that he could look up to where the line of bushes and trees broke at the entrance to the cottage. His left hand held the steering wheel, the skin taut over his knuckles.

He drew in his head and sat back in the driving seat, forcing his thoughts to concentrate on his business with Andy Dolan and the task of saving the hay in the coming days. He had to wait a few minutes while the engine of the old Ford struggled to find a stabilized rhythm before throwing it into gear.

6

In her bedroom, Annie gratefully sponged her neck and shoulders with cool water from the well, shivering as tiny rivulets ran down her naked body, tracing miniature islands of dust and water on the boarded floor. She closed her eyes, exhaling softly, her breasts responding to the slow, clinging caress of the sponge. For a brief moment she felt a raw hunger envelope her and she willed it away, opening her eyes to the emptiness of the cottage.

She reached for a towel and paused, staring into the mirror. What was it about the eyes? People spoke with their mouths, laughed with their mouths but their eyes told a different story.

The eyes of the whole parish had been on her and Seánie on that first Sunday that she had gone to Mass after her return to Ballycrag. Clutching his hand, her head high, she had deliberately come in late, facing them all at once; giving them the time it took for the priest to say Mass, to come to terms with her homecoming. Kneeling in the front seat, eyes fixed on the priest's back as he intoned the words of the mass in Latin, she could hear the unrest, the rustling, and the whisperings around her. During the fifteen or twenty minutes of the sermon she had focused on the priest, not hearing a word he said.

"Ite missa est!" *Go, the mass is ended.*

As the priest left the altar, she had filed out with the congregation, acknowledging a slow nod of the head here and there. Outside, they had come singly, or in couples or in small groups, not to welcome her back but to sympathize with her on the death of her father. Some had avoided her and just a few had been bold enough to ask her why she had not been at his funeral. "I was too ill to travel" she had answered and had left it at that. Mollie Sullivan had come to her rescue as the strain had begun to affect her: "Are you coming home, Annie? We have to walk today. Joe went off early to a hurling match."

That ordeal had passed, but the stigma would remain. It didn't matter. That was a problem for other people. She began to dress, feeling the coolness of the air under the thatch.

In the kitchen, the flagstones cold against her bare feet, she put away the last of her shopping and glanced at the clock on the wall. It was too soon for Seánie to be home yet and too early to begin making supper. She could relax outside for a while and enjoy the pleasure of the summer evening.

Twelve miles away, in the village of Kilcrone, schoolmaster Owen Dara drove slowly through the wrought iron gates of the creeper-covered glebe house that he had inherited from his uncle, the late Dr John Dara, conscious that the lawns on either side needed attention.

Throwing the small stack of third class compositions he had taken home with him, on the kitchen table, he took a tumbler from the cabinet near the sink and filled it with cool water from the tap, downing it in one long motion. Drawing the back of his hand across his mouth, he stood gazing through the window, until a tremor passed through his body and he turned away.

Slinging his coat on the back of a chair, he dragged the chair over to the table and settled the bundle of compositions at his elbow. Red pencil poised, he drew the first one to him and began making corrections.

His task completed, he rose from the table and walked out into the garden, blinking against the sunlight, his eyes taking in the smooth, rounded shape and texture of leaf and flower and stem, blending together in an indolent intimacy. He had loved the summers, with the richness of things growing and ripening all around, but now they brought only memories of Annie and of the summers when they were together. And they brought back the pain.

Unconsciously reaching out, his fingers closed over a rose, and he crushed the petals into the palm of his hand. He stared at the crumpled remains. He would have to go and see her. He could not put it off any longer.

It was fear that had held him back, fear that she would reject him. And the fear had brought a return of the blackness, the sleepless nights, the endless days.

He walked back into the kitchen and poured another glass of water, emptying it in one gulp. He had an added fear now, fear that he could lose his position as schoolmaster. Lose the only thing that had held him together over the last years. It had not crossed his mind until the new parish priest, Canon Bates, had made that possibility very clear.

The canon had arrived into the school quite casually one morning only days after Seánie Luhan had been enrolled in the school. After a number of harmless observations, he had startled Owen by asking: "Did you ever think of considering that nice young assistant teacher of yours, Aoife Duffy, as a wife?"

For a moment Owen thought it was just an effort at frivolous conversation by an otherwise dour, blunt man, not given to light talk but rather to making his uncompromising wishes known and ensuring that they were carried out. Realizing that the canon was serious he answered simply: "No."

"It's something you should give thought to. How old are you now?"

"Thirty six."

"Young enough…but old enough to be settled down with a wife and family. A schoolmaster has an example to set, you know. He can't afford to be the subject of idle gossip, or have his moral character used as a talking point in pubs or around kitchen fires late at night." The canon tugged at his soutane, stretching it over his ample stomach: "Ah no, that would not be a good thing, not for him, nor his pupils, nor their parents. It wouldn't do the parish any good at all…or his parish priest either. What better way for him to avoid all that than to have a good decent girl as a wife, healthy and strong for child-bearing."

Owen just stared at the canon.

"A young man in your position could easily fall prey to a particular kind of woman, especially…" the canon bent his head a little, his eyes peering at Owen over the rim of his spectacles "…especially one whose only chance might be to marry someone whose position in the parish would give her some kind of respectability. Her need…" he cleared his throat "…her need to find a man like that would be all the greater if she happened to have a bastard son as well."

The blood drained from Owen's cheeks.

"Of course…" the canon stepped back a pace "…there would be no fear of such a thing happening in your case. And now, I must go…so many things to attend to. The duty of a parish priest is not always an easy one."

He turned and walked down the steps leading out of the hall where they had been talking. He paused at the bottom: "You might take time to consider my suggestion. You could do a lot worse than make that young Miss Duffy your wife."

Owen left his classes to care for themselves and walked outside to the lavatory. He sat for a long time on the lavatory seat, his arms tight around his stomach, his eyes closed. Only when the nausea had subsided and the trembling in his body had ceased did he return to the schoolroom.

He cursed himself now, for his fearfulness and for his silence in the presence of the canon. He took the bundle of compositions from the table, sifting through it until he had found the one he was looking for. He just stood there, staring at the name *Seánie Luhan* at the top of the page.

7

Stretching her legs and wriggling her toes, Annie relished the freedom from the stockings and the cramping, pinching shoes she'd worn to town. She sat on the wall near the back gate, shaded by the spreading branches of a beech tree, looking westward to where the sun was still high above the horizon. Away in the distance, the sound of shouting and laughter carried easily in the otherwise tranquil air. Seánie and the Sullivans were playing in the quarry! She was so glad he had them to play with and so glad that she had come home.

She began to hum a little tune, swinging her legs in time to the music. She smiled when she realized what she was doing: it was so long since she'd felt so contented.

A donkey brayed somewhere a long way off, shattering the peace of the evening. She stopped humming and listened to the gasping, snorting cry, like the painful, lonely wail wrenched from the very heart of a wounded creature. A dog barked and was answered by another and here and there other dogs took up the call. The hollow rumbling barks of bigger dogs mingled with the sharp staccato noise of smaller ones and for a time the air rang with the agitated cries of animals disturbed from an uneasy, lazy sleep in the warmth of the sun, and then - silence.

Her eyes had been unconsciously searching for the origin of the sounds, even after they had died away. They came to rest on the dark outline of a distant wood, the wood that marked the boundary of the estate at Fernmount, almost lost now in the haze that was gathering over the landscape.

She had refused to dwell on the memory of Fernmount since her return, pretending to herself that it did not exist anymore. She had been tempted once or twice to ask Mollie Sullivan, or Joe, or the postman, in an offhand way about it, but she had resisted the impulse. It was better for them all that it remained sealed up in her mind just as the estate had been sealed away from the rest of the small farmers and labourers from the time it had been established.

The braying of the donkey and the rise and fall of the barking dogs fading into silence, awakened the thought that maybe it had been like that during the war: the shattering noise of the big guns, the screams of the wounded and dying, the rumbling of tanks, the cries of men, and then – silence.

It was the silence that would be her most abiding memory: the silence that had surrounded that night in Fernmount; the silence that had caused so much hurt. She sat mute then, thinking of her father, tears tracing a glistening film down the warmth of her cheeks.

It was at that moment that Hungry Jack Maran caught sight of her.

Hungry Jack had taken the shortcut across the fields, his need to reach the pub in a hurry prompted by the heat of the day. The ground had dried out and was firm enough for the bicycle. He had cycled slowly along, close to the tree-lined hedge dividing one field from another, the ground worn down by the constant milling of cattle seeking shelter under the trees. The bicycle had wobbled now and then as the front wheel struck a rutted patch but he had managed to keep from falling, making slow but steady progress.

The warmth of the sun had drawn every drop of moisture from his body and nothing but a good pint of stout would restore him. The short cut across the fields, along the bottom of the hill, would take a mile and a half off his journey to Horgan's pub and the slaking of his desperate thirst.

At a low point in the hedge he noticed a flash of white. He got off his bicycle, and screwing up his eyes, it was a while before it dawned on him that he was looking at a pair of pale-skinned female legs dangling from a wall, the rest of her body hidden by the branches of a tree. *Her legs! Jaysus! It must be true all right what Willie said. She's askin' for someone to go up there now, grab them and tumble her on the flat of her back and give her a right good one.* His heart began to thud in his chest: *I could sneak up there, right this minute and given her one she'd…*

He jerked his head around as the sound of voices drifted towards him. *Blasted children!* He stood, stock-still, and watched as a boy came through a gap in the hedge in the next field and ran up the hill. *He must be the son!*

"Mama! Tommy and Mikey drowned Bouncer in the pond in the crag but he…"

"Oh…Seánie!"

I had startled her. She had not heard me approach.

"Tommy put him in a sack and tied a huge big rock to it, and Bouncer went straight down into the pond and never came up again, but when we went back to Sullivans he came home after a while an'…are you crying, mama?"

"I…no, it's just the sun affects my eyes sometimes. It's…it's a kind of hay fever?

"What's hay-fever?"

"It comes from the…the…pollen."

"What's pollen?"

"It's a yellow powder that bees take from plant to plant in summer. It helps the flowers to grow."

"Did you get it from a bee?"

"No. It floats in the air as well."

"Will I get hay-fever too?"

"No! You're too young…come in and have your supper. And don't forget you have homework to do."

She swung her legs over the wall and climbed down.

Hungry Jack waited, breathing heavily, until the boy and his mother disappeared around the side of the cottage before continuing on his way to Horgan's pub, his mind a whirl of confused emotions that only a good pint would ease.

8

"It's time for your homework, Seánie."

Supper was over and the table cleared.

"Couldn't I go down to Sullivan's for a little while, mama? I have only a few sums to do…and spellings. I nearly know those already."

"You'll do your homework first. Then we'll see."

I could never get away with lying to my mother. There were sums to do from the previous night, which I had conveniently forgotten about, and another batch from that day. Spellings were always easy for me. Arithmetic was not my strength but I managed. She left me now to work at the sums on my own. Later she would go through them with me. That was the rule.

Pouring a glass of sherry from the bottle she had bought on a whim earlier in the town Annie sat on one of the armchairs by the hearth. As she sipped from her glass, the discomfort of her recent thoughts began to recede and was slowly replaced by fond recollections of her childhood. She settled herself more comfortably and began to savour these memories, basking in the warmth of the summer evening and surrendering to the mellowing effect of the sherry.

The chair she sat in, the worn, knotted seat hidden beneath embroidered cushions, had darkened with age and with countless hours of exposure to turf smoke. It had been her father's chair and she had sat on his lap, feeling warm and secure, while she had listened to his stories all those years ago.

She smiled now at the memory of the worn old cap he had called his "considerin' cap". He could not tell her a story unless he was wearing it and when, somehow, it got mislaid at times, she would search frantically for it, while he sat in his chair shaking his head and sighing: "There'll be no story tonight…not without my considerin' cap." If her search took too long he would suggest one or two places where it might be and always he was correct.

She rested her hand idly on the iron wheel bellows, fixed into the floor near the fireplace, its wooden handle gleaming like polished granite from the touch of generations of turning hands.

"When you turn the wheel, it wakens the good fairies asleep under the hearth…they know then that the fire is dyin' down. They like to keep warm so they all blow together until the fire lights up again", her father had told her on one occasion.

"Would you stop filling the child's head with nonsense!"

Her father had laughed sheepishly at her mother's intervention and Annie had not been sure whether she was disappointed or relieved when he had explained to her about the little tunnel underneath the flagstones.

The unpainted pine settle that stretched almost the length of one wall, its paneled back reaching halfway up the window, had been her favourite seat on winter nights when Charlie Wixted came to the cottage with his fiddle and Bob Frawley brought his banjo. She would sit between them while they played, and sometimes, when her father put more turf on the fire and the flames blazed in the chimney, strange, shadowy figures would appear on the walls and quiver and dance in step with Charlie's fiddle or tremble to the rhythm of Bob's banjo.

With just a little persuasion from her father, her mother always sang a song before the evening ended, and Annie would feel a warmth growing inside her, a warmth that made her throw her arms around her mother and hold her tight.

"Do you want to see my sums now, mama?"

"What?"

"Do you want to see my sums?"

She took me quickly through them, explaining the mistakes I had made and returned to the armchair, leaving me to fill in the corrections.

Her eyes lingered now on the large wooden, dome-topped

travelling trunk almost hidden by the open cottage door. She had believed her father when he had told her:

"A long time ago before you were born, and I was a fearless young sailor-lad sailin' the high seas, on a dark and stormy night I stole that trunk from a pirate ship while it lay at anchor in Madagascar. I crept up the gangplank in my bare feet and sneaked in between the bodies of the ferocious, black-bearded pirates who were asleep on deck and stole it right from under their noses."

She had snuggled closer to him, the light from the oil lamp not strong enough to brighten the dark corners in the kitchen that could easily have hidden the ghosts of pirates, darker than those in Madagascar.

"Do you know why I stole that trunk? Do you know why I risked my life among those terrible cut-throat pirates?"

She had looked up at him, wide-eyed: "No, Daddy."

"I stole it so that I could use it to rescue your mother from the captain of the pirates who was keepin' her a prisoner in a dungeon in a castle on the island until she would give in and agree to marry him."

She had gasped with dismay and had looked over at her mother, who had smiled reassuringly at her: "Oh, I wasn't a bit afraid or worried. I knew your daddy would come and save me."

Her father had broken into the dungeon and knocked out the pirates guarding her mother with two mighty blows from his fist. He had quickly untied her and had put her in the trunk. He had staggered up the stone steps with the trunk on his back and had smuggled it on board another ship that sailed the whole way home to Ireland.

Her eyes wandered to the big, blue-painted pine kitchen dresser, the shelves crammed with willow pattern dishes, and plates of varying shape and colour. Milk jugs with roses on them, hung from hooks, or stood on the shelves beside sturdy mugs, delicately painted cups and robust china teapots. On the unpainted top over the cutlery drawers and food cupboard, wooden dairy bowls sat side by side with baking bowls, butter pats, butter stamps and bread boards carved with corn sheaves.

Near its edges the white of the wall had faded into grey. Each Spring her father would decide suddenly to renew the coat of whitewash in the kitchen and each time he did so her mother would complain:

"If you only warned me in time I could clear off the dresser and you could do the wall behind it. There must be God-knows-what back of it."

There is still God-knows-what at the back of it, she thought, *spiders and cobwebs and all sorts of creeping things. I will have to move it out this summer and do the wall behind it…*

I interrupted her thoughts again:

"I'm finished, mama. Can I go down to Sullivan's now?"

I had made the corrections and easily ran through my spellings.

"All right, but tidy up your books first. Don't stay too late. You have school in the morning."

She was pouring another glass of sherry as I ran out the door and down the hill to Sullivans, the prospect of pleasure speeding my feet, the sights and sounds of a somnolent summer evening everywhere around me: daisies barely wavering on their stems in the gentlest of breezes, the silent flicker of butterflies among the yellow tips of the gorse; the chirring of wrens from somewhere deep in the bramble bushes and the throaty calls of distant rooks.

It was a moment in time in which I was utterly content with my world.

Billy ran to meet me the moment I appeared in the yard: "Seánie! Will you play a game of cowboys with me?"

I hesitated. Behind him, Tommy and Mikey were busy doing something. I wanted to be with them. I was about to refuse when Tommy called out: "Play with him, Seánie! He's only annoyin' us and gettin' in the way!"

"Here!" Billy handed me a home-made wooden gun as I reluctantly followed him out into the haggard. "You can be a cowhand minding the cattle and I'll be a rustler trying to steal one of the cows."

9

Hungry Jack Maran downed the remaining half of his pint of stout in one continuous swallow, wiped the back of his hand across his mouth, belched and patted his stomach.

"I'll be off now!"

He left Horgan's pub feeling comfortably mellow and with a growing tightening in his groin. He might have had one or two more but as the evening wore on he had felt the desire growing stronger and stronger. The sight of Annie's legs and the thoughts that had been in his mind had stayed with him all evening. The possibility that she might object to his dropping into the cottage uninvited began to fade as the alcohol took its effect.

At the same time as Hungry Jack left Horgan's pub Owen Dara finished taking a bath and began changing his clothes.

He had spent the previous couple of hours mowing the front lawns in a frenzy of effort, sweat streaming from every pore in his body. He had damaged some of the shrubs in the process and had cursed at the mower as though it was a thing apart, operating under its own guidance. His task completed he had not bothered to change, but had thrown himself into an old canvas-backed chair under a tree in the back garden.

He had slumped in the chair, but only briefly. Visions of Annie, more beautiful now than he had ever remembered, and the thought of what he must do, regardless of the consequences, brought him springing to his feet again. His fingers tore at the buttons of his shirt. Dragging it off, he threw it over a chair on his way through the kitchen. His body trembled as he rushed upstairs to the bathroom to make himself ready.

"You're dead, Seánie!"

"No I'm not, Billy." I climbed over the dry-stone wall that separated us: "You couldn't shoot me through the wall."

"I didn't shoot you through the wall, Seánie. I saw your hair sticking up over the top and I shot you."

"You can't shoot me in the hair!"

"Yes, I can. I saw a sheriff in the pictures shooting a rustler in the hair."

"No one would be dead if they got shot in the hair."

"Yes, they would."

"No, they wouldn't…ask Tommy or Mikey."

Tommy was completing the making of an Indian bow from an ash sapling, when Billy and I came into the yard, still arguing. He was cutting notches in each end to take the string and Mikey was pointing arrows, cut from willows, with a knife taken from the kitchen drawer when Molly Sullivan's back was turned.

"Tommy, Billy says you can shoot someone in the hair and he's dead."

Tommy had tied a string to one end of the sapling and was now bending it and tying the string on the other end.

"He wouldn't be dead. He might only be creased." The string went taught as Tommy finished tying it and the sapling strained against the arc he had bent it into.

"See! I told you, Billy!"

"No, you didn't. You never said I greased you. "

Tommy and Mikey laughed.

"It's not *greased*, Billy, it's *creased*" Mikey said.

"See! I was right, Billy. I'm not dead."

"What's creased?" Billy was annoyed

"It means you only winged him." Mikey always had at least two different words to describe something when the need arose.

Billy was even more annoyed and frustrated now, not understanding 'winged' either: "You're only making it up, Mikey. You're always making things up. Like you said the pond has no bottom and…"

"I'm not making it up. Anyone knows that cowboys get creased or winged and they just fall down for a minute and then get up and start shootin' again."

"Tommy, is Mikey just making…?"

"Be quiet, Billy. Mikey, gimme an arrow."

The argument ended as all interest focussed on Tommy.

"I'll have to have something to aim at."

After a search of the yard and the outhouses, an old coat was stuffed with straw, buttoned up and propped on an upturned wooden butter box.

"Who's it supposed to be?" Billy studied the dark, headless and legless effigy.

"It's not supposed to be anybody," Tommy answered and walked fifteen measured paces away and turned to face his target.

"Stand out of the way."

He lifted the bow upright, holding the end of the arrow close to his jaw and took aim, pulling on the string and arrow, locked between his thumb and finger, as hard as the bending sapling would allow, without breaking in half. We held our breaths while he held the tension between bow and arrow for what seemed an eternity.

The bowstring *blipped* rather than *twanged* as the arrow was released and only travelled a disappointing halfway to its intended victim.

"These arrows are useless, Mikey. We'll have to put a weight on the tips, otherwise they'll go nowhere."

"You should have stood closer, Tommy. You're too far away."

"Bang!" Billy shouted, aiming his wooden gun at the target. At that moment, the headless nobody toppled off its perch on the butter box.

"I shot him! I shot him!"

"No you didn't. He just fell off the box," Tommy said crossly, feeling let down by the failure of the arrows. He turned to Mikey: "Mikey, do you know that tin banding on the tea chests that daddy got? If we take that off, maybe we can cut it into thin strips and wrap it round the tips."

"It's too hard to cut. I tried it before. Couldn't we wrap wire around them?"

While they were considering this and what other material they might use the voice of Joe Sullivan called loudly from the back door: "Tommy, get the others and come in! It's time for the rosary."

The four of us walked reluctantly across the yard.

"I'll go home," I said. "I don't want to say the rosary."

Billy caught my arm: "It'll only take a few minutes. You know my father always says it fast and anyway, we have to finish the game. You weren't dead when I shot you."

This admission from Billy encouraged me: "I'll stay so."

Owen Dara did not see the cyclist until the very last moment. He braked hard, the car travelling a long distance before slewing sideways and coming to a halt.

The young man on the bicycle, sensing imminent danger, had reacted instinctively and had swerved off the road straight into a clump of briars

He emerged angrily from it now, his trousers torn, scratches on his face and hands. After a cursory examination of his person, he retrieved his bicycle and checked it for damage. Satisfied, he placed it carefully against a bush and walked towards the car.

Owen sat shaking behind the wheel. He did not move until the young man grasped the door handle and dragged open the driver's door: "You nearly killed me!"

The young man's eyes were blazing, his face white.

"I'm sorry. I…" Owen turned to face him.

"You were drivin' like a madman! Look! My bloody trousers is all torn."

The young man stood back as Owen slowly got out of the car: "I'll pay for your trousers."

Owen dropped the wallet he had just managed to take out of his pocket with trembling hand. He bent down to pick it up, but the young man reached it first and handed it to him.

"You're the master in Lisbeg, aren't you?" The young man had calmed down.

"Yes."

"My sister's child goes there…Michael Hayes…he's only in infants."

Owen handed him the bank note he had taken from his wallet: "Is this enough?"

"It's too much. My trousers only cost…"

"Take it…please."

The young man folded the note and shoved into his pocket: "Are you all right?"

"Yes…yes."

He waited until Owen had restarted the engine, straightened the car and had driven slowly away.

Later that night the young man briefly described the incident to his parents. Within weeks he would retell the story over and over again to a much wider audience of eager listeners, only this time not even the tiniest detail would be overlooked.

10

Joe Sullivan was mid-way through the second decade of the rosary when Billy began to feel the onset of drowsiness. He made an effort to stay kneeling upright, but slowly, very slowly, he sagged down on his heels and slumped against the chair seat.

He was beginning to relax completely now as the Hail Mary's were intoned one after the other, like a soothing chant, lulling him to sleep. His heels finally took all the weight of his body, his stomach muscles loosened and the accumulation of gas inside him exited like the gentle sigh of the wind under the eaves.

"Silent, but deadly," Mikey whispered out of the side of his mouth to Tommy as the unpleasant odour wafted towards him.

Tommy pretended not to hear, clasping his face in his hands in what looked like pious concentration.

Billy repeated the performance and this time Mikey kicked him in the foot. Billy slid sideways off the chair and came alert instantly.

"What'd you do that for?"

"You farted!" Mikey hissed at a bewildered Billy.

"I didn't!"

"You did!" The sight of Billy's uncomprehending face and his wounded voice was too much for Mikey and he began to heave and splutter, infecting Tommy who laughed out loud.

Joe abruptly stopped giving out the rosary: "Is there to be no respect for prayer in this house?"

Muted laughter was the response.

"There's no point in continuin' on, when there is no respect shown for the Holy Rosary!"

Joe's apparent ignorance of the reason for the disruption caused Tommy and Mikey to laugh all the harder. Unable to help himself, Billy joined them and I too was unable to resist.

Joe jumped up: "The three of you can take yourselves off to bed this minute!"

"Sorry, daddy!" Mikey and Tommy said simultaneously, the threat of immediate bed prompting their contriteness.

"Kneel down, Joe." Mollie reached up and caught his arm, giving it a gentle tug.

She turned to Mikey and Tommy: "Settle down now and let your father get on with the rosary."

The rosary continued with no more interruptions or distractions except the deep, easy breathing of Billy as he drifted off to sleep.

A short distance beyond Sullivan's gate, Hungry Jack got off his bicycle and began a slow walk up the hill. The light was a soft, bluish haze, the moon beginning to rise higher in the sky. It was a bit too bright, he thought. Maybe he should have waited for a darker night.

The incident on the road with the young man had frightened Owen Dara. He had lost track of where he was and what he was doing. Had the young man not swerved off the road he would surely have struck him with the car, injured him, maybe even killed him.

This thought frightened him even more and the certainty he had felt an hour or so earlier, that his meeting with Annie would have the outcome he hoped for, began to desert him.

As he neared the hill leading up to the cottage, he drove slowly, his body sagging in the driver's seat, the blackness that had been lifting from behind his eyes beginning to descend again.

The prayers had barely ended when Joe Sullivan looked over at Billy stretching himself into wakefulness across the chair: "It's bedtime for you."

"Aw, daddy can't I stay up a bit longer? I wanted to finish a game with Seánie."

"No! It's time for Seánie to go home." Joe stood up: "Come on, Seánie, I'll walk up with you."

Mollie, still on her knees, looked up at him: "There's no need. It's still bright. He'll be alright on his own."

"The bit of a walk will do me no harm. I'll only be a minute."

Joe walked up the hill in silence, the distant sound of an approaching car and the tread of his boots on the rough surface, drowning out my lighter step.

The gate to the cottage was open and Hungry Jack left his bicycle by the wall just inside it. Walking along the path to the door he stopped abruptly, hearing the noise of a car as it crested the hill. Keeping his back to the road, he hunched his shoulders and leant forward. He bent lower as the car slowed and appeared to be coming to a halt outside the gate.

The pounding of Owen Dara's heart pulsated in his stomach as the car rolled to within yards of the cottage. He reached for the gear lever to disengage the gears, and paused, the headlights picking up two figures further down the hill. His heart lurched, and grasping the steering wheel tightly, he pressed his foot down hard on the accelerator pedal.

Joe Sullivan half-turned and shoved me closer to the ditch as the car roared past.

"The master's out late tonight…an' he's in a terrible hurry, wherever he's off to," he said.

Hungry Jack remained as he was until the car accelerated away. Straightening up, he took a step forward, only to stop short once again. This time, he turned back on the path and hurried to the gate, the sound of footsteps close by on the road, spurring his action. Grabbing his bicycle, he lifted it off the ground and as quietly as possible carried it behind the gable-end of the cottage.

He held his breath as the heavy sound of boots moved off the road and crunched along the gravel path to the cottage door. He heard the click of the latch being lifted and, after a brief pause, the indistinct sound of a man's voice and then the noise of the door being closed.

"Blast it to hell!"

He quickly bundled his bicycle out over the hedge between the yard and the road, swearing as the barbs of a hawthorn raked his hands and his face.

He straightened his bicycle, allowing it to rest against his stomach and drew his sleeve across his face to wipe away the blood the thorns had drawn from it. He lifted each hand in turn and sucked at the blood that oozed from the backs of them, losing his balance, his bicycle falling back against the hedge.

Inside the cottage, my mother stood up: "Joe!"

"Hello, Annie! I just brought Seánie up."

"There was no need. Thanks all the same."

Joe stood awkwardly: "It's a grand night."

"A lovely night, thank God."

"It's hard to go to bed early when there's such a long stretch in the evenin's."

"Long stretch or not, it's time Seánie was in bed."

Joe swallowed and cleared his throat: "Late an' all as it is, maybe you could do with a bit of company for a while."

The smile that had played on Annie's lips disappeared: "Another time maybe, Joe. I was just waiting up for Seánie before going off to bed myself."

Joe moved to the door: "I should be gettin' home to bed myself."

"Good night Joe. And thanks again."

"No trouble, Annie."

Hungry Jack bent down to retrieve his bicycle. The click of the latch on the cottage door, loud in the stillness, jolted him and he tripped on his bicycle, falling forward, his face buried in the ditch. He lay still, listening to the footsteps on the hill road until they faded into silence. Breathing hard, he disentangled himself gingerly from the thistles and briars. He waited a moment, staring back at the cottage, before shoving his bicycle closer into the ditch.

Joe Sullivan paused, his hand on the doorknob of the back door to his house. He'd made a fool of himself in mistaking Annie's flushed face and brighter than usual eyes for something more than just pleasure at his appearance. He'd been wrong and he'd made Annie feel uneasy. It was unfair to the girl. He'd be more careful in the future, and anyway, what in God's name had he been thinking of? It occurred to him then, that if he didn't know any better, it looked like the master was going to stop at Annie's gate but had changed his mind. Mollie would have a better idea of what was goin' on. *If somethin' was goin' on.*

Owen Dara parked his car close in by an old wooden farm gate, and made his way slowly across the marshy ground that lay between the road and the more solid bank of the river that rose and fell with the cycle of the tide from the estuary.

He stared into the void of the river, the shadow of the outgoing tide in the channel at its centre, darker than that of the sloping mud flat that disappeared somewhere into the quietly receding water. It would be hours yet before the tide turned and the empty space between the riverbanks would be filled. He lifted his head, gazing up the moon: "Oh God! Oh God!"

The sharp, piercing, echoing calls of disturbed seabirds rose in answer to his cry and he turned away, stumbling over a tuft of grass.

He drove onwards from the river, not conscious of the direction he was travelling in, until he reached the church at Ballycrag, recognition of where he was dawning on him. He stopped the car and after a moment's hesitation, drove onwards, his destination clear in his mind.

11

Mikey Sullivan tossed and turned, unable to sleep. He usually drifted off to the comforting sound of the murmur of conversation rising through the floor of the bedroom, but not tonight. Disturbing shadows rose in the moonlight and hovered in the bedroom he shared with Tommy and Billy. Each time he closed his eyes and tried to sleep he had to open them again, the deep, dark waters of the pond ebbing and flowing in his memory.

His bare feet made no sound as he slid out of bed and padded across the floorboards to the landing. The linoleum on the stairs was cool under his feet. He could hear the voices of his parents louder now as he reached the last steps, pausing in the hall to hoist his pyjamas. He gently turned the doorknob on the kitchen door. Before the door was fully open, he slid noiselessly into the kitchen, blinking in the light.

Joe was leaning against the mantel-shelf, his back to Mikey. Mollie sat at the kitchen table knitting, her eyes on the clicking needles as she spoke to Joe.

"…only gossip, anyway. The day I had a cup of tea with Mary Sugrue in town, she started talking about the master and Annie. Then she started on about who Seánie's father's might be. She said it could have been the son or the father or one of the farm workers. Wouldn't you think that they'd forget about all that, an' give the poor girl a chance to get on with her life? They're bothered because no one knows who Seánie's father is. It must be…" Mollie raised her head "…what are you doing out of bed, Mikey? Why aren't you asleep?"

"I was thirsty."

Joe turned round: "Have a drink of water, then, and go back to bed."

Joe walked to the dresser. Taking down a mug, he dipped it into the bucket of water standing on the small cupboard near the back door and handed it to Mikey.

"Drink up, now."

Mikey didn't feel that thirsty, but he drank the water anyway, emptying the mug.

Joe held the kitchen door open.

"Off to bed now, Mikey, and settle down and go to sleep."

Climbing the stairs, Mikey wondered why nobody knew who Seánie's father was. Did Seánie not know either? He must ask him about it. He wouldn't like it himself if he didn't have his daddy or if he didn't know who he was.

He snuggled down under the blankets listening for the murmur of the voices downstairs. They were speaking very quietly now, and only the sound of a word here and there floated upwards. He listened and listened until it was too hard to try and listen any longer and he fell asleep.

Up the hill, Hungry Jack Maran peered through the window of the cottage that gave a view of the hearth and of Annie, her back to him, seated in an old armchair. Beside her, on the floor, the bottle she'd been drinking from, empty now, lay on its side. She had been speaking to the boy sitting opposite her for ages, her head, bobbing and weaving, and only the regular swigs from the half-bottle of whiskey that he had in his coat pocket had helped him to keep at bay the urge that was building and building inside him.

The boy, half-asleep, slid from the chair on to the floor and Annie struggled to her feet, staggering as she moved forward to him. Jack raised the whiskey bottle to his lips and when he lowered his head they had passed from sight.

He moved to the window at the other side of the cottage door when the light inside came on, watching until the boy was finally in bed and Annie had left the room. Moving back to the other window, he watched as she pottered around the hearth, tripping over the empty bottle before she moved out of sight again. He waited a moment for her to reappear before he staggered his way round to the back of the cottage.

Annie could not stop herself from stumbling and bumping into the side of her bed as she undressed, allowing her clothes to fall where they would. Naked, she crawled under the covers and lay flat on her stomach, feeling as though she was lying on water that undulated beneath her.

Cresting the hill at Ballycrag for the second time that night, Owen Dara cut the engine and turned off the lights, only the rumble of the wheels and the odd thumping of the suspension audible as his car came to a halt a short distance beyond Annie's cottage.

The light was still on in the kitchen and in the bedroom to the side. He peered through both windows in turn, the sleeping figure of the boy unnoticeable beneath the bedclothes drawn completely over him. He walked back to the cottage door and knocked softly.

Annie grappled with the pillow that was stifling her breathing, knocking it to the floor. Before unconsciousness overtook her, she had a fearful pinprick of knowledge that, that was how she had felt that night in Fernmount.

In the shadows cast by errant clouds sliding across the moon, Owen Dara saw a dark, ethereal figure emerge from around the gable end of the cottage. Hungry Jack saw only another man standing between him and Annie and he lunged at Owen. The wildly swinging fist that struck Owen's collarbone had the crunching impact of iron and Owen fell backwards against the wall of the cottage. Jack reached for Owen's throat, as the schoolmaster rebounded off the wall, ducking beneath Jack's hands, his head striking Jack's throat, forcing him to step back and gasp for air. Jack clawed at the schoolmaster, his broken nails failing to get a grip as Owen's shoulder struck him in the chest. Arms flailing, the unbalanced Jack fell awkwardly onto the path.

Owen ran to his car, fumbling for the ignition key, unable to find it. He scrambled into the driving seat, rocking his body forwards and backwards, the car quickly gathering momentum as it careened down the hill, bumping and scraping against the hedges on either side, the driver's door swinging loosely, the lights off.

Jack lumbered to his feet, his unfocussed eyes searching for his adversary, his mind fixed on exacting violence. He lurched through the gate and out onto the road, hearing sounds that made no sense. He stumbled about, lunging at shadows, swinging balled fists at an imagined assailant, until his efforts petered out, his passion quelled. Lifting glazed eyes to the lighted cottage he made to go forward to the gate and stopped, his head drooping. Turning his steps upwards to the hill he wove a meandering path to his bicycle.

Owen's car came to a shuddering halt, a short distance beyond Sullivan's gate, the momentum it had gathered on its downward journey on the hill finally running out. He got out and listened for any noise that he was being followed, his body trembling, his stomach turning over; his mind unable to make sense of the nightmare that had enveloped him.

In the long, unbroken silence surrounding him, his body quieted and he located the ignition key.

Tommy Sullivan was awakened by the noise of a car engine starting up, a noise rarely heard in the quiet of the late night in Ballycrag. He lay still for a moment his fogged mind clearing to the events of earlier in the day. Rising, he crept out of the house, taking with him an old jumper. Putting it in the cardboard box that he had earlier placed for Bouncer under the beech tree, he waited patiently while the puppy pulled and tore at the jumper until he was satisfied that his bed was to his liking and he lay down.

As soon as Tommy had left, the puppy stood up again, watching and waiting, until Tommy had reached the silent house and the back door had closed behind him. Fixing his bed once more, Bouncer lay down again, cocking a comfortable eye at the full mid-summer moon, floating like a ball among the dark, hushed leaves.

12

Many things happened on this road on the way to school. Little adventures were played out; outrageous dreams were unfolded; truth was coloured through the eyes and ears of innocence; claims and counter-claims of burgeoning adolescent love were made; friendships were forged and friendships were broken, only to be repaired again, sometimes quickly, other times taking a little longer. Always for me, at least, there was the unpleasant feeling of the morning and the relief and renewed energy of the afternoon as I made my way home.

After the third call from Mollie and the threat that she would go up and drag him out of bed, Mikey Sullivan came downstairs, the morning after Bouncer's miraculous escape, knuckling the sleep from the corners of his eyes. Billy was seated at the table, his head bent over a bowl of porridge. Mollie was busy putting small bottles filled with milk and sandwiches, wrapped in brown paper, into their schoolbags.

"Hurry up, Mikey…go and get yourself washed."

Mikey made his way to the back kitchen.

"Don't forget to wash behind your ears…and comb your hair."

Through the open door Mikey heard the clucking of hens and the excited yelping of Bouncer as he played with Tommy. He barely splashed his face with water from the basin, ignoring the soap and the face cloth. He dried himself quickly, picked up the comb and drew it a few times through his straight black hair.

Billy, his porridge eaten, hoisted his schoolbag over his shoulders, fastened the strap across his chest, and went out to the yard.

"Don't be long!" Mollie called after him. "And hurry up, Mikey. You'll be late for school."

Mikey ate a few spoonfuls of his porridge, picked up his mug of milk, drained it and stood up from the table: "Why does no one know who Seánie's father is, mammy?"

"What are you talking about?" Mollie noisily dropped a bowl into a basin.

"I was just asking…?"

"Stop your nonsense," Mollie said crossly, "…and put on your schoolbag. Hurry up, now."

Bouncer rushed into the kitchen, Tommy and Billy close behind, and jumped up on Mikey. His front paws became entangled in Mikey's jumper and for a moment he just hung there.

"Get that dog away! Your jumper will be in shreds."

Just as Mollie spoke the threads gave way and Bouncer fell back on the stone floor. Mollie bent down and scooped up the puppy in her arms.

"Go off to school now," Mollie was holding the struggling Bouncer with difficulty, "and don't delay on the road."

"Seánie!" Mikey called. "Seánie! Seánie!"

Mikey's voice, and the banging on the door, woke me. I struggled out of bed, but only in time to hear Tommy shouting: "Come on, Mikey, or we'll all be late for school!"

They had gone by the time I had unlocked the door.

At Riordan's cross the Sullivan brothers turned left into the road that was barely the width of a car. Heavy showers had blown in from the northwest just before dawn, battering the rough uneven surface, leaving behind potholes filled with brown water and the road streaked with mud. The rain had passed over quickly and the morning sun was already siphoning away the water, hardening the mud.

Up ahead Hungry Jack Maran and Willie Cray were at work, filling the potholes with shovels of rough stone chips from one of the heaps the council lorry had dumped on the roadside, at intervals of a few hundred yards. They leant on their shovels now as the boys approached.

Hungry Jack, usually intolerant towards children, felt even more intolerant that morning. His aborted efforts of the previous night had left him in a mean humour. He had arrived late at his work, the half-cooked breakfast of sausages, rashers and eggs churning in his stomach, the scratches on his face and hands clearly evident. Willie Cray's jibes at Jack's general condition had angered him but he had been unable to return in kind, having had to make, to the undisguised amusement of Willie, frequent and hurried visits over the ditch to lower his trousers.

"Hah!" Jack growled now. "The future of the country is comin'."

Willie nodded: "It's goin' to be a great country, sure enough, Jack."

Hungry Jack, the nickname *hungry* having followed him all the way from his schooldays, from his habit of asking other children for uneaten scraps of their lunches and from the ravenous way he devoured food whenever it was offered to him in the house of a neighbour, was lean and tall. Black, bushy eyebrows peeked out from under the cap he wore, pulled well down over his forehead. His chin was covered with black stubble. Irregular yellow teeth were exposed as he stretched his chewed up lips in the semblance of a smile.

"Mornin' boys!"

"Mornin', Jack! Mornin', Willie!" Tommy, bringing up the rear, pushed against Billy and Mikey, urging them on.

"Where's your hurry?" Willie's short, bulky figure moved in front of Billy bringing all three to a halt. His mouth opened in a twisted grin, showing gaps in teeth that matched the colour of Jack's: "No time to talk to the neighbours? That's not a right thing now, Jack, is it?"

"No, Willie."

"We'll be late for school", Tommy said, trying to shove Billy and Mikey past the overweight Willie.

Jack reached out and gripped Tommy's shoulder, leaning down to leer into his face, his alcohol-laden breath almost turning Tommy's stomach: "Stop your shovin' an'pushin!"

Willie looked over Mikey's head at Tommy: "How is it your little pal's not with you at all this mornin?"

"What pal...oh! Seánie? No! He wasn't up when we called."

Willie gave a sly look in Hungry Jack's direction: "Still in bed is he? Maybe he's in bed with that fine mare up on the hill. Who'd want to get up if he was snuggled up close to that?"

"We have to go or we'll be late," Tommy said.

Jack's tightened his grip on Tommy, restraining him as Willie poked the handle of his shovel between Billy and Mikey and nudged Tommy in the stomach: "Doesn't like talkin' about the girls, now, does he, Jack?"

"Let go of me!" Anger began to redden Tommy's face.

"Maybe…" Willie leered "…maybe he's got a little bit a skirt…"

Tommy swung his fist upwards, striking Jack's arm, attempting to twist free at the same time.

"Aisy now!" Hungry Jack growled, and dug his fingers deeper into Tommy's shoulder, hurting him.

Tommy drew back his right foot and kicked Hungry Jack hard in the shin. Jack loosened his grip. Sucking air through his teeth he roared: "You little bastardin hoor you!"

Tommy twisted away from Jack and made a grab for Billy, but Mikey had already grasped Billy's hand and had rushed forward, managing to brush past the slow-moving Willie. Tommy darted sideways and the three of them ran at full speed away from their tormentors.

"Little bastards, come back here!"

Jack brandished his shovel in the air and set off after the fleeing trio: "If I catch you I'll beat the lard out of you!"

Jacks threat and his thundering boots added speed to their legs and they ran on and on, not daring to look behind, Tommy and Mikey each holding Billy by the hand. Minutes later, the sound of Jacks boots faded. Tommy looked back over his shoulder. Hungry Jack was standing in the middle of the road, still shouting and still brandishing the shovel. Willie hadn't moved.

They were able to relax now and take time to catch their breaths. The fear of being smashed to pieces with a shovel showed on Billy's white face. Tommy was breathing hard, the anger still in his eyes. Mikey was bent over, his hands on his knees, gasping for breath.

"They're savages," Tommy said. "Don't ever go next or near them again. The next time you see them on the road, climb over the ditch and cut across the fields."

They walked on now, taking the odd glance behind them, especially Billy, making certain that Hungry Jack hadn't jumped on his bicycle and followed them. As they rounded the last bend on the road, they were almost relieved to see the school gate.

A long way behind the Sullivans, I ran along the road in short bursts, lack of sleep and an uneasy feeling slowing me down. I had dressed hurriedly after the Sullivans had left and gone into my mother's room but she seemed to have difficulty trying to wake up. I grabbed a few slices of bread and butter and taking my schoolbag, I rushed towards the door at the same time as my mother, a coat thrown over her, shuffled into the kitchen.

"Wait, Seánie!"

I hesitated.

"Did you take some lunch?"

"Yes, mama," I answered, as I ran through the doorway.

I was unprepared for Hungry Jack Maran's roar as I passed by him and Willie Cray: "Another little bastard!"

"A real one this time!" Willie Cray banged the shovel hard against the road. Fear gripped me then and I ran on as fast I could. I heard him shout after me: "You could be havin' another little bastard for a brother before long."

The sound of his snorting laughter fell away and I slowed down, my heart pounding.

13

Mikey Sullivan waited with the rest of fourth class for the master to turn his attention to them. He had already given his instructions to the other classes, setting them easier tasks than usual, and had not raised his voice once, not even when he had returned the corrected compositions to third class. Every so often he had paused to massage a spot just below his left shoulder but now he sat behind his desk, his hands on his knees, staring over the children's heads at the back wall. The schoolroom was quiet, the children sensing something amiss.

It seemed like a long time before Owen Dara ended the silent puzzlement for fourth class: "Take out your English readers…and turn to page forty seven."

A scraping of leather against wood as the appropriate book was fished out of schoolbags.

"Sullivan!"

Mikey shot up from the seat of the desk he shared with Lucy Joyce.

"Yes, sir!"

"Read out the poem on that page, Sullivan."

Mikey gave a little cough:

Where glows the Irish hearth with peat…

"Read it slowly, Sullivan!"

Mikey took a deep breath:

Where glows the Irish hearth with peat,
There lives a subtle spell -
The faint blue smoke, the gentle heat,
The moorland odours, tell

Of long roads running through a red
Untamed unfurrowed land,
With…

The sound of the schoolroom door opening distracted Mikey and he paused, but only for a moment:

…curlews keening overhead
And streams on either hand.

"Stop, Sullivan!"

Mikey stopped and looked up at the master, and then, turned his head to look in the same direction as all the other eyes in the classroom.

I had pushed at the creaking door, vainly trying to enter unnoticed. I closed it behind me now and bowed my head against the silence.

"You're late, Luhan."

I kept my head down, my schoolbag hanging by my side, my back to the schoolroom door.

"Why are you late?"

"I slept it out, sir."

"Raise your head when you speak to me. You did what?"

I muttered the same reply.

The master's voice rose now, cutting through me: "Raise your head, Luhan! Raise your head and spit it out so that everyone can hear you!"

"I slept it out, sir!" I shouted.

"You…slept…it…out," he dragged the words. "And… where…did…you…do…that? On the grass? In the outhouse?"

Nervous titters erupted here and there.

"You did not *sleep it out*. You *slept in*, Luhan. You *slept in*. What did you do?"

"I slept in, sir."

"And why did you sleep in? Well?"

"I don't know, sir."

"You don't know. What don't you know, Luhan? Whether you slept inside or outside or what?"

There was no more tittering now.

"Stand over by the wall."

I moved over to the wall, my eyes on the floor, my schoolbag raising a little flurry of dust from the boarded floor.

"Continue, Sullivan."

The sound of Mikey's voice was a kind of comfort:

> *Black turf-banks crowned with whispering sedge*
> *And black bog- pools…*

I stood by the wall, without once looking up, feeling no sense of shame, only the sense of isolation that I had felt at other times. The schoolroom and the children and the master ceased to exist. I did not belong there. I belonged somewhere on the faded yellow map of the world that hung high up on the wall over my head. But not there.

"I'm going to go far away," I spoke through clenched teeth "an' I'm never going to come back"

"You're only saying that 'cause you were late this mornin' and the master was mad at you."

Mikey stuffed the last piece of his lunch into his mouth and lay back in the grass, dry now from the hot sun that had been shining from a clear blue sky since early morning.

We were eating our lunches by the side of the large field in front of the schoolhouse. Tommy and a number of the older boys were hurling at our side of the field. The clash of wood against wood and the sharper *crack* of the leather ball rose amid the clamour and shouts of:

"Pass it here!"

"Go on, Mac!

"Here…ah!"

"Pull on it, pull!"

"That's a foul!"

At the other side of the field, girls skipped or played *ring-a-ring-a-*

rosy, or chattered to each other in small groups. A few were making daisy chains. Smaller children played tig or simply ran around relishing the freedom of lunchtime. Here and there boys pulled at and wrestled with each other and a few fought briefly, small fists flailing.

"Hungry Jack was going to nearly kill us this morning," Mikey said.

I sat with my back against an oak tree, my arms clasped around my drawn-up knees, my half-eaten lunch of bread and butter on the grass beside me.

"He was really mad because Tommy kicked him in the shin and…"

I stared into space, paying little attention to Mikey's words, as he related the incident. He turned his head: "You're not listening at all."

"I hate school." I reached down and picked up a piece of bread. Taking a small bite, I threw the rest on the grass: "I hate it!"

Mikey laughed: "My father always says that schooldays are the best days of our lives. I don't…"

A shrill whistle announced the end of the lunch-break.

Mikey stood up: "Come on." He set off at a trot and stopped: "Come on, Seánie!"

I got up slowly and just as slowly began walking towards the schoolhouse.

"Hurry up! I'm not waiting for you." Mikey broke into a run.

Head down, I continued my slow walk. Entering the classroom behind the others, I walked up to my desk, picked up my schoolbag and walked back out the door into the afternoon sunshine.

"Quiet! No more talking!"

During the few minutes it took the children to settle after the break Mikey realized I was not in the schoolroom and raised his hand.

"Sir!"

Owen Dara was busy with third class at the front of the classroom.

Mikey raised his voice: "Sir!"

"What is it, Sullivan?"

"Please sir, I have to go out."

"You're just in."

"Yes, sir. I have to go out, Sir."

"Go on…and don't let it happen again, Sullivan."

"No, sir."

Outside, Mikey ran up and down calling my name as loudly as he dared without being heard inside the schoolroom. He ran round the back, looked in the lavatory, ran round to the front again and scanned the playing field, all the time calling my name. I resisted the temptation to answer him. For all I knew the schoolmaster had sent him to look for me and I did not want to be found. I watched him run along the long avenue to the gate and look up and down the road. Finding no sign of me he ran back even more quickly.

Perspiration streamed down Mikey's face and he drew the sleeve of his pullover across it before he re-entered the classroom and sat down.

"Seánie's gone," he whispered to Lucy Joyce.

"Where's he gone to?" she whispered back.

"I dunno."

"Maybe he's gone home."

"I don't think so."

"Sullivan!" From his position behind his desk, the master glared down at Mikey.

"Yes, sir?"

"You're disrupting this classroom again…what were you talking about?"

"Nothing, sir."

"You mean your mouth was just opening and closing of its own accord."

"No, sir."

"Stand up!"

Mikey stood up, his mouth going dry.

In his seat at the back with the other sixth class pupils, Tommy began to feel the slow anger building up inside him.

"Now, Sullivan, tell the class in a loud clear voice what you were talking about."

Mikey said nothing.

"You have one more chance, before I teach you a lesson you won't forget…well?"

"Leave him alone!"

All eyes turned to the back of the classroom. Tommy, standing up in his seat at the back, his face red, looked directly into the master's eyes. Billy, up near the front with third class, had just begun to feel nervous for Mikey, but now he was terrified at what the master might do to Tommy. His knees began to tremble under the desk and his face grew pale.

"What…did…you…say?" The master's eyes were almost popping out of his head.

"I said…leave him alone."

Owen jumped up from behind his desk, sending his books flying and his chair crashing to the floor, his face turning chalk-white, his nostrils flaring. He rushed down the room, reached in and grabbed Tommy by the arm, dragging him out on the floor past two other boys. His left hand still grasping Tommy, he curled his right hand into a fist and drew it back.

"Stop, Owen! Stop!"

Aoife Duffy, at the noise of the crashing chair, had come through the door that connected the two classrooms. She ran down and caught the upraised fist.

"Whatever he did, this isn't the way to deal with it."

She held on to the upraised fist until the master released his grip on Tommy's arm and his breathing began to sound almost normal again. She spoke to Tommy: "Go out into the hall and stay there until I come out."

Tommy, trembling all over, did as he was told.

She turned to the children: "Take out your books and sit quietly. I have to speak to the master for a minute. If there's any noise you'll all hear about it."

Taking Owen's arm, she led him through the door to her

classroom, issued the same instructions to her own classes and walked him out into the yard.

High up in the sycamore overlooking the yard I stayed absolutely still, not daring to breathe. I watched through the screen of heavy foliage as the master and Miss Duffy came out into the yard and stood talking to each other. Holding my breath, I drew my body tighter into the crook of the tree. I heard the sound of their conversation, quiet and low, but no word was audible.

I had used the wall to reach the lower branches of the tree and had laboriously hauled myself up, pausing now and then to untangle my schoolbag, until I had climbed to within ten feet of the topmost branch. When I looked down, for a moment it was like being on Jim's shoulders when I was younger, only this time it was much higher. I had a brief surge of near panic, but it passed quickly. I was looking down on the roof of the school, the yard, the avenue. I could even see the road and the trees and fields beyond. I intended to stay up there until school was over and the master had gone, before making my way home.

The master and Miss Duffy went back into the school. I felt safe then. The whirr of wings startled me. A pigeon landed on the branch over my head, swooping away again almost immediately. All was quiet now except for the hum of a car on the road, the chattering call of a magpie and the soft cooing of pigeons somewhere in the distance.

I fixed myself more comfortably and settled down to wait.

Aoife Duffy faced Tommy in the hallway.

"You'll apologise to the Master. You'll go in this minute and apologise."

"I don't want to."

"Whether you want to or not, you'll apologise. You're leaving here for good in a week's time and you're not leaving without showing proper respect for the master and for all he has done for you over the years."

Tommy dropped his head.

84

"He shouldn't have been so hard on Mikey. He was only talking."

"Mikey was disrupting the class. If Mikey wants to make trouble for himself, then it's up to Mikey to deal with the consequences. He'll have to learn that sooner or later."

Tommy raised his head.

"If I do it, what about Mikey? What'll happen to him?"

"That's not your concern," she paused, "but it will be better for him if you do what's right."

"I'll do it so."

Tommy closed the door quietly. Mikey was standing out by the wall, looking none the worse for wear. Owen Dara, face still pale, was back at his desk. He appeared to be reading something.

All eyes, except those of the master, focussed on Tommy as he raised his hand: "Sir!"

His voice was low, but carried easily in the hushed room.

Owen Dara did not acknowledge him. Tommy, his hands twisting behind his back, shifted from one foot to the other. Not a sound was heard in the room.

"I…" Tommy cleared his throat, his voice sounding unnaturally loud in the hush, "…I…I'm sorry, sir."

Owen, all eyes on *him* now, raised his head, and looked down at Tommy, a blank expression on his face.

"What?"

"I'm sorry, sir."

The master stared at him for a moment: "Sit down," he said quietly and bent his head again.

Whispers and shuffling began to rise in the classroom and ceased instantly as Owen Dara raised his head again. His eyes scanned the room, coming to rest on Mikey: "What are you…?" he began, and stopped, turning to look out the window. He shook his head, as if to clear it, and turned back to Mikey: "What were you talking about?"

In the face of all that had happened Mikey gave in immediately: "Seánie Luhan went away after lunch, Sir."

"He *what*?" The sudden rise in tone startled the children.

"He's gone away, sir."

"Gone where? Home?"

"I don't think so…he said he was going to go far away."

"Did you search for him when you went out again after lunch?"

"Yes, sir."

"Where did you search?"

"Everywhere, sir"

Owen sat still, while the children waited. He raised his head: "All of you… go home now. Go home."

The children left quietly, the younger ones still frightened by the events of the afternoon, the older ones trying to come to terms with the violence of the outburst from the master. They had seen him angry before but nothing had prepared them for what had just taken place.

Tommy, with Mikey and Billy close beside him, cut across the fields the moment they caught sight of Hungry Jack Maran and Willie Cray in the distance, but not before Mikey had spotted the master's car.

"Seánie's in right trouble now…the master must be goin' to see his mother to complain him."

14

I have walked around the last bend before the school gate and have arrived at the spot where I left the road and climbed over the ditch, on the afternoon that I was supposed to have run away. I left the road because I did not want to meet the master on his way back from visiting my mother; and because I feared meeting Willie Cray and Hungry Jack Maran on my own.

I had watched Tommy, Mikey, and Billy, and the other children, leave the school, waiting for what seemed like an age, before Owen Dara and Miss Duffy emerged. The master got into his car and drove off, not in the direction of Kilcrone, as I had expected him to do, but towards Ballycrag. I knew then that he was going to see my mother.

My descent from the sycamore was painstakingly slow. I had never climbed anything near that height before and, more than once, I clung to a branch and thought to cry out for help, especially when my schoolbag slipped from my grasp and seemed to take an age to reach the ground below. Each time, I would inch my way down, until the next bout of fear halted me. Eventually, I reached a height I was used to and it was easy from then on.

Climbing over the ditch, I ran across the first couple of fields, not caring about the direction, my only thought being to put as much distance between me and the road as quickly as possible.

Annie Luhan was endeavouring to drink yet another cup of tea in an effort to cure the headache and the rawness that she had felt all day, when the sound of a car door being slammed shut alerted her. Whipping off her apron and giving a quick pat to her hair, she went to the door of the cottage. The sight of Owen Dara disconcerted her totally and her immediate thought was to be rid of him as quickly as possible.

The only time they had come face to face since her return to Ballycrag was on the morning she had brought Seánie to the school to enrol him. Except for a formal greeting, Annie had kept to the matter in hand and had blocked any attempt on Owen's part to engage her in casual conversation. The short time it had taken to conclude matters had been strained and awkward and she had left quickly with a simple "Thank you" and had hurried from the schoolroom not giving Owen a chance to engage her further.

The look on his face disturbed her now and his opening question: "Is Seánie here?" sent a wave of worry through her.

"No…why? What's wrong?"

"It…it's just that he didn't come back into school after lunch."

"You mean you don't know where he is?" Fear brought her two hands across her chest.

"I…no. I thought he might have come home?"

"Have you searched for him?"

"Yes…well, Mikey Sullivan did."

"Mikey Sullivan?"

"I didn't realize he hadn't come back until Mikey Sullivan told me. I sent the children home and came here."

"We'll have to find him."

Annie ran to her bedroom. She was fixing on a cardigan when she returned: "Did you do anything to upset him?"

"I…I told him to stand by the wall."

"Why?"

"Because he was late for school."

Annie brushed by him: "We'll have to go in your car and find him."

"Wait, Annie! Wait a moment!"

"We have to find him."

Owen raised his hands in a gesture of helplessness or hopelessness and followed her along the path.

I lost my sense of direction almost immediately. I was crossing an open field with cattle grazing peacefully in the sun. One or two were lying down, lazily flicking their tails. Suddenly, one of them jumped up and charged straight at me, or so it appeared. My actual experience of country life was limited during my time in the midlands and all I could think of at that moment was that I was going to be trampled to death. I knew little of the extreme nervous reaction of cattle to the presence of gadflies. I stood transfixed to the patch of grass I stood on for two or three seconds and then I ran back the way I came, faster than I had ever run in my life, crying out in terror.

I tore my hands and knees, running blindly through thorn trees at the other side of the wall that I had no memory of getting over. I ran on and on until, sobbing for breath, I tripped and fell on my face by the side of a hedge. I lay there, panting and heaving until the tears and the thought of my mother's comforting arms brought relief.

Tommy Sullivan remained standing on the wall he was about to jump down off when he saw the schoolmaster's car approaching. Mikey's head appeared on the same level as Tommy's shins and he too remained in that position.

Billy called from below them: "What are you waitin' for? I can't go up, 'till you get down?"

"Be quiet, Billy! The master's comin'."

Billy lapsed into immediate silence, the memory of the events of the afternoon in school still fresh in his mind.

Tommy was surprised to see Annie in the car. She it was who got out first when the car came to a halt.

"Tommy, is Seánie with you?"

"No, Mrs Luhan."

"Have you seen any sign of him?"

"No."

"If he's not at your house when you get home tell your mother he's missing. If your father's there please ask him to search for him."

"Wait a minute, Annie…" Owen Dara came round the front of the car "…there's no need to…"

Annie interrupted him: "We have to find him. He could be lying hurt somewhere."

"There's just no need to over–react. He could be further back along the road. Why don't we go back as far as the school first and…?"

"We'll do that then. Tommy, get into the car! You too, Mikey."

Tommy hesitated, looking to the master for confirmation.

"Do as she says, Tommy."

Tommy jumped off the wall. Mikey looked down at Billy: "Come on, Billy!"

"Please hurry up and get in the car." Annie's voice was rising.

"Billy's here as well." Tommy was nervous.

"For God's sake, tell him to come out and get in the car."

A search of the school grounds, and the immediate area around it proved fruitless. Stopping here and there on the road back, they called out: "Seánie! Seánie!," to no avail.

Approaching Ballycrag, Owen took a deep breath, trying to keep his voice even: "He could be at home already."

"What time is it now?"

Owen looked at his watch: "Twenty past three."

"My God! He's gone since lunchtime."

"There's no need to be so worried. He's not the first boy to have run away. He'll be all right."

"You don't know that…and you don't know, my son."

Owen was silent.

In the back of the car Mikey whispered to Tommy from behind Billy's head: "He doesn't know who Seánies's father is either."

"What?"

"No one knows who Seánie's father is."

Tommy looked surprised: "How do you know…?" he began and then checking himself, hissed: "Be quiet, Mikey."

A rustling in the hedge brought me to my feet. I set off in the direction of one of the low hills that were so much a feature of the area. It seemed to offer more safety for the moment and it would be a high point from which I could survey the country around. Relief from what I thought was an escape from sure death gave me renewed confidence and a sense of exhilaration. I climbed a tree and, from half way up, I thought I recognised in the distance, the contours of the hill at Ballycrag and other landmarks that looked vaguely familiar. I felt better now and ran down the hill.

Billy was first into Mollie Sullivan's kitchen, with Mikey hot on his heels: "Seánie ran away from school an' the master is here with his mammy an' he brought us home in his car an'…"

"Mollie! Have you seen, Seánie?" Annie ran through the kitchen door.

"No, Annie."

"He's gone, Mollie. We can't find him anywhere."

"Ah, Annie, he's probably just…"

"He told me he was goin' to go away and he was never comin' back," Mikey interjected.

"When did he tell you that?" Annie's alarm was increasing.

"He told me…" Mikey hesitated as the master appeared in the doorway, Tommy behind him.

Annie grabbed his arm: "When did he tell you, Mikey?"

"He told me at lunchtime."

Annie dropped Mikey's arm and held her head in her hands: "We'll have to find him." She turned to Owen Dara: "You'll have to go for the guards in Kilcrone."

Mollie moved close to Annie: "You go with the master. I'll send Tommy off to get some of the neighbours. They can search the fields around…and don't be worrying, we'll find him."

"I don't think…"Owen began, but Annie cut him short: "We'll go now, and not be standing here wasting time."

While Owen Dara and Annie left for Kilcrone, Tommy set out to alert the neighbours. A search party would be organised to work its way back to the school across the fields and as soon as Joe Sullivan came home, he would be asked to drive along the road that ran in an uneven triangular shape around Ballycrag. A quarter mile of this road passed by the bank of the river that fed into the estuary.

This river would become the focus of the search party. It would induce the greatest fear my mother would ever again experience and may have been the final element that drove another human being to the darkest despair.

15

The first, and only time I had been to the river with the Sullivans was two weeks before. I had asked my mother's permission and she had refused. It was one of those occasions when the promise of a new adventure overrode conscience and so I went with them, telling her that we were going to the quarry instead.

The water was low, the level slowly rising, as the incoming tide pushed all the way from the estuary between dark-green banks and tall rushes. The river was spreading itself upwards and outwards across the steeply sloping beds of soft grey mud on either side of its centre.

I had no swimsuit and nothing would persuade me to enter the river naked. Tommy, Mikey and Billy had no such inhibitions. The whipped off their clothes the moment they arrived. Waving their arms and whooping, they ran across the riverbank and jumped straight in, sure of an easy landing in the yielding mud. They rolled in it then and daubed their bodies, until they began to look like remnants of some ancient tribe engaged in a ritual, the reason for which was lost a long time ago or known only to themselves.

I did not know how to react to this unbridled communion between bare, vulnerable flesh and the raw elements of nature. I had only experience of the stream I visited with Francy Hogan and the memory of one day at the seaside when I was very young. I enjoyed them, but I had no sense of unity with them. This was different. It was as though the Sullivans belonged in, and with, the natural world around them and saw themselves not standing aloof or above it but at one with it. That is what I had been learning from them since I'd come to Ballycrag but I would not have known or thought about it then.

They reserved the heaviest applications of the mud for their genitals piling it on in what might have been a gesture of modesty but was more likely to have satisfied a different instinct altogether. I watched from the bank as the three of them, bodies the colour of wet ashes, threw themselves into the cloudy water, laughing and splashing.

I had taken off my boots and socks and had climbed down the bank, tentatively testing one foot and then the other until I stood knee-deep in the opaque, silted mass, fearing for a moment that it would draw me down into its very depths. I went no further and began to climb out again, stopping dead at the sound of the laughing voices, coming from the same level as my head.

I gaped at the two girls who had appeared from nowhere.

"He's afraid to come out."

I recognised them from school. Lucy Joyce was in Mikey's class and Mary Hanafin was in Tommy's. They were sitting a little back from the edge of the riverbank, leaning into each other, and giggling.

"He's afraid to come out in case we'll see."

I hauled myself up on the bank and stood looking at them.

"He has his trousers on," Mary said.

They giggled all the more and I felt the crimson tide of embarrassment flood my cheeks. To me they were quite grown up, especially Mary Hanafin. Mary, the plumper and older of the two, and already on the way to developing ample breasts, was smaller than Lucy. She had red hair and freckles and was always laughing, her eyes twinkling. They were twinkling now: "You're Seánie Luhan, aren't you?"

"Yes."

"Why aren't you in the water with the others?"

"My mo…I don't…I have no swimming togs."

They were giggling again.

"Tommy and the others have none," Lucy said.

She was slim and as tall as Tommy with an oval face surrounded by dark hair. Her eyes, equally dark, appeared as though they magnified everything they looked on.

They giggled all the more now while I began to blush at the sudden knowledge that, behind me in the river, were the three naked brothers splashing and shouting and completely unaware of what I saw as a truly awful situation. I had to warn them.

Without thinking, I turned round and slid down the bank into the mud, managing miraculously not to fall into it.

"Tommy!" I shouted, through closed teeth. "Mikey!"

I began waving my arms. Billy was the first to notice me. He came out onto the mud.

"There's girls!" Some instinct in me kept me from opening my mouth and shouting out loud.

"I can't hear you!"

I tried again. "There's girls watching!"

Billy turned and called out to Mikey, pointing at me. Something about my strangled vocal efforts and my body movements caused Mikey to call Tommy.

"What's wrong?" Tommy stood up in the water.

When I failed yet again to warn them, they looked at each other questioningly and began walking towards me. I gave up then. Dropping my arms to my sides, I tried to shrink into myself while I waited for the inevitable.

Emerging from the water, their bodies now seemed whiter than before and Tommy's sparsely growing pubic hair seemed to accentuate his dangling penis. Slowly plodding through the mud, they were half-way to the riverbank when the two girls stood up and ran to the edge.

Three pairs of hands instantly covered the source of immediate embarrassment for what looked like three open-mouthed, knock-kneed statues, anchored in mud.

The two girls were silent for a moment, and then, their laughter rang out across the river. I, almost fully-clothed, felt the shame of the others and cringed as each girl sang out: "You…hoo! You…hoo!" and, each lifting a hand, wriggled their fingers at Tommy and the others.

The wriggling fingers galvanised the statues into life, Billy being the first to react.

"They'll see me! They'll see me!" he shrieked and knelt down into the mud, bending over until his chest hit the surface. Mikey jerked out a foot, turned back to the water, fell flat on his face, picked himself up and scrambled downwards through the mud like an awkward, immature reptile.

Tommy stood his ground, his face crimson, and shouted: "G'way! G'way!"

"We...can...see...you," the girls sang out

Billy began to cry and Mikey, waist deep in the water, shouted: "It's a sin for girls to...to..." he foundered "...you'll have to tell it to the priest in confession."

The girls, hands on their knees for support, laughed all the harder.

It was too much for Tommy. Covering himself with one hand he scooped up as much mud as possible and began to apply it to his nether regions. He worked fast, scooping and applying until he must have decided that he had covered himself sufficiently. He began to run upwards towards the bank, clawing the air with one hand, trying to make reasonable progress through the impeding mud. He had covered only a few yards when he tripped and his appendage freed itself enough to swing comfortably.

The sight made me squirm all the more and, it was with relief, that I heard Lucy Joyce's voice: "Run, Mary! Run!" and screaming with laughter they were gone.

The interruption from the girls shortened our time spent at the river. The mud clinging to feet and hands we washed off in a nearby stream. Barefooted we made our way home.

"I'm never swimming ever again without my togs," Billy said.

It was when we were putting on our boots, as we neared Sullivans, that I realized I had lost one of my socks. When I got home I found another pair and hid the odd sock where my mother would never find it.

Mikey and Billy, having fortified themselves with sandwiches, planned their own search.

"He could be hiding in the quarry," Mikey said.

"Maybe he was kidnapped." Billy wasn't sure if he wanted to go alone with Mikey. Maybe they should wait for Tommy and the others.

"He isn't kidnapped. He's only afraid to come home that's all. You'd be afraid too if mammy and the master were waitin' for you."

"What'll happen when he comes home?" Billy's thoughts moved away from the possibility he had been considering. The thought Mikey had put in his head seemed more frightening in its contemplation.

"He'll be killed for sure."

Mollie stopped them on the way out.

"No," she said flatly. "I don't want any more worries. One at a time is enough."

"Can't we go with Tommy and the others then when they come back?"

"No! You'll stay here."

"Ah, mammy."

"What you *can* do, Mikey," Mollie smoothed her apron as she did when she had finished with an argument or had reached a decision, "is...you and Billy can to go up to the cottage and wait in case Seánie comes home. Come down straight away and tell me if he does."

"But, mammy…"

"Go up now and wait."

The route I took that late afternoon and evening made it very difficult for any search party to find me. I had taken a shortcut on the way to school with the Sullivans on one or two mornings, to avoid being late. I had done the same on the way home on a couple of occasions when they brought me to a deep, water-filled trench which was good for practising jumping across, or when they wanted to show me the remains of an old cottage that was said to be haunted. Now, I thought I recognized in the distance the places we had passed by, but each time I neared them I knew I was wrong.

In the weeks since I had come here, the increased growth of foliage on trees and hedges, and the taller grasses in fields and meadows made it all the more difficult for me to recognise familiar places. I confused myself even more by skirting fields with cattle in them, in my anxiety to evade the possibility of another fright from another charging animal.

I kept away from the few farmhouses and cottages dotted here and there. The questioning that would surely result if I called in to ask directions was also something I did not wish for. I was confident I would find my way home. I didn't need any help. The worst that could happen would be that I would arrive late and my mother would be angry. I could cope more comfortably with that.

16

On the way to the guards' barracks in Kilcrone, hardly a word passed between Owen Dara and Annie. She twisted and turned, looking this way and that, rising in her seat to peer out the rear window, requesting him to slow down, to speed up, to slow down again. They reached Lisbeg in silence.

"He might have come back to the school," Annie said. "Maybe we should stop and check around again?"

"If you want to…but I don't think you'll find him there. I still think…"

"We'll go on…no…stop!"

Owen followed reluctantly as she ran through the school gate calling out. She was on her way back before he had reached the end of the avenue.

"He's not here! We'd better get on!"

"Listen Annie, you're getting all…"

"I have to find him…if we don't find him before it gets dark I don't know what will happen."

"I'm sure he'll be…"

She hurried to the car and sat in, waiting impatiently until they were moving again.

Nothing was said for a mile or two.

"He's never been alone in a strange place. He doesn't know this area at all." Annie spoke quietly. It was as though, being distanced from the school and from Ballycrag, the problem of Seánie had become, momentarily at least, distanced in her mind and she seemed to relax a little.

"He'll be all right. Nothing will happen to him."

Owen was relieved, but the events of the previous night surfaced now. He had driven back to Liscrone with no memory of the journey home. Sleeping fitfully, he had relived the living nightmare surrounding his attempt to see her. In the half-light of dawn he had paced his bedroom, fear and despair besetting him, his over-burdened mind wrestling with agonising questions: was his attacker somebody that Annie had already taken up with? Had whoever it was who had been on the hill when he had passed her cottage, earlier in the evening, guessed at his intention and had lain in wait for him to return? Had he had been followed to Annie's? Was the canon behind it and had the locals been watching out for him all the time? Had his actions destroyed his life, his career, his hope of ever getting back with Annie?

He had knelt then and begged for his pain to be taken onto the cross; for his life to be restored; for peace in his heart.

Annie's closeness now and the soothing aura of her beauty eased and strengthened him. Were these moments of their being alone and comfortable together, for the first time in almost a decade, the answer to his prayer? He glanced across at her. She was turned away from him, looking through the side window.

"Annie…we…we haven't had the chance to talk since you came home." He moistened his throat: "I still don't know what really happened. Your father wouldn't tell me anything except that you'd gone. There wasn't a word from you…not a goodbye…nothing…all there was, was rumour and…"

"This isn't the time for that." Her voice was still quiet

"I know…but…" he glanced at her again, "…what I really wanted to say is that it doesn't matter anymore. I'm glad you're home…I hope that we can…"

"I told you…this isn't the time."

"I never stopped thinking about you, Annie…" he shifted the car down a gear "…I think of you every day."

"Why are you slowing down?"

"Annie…I…" the car rolled to a halt.

"What are you doing? Why have you stopped?"

Owen turned to face her: "I love you Annie…I don't care about anyone or anything else…we can…"

"We have to get on…" Annie's agitation was increasing again

"…we have to find Seánie."

Owen reached out, touching her cheek: "Please, Annie…"

"Don't!" Annie pushed his hand away.

"We can leave here, Annie…get married…make a new life."

"I don't want to marry you!"

Owen stared blankly at her for a moment before he slumped back in his seat.

"Where's Dan?" Sergeant Mahaffey turned to the tall moustached figure of Guard Hannigan.

"He's gone down to Fitzpatrick's to check out a dog licence."

"Go down and get him and bring him up here."

After a speculative look at Annie and particularly at the master, Guard Hannigan fixed his cap and walked slowly out the door of the guards' barracks.

"Now…" Sergeant Mahaffey turned to Annie "…as soon as the two lads come back I'll leave one of them here, and myself and the other fella will go with you to see what we can do."

"Will they be long?" Annie had tried her best to stay calm and not show her growing impatience with the round-faced, easy going, big-bellied sergeant.

"Ah no…two shakes of a lamb's tail. 'Tiz only down the street. The dog took a bite out of young…"

"Will you get extra guards to help in the search?"

"Well now, before I do anything I'll have to phone the inspector in town and let him know what's happening."

"Won't that take up a lot of time? Don't you understand? My son is missing. He could be lying somewhere…"

The sergeant placed a big hand gently on Annie's shoulder: "If I was you…and I'm sure the master will agree with me in this…", he looked across at Owen Dara, standing by the window, his eyes on the floor "…if I was you I wouldn't be too worried. Young lads like that…"

Annie shrugged off his hand: "You're not me. Seánie's not your son and you don't understand."

The smile began to leave the Sergeant's face, a look of resignation replacing it: "I'll go and phone the barracks in town."

Annie left the barracks in the sergeant's car while Owen Dara followed behind in his car with Guard Hannigan. They would leave the cars at the school and work their way in the direction of Ballycrag. The sergeant had suggested that the master should take my mother home but she had declined. She had not even replied to Owen when he had asked her to follow the sergeant's suggestion. They had not spoken a word to each other since the incident on the road to Liscrone.

Walking and running I had set off in a kind of diagonal across the fields and low hills believing all the time that I was getting nearer to home. I thought I recognised yet another landmark and swung off in its direction. After travelling in a wide semicircle I re-crossed the path I had been on earlier, realizing only then that I was back at the hill I had started out from hours before. Exhaustion, disappointment, loneliness and hunger took hold. I foraged in my schoolbag for remnants of the lunch I had made that morning. Only a few grimy crumbs remained. I ate the leaves of whitethorns then and plucked sour-tasting sorrel from among the grasses in the way Mikey Sullivan had shown me and had assured me were edible by eating them himself. I found a trickling stream from which I drank. I curled up at the base of the tree I had done my survey from earlier and closed my eyes.

17

The news of my disappearance did not filter through into Horgan's pub until about ten o'clock that night. By then, a word here and a word there had led to all kinds of speculation as to the reason for my running away. Owen Dara suffered most from wagging tongues; and when a passer-by called into the pub, a short while later and let it be known that my clothes had been found on the riverbank, the whole circumstances took on a new significance.

It was my sock that had been found, nothing else. The sock had grown in the telling until it became my boots, then my jumper and finally all my clothes.

When my mother and Owen Dara along with the sergeant and the guard met up with Tommy Sullivan and a number of near neighbours who had set out from Ballycrag, without either group having had any success, it was decided that my mother and the guard would return to Ballycrag while the sergeant and the master went to collect their respective cars. They would all meet up again at Sullivan's and, hopefully, I would have returned by then. If not, a further course of action would be determined upon.

Mollie and one or two of the wives of the searching neighbours had been busy making sandwiches and these were set out on the Sullivan kitchen table along with several pots of tea. The eating of the sandwiches and the drinking of the tea had barely begun when Joe Sullivan returned, following his own search. He had stopped at the river on a whim and had walked along the riverbank. At the very end of his search he had found a sock, which my mother identified straight away as belonging to me.

It took several of the women, not least among them, Mollie Sullivan, all their powers of persuasion and comforting to prevent my mother, shattered now by this turn of events, from immediately taking off on foot for the river.

The sergeant, who had just reached Sullivan's, with Owen Dara following close behind him, viewed this latest development with concern. The three cars, the sergeant's, Owen Dara's and Joe Sullivan's, along with several volunteers, were despatched straight away to begin a new search, this time concentrating on the river. Two local fishermen were to be contacted directly and requested to launch their boats. My mother was prevailed upon to return to the cottage and wait there in the company of Mollie and three other women who accompanied her. They stressed to her that the dreaded thought that I might have drowned was not to be considered and that I would either turn up at any moment or be found safe and sound. Privately they began to pray.

Mikey and Billy were sent home with strict instructions from Mollie to eat only as many sandwiches as were necessary to appease their hunger. They were *not* to stuff themselves. Should I appear they were of course to bring me up to the cottage without delay.

Hungry Jack greeted the news in the pub with anger and disappointment. *Blasted children!* He had been drinking in the pub all evening, fortifying his determination to succeed later in the night where he had failed the previous night. While some of the drinkers left the pub to join in the search at the river he ordered yet another pint of stout to console himself. He left Horgan's, barely able to hold on to the bicycle he walked beside and, after a mile or two, let it stay where it fell and staggered onwards to his cottage, pausing frequently to relieve himself.

It was about that time perhaps that I awoke, fearful, hungry and disorientated. Clouds passing across the still rising moon changed everything around me. The countryside was no longer open but was enclosed now: enclosed in whispering silhouettes of trees and hidden places and grotesque dark shapes that moved and changed whenever I looked away. I could die here or be killed by a creature that nobody knew had lurked here all this time waiting its chance, waiting for night. I was terrified.

I saw the light then. I had to go there. It was that or perish alone in this alien place. Skirting a hedge, my heart almost stopped beating. The heavy breathing of cattle at rest at the other side sounded like the stealthy approach of a flesh-eating monster. I panicked then and ran blindly towards the light, falling down and getting up, tearing my face and hands on briars and thorn bushes. I fell getting down off a wall and landed on a rock that crushed against my ribcage, despite the cushioning that my schoolbag provided. Crying and wailing into the emptiness of the eerie half-light, I crawled to my knees and stood upright before stumbling towards the light that spilled onto the boreen I found myself on.

The door of the cottage was wide open. Hungry Jack, hidden by the shadows outside, was relieving himself, and as I reached the doorway, he reached out and grasped my shoulder. The terror I had felt on that first occasion I'd gone to the pictures with my mother when the convict Magwitch rose suddenly like an evil apparition from among the gravestones and grabbed the boy, Pip, as he ran across a graveyard came back. I had screamed then and I screamed now, struggling vainly in Hungry Jack's grasp. Still struggling he dragged me into the cottage.

18

Owen Dara, normally deferred to by the men who had gathered to search for me, found himself isolated when he returned to Sullivans. He did not want to be there, and yet, he could not bring himself to leave. That he had done something to me that caused me to run away was whispered about, but he was not confronted with it. It was inconsequential in the bigger picture and, anyway, it was the sergeant who had taken charge.

Owen had driven in silence to the river, paying no heed to the muttered conversation of the men who had travelled with him. When his passengers had discharged themselves he had remained sitting behind the wheel, alone with his thoughts, until the appearance of the two fishing boats aroused his attention. He got out and began walking mechanically in the direction of the river mouth.

The outgoing tide worried the searchers as much as the possibility that I had somehow gone into the river. Some had already preceded the master in heading for the mouth of the river where it joined the estuary. Others poked among the reeds by the riverbank. The boats trawled up and down, those in them conscious of the fact that their time for searching was limited by the falling levels of the water.

Lanterns winked from the boats and threw flickering images on the water as Owen Dara made his way back to his car. Muted conversation drifted along the riverbank and the blurred shapes of men moved soundlessly in the silvered half-light. The setting was as unreal in his mind as the events of that day.

My whole life is unreal. He did not know if he had spoken the words aloud or not. It did not matter. His life *was* unreal and it was ebbing away from him like the ebbing of the river in the receding tide.

When the moon was no longer visible and the light brought back a familiar world, the water would return to the river again, whole and undiminished as before. His life would not do the same. It was being drained from him into a void from which Annie and everyone around him had withdrawn. In that emptiness there was only pain: an unrelenting, unremitting pain, from which there was no relief and no coming back.

Neighbours and the curious came and went until obligation to their own affairs, weariness, fruitlessness and the receding tide demanded the search be called off, for a few hours at least, until the dawn light would make the task a little easier.

"Sit down!"

Hungry Jack shoved me down on the old car seat he used as a kind of settee and threw himself into a chair in front of a half-eaten meal. The single naked bulb that had seemed so bright a moment or two ago, when I came in out of the night, was now barely adequate to light up the dark and cluttered kitchen. The heavy smell of recent frying, mixed with the odour of sour milk, unwashed plates and mugs, and bits of stale and rotting food, and the stench rising from a pile of dirty clothes on the floor right beside me, sickened and terrified me. It might easily have been the smell of death. That he would kill me lay at the forefront of my terror. Sitting at the table, alternately slugging from a bottle of stout and shoving food into his mouth, his head close to the plate, he might have been a monster devouring its prey. When he raised his head to drink from the bottle and looked across at me, with the grease on his beard and the wet rim of the stout around his mouth, he was a slavering animal contemplating his next mouthful of flesh.

"You'll have…to…goin' home!" The words were slow and guttural, like a menacing growl. He shoved away his plate and opened another bottle of stout: "Goin' home!" he repeated. I did not believe him. He was only stalling. When the moment was right my life would be over. I would be killed in this horrible place.

I sat watching him like a rabbit mesmerised by a weasel, unable to take my eyes away. It was a long time before I could muster up the courage to accept that he was lying back in the chair fast asleep, his snuffling and snorting head sideways on his chest.

I ran from the cottage then, down the boreen, looking back only once. I almost ran under the wheels of Sergeant Mahaffey's car.

Minutes before I made my escape Owen Dara passed by the opening to the boreen. He had left Ballycrag without a word to anyone, stopping briefly outside our gate, before driving on again.

He normally left his car in front of the door of his house, but this time, he drove in around the back to the yard. Taking a pen, and tearing a sheet of notepaper from the pad on the desk, in what was once his uncle's surgery, he walked through to the kitchen and placed them on the kitchen table. He hung his jacket on the back of a chair and sat down, staring at the blank sheet of paper as though it was something strange or unusual. More than an hour passed before he picked up the pen and began to write.

The sergeant had left Guard Hannigan to keep watch on Hungry Jack believing, from the incoherent and sobbing story I had only half-told him, that Hungry Jack had been holding me against my will and had threatened, if not to kill me, to at least inflict serious injury on my person. I was in such a dire state both physically and mentally that anything was possible.

My mother's undisguised relief at seeing me was quickly followed by an outburst of crying and then horror at my condition. Again, the nightmare of being Hungry Jack's unintentional prisoner still fresh in my mind, I confirmed the fact, especially in the sergeant's mind, that he was responsible, if not entirely to blame, for the delay in my homecoming. Stripped to the skin, my physical condition was soon ascertained as the result of having being scratched and torn by thorn bushes and briars. The soreness in my ribs I did explain as having been caused by my falling off the wall. Satisfied that I was in reasonable condition the sergeant left to arrest Hungry Jack and to take him to the barracks for questioning.

Wrapped in a blanket and comfortably warm my mother put me to bed, leaving the bedroom for only a brief period to say goodnight to Mollie Sullivan and another woman who had stayed with her. Joe Sullivan would be asked to drive around and advise as many as possible of my safe return.

Mikey Sullivan, awake when Mollie returned, came down into the kitchen and was quickly shooed back to bed again after being assured that I was already in bed safe and sound. Tommy and Billy were long since asleep.

Hungry Jack added to the predicament he found himself in by reacting badly to being awoken from his drunken slumber and by throwing a wild punch at Guard Hannigan who wasn't fast enough and Jack's callused knuckles grazed his chin. The sergeant had to restrain the urge to flatten him with a right hook that would have been honed to perfection during his early days as a champion amateur boxer. Between them, the sergeant and the guard bundled Jack into the car and on arriving at the barracks, locked him up and left him to recover from the manhandling and an excess of porter.

Owen Dara got up slowly from his chair and walked outside. The early morning was alive now with the activity and singing of birds. He entered the shed at the end of the garden and peered into the shadows until he found what he was looking for. Outside again, he paused, looking up into the branches of a chestnut tree. Taking a ladder from the side of the shed he placed it against the tree trunk and began to climb.

19

An enormous black dog rose out of the pond and towered over Billy and Seánie. Green slime poured out of its eyes and its roaring mouth. He tried to cry out, to warn them, but the words froze in his throat. From a long way off Tommy's voice called out: "Pick up the shovel, Mikey!" He couldn't move. The master shouted at him this time: "Pick...up...the...shovel." He bent down and grasped the handle of the shovel, lifting it. It was torn from his hands. Hungry Jack was beside him, his yellow teeth bared. He tried to run away, but Hungry Jack held him back. He heard a noise behind him and turned his head. The black dog had changed into a huge, green ugly thing with dark holes where it eyes should have been. Heart pounding, he looked for Billy and Seánie. They were gone. The horrible thing was nearer now. It was roaring and roaring and roaring...

Mikey opened his eyes and sat up, staring fearfully around. Sunlight streamed through the window, but the sound of the monster was still in the room. He grabbed at a blanket holding it up to his chin. He was covered in sweat and shaking all over. Tommy's and Billy's beds were empty. Slowly, the noise of the monster abated, and became the steady clacking, humming sound of a mowing machine.

Mikey threw off the blanket and went to the already open window, leaning out. Through a gap in the hedge he caught a glimpse of two horses, plodding steadily up the hill field, drawing the mower behind them.

He quickly pulled back from the window pleasure rippling through him. *Today is Saturday! No school!* He dressed hurriedly, remembering the events of yesterday. He had to see Seánie as soon as possible. He had to find out where he'd been and what was going to happen to him now.

Hungry Jack, feeling physically sick and suffering from severe dehydration, roused himself sufficiently to face Sergeant Mahaffey.

"You'll be off to the town in a couple of hours, Jack. They'll want to talk to you over there. 'Tis a serious thing now, assaultin' a guard in the line of duty."

Jack fixed uncomprehending eyes on the sergeant, the memory of the previous night almost totally lost in his throbbing head. The sergeant nodded: "You're in serious trouble on that one, Jack. Serious trouble and if that isn't enough…" the sergeant stopped, shaking his head.

Jack looked around, doing his best to try and remember. He'd been in Horgan's and…

"The boy" he said, vaguely remembering me.

"Yes, Jack," the sergeant said gently, "the boy! Supposin' you tell us now what happened?"

Jack tried to focus his mind, swallowing non-existent saliva, his throat burning.

"Well, Jack," the sergeant continued with the soft approach "…what was it exactly that you intended to do last night?"

"I wasn't goin to do nothin'. I…I was goin' to wait."

"Wait for what?"

"Wait 'till there was no one else there."

"Where?"

"At her house."

The Sergeant moved a bit closer to Jack: "Whose house?"

"The…the Luhan lady's."

"Ah!…so…so you were goin' to go to her house? When were you goin' to do that?"

"I was goin to go on…on…" Jack attempted to scratch his head with a trembling hand and then held on to it as if it might fall off, "…on Thursday night but someone else was there so I went home instead. I thought I'd go last night but…" Jack's concentration failed him.

"So you planned the whole thing?"

"Well I…no, I didn't…I wouldn't a gone atall only for Willie Cray."

The sergeant drew a deep breath. He was beginning to get the whiff of a conspiracy. He looked up at Guard Hannigan with a *there's-a-whole-lot-more—to-this-than-meets—the-eye* look. Guard Hannigan gave a nod and a wink of assent reminding himself to listen even more attentively. His wife would quiz him as soon as he got home and he wanted to be sure of his facts. His confidences, she always assured him, stayed within the confines of their four walls. He appeared to be totally unaware that his wife reported, if not daily, at least weekly, to their next-door neighbour, also in strictest confidence, on everything that happened at the barracks. The neighbour was only too glad to display her knowledge of situations that did not concern her and so almost everything of significance that happened in the barracks was broadcast to the entire village of Kilcrone and further afield. For now, Guard Hannigan was happy to give his full attention to what Hungry Jack had to say.

"Would you like somethin' to drink?"

Jack's tongue felt like a lump of wood and his throat was still burning: "You wouldn't have a…?"Jack blinked his eyes at the sergeant, who smiled a tiny *you-won't-get-any—porter-here* smile "…mug of water!"

The sergeant smiled broadly: "Get him a mug of water, guard."

They waited patiently while Jack managed to steer the mug clasped in his quivering hands to his mouth, emptying it in one long, painful gulp.

The sergeant felt good. He would have a nice little collection of facts for the inspector when he would phone him later. He'd let him see that he was no fool when it came to getting to the bottom of a case. He'd let Jack tell it his way first. After that he'd get a signed statement from him.

"Would you like more water, Jack? No?.. right! Take your time and tell us your story from beginnin' to end."

Willie Cray, a crate of empty bottles cradled in his arms, was about to exit the shed in his backyard when he noticed the sergeant's car approaching. He turned quickly and threw the crate onto a heap of straw, covering it as best he could. Brushing loose strands of the straw from his clothes, he grabbed a spade and emerged from the shed just as the sergeant drove into the yard. The sight of Hungry Jack sitting in the back seat with Guard Hannigan gave him an uneasy feeling.

"Willie!" the sergeant's tone was pleasant.

"Sergeant!"

"Goin' to do a bit of digging, Willie?"

Willie raised an arm, waving his hand in no particular direction: "Cleanin' out an ould drain, over beyond, sergeant."

"Good!" The sergeant nodded slowly and turned to Guard Hannigan who had just then come up beside him: "That's a good thing now, isn't it, guard?"

"What is?"

"Cleanin' out bad old stuff that can block up things."

"'Tis, sergeant," Guard Hannigan poked at his ear," 'tis."

Willie stepped back half a pace as the sergeant leaned forward and plucked a bit of straw from his hair: "The bad old stuff is good for nothing or no one…you know that yourself, Willie."

The repetition of 'the bad old stuff ' instantly formed the suspicion in Willie's mind that Jack had told the sergeant about the poitín that Willie and a few others were making up in the hills. *The hoor informer,* he though. *I'll kill the hoor!*

"Bad old *words*, Willie," the sergeant continued, "can block up the brain in a certain type of individual with *bad old stuff*…and serious…very serious consequences can result. Are you following me, Willie?"

Willie, his mind racing, was trying to work out what the sergeant was getting at. Had Jack guzzled the bottle of poitín that Willie had sold him and lost the head or what? Was the sergeant going to arrest him? Would he have a chance to warn the lads to get rid of the still?

"So, Willie, to clean out the bad stuff and to get things straight, tell me now what passed between you and Hungry Jack Maran on…which day was it, guard?…"

"Thursday, sergeant."

"…on last Thursday, Willie, concerning…"

"There was nothin' passed between us, sergeant."

"There were words, Willie! Words that could land a man in jail."

"Words?" *Christ Almighty! What was Jack up to?*

"Yes, Willie! So, now, what did you tell Jack con…"

"I told him nothin', sergeant."

"Willie! Willie!" the sergeant's voice hardened and he laid a heavy hand on Willie's shoulder: "We can go and talk in the barracks…or you can tell me now, what words passed between you and Willie concerning the Luhan lady from Ballycrag last Thursday."

Willie exhaled, the reticence he would normally have employed when confronted by any representative of the law deserting him and he gave the sergeant as near as could be an accurate and detailed report of all that had transpired between himself and Hungry Jack Maran on the Thursday afternoon.

Barely a mile out from Willie Cray's, Guard Hannigan leaned forward: "I think you should stop the car, sergeant…Jack's goin' to vomit any minute."

While Hungry Jack threw his guts up, over the stone wall that he held on to for support, Sergeant Mahaffey contemplated his morning's work. One fool leading another fool, the sergeant decided, only one fool was a bit smarter than the other. Dangerous bloody fools when it came down to it. He'd made his feelings on that score known to Willie Cray. The fellow was hiding something though. He'd been too anxious to cooperate. He'd keep a close eye on him in the future. Jack was a different animal. Aggressive when thwarted. He'd shown that when they were arresting him last night. What could he charge him with in relation to Annie Luhan? Intent? Or for that matter could Willie Cray be indicted for incitement? The whole thing was beginning to give him a headache. He'd leave it alone until after they had visited Annie. Anyway, bringing anything to court would only cause more trouble for her - and she had enough to cope with as it was. He looked across to where Hungry Jack was now standing upright. The bile began to rise in his stomach at the sight of him. The sound of Guard Hannigan whistling through his teeth, while he lounged in the back seat, the car door open, grated on him. He had enough now.

"Get that fellow back in here, guard!"

20

I had eaten breakfast and was in the backyard, leaning comfortably against the stone wall that seemed to rest against the line of trees in front of it. I had been warned to stay within the limits of the yard by my mother.

At the bottom of the meadow, stretching downwards from the gable end of the cottage, I watched Andy Dolan make his first turn around the perimeter of the hill field on the mowing machine. The pair of horses, tails swishing, coats already glistening, hauled it along effortlessly. From his iron seat on the mower Andy controlled the horses with the reins held in one hand, the other hand resting on the lever that raised and lowered the mower blade. Some distance behind him, Joe Sullivan and Tommy were using the two-pronged hay forks in a side to side swinging motion, throwing out the backstroke: the first swathe of the long ripe grass the cutting blades of the mower had laid low.

The sweet warm scent of the new-mown hay drifted upwards, reaching deep down inside me. It was like tasting something wonderful, something magical; something that I could not see or reach out and touch but something that I could feel that I had tasted. I would always remember it as the taste of summer.

"Seánie!"

A hoarse whisper from the other side of the wall almost made me jump out of my skin. Mikey's head appeared briefly and disappeared again.

I stood on my toes and peered over the wall. Mikey was on his hunkers, Billy crouched beside him.

"Why are you hiding?"

"Is your mother there?" Again a hoarse whisper

"She's inside."

"Are you going to be killed?"

"No! I don't know."

"Is your mother mad?"

"I don't think so."

"Are you sure?"

"She doesn't seem to be mad."

Mikey stood up: "We'll come in so."

"Where did you go? Everyone thought you were drowned in the river...Billy thought you were kidnapped." Mikey settled himself down, his back to the wall, Billy beside him.

"Mammy said Hungry Jack got you an' was goin'..."

Mikey interrupted Billy: "No she didn't. She said you went into his house but he wouldn't let you home until the sergeant came. Were you there all the time?"

"No. I only went in there when it got dark and because I got lost."

"How did you get lost?" Mikey frowned. He couldn't understand how that could happen.

"I got lost after I got chased by a...a huge big bull."

"A bull! You must have been runnin' towards Ballinaclough so."

"I don't know where that is."

"You couldn't have got lost if you were runnin' this way."

"The master was out lookin' for you as well," Billy said, "an' the sergeant an' the guard."

The mention of Owen Dara and the sergeant brought a shudder: "Why?"

"I dunno. There were loads of people out lookin' for you."

I hadn't considered this at all. My mother I could understand and Mollie Sullivan maybe, but anybody else...

"Why?"

"Because they thought you were drownded or dead or kidnapped." Billy's face reflected the fear with which he had thought about these.

"Or murdered," Mikey added. Then, as if this possibility had triggered a like thought he shook his head: "I don't know what's goin' to happen when you go back to school on Monday."

I had felt quite contented up to that moment. It was Saturday. I was safely at home. My mother hadn't said anything, except not to leave the yard. Now I began to get the shivering feeling that somewhere there was an axe, a deadly axe, waiting to fall on me.

"Did he beat you?" Billy asked.

"Who?"

"Hungry Jack." Jack seemed to be foremost in Billy's mind.

"No. He…he grabbed me an' pushed me. I nearly broke my back when I fell off a wall."

"Were you really frightened?"

Before I could answer Billy, Mikey cut in: "I had a terrible nightmare. I was glad when I woke up."

"What was it about?" I asked him.

Mikey had entertained us on previous occasions with stories from films neither Billy nor I had seen, particularly stories about cowboys and Indians and Tarzan. Now, as he embellished every detail of his dream, I sat down next to Billy, drawing closer to him on that warm summer morning as Mikey's words cooled the air. Every so often he would shove his glasses back up off his nose or push back the lock of black hair that fell down on his forehead. He gazed into the distance like a fortune–teller might gaze at a crystal ball, his slight frame exuding energy that matched the animation of the words that flowed so easily from him. I drew a deep breath of relief when he had finished, realizing only then how menacing the mowing machine sounded.

"If Hungry Jack touched me," Billy was agitated, "Mammy said that daddy would go after him an' he'd never touch me again."

"Tommy would…" Mikey changed his mind about what he was about to say, suddenly remembering the question he had been meaning to ask me: "Seánie, mammy said no one knows who your daddy is. Does your mother not know? I thought you said he was killed in the war."

"I didn't say that," I said defensively, "I said he might have been a soldier."

"A soldier?! I never knew that," Billy said. "Was he killed fighting the Germans?"

"I don't know."

Mikey had one of his divergent flashes of recollection: "My father was nearly shot by the Black and Tans when he was young. He only escaped because he ran into a wood. They fired lots of shots after him but they missed"

"Did they follow him into the wood?" I asked.

"No! They just stayed in a lorry firing away. They were all laughing."

"I might be a soldier when I grow up," I said, wanting to impress.

"I don't want to be a soldier," Billy said, "you can get shot or blown up or…"

My mother's voice rang out just then: "Seánie!"

The three of us jumped at the call from around the side of the cottage.

"Seánie! Come here a moment! Sergeant Mahaffey is here to see you."

My heart missed a beat and Mikey, with Billy at his heels, made a rush for the back wall. They went over it very fast and ran down by the side of the meadow not bothering to look back.

Neither Billy, nor Mikey, nor I had heard the sound of the car above the noise of the mowing machine. The sergeant had left Hungry Jack waiting in the passenger seat and had gone in alone to speak with my mother.

I approached the kitchen now in a state of nervous anticipation, not knowing what to expect. The thought crossed my mind that maybe, just maybe, a boy could be arrested and taken away for leaving school unannounced, for getting lost and for being the cause of so many people, including the sergeant and the guard and the schoolmaster, having to search for him.

I need not have worried. The sergeant was seated at the kitchen table a cup of tea in his hand. He smiled as I sat opposite him, my mother standing behind me, her hands resting lightly on my shoulders. I told him how I had seen the light in the cottage and had run there for shelter; how Hungry Jack had grabbed me and pushed me into the cottage; and how I had feared for my life when I had remembered the picture, *Great Expectations,* that I had seen on the day of my First Holy Communion.

"Did he say anything to you, Seánie?"

"He only said I had to go home."

"Did you run out onto the boreen then?"

"No."

"Why didn't you?"

"Because I thought he was going to jump up and grab me and kill me if I tried to run out."

"Oh, Seánie!…", My mother bent down and pulled me close to her, "…and because he told Mikey Sullivan that he was going to kill him…and Billy and Tommy…and he roared at me as well."

"And when did he do that?"

"Yesterday morning when we were going to school."

After a pause the sergeant asked: "Did he say anything or do anything else to you at his house, Seánie?"

"He only said, *home.*"

"And that's when you ran out?"

"No. I ran out when he went asleep."

"Well now, Seánie, I'm going to go out to the car for a while and then I'm going to bring Jack in to…"

"Do you have to do that, sergeant?" my mother asked, her voice sounding worried.

It took some time for the sergeant to persuade my mother that it was right and proper that Jack be made to face her and me. It seemed a long time before the sergeant came back in.

I stood with my mother's arm around my shoulders as Hungry Jack, in his filthy clothes, was brought into the kitchen by Guard Hannigan. I was nervous and confused when, with his head hanging sideways, he told me he was sorry for anything he had done or said that had frightened me. He simply said sorry to my mother. He did not lift his head to look at either of us.

When Hungry Jack and the guard went outside to the car, the sergeant turned to me: "Runnin' away from school or runnin' away at any time is not a good thing now, is it Seánie?"

"No."

He was looking down at me, his face serious.

"We can't have your mother, or the neighbours or the master out all night lookin' all over the country for you, now can we?"

"No."

"Be a good boy now and don't be causin' your mother any more trouble.

Instead of driving directly to the barracks in Kilcrone the sergeant brought Jack back to where his bicycle lay tangled in a clump of briars. He left Guard Hannigan in the car and while helping Jack to retrieve his bicycle he told him that if he went anywhere near my mother again that he would personally beat him to pulp before throwing him into jail; and that if he ever threatened, roared at, or laid a finger on me or any other child again that the same punishment would apply. Feeling better now, the sergeant also decided to call on Owen Dara to put his mind at rest. The schoolmaster hadn't looked at all well the sergeant had concluded. His concern over the boy seemed to have taken a lot out of him.

There was no sign of the master's car outside the house. Maybe he'd gone over to Ballycrag to see what the story was, the sergeant thought, although he hadn't passed him on the way. Or maybe he was gone to town, or maybe he'd checked at the barracks first.

"No," Guard Guilfoyle told him, "the master hasn't been here at all."

"If he does come in, tell him there's nothin' more to worry about."

Having completed his report in which he detailed the previous day's search; his discovery of the lad; his taking in to the barracks for questioning of one, Jack Maran, in whose house the lad had sought shelter, to ensure that the said Maran had neither detained the boy against his will nor molested him in any way; his interview with a co-worker of Maran's one, Willie Cray, to ascertain the veracity of personal details that Maran had provided during questioning; and finally, his visit to the lad's home along with Maran to meet with the lad's mother as a gesture of goodwill, the sergeant signed it and called Guard Hannigan.

"Read that," he said, handing the report to Hannigan, "and see if there's anything in it you don't agree with, or if there's anything you want to add to it."

"I'm sure it's grand, sergeant." Hannigan was starving and was in a hurry home

"Read it!"

As was his wont with everything he read, Hannigan read slowly, his lips moving.

If I could lip-read, the sergeant thought, *I'd say his reading every bloody word the same way he did when he was in first class at school.* A long sigh emanated from him as he sat back in his chair: *'Tis some country when a grand young woman, with a life to live and a young son to look after on her own, has to put up with the likes of Willie Cray and Jack Maran and a lot of others besides. The whole lot of them wouldn't recognise honest-to-God decency not even if it came up and slapped them in the gob.*

"Everything's grand, sergeant."

"No more to be said then, guard?"

"No, Sergeant."

"So...all's well that ends well, guard."

"'Tis, sergeant. 'Tis."

Guard Hannigan, reflecting on the neat way that the sergeant had presented the facts on the Seánie Luhan case, thought that maybe it would be better to tell his wife about it the way the sergeant had written it.

His wife, however, still resenting the graze evident on her husband's chin and sensing that there was something more, had prodded and poked at him until, finally, he had given in and told her the whole story.

My mother and I were seated at the kitchen table. I had asked if I could go and play with Mikey and Billy.

"We have to have something to eat first."

"I'm not hungry, mama."

"You can eat a small bit."

I was restless. I wanted to go and play. It was Saturday. I did not want to dwell any more on past events.

"Tell me what happened at school yesterday, Seánie?"

"The master put me out by the wall for being late?"

"Is that why you ran away?"

"I didn't run away. I hid in the tree. I was waiting 'till the master left and then I was going to go home."

After a moment's silence she asked: "Why did you leave the school?"

I didn't really know. It was only a feeling. I searched my mind for something definite.

"The master hates me."

"How do you know that?"

"He looks at me and he says things."

"What things?"

How could I explain to her that it was not what he said but the inflexion in his voice, the way the words seemed to cut through me, and the uneasiness I felt anytime he came near me or addressed me.

"What things does he say?" My mother's voice was even, controlled.

"I don't remember."

"Has he ever mentioned me?"

"No...can I go down to Mikey's now, mama?"

"Are you sure he didn't mention me at any time?"

I thought hard: "Once he said I was very bright like my mother. He didn't say anything else."

My mother allowed herself a tight little smile: "He said nothing else?"

"No. Can I go...?"

"All right" she said quietly, "but only for a little while. I want you back here in an hour. Is that clear? Oh…and Seánie…"

I was out the door and gone.

21

I've reached the school gate. I'm looking in at the avenue which appears not near as long as it did fifty years ago. The gable end of the school, facing it, has been altered to accommodate a modern extension that seems to fill what was the schoolyard. There are people at work inside and out, probably teachers and volunteers preparing for the celebrations.

I won't go any further. I don't wish to meet with anybody, not today. Right at this moment I can only think of the afternoon that I watched the master pass through this gate, not knowing then that I was watching him do so for the last time.

It was Canon Bates who found Owen Dara's body. The canon had just finished a satisfying lunch when his housekeeper announced that a particular parishioner wished to see him. The Canon was tempted to plead indisposition but thought better of it: "Show him in and tell him I'll be along shortly."

The parishioner that the Canon had mentally nick-named *Sleeveen* was useful in his way. His primary virtue was the value of the donations he insisted on presenting to the canon to be used at his discretion. His secondary virtue, which the Canon considered a little dubious, was his concern for the welfare of the members of the parish, in all areas of their lives. While the canon walked along the hallway to the parlour, he couldn't help thinking that the man might in any other circumstance be thought of as a prime nosy parker; and a real pain in the backside at that.

He listened patiently, nodding his head from time to time, as *Sleeveen* related the news of my escapade and the ensuing negative attention it had visited on the school. Luckily for everyone concerned he had just met with Guard Hannigan who had informed him that the boy was at home safe and sound. However, it had thrown together the master and *"that woman"* that he had already advised the Canon about. It was still his opinion that *"that woman"* was nothing but trouble. Something would have to be done about her before something worse happened.

The canon promised to give it his attention, thinking at the same time that *Sleeveen* might just be a little over-zealous in his adopted role as guardian of the parish. Still, he might as well stay on the right side of him and anyway, boys running away and causing upheaval in the school and in the parish would have to be investigated. He would go and have a word with Owen Dara.

Unlike the sergeant, the canon parked his car at the front door of the master's house and knocked on the door. On a whim, he tried the door handle and found it unlocked. He stood in the hallway, calling Owen's name. He walked through to the kitchen and out into the garden.

His initial reaction was to run away. Fighting the nausea that threatened to overcome him, he steeled himself not to lose control and climbed the ladder until his head and that of the dead man's were on the same level. Leaning forward, his eyes closed, he whispered an act of contrition into the master's ear. Still fighting the nausea he climbed down.

In the kitchen he drank a glass of water and went directly into the hall and picked up the telephone. For the first time since childhood he chewed at the nails of his left hand while he waited for the operator to answer. By the time he had been connected with the bishop's palace, and the bishop himself had, finally, come on the line, he had bitten off three of the tips of the fingernails of his left hand.

"What is it, Canon?"

"It appears the schoolmaster of Lisbeg national school, Owen Dara, has hanged himself."

"Good Lord! When did this happen?"

"I don't know…this morning, maybe…or last night. I really don't know. I only found him a few minutes ago."

"Where?"

"In his garden…he's still hanging from a tree outside."

"Does he have a family…a wife…children?"

"No! He's single. His father is dead. The mother is still alive. She lives with an older brother. They have a farm…it's a good distance from here."

"They'll have to be notified. I would…"

"He has a brother out on the Foreign Missions."

"Ah!"

"That's the reason I called you."

"Right…are you alone there at the moment?"

"I am."

"You're sure it's suicide?"

"I'd say so, yes."

"Any reason you know of that might have driven him to it?"

"No…well…there was a bit of an upset at his school yesterday. A young lad ran away, got lost for a bit and it seems that the boy involved is the illegitimate son of a young woman that by all accounts the schoolmaster was very keen on some years ago."

"Are you saying he's the father?"

"No! No! Only that he appears to have been very attracted to her. Took it very badly after she left to go and have the baby, it seems. She returned to the parish a couple of months ago."

"Well, well! By the way, did you administer the last rites?"

"I said an act of contrition for him."

"That's all right. You can administer the last rites when he's down off the tree. Look, Ignatius! Stay where you are. Don't allow anyone into the house. I'll phone you back as soon as I can."

It was all arranged quite quickly.

"Superintendent Egan will be with you in less than an hour. Dr O'Grady will accompany him and an ambulance will be dispatched about the same time to take the body to the hospital. The superintendent will begin the process of notifying his family. A post-mortem will have to be carried out, after which a discreet undertaker will look after the remains. All right?"

"Yes."

"Anything else?"

"I have to think about what to do in relation to the school."

"When is it due to close for the summer holidays?"

"Not for another week."

"Close it straight away."

"I'll have to notify the parents."

"Can't you do that at tomorrow's Mass?"

"I thought about that. It's just that the circumstances of the master's death...well..."

"I know what you mean...couldn't you just say something like...ah...following a sudden illness...?"

"You mean like heart-failure?"

"Well it could be said his heart stopped beating alright. I suppose it might also be said that he had an accident"

"An accident?"

"Well, you know. It is possible that he may have changed his mind at the last moment but left it too late."

"An accident could be the most likely explanation, I suppose."

"Well then, Ignatius, that's all I can help you with at the moment. Oh! One more thing. Did he leave a suicide note?"

"I forgot about that. I'll have a look now."

"If you find one, you might let me know."

The canon, his back resting against the sink, his lips compressed, read quickly through the pages of notepaper he had found on the kitchen table. He stood still for a moment and then turned to the window, angling his head until he had partial sight of Owen Dara's body.

"Jesus Christ Almighty!" he swore aloud, and turning away, walked back into the hall to the telephone.

The bishop took the call straight away.

"Yes, Ignatius?"

"He left a note."

"Ah!"

"The woman I told you about is mentioned in it...and her son...the young lad that ran away from school yesterday. He seems to be blaming himself for everything that happened."

"And did anything happen to the boy?"

"No. He's at home safe and sound. He also mentions me in it."

"In what way?"

"He…he seems to have thought that I was working against him. I don't know why."

"Read the note, Ignatius."

The Canon's cleared his throat: "*The blackness is back. It will never go away now. There is nothing left. Nothing. There is only the blackness and the pain. I brought the pain to Annie, to her child, to everyone and I killed our love. I have to end it. It is the only way. I…*"

"That's enough, Ignatius."

"There's a lot more."

"It doesn't matter. Just tear it up, Ignatius. Tear it up and throw it away. You have enough to deal with as it is. You don't need any more strings around your neck…oh, sorry! Not an appropriate choice of words in the circumstances."

The arrival of the ambulance in Kilcrone did not go unnoticed. By the time it had driven round the back of the glebe house, onlookers were already gathering. The superintendent, who had arrived only minutes earlier with the doctor, found himself guarding the gates to prevent anybody else from entering. He thought it prudent to let it be known that the schoolmaster had had an accident but that the extent of his injuries was not yet fully known. When pressed further on the matter, he expressed the personal opinion that there was no need for anyone present to be concerned about it. He would not allow himself to be drawn further on the subject.

While the presence of the canon, the doctor and the ambulance was readily understood, the presence of the superintendent was less so. Why Sergeant Mahaffey had not been called caused some speculation. The matter was laid to rest when someone observed that the superintendent's presence only served to prove just how important the schoolmaster's position in the community was.

As the ambulance emerged, the telephone exchange operator from the village post office, who had just finished work, stood at the back of the group at the gates, in a highly agitated state. She had listened in to the calls between the bishop and the canon and the information she now had, she dared not impart to anyone else. The abuse of her position, if it were discovered, would not only lead to her losing her job, but could have all sorts of dire consequences. She took a vow of complete silence on the matter there and then.

On the following Sunday morning the faithful of Ballycrag gathered for Mass at the usual time in the little barn church that had served their needs for generations. Only a few had heard the report of the master's accident that had come out from Kilcrone the previous evening, and those who had heard were led to believe it wasn't at all serious.

Having arrived at the church, in the Sullivan family car, my mother told Mollie that she wished to stay for a while after Mass and was quite happy to walk home afterwards. Mollie accepted this without question, understanding that it was my mother's way of avoiding any confrontation, good or bad, in relation to my recent escapade. The moment we got out of the car she whisked me inside, not hearing even a whisper relating to Owen Dara's accident.

Mass was usually said by one of the curates, but not on this particular Sunday morning. The men gathered outside the church, awaiting the start of the service, were surprised when the canon's car, ten minutes late, arrived in a flurry of dust and he made his way to the sacristy without acknowledging any of the greetings offered to him.

On the rare occasions he did say Mass his delivery of the Latin words of the liturgy was slow and ponderous. This time it was muttered and hurried, while at times he appeared to lose concentration. Communion over, he turned to face his parishioners: "My dear people, it is with regret that I have to inform you that the schoolmaster, Owen Dara, is at this moment lying seriously injured in hospital."

Sharp intakes of breath all around. I looked up at my mother. Her face had grown pale and I felt her body tremble.

"It would appear that the master had a fall from a tree in his garden and severely damaged his neck."

Gasps now at this revelation followed by total silence.

"He is being attended to at this moment and news of his condition will not be made known until later tonight…or tomorrow morning. In the meantime, I would ask you to pray earnestly for him and his family." The canon cleared his throat: "Lisbeg national school will not re-open on Monday. It will remain closed until after the summer holidays."

He turned away abruptly and continued with the concluding rite of the Mass.

My mother remained kneeling, head bowed, while the church emptied quickly. The worshippers had much to discuss outside. Curious stares were directed at her and the whispering grew apace as they made their way down the aisle. I waited restlessly, particularly anxious to share with Mikey what I thought was surely good news indeed.

The door to the sacristy opened noisily and the canon came striding through onto the altar. He paused in mid-stride, his eyes riveted on my mother's bowed head. Conscious of his staring she looked up.

The canon walked to the centre of the altar steps and stopped, looking down.

"You're Annie Luhan?"

My mother stood up to face him: "Yes."

His eyes searched her: "You knew the master."

It was a statement and my mother grasped the back of the pew in front of her: "Yes."

The Canon's face flushed: "Yes, you knew him…" his voice rose and there was a bite to his words…"you knew him…it was to his cost that he knew you."

I could feel the trembling in my mother's hand as she grabbed mine. She dragged me into the aisle and began walking to the church door.

"You are here to wind up your father's affairs I take it, and then you will be off to wherever it was you came from."

My mother turned, her voice sounding unnaturally loud in the empty church: "No!"

The canon held her eyes for a long moment, before turning on his heel.

22

I'm retracing my steps now, not leisurely but impatiently, anxious to reach my car. I want to leave this place. I have no business here, really. I'm undecided now as to whether I will attend the Centenary Celebrations or not. I won't know anybody and I have no fond recollections to exchange with anyone either, except Mikey, and I can do that without having to go near the school. All I have at this moment is a feeling of anger for the pain and humiliation my mother had to have suffered at the time of the master's death, and again in just a few short weeks after his burial.

The Requiem Mass for Owen Dara took place some days after the announcement of his death. The Sullivans and I, together with the rest of the pupils from Lisbeg, knelt together in seats reserved for the school. My mother was somewhere else in the church, with Mollie and Joe Sullivan. My memory of it is of a huge crowd of people, of several priests surrounding the canon on the altar, and of the long time he spent, speaking about Owen Dara.

I heard little of what he said. My eyes and attention kept returning to the coffin in front of the altar. I found it difficult to comprehend that the master was no longer alive; that he would never be able to confront me again; that the wooden casket contained his lifeless body. When Mikey began whispering in my ear, it was not the censuring gaze of Miss Duffy that I expected, but the intense, disturbing eyes of the master.

I do remember the canon talking about "…the tragic loss to his family and to the community and in particular to the children, who have lost a dedicated teacher…" and the sight of Miss Duffy wiping away her tears.

At the end of the ceremony we were the first to leave and were lined up in two rows outside the church door. After the church bell began tolling a series of plaintive, measured peals, the priests emerged through the doorway, followed by a number of men carrying the coffin shoulder high.

We had to walk a long way behind the hearse. I did not know then that my mother had remained behind in the church and would walk home alone after everyone had left.

Alternating groups of men carried the coffin three times around the stone wall perimeter of the graveyard before entering it and finally laying the coffin down by an open grave.

"Come on, Seánie!"

Grabbing my hand, Mikey moved away from the rest of the children, and burrowed through the adults that were bunched closely around the grave. We emerged to the front as the coffin was lowered on ropes into the pit.

"Look, Seánie! The stuff pirates put on their flags," Mikey whispered, pointing at the skull and various bones that lay at the base of the mound of fresh earth beside the grave.

Men with shovels appeared and began, with furious intent, to fill in the grave. The skeletal remains that had been unearthed during the digging of the grave were thrown in by hand and I thought I heard the sound of bone against wood, but it might have been just the pebbles that peppered the clay. Final prayers were said, and the event that was to have such a significant effect on the lives of my mother and me, came to an end.

My mother was lying down in her room in the cottage when I returned with the Sullivans in their car. Mollie came in with me, and stayed with her for a few moments, speaking quietly.

"You're coming down to the house to have your supper, Seánie," Mollie said when she was about to leave, "your mother needs to rest for a while."

Over the next few weeks, I spent more and more time with the Sullivans, especially with Mikey. I had the freedom to come and go with little censure from my mother who seemed to be tired all the time and much quieter in herself. Perhaps she was regretting her decision to return to Ballycrag, reconsidering it maybe.

Whatever the situation, it was made much more difficult when the telephone exchange operator in Kilcrone found that she could no longer carry her awful secret alone without having a nervous breakdown. She confided in her best friend. The best friend promptly told her own mother. The mother whispered it to a neighbour and the neighbour whispered it to another neighbour. By late afternoon, everyone in the village of Kilcrone knew. Before the day had ended, the whole parish, including Ballycrag, was made aware that Owen Dara had committed suicide and why.

The end of our time in Ballycrag that summer was a just a week or two away on the day that Mikey told me: "Maggie Dolan called your mother a hoor."

I had heard Andy Dolan shout: "Get on there, you hoor you!" to a straggling bullock or listened now and then at school to a boy refer to another boy as "a right hoor" but it had not meant anything to me other than as a strong swear word. That Maggie Dolan had used it in relation to my mother raised an instinctive feeling inside me that it meant something ugly; something to be ashamed of. That awareness did not leave me for a very long time even after we had left Ballycrag. I did not know how to express that feeling to Mikey now and so I said nothing.

"Maggie said the master would still be alive only for your mother. Mammy was very angry. She told her not to be sayin' things like that."

I did not understand any of this.

"She said that she heard that someone wrote everything down about the master and sent it to your mother. Mammy was really mad then and told her to go home."

The mention of the master made me think that my running away from school had something to do with the whole situation. I felt uncomfortable now.

"Are you goin' away?"

Mikey's question worried me.

"No."

"Daddy says the best thing for you and your mother to do would be to go away."

The thought that we might leave Ballycrag had not entered my head until that moment. My mother had made no reference to it but now, in an instant, I understood that the possibility was there.

"I don't want to go."

"You'll have to, if your mother is goin'."

We were sitting on top of the big crooked rock in the crag, the sounds of warm summer all around us: the clear notes of an ascending lark; the muted lowing of cattle; the soft note of a pigeon somewhere far away.

Mikey jumped to his feet: "Look, Seánie! A kestrel!"

The kestrel wavered high above the crag, holding position for a moment, then swooped and rose again, repeating the manoeuvre over and over until it hung in the sky for what seemed like a long time before it dropped quickly towards the earth at a steep angle away from us. We lost sight of it then and strained our eyes against the brightness of the sun but it was nowhere to be seen.

"He's got a field mouse or a grazer," Mikey said.

"What's a grazer?"

"A young rabbit…it kills chickens as well if you're not careful."

There was always something new to be discovered while I was with him or Tommy or even Billy. There was the following of a worn narrow track through the long grass and the finding of a hare form, the beaten down hollow still warm. There were the tiny lizards that lay hidden under rocks; the little creatures that would jump down your throat into your stomach and grow and multiply down there unless you kept your mouth firmly closed. There was the slippery translucent frog-spawn with thousands of tiny black dots waiting their time to grow into tadpoles and eventually into frogs if they survived. There were the habits of field and woodland creatures and the stories that went with them.

I did not want to leave all this. It was the opening to a world I could not discover on my own or perhaps never would at all.

Later that afternoon, as I ran up the hill, my heart palpitated when

I saw the canon's car come to a sudden halt outside our gate. Reaching the cottage I heard the raised voice within. The conversation I had had earlier with Mikey had prepared me in some small way for what was to come.

Sleeveen had wasted no time reacting to the news of Owen Dara's suicide and my mother's supposed part in it. He had not waited for the housekeeper to announce him but had brushed by her and had confronted the canon in his study: "You have transgressed the laws of God and the Church!" he shouted.

"What do you mean?" The canon rose quickly from behind his desk, anger at this intrusion flushing his face.

"You have buried a suicide in consecrated ground!"

The canon was stunned. His composure faltered for a moment and then quickly reasserted itself: "You have a cheek to barge your way in here making accusations you know nothing about."

"The whole parish knows about it! You have led them astray and defiled…"

"Get out of here!" The canon was furious: "Get out of here and do not attempt to call at this house ever again! D'you hear me?"

Sleeveen turned pale and was speechless for a moment. He turned away and instantly turned back again: "I warned you about *that woman* I warned you about her but you did nothing…"

"Get out, I said!"

"…and you have brought scandal and desecration…"

The canon came out from behind his desk and rushing forward, grabbed *Sleeveen* by the arm. Half-dragging, half-pushing him, he propelled him into the hall, past the disbelieving look on the housekeeper's face.

"I'll report you to the bishop! I'll have you…" was as far as *Sleeveen* got before the canon bustled his unwelcome visitor out the front door, slamming it shut behind him. Ten minutes later he drove at reckless speed towards Ballycrag. His anger was still burning when he strode into our cottage, startling my mother: "I

136

want you out of here! I want every trace of you to be gone before the week is out! You scandalized this parish before but it is nothing compared to what you have done now!"

My mother turned chalk-white and it was at that moment I entered the kitchen. I ran to her and felt her trembling arms tight around my waist.

"If you do not go of your own accord I will see that you are dragged out of here by the decent people of this parish!"

"I will not go."

"You will!"

"No! I will not."

"You will." He paused, his eyes boring into mine: "You will when the people fully realize that you and that…that…" I cringed in fear "…bastard…" he spat out the words "…are responsible for the death of a good man."

I clung to my mother then as her strength deserted her and she broke down into convulsive sobbing. It did not soften the canon: "I do not care where you go or how you go, but you will not be here in this house, in this parish by this time next week." He looked down at me once more and breathing heavily he turned on his heel and left.

The closing of the car door sounded like a gunshot and as he drove away down the hill the engine screamed from the hard pressure of his foot on the accelerator pedal.

I cried with my mother and she held me all the tighter. We were in that position when a breathless Mollie Sullivan ran through the open door: "Oh, Annie!"

She had her arms around both of us in an instant.

I did not understand anything of the circumstances that had brought our lives to such a state. I only knew that something terrible had happened and that I was somehow to blame.

Molly Sullivan stayed with us a long time that night. When Joe came up to the cottage she told him to go home and wait and that she would come down when she was ready. She it was who forced my mother to eat and put me to bed after I too had eaten, but I was too fearful to be alone in my room. Mollie brought my quilt and a pillow into the kitchen and placed them on the settle near the fire. I felt secure as I lay down, the low pitch of her voice and that of my mother's comforting me.

23

As I walked through the hotel lobby on my return from the school, some eight or nine hours ago now, one of the girls in reception called me: "Mr Luhan?"

"Yes."

"A gentleman left a message for you…he was here only about ten minutes ago."

She handed me the note:

> *Glad you could make it. Looking forward to meeting you on Sunday. Sorry I can't meet you before then. Am on my way to a wedding in Dublin. By the way, I have some news that should interest you.*
> *Mikey.*

I couldn't help but smile. It was always the same with Mikey when we were children. There was always the bait, the promise of something interesting to be seen or told about. After all these years it was '*news that should interest you.*' I would have to go to the celebrations, I decided at that moment, if only to keep faith with Mikey.

I had a snack then and afterwards came up here to my room to relax but I could not. The memories would not leave me alone and I returned to reading a journal my mother had given me - one of a large and unexpected collection she had pressed on me just a year or so before.

I had called to her home one afternoon just to see that she was well and that she was managing all right on her own. She had insisted on my having tea and we sat talking in her kitchen. When I had told her that I would have to leave shortly to keep a business appointment she stood up, leaving the cup of tea she had been drinking: "There's something I've been meaning to give you."

"What?"

"If you come with me, I'll show you."

I followed her upstairs to her bedroom and then to her dressing room.

"I want you to have these," she said, pulling out one drawer and then another, and more drawers, all of which contained what looked like books and papers.

"What are they?" I asked her, quite perplexed.

"The story of my life…" she did not look at me "…and yours too, in a way. I want you to have them."

"But…?"

She began taking out books and papers: "Just take them and keep them."

"Is there anything…?"

"I'm fine and there is nothing wrong." She was piling copybooks, loose sheets of paper and hardback journals and diaries on the floor: "I don't want them thrown out into some rubbish bin…or to fall into someone else's hands if anything should happen to me…there are some cardboard boxes down in the scullery which you can pack them in.."

She offered no further explanation and I did not press her. I did not ask her if I should read them. I just assumed that she was leaving that decision up to me, to do so in my own time.

The boxes filled the car boot and the back seat of my car. Back in my apartment I stacked them in a corner of one of the bedrooms, covering them with a wall-hanging I had brought from Marrakesh. I did not look at them again until last evening and then it was just a hurried search for any of the journals that related to our time in Ballycrag. I found a few likely ones and shoved them into my overnight bag except for the one I began reading while I was waiting at Heathrow, and again, on the flight to Ireland.

Having read a few pages of the journal now, I turned to the others I had brought with me, and found a letter from Mollie Sullivan, tucked between the pages of one of them. I realized only then that my mother had maintained contact with Mollie for a long time after we had left Ballycrag. In her letter, and in others that I found, Mollie had detailed inconsequential things, mostly about Joe and the boys. Reading them lifted my spirits a little and I relaxed then, drifting into a half-sleep for an hour or more. I showered and changed, feeling almost buoyant as I went downstairs to the hotel dining-room for an early dinner.

There was just a sprinkling of diners and my attention was immediately drawn to an attractive young woman and a small boy, eating together a few tables away from me. Mother and son I thought idly. She looked to be in her mid to late twenties and the little boy around seven or eight. Their ages could have been the same as my mother's and mine on the morning we had left Ballycrag.

My mother had arranged with a solicitor, the same one that had handled her father's affairs, to have the land sold, as soon as Andy Dolan's lease was up at the end of the year. She had decided to hold on to the cottage and the ground it stood on. She had told Mollie Sullivan to take whatever she fancied and had turned the key in the lock, believing then, perhaps, that someday one of us would return to dwell in it. It would be six or seven years later before she could finally bring herself to have it sold off.

Joe Sullivan drove us to the railway station. I sat in the front seat with my mother, the distribution of our luggage between the boot and the back seat allowing just enough room for Mikey and Billy to accompany us. A disappointed Tommy remained behind with a tearful Mollie.

As the train began its slow, shunting exit from the station, I stood beside my mother in the corridor and raised my hand to wave to Billy and Mikey. I was taken by surprise at how quickly they drifted away from me into the blurred interior of the railway station; like shadows slipping into a darkening sun.

We stayed for a few nights, maybe more, in a boarding house in Dublin. I remember our room as a dull unwelcoming place, stranded in the midst of noise and semi-darkness, already cluttered by the addition of our clothes and the cardboard boxes containing the bits and pieces my mother had taken with her from the cottage.

We moved from the boarding house to live with an old lady in Sandymount, the closeness to the sea bringing relief and excitement back into my life. When we left for England some weeks later, in the boat that I had regarded as a great ship, the passage from Dun Laoire to Holyhead seemed more like the substance of dreams than that of reality. The train journey to Euston Station in London was a long, endlessly moving, shifting corridor of colliding bodies, babbling voices and broken, restless sleep.

"Daddy!"

The face of the little boy lit up with the excited glow of recognition and he jumped from his chair. The figure of a man passed by my table and dropped on one knee, arms wide open, to meet the headlong rush of the child.

I watched them for a while, feeling the onset of a yearning that I have felt at various times over the years: a yearning to have known what it would have been like to have shared my boyhood with my father and to have had both my parents in my life. I finished eating then and walked out into the warm, bright evening, leaving the more sanitized and formal surrounds of the hotel grounds, and turned off into a by-road.

Low-lying hills splashed with the yellow of gorse and the purple-brown of heather, rose above a landscape rich in the green and fruitfulness of summer. I clambered over a wall into a field, dislodging some of the stones, glancing guiltily around as I replaced them, half-expecting an irate farmer to come running in my direction.

The light faded into the quiet and the shadows, as I made my way back here to my hotel. I decided against having a drink in the hotel bar, opting instead for room service. I was tired, but it was not a physical tiredness, more a heaviness of spirit. I had hoped that a nightcap or two would relax me enough so that I would fall into bed and drift into restful sleep, but it did not happen. In fact I've been sitting here for quite a long time, at the writing table, wide-awake and reading another of my mother's journals.

The journal is one that I had shied away from reading; one that referred directly to the early part of her life, from the time when her mother had died, to the time she had first left Ballycrag. The content was probably originally written down elsewhere as a daily or intermittent diary of events as they happened at the time, but at some later stage in her life she must have re-written it as one continuous story.

I had looked at it briefly before going to dinner and then I had left it, feeling that it was too personal, too revealing of my mother's life. Instinctively I knew that it would detail the circumstances surrounding my birth and I was a little frightened of it.

I have always had a kind of ambivalence towards the discovery of the truth about my origins – one part of me has always wanted to know everything there is to know about my birth, about my father - the other part of me has feared the answer. I tried asking my mother about him a long time ago and her reply then was vague and incomplete. Some instinct throughout the years told me not to ask again but to wait; to wait until whatever it was that held her back from telling me had been removed.

Reading through her journal now, I realize that she had not been holding back. She had given me the answer - the only answer available to her.

The Mother

1

West of Ireland
1938/43

Annie Luhan's breath caught in her throat when the master answered the knock on the schoolroom door and she saw her father standing outside in the hall. Her father muttered something to the master who shook his head and after a few minutes came back into the room and spoke quietly: "Annie, get your schoolbag."

He put his arm on her shoulder as they reached the door: "I'm sorry" he said, and closed it behind her.

Her father looked very pale as he reached out to her. Holding her close, his cheek resting against the blue ribbon on her hair, he told her.

Blue was her mother's favourite colour so Annie wore the same colour ribbons almost all the time her mother was in the hospital. She thought her mother would come home again. She never thought she would die.

She couldn't remember how many days or nights had passed before she stood beside her father, holding his hand tightly, as the brown earth thudded on the coffin with her mother inside. Back home in the cottage, sitting by the cold hearth with her father's arms around her, she started at every sound expecting her mother to come through the door even though she knew she was dead. She cried a lot and her father had to sit with her by the side of the bed until she cried herself into an exhausted sleep.

She cried again when she went back to school and the other girls were nice to her and talked about her mother. The master brought her next door to the mistress, Miss Conway, who didn't mind, and told her that her mother was in heaven and was her guardian angel now and that she was looking after her and that she would be all right.

The boys were quiet and didn't say anything. When one of them forgot and pulled her hair the others chased him across the yard.

It was the beginning of October then and she was thirteen. She would be fourteen the following July.

The week before the Christmas holidays Miss Conway came late to the school gate where they were all waiting in the rain and told them that the master had died suddenly and that the school would be closed until January. Annie was worried about her father and ran the whole way back to Ballycrag. She was relieved when she came into the kitchen and found him kneeling near the fire, a pile of sally rods beside him and a creel taking shape under his hands.

Her mother was a dressmaker and every Christmas she made Annie a new dress or a new coat or both. There was none that Christmas.

Her aunt Nora, her father's sister, asked them to come to her house for Christmas Day but her father said no, so she brought them a goose and a cake and told them what to do.

Walking across the fields to midnight Mass, the frost crunching under their feet Annie asked her father: "How old are you, daddy?"

"Forty two."

"How old was mammy when she died?"

"She was thirty four."

"Is forty two old?"

Her father held her hand tighter: "No. It's not old."

The parish priest, Fr. Hayes, had announced at mass that the schoolmaster's son, Owen Dara, would be coming up from Cork to take his father's place in the school when it reopened.

"I have no doubt but that he will continue the good work of his late father. The Dara family's contribution to both education and the church is exemplary. Some of you will already know that one of Mr. Dara's brothers is a missionary priest, bringing the word of God to the poor people of Africa."

The new master looked just a little bit like his father, only that he was taller and a lot younger, with dark hair and brown eyes. He didn't smile very much, 'though he did smile at Annie when she answered a question. She felt his eyes looking at her at times when her head was down and she was busy writing or doing arithmetic.

He knew about her mother because he said to her when she was hanging up her coat in the hall: "It's just you and your father at home, Annie?"

"Yes, sir"

"How is your father?"

"He's well, sir."

In March he gave her a note to take home. Her father read it and Annie waited for what seemed like an age before he said: "The master wants me to call to the school."

"Why?"

"He wants to talk to me about you."

"Show me the note."

The master told her father she was very bright and that she ought to go to the Convent Secondary School.

"It's not much use to her doin' that. What would she get out of it?"

"It would open up opportunities that she would not have otherwise. She might become a teacher or join the civil service. It would be a shame not to give her the chance of an education."

"We can't afford it. If her mother was alive it might be different."

"It's a great pity all the same. Is there no way at all you could manage it?"

"I'll see."

She was surprised when she came home and her father asked her if she would really like to go to the Convent Secondary School the following September. She had liked helping her mother with the dressmaking and she had thought that she too would be a dressmaker when she was older.

She had seen the convent girls when she was in town with her mother and had admired their uniforms and envied them as they entered the gates of the big grey school behind the high stone walls and the tall trees. Through the black iron gates she had caught glimpses of the wonderful flowers and shrubs that grew either side of the gravelled drive leading up to the heavy wooden doors that she thought must surely open into a lofty and exotic world.

"I would like to go, daddy."

"I'll see what I can do."

Two weeks later he said: "Tell the master it's all right for you to go."

The schoolmaster was pleased when she told him.

"Now we'll have to prepare you as best we can."

Some days she was late getting home when he kept her back to work out an equation in algebra or a theorem in geometry or to translate a simple sentence into French. She began to enjoy these extra subjects and it gave her the feeling that she had grown up and had already left the days of national school behind her.

Her mother had coughed up blood before she went to the hospital so she was terrified when the blood appeared and screamed and screamed: "Am I going to die? Am I going to die?"

Miss Conway had taken several moments to assure her that she was not and explained quietly to her that she had indeed grown up. She didn't tell her father when she got home.

She went to the dressmaker with Aunt Nora before her Confirmation. When she tried on her veil, the dressmaker said: "Beautiful…like her mother."

Her father had tears in his eyes when she put on her confirmation outfit for him.

On the way out from the church after the ceremony was over, Conor Lawlor, who had pulled her hair after her mother died, pushed a love note into her white-gloved hand.

On the last day at Lisbeg the girls hugged each other and some cried. The master told her he was sure that she would make the school proud of her.

A week later she went to the convent with her father. Passing through the big iron gates and walking along the curve of the drive to the stone steps she felt the thrill of a new sense of promise to her life.

The little nun that answered Paddy's tentative tug on the bell pull seemed to Annie to be very old, very tiny, with the bright shining eyes of a bird peering out at them from the habit that swallowed up the rest of her body. The nun's feet made no sound on the polished wood floor as they followed her across the entrance hall. She glided ahead of them, the rustle of her clothes like disjointed whispers. In the parlour, where she left them to wait, the strong odour of wax polish and a weighty sense of grandeur caused Annie to reach out unconsciously and grasp her father's hand.

The headmistress, Mother Paul, a smile softening the stern-face she invariably presented to the world, withdrew a marble-white hand from the folds of her sleeve and extended it to Paddy in formal greeting, her eyes measuring them both.

"Please sit down." She indicated chairs around a circular mahogany table: "You too…ah…Annie, isn't it?" adding sternly as Annie nodded her head in reply: "Answer *yes mother* or *yes sister* and *no mother* or *no sister* when you are spoken to. You do have a tongue, don't you?"

"Yes sist…Mother."

Paddy felt a quickening in his pulse: "Annie's a good…"

Seated across from him, Mother Paul cut him short, her features relaxing once more into a smile: "Now, Mr Luhan…"

Annie's slight feeling of discomfort at Mother Paul's rebuke left her immediately. She paid scant heed to the conversation between the nun and her father, her eyes busily taking in the lofty ceiling, the huge gilt-framed portraits of nuns, the religious paintings and the ornate cabinets filled with ornaments and objects she had never seen before.

"You are paying attention, Annie, are you not?"

The measured tone of Mother Paul brought her back to the conversation. She listened then as the nun outlined the term fees and had handed Paddy a list of requirements while informing him of the shop in the city that supplied the uniform for the girls. The code of conduct she also gave them, reminding Annie of its importance and her need to ensure that she abided by it.

Paddy had reluctantly agreed that Annie would stay with Aunt Nora who lived on the edge of town with her carpenter husband and the son who had been born to them late in their marriage.

"It's a long enough journey from Ballycrag…" Nora had argued "…let her stay for a few weeks, at least until she settles in." Noting Paddy's crestfallen face she had added quickly: "Of course she'll go home on Saturday afternoons and come back Sunday evenings." Paddy's face had brightened at that.

About to enter the convent gates behind two other girls on her first day at school, Annie did not notice her father standing across the road. He had risen early and cycled into the town.

"Annie!"

She ran across the road and hugged him.

"I just wanted to be here on your first day," he said.

He waited until she had walked along the drive and had passed through the convent doors before mounting his bicycle and beginning the return journey to Ballycrag.

2

Owen Dara's faith in Annie's ability had not been misplaced. He had been calling at regular intervals to the cottage to inquire of her father about her progress at the convent. He was pleased, but not surprised when, at the end of her first year, Paddy Luhan proudly told him that Annie had been chosen to sit the Intermediate Certificate Examination on the following June, skipping an entire year in the process.

"It will be a hard year for her, but she'll be well able for it," Owen said. "I could come over the odd weekend if you like, when she goes back after the holidays, and give her a little help."

Annie did not welcome the idea.

"I can do it on my own. He doesn't have to come over here."

"Where would be the harm in him givin' you a bit of help?"

"I can get help from any of the nuns in the convent if I want it."

"I know…but you wouldn't be goin' there at all only for him…'tisn't every master would try an' do what he did for you."

Annie gave in and when the school year began, Owen came every second Saturday to the cottage. After Christmas, he came once a week, always on a Saturday evening. For the final two months, he came every weekend, sometimes on both Saturdays and Sundays. Annie had grown used to his visits, but had often wished that she could have spent the time differently. Some of the girls in the town were allowed to go to the pictures on a Sunday night, or visited each other's houses, but for Annie there was no choice in the matter.

While they waited for the examination results that summer Owen still visited the cottage regularly, just to assure Annie and her father that there was nothing to worry about and everything to look forward to. When the results were known, Annie had taken first place in her class and had finished among the top group of all the students in the country.

Returning to the convent at the end of that summer, Annie settled in to what was a relatively comfortable and relaxed period for her at school, with the Leaving Certificate Examination not taking place for two more years.

Having moved up a year, she made friends with Elizabeth Ross, a year older than her, with whom she had had only a passing acquaintance up to then. Elizabeth's family owned the biggest drapery shop in the town and Aunt Nora was happy to encourage the friendship, particularly since Elizabeth's father had the reputation of being able to acquire the scarcest of items despite the wartime rationing.

Elizabeth was the youngest of the Ross's three children. Her sister, a nurse, the eldest in the family was married to a doctor in London and her brother, also married, worked in the family business.

Smaller than Annie, with short wavy hair and the round smooth, cheeks of a cherub Elizabeth looked younger than her age, despite her efforts to contrive a more mature appearance. She affected knowledge of sexual matters that sometimes shocked Annie and at other times caused her to laugh and to question the accuracy of her friend's revelations. Elizabeth's preoccupation in this regard was not lost on her parents who hoped that Annie would exert a good influence on her.

As the year progressed, Annie began to spend the odd night at Elizabeth's home and eventually, some weekends. Sometimes they went to the cinema and, on a rare occasion, to a dance, in the company of Elizabeth's brother and his wife.

In springtime, when daylight began to extend well into the evening, they were permitted to stroll around the town square for an hour or so after supper. More often than not, Elizabeth used these occasions to relay the town gossip and the town scandals to Annie, usually prompted by the sight of, or following the greeting of someone or other of the townspeople.

"See the woman coming towards us, Annie?"

"Which one?"

"The one in the brown coat and the hat…with the little boy."

Elizabeth dropped her voice: "Her name was Mary Fahey, but she's now Mary Furlong. Her husband's not the boy's father at all...Joe Lillis is...he was great with her before she married Petey Furlong. Her parents wouldn't hear of her marrying Joe at all and when they found out that she was going to have a baby they made a match with old Petey and she had to marry him."

Annie couldn't bring herself to look too closely at the approaching woman, the little curly-haired boy trotting beside her, and glanced down at the footpath as the woman passed.

"A lovely evening, Mrs. Furlong," Elizabeth said sweetly.

The woman replied inaudibly and quickened her pace as she passed on.

"Does her husband know that the baby isn't his?" Annie asked, after a moment or two.

"He doesn't care...he's delighted...he's too old and withered to give anyone a baby."

"What about the real father?"

"He's gone away...Mary Fahy's three brothers made sure of that. They beat him one night until he was nearly dead...he was gone a few weeks after that...Mary was going to throw herself into the river only the priest was called."

Annie was appalled: "That's awful...but how do you know that it's all true?"

"It's true all right."

Elizabeth's information came mainly from her father's more important clients who were regularly entertained by her mother in the kitchen behind the main drapery section. From quite early on, Elizabeth had discovered that by sitting quietly on the stairs, hidden from view, she could easily hear every detail of gossip and the retelling of scandals that seemed to be the sole preoccupation of her mother's visitors.

"How can you be so sure?" Annie asked now

"I heard my mother and Mrs. Ryan talking about it."

"But...?"

When she had no wish to be pressed further on the truth, Elizabeth always found some means of distracting Annie:

"Look! There's Simon Enright…come on!"

If it wasn't the sight of some boy or other, or yet again, another foray that brought them past the whistles and cat-calls of the boys gathered at the Munster and Leinster Bank corner, there was always something or somebody to aid Elizabeth in preventing Annie from any further questioning.

Twice, in the weeks before her seventeenth birthday, they had met Owen Dara in the town square. On the first occasion, he had walked hurriedly towards them, stopping only to ask Annie how she was getting on and how her father was and to nod to Elizabeth.

"He's after you," Elizabeth observed the moment after he had left them.

"No he's not!"

"Yes, he is."

"He's not!"

"I wouldn't mind it, if he was after me. He's handsome enough… and not too old."

"It doesn't matter whether he is not."

Elizabeth shrugged, her face serious for a moment: "The older ones are better, you know. The younger ones only talk about stupid things or grab at you."

Annie quickened her pace and Elizabeth had to run to catch up with her.

Later, in the quiet of the bedroom, when she and Annie were studying, Elizabeth brought up the subject again.

"They do it to themselves, you know."

"Who do?" Annie's head was bent over a textbook.

"Boys…men."

"Do what?"

"Pull at their things."

"What?" Annie was only half-listening, her thoughts on Owen Dara.

"They go around thinking about it all the time as well."

"Thinking about what?" Annie's head was still bent over the book.

"About…about putting their thing in a girl."

Annie's head jerked up straight: "Elizabeth!"

Elizabeth crinkled her nostrils: "That's why you have to…to…to do it for them sometimes."

"That's disgusting!"

Elizabeth rested her chin on her palm, and looked pensively into space: "At least that way you don't have to worry about getting a baby."

"Stop, Elizabeth!"

Annie went back to her textbook. She had sensed for some time that Owen Dara's interest in her was more than just that of a schoolmaster for his pupil but she had thought that it would cease to exist after she had finished at the convent. Elizabeth's remarks made her think differently now. She shook her head to clear her thoughts, trying to concentrate on the text before her.

On the second occasion when they had met Owen, again in the town square, Elizabeth had made an effort to engage him in conversation, blinking her eyes at him and smiling her most alluring smile, but he had barely acknowledged her, his attention focused on Annie. This time he stayed a few minutes, asking Annie about her father and about her studies.

"What will you do for the summer holidays?" he asked her, as she was about to move away.

Annie had hoped to stay the odd weekend in town with Elizabeth, but Elizabeth was spending the summer with an aunt in Dublin.

"She's a bit of an old snob," Elizabeth told Annie, "even though her husband's only a coal-man."

"You mean he delivers coal?" Annie had assumed that all of Elizabeth's relations were in important positions. One uncle was a doctor and another owned a large farm.

"No. He has men working for him who do that."

"Oh!"

"They have a lot of money…but coal! Coal is black and dirty," Elizabeth affected a shiver, "I'd never marry a coal-man."

Annie had thought about staying with Aunt Nora but it was not the same as staying with Elizabeth and there was no likelihood of her being able to visit her friend in Dublin or that Elizabeth would come and stay with her. On the one occasion Elizabeth had done so, she had complained that it was "just too quiet" with nothing to do and "nobody around."

"I'll be at home helping my father," Annie told Owen.

In July, as the holidays progressed and Annie was back home full-time in Ballycrag, on a Saturday afternoon, the day after her seventeenth birthday, she was alone in the cottage when Owen Dara called.

"I brought you this." He handed her a package wrapped in brown paper: "For your birthday. It's only a small thing."

She bent her head as she unwrapped the package, hiding the blush that rose in her cheeks. It was the first present she had been given by a man, other than her father. She held the slim leather-bound volume of poetry in her hands for a moment, not really seeing it, trying to control the trembling that the unexpected gift had caused her.

"Thank you," she said simply and laying it aside on the table, she busied herself preparing tea.

They sat facing each other across the table, bright shafts of June sunlight touching the embroidered roses on one corner of the tablecloth. They had talked about school until Owen said: "I hope you like your present…it's not very much."

"It's a lovely present." Annie picked up the book, thinking that perhaps she ought to have made more of the gift, shown more appreciation. She ran her hand over the soft smooth surface of the green leather binding: "It's a beautiful book."

"I like Tennyson…would you like to hear a little of it read aloud?"

Annie hesitated. She thought that she wanted him to be gone so that she could consider his gift, hold it, savour it and decide how she felt about it all.

"Yes…I'd like that," she said.

She extended the book across the table and Owen gently took it from her hands. He riffled through the pages slowly, not wishing to find too quickly the lines he had read and re-read while he had thought for the hundredth time on the inscription he would write in the fly leaf, finally settling on '*Happy birthday! Owen.*'

"This will do…a few lines from *Maud*." Covering his face with the slim volume, he cleared his throat with a little nervous cough:

> *She is coming, my own, my sweet;*
> *Were it ever so airy a tread,*
> *My heart would hear her and beat…*

He read slowly, a tremor in his voice, and Annie felt a quickening in the beat of her heart and the heat of the colour beginning to rise in her cheeks as the words of the poem flowed over her. There was a moment of silence when Owen lowered the book and looked across at her. She had kept her head bowed while he was reading and she raised it now to look at him.

She spoke softly: "It's beautiful."

When Owen was leaving, they stood at the cottage gate, uncertain now in each other's presence.

"I'll have to be going."

"Thank you for the present."

"It's nothing. I…" Owen stood awkwardly for a moment and then, leaning forward, he kissed her, a fleeting kiss that barely touched her lips.

He straightened: "I could come over some evening during the week after school if you like…we could go for a walk maybe."

"All right," Annie said and turning quickly away, she ran along the path to the cottage door.

3

There had been occasions in the town, when Annie was either alone or with Elizabeth, that her eyes had briefly met those of some man or other, causing her heart to flutter. She had even retraced her steps more than once in the hope of catching sight of the man again. For a long time she had been certain that that was how it would happen when she fell in love: she would meet a handsome man, they would look into each other's eyes and know straight away that their destinies were inextricably linked together forever more. With Owen Dara it was not at all like that.

For the first few weeks, she was confused and uncertain, and yet, when they were together, and he held her in his arms and kissed her, she felt warmth growing inside her. It was a good feeling and stayed with her after he was gone and until she fell asleep at night. Some mornings she wasn't sure if she wanted to see him again, but then, when he came back she would feel the warmth even before he touched her.

She wished she had somebody to talk to about it, but Elizabeth had already gone to Dublin and that left only her father or Aunt Nora. Whatever about her father, there was no way she would dare mention it to her aunt. Aunt Nora would surely get too excited and make the whole thing into something it wasn't at all.

As the days passed, and she began to look forward more and more to his company, she felt the blossoming of a new kind of desire within her. Her doubts troubled her less often and despite the world being in the throes of a war that threatened to desolate it, she felt the beginning of the promise of something new and wonderful unfolding in her life.

In July, when Owen had his school holidays, he came to the cottage more often, staying only briefly if Annie's father was there. If her father was absent they sometimes lay on her bed, jumping up guiltily at every unexpected sound. Fearful, she pushed Owen away, whenever his passion led him to seek more intimate satisfaction.

"We should go somewhere together," Annie said, easing her body away from Owen's embrace.

"Where?"

"Anywhere. We spend all our time here in the cottage. We don't go anywhere together."

"We go for walks."

"Yes…around the field."

"I have to be careful, Annie."

"Why?"

"People would talk."

"You don't want to be seen with me?"

"It's not that, Annie…it's just that you're still my pupil in people's eyes. They might think I was taking advantage of you. It might be best to keep ourselves to ourselves…until you finish at the convent."

"You're not ashamed to be seen with me, are you?"

"Oh no! It's just that we have to be careful. It's as much for your protection as it for mine."

For a while Annie did not like the idea of having to keep their courtship a secret, but then, when she thought about it, she believed that she could understand Owen's concern. She even began to enjoy the feeling of intrigue that served to heighten the pleasure of every moment they spent together.

Annie was sure her father knew, but he said nothing about it. He liked the schoolmaster and he seemed to be happy to see them together.

Owen did bring her to meet his mother. When he suggested it to her a couple of weeks later she was surprised.

"I thought you didn't want anyone to know?"

"My mother's not just anyone…anyway, it's only a visit…nothing more."

"What did you tell her about me?"

"I just told her that I might bring a friend to visit, that's all."

"Who else will be there?"

"Just my mother and my brother."

It was a very long cycle and Annie was already tired by the time they got there - tired and nervous. After an hour or so, Owen left Annie alone with his mother and went in search of his brother who was somewhere out in the fields. Annie was relieved when he returned and she was able to signal to him that it was time to begin the long cycle back.

"Well...how did you get on with my mother?" Owen asked her on the way home.

"All right...I don't think she was too happy to see me."

Owen laughed: "She was."

"She asked me how old I was. She made a face when I told her."

"That's just her way."

"She thought it was a pity that my father's farm was so small and that he had to work for others in order to support us."

Owen tried to laugh off his mother's barbed conversation: "Ah, she was only making talk..." he cycled close to Annie and put his arm across her shoulder "...she'll be different the next time, you'll see."

Annie had the disquieting thought that there might never be a next time. She hadn't even met his brother. Owen had been unable to find him. Perhaps the brother hadn't wanted to meet her. It took effort for Annie to shrug the thoughts away.

At the end of August, as the holidays came to a close, she asked Owen to go with her to a céilí about three miles beyond Kilcrone.

"It's a long way on a bicycle. It'll feel even longer on the way back, Annie. We wouldn't be home until all hours."

Annie was disappointed. She had wanted to go somewhere exciting before she went back to school.

"It's not just the distance, Annie...remember what we said about being seen together?"

"It's shorter than the journey to your mother's house...and you didn't mind about us being seen together then."

"Look, Annie…"

"It doesn't matter. I only wanted to go to a dance. It's not even a modern dance. I just love dancing…that's all. I haven't been to a dance for ages."

"I'm not much of a dancer…I have two left feet…but if you really want to go…"

The céilí was held in an old converted coach-house in a farmyard. The farmer, with growing children of his own, had decided to open it up for young people who had little or no access to a place of entertainment. The entrance fee covered the musicians and no more.

Owen and Annie had just arrived when Fergal, a friend of Owen's, came in. Shorter than Owen, with unruly fair hair falling across his forehead, his blue eyes opened wide as he caught sight of Annie first, then Owen.

"Owen Dara! The last person on this earth I expected to meet here."

Owen turned to Annie: "Fergal O'Dwyer…Annie Luhan. Fergal and I were at the teacher's training college together."

Fergal made no effort to hide his admiration of Annie's good looks: "You're beautiful…beautiful!"

His broad, open smile was disarming and Annie smiled back, acknowledging the compliment.

Owen had not understated his inability to dance, but nevertheless Annie enjoyed just being there. Fergal danced two set-dances with her while Owen sat glumly on one of the benches along the wall, staring at the floor. He brightened up when Annie came back to him after the second set-dance and suggested that they go outside for a while.

The doors and windows had already been thrown open to allow the warmth of body and air to cool in the late summer night. While the fiddler, the bodhrán-player and the banjo-player were still giving heart to the music, they left the coach-house, the heat still in Annie's blood from the fiery rhythm of the music and the exertion of the dance. Passing through a gate leading out of the farmyard, they found a haystack, away from the talking and the shouting and the calling of the dancers milling about in front of the coach-house.

They pressed into the softness of the hay, their hands caressing and clasping and stroking, the sweat from their bodies dampening the harvested grass, the scent of the matured fruit of the meadow all around them.

Owen reached down, lifting her dress, sliding his hand upwards along her thigh, his fingers searching and finding her most intimate part, his embracing arm drawing her close. Annie pushed at his shoulders and he withdrew his hand, falling to his knees. He ruffled her clothes to her waist, his head moving downwards, coming to rest against the pulsating rippling in her belly, his lips softly pressing against the fragile protecting fabric between her legs.

Annie locked her fingers into the damp strands of his hair, gently moving his head back. Struggling to stay on her feet, she uncoiled her fingers and drew him upright, holding him to her, until the shuddering in his body ceased and his breathing became even again.

"We'll go back inside," Annie said, brushing the back of her skirt and fixing her hair.

"I…I can't," Owen was embarrassed.

Annie paused fractionally: "We'll get our bicycles and go."

A mile or so on the road, Fergal caught up with them: "I went looking for you to say goodnight, but you'd gone. I knew you couldn't be too far ahead of me."

After Fergal had turned off at Kilcrone, they were quiet and Annie began to feel the tiredness settling over her. She would have fallen off her bicycle more than once, on the last mile or two, but for Owen's steadying hand.

"I have to go to my bed before I fall asleep standing up," Annie said as Owen took her bicycle and wheeled it in the path and around the side of the cottage. She stood inside the half-open door until he returned: "I don't how you'll make it back to Kilcrone."

"I'll be alright, Annie."

Owen bent to kiss her, his lips brushing her hand as she raised it to her forehead.

"I just have to go to bed," she said, gently closing the door.

Annie curled up beneath the bedclothes, the céilí music still in her head, Fergal's smiling mouth merging into Owen's glum face in the seconds before she fell asleep.

4

On the Saturday afternoon that Annie completed her last test paper of the Leaving Certificate Examination, Owen waited for her, sitting on the wall at Riordan's Cross. As soon as he saw her coming in the distance he jumped off and cycled to meet her.

"Well! How was it?"

"Thank God! The last one!" She got off her bicycle: "It was alright. You can look at the exam paper afterwards."

Leaning on the handlebars of his bicycle Owen smiled: "Well, if you say it was alright that means you had no trouble getting through it."

"When the results come out in August we'll know…it was easy enough though. I had to sit twiddling my thumbs for the last fifteen or twenty minutes. There were just two other girls who finished the paper before time was up. The invigilator kept looking down at me as if I was up to no good."

"How old was he?"

"About your age…Lord! I must get home and get out of this uniform…come on!"

Placing her foot on a pedal, Annie did a little hop run and jumped up on her bicycle. She hadn't gone very far before Owen drew level with her.

"What are you thinking about?" he asked.

Annie's front wheel ran straight into a pothole and her bicycle wobbled precariously before she brought it under control: "I was thinking about avoiding that pothole until you distracted me."

"Oh, sorry!"

"I'm only joking."

Owen looked across at her: "Would you like to know what *I'm* thinking about?"

"What?"

"I'm thinking that we could go to a dance tomorrow night"

Annie's face lit up: "Oh! I'd love that! Where?"

"Carrigroe."

"Carrigroe! That's about twenty miles away."

"You don't have to worry. Fergal will drive us there."

Fergal's father had a large dairy and poultry farm and despite the wartime restrictions, he was able to get a reasonable quota of petrol for the motor van he had acquired for his deliveries. At weekends, with no school to teach, Fergal sometimes helped his father out, giving him access to transport he would not otherwise have had. Whenever he was in the vicinity of Kilcrone he called to see Owen. He had come by earlier that Saturday and had told Owen about the dance in Carrigroe.

"It's to raise funds for the Local Defence Force. It'll be a great night. Why don't you come and bring Annie?"

"I don't know…" Owen wasn't comfortable with the thought of going to a dance "…it's too far away. We'd never manage it on the bicycles."

"Don't worry about that…I'll take you in the van."

"But tomorrow is Sunday. How will you explain to the guards if they stop you? I hear they're gone very strict on the use of petrol."

"I'll just say I had to make an urgent delivery in Carrigroe…I'll throw a couple of chickens and a few eggs into the back of the van just in case."

"What are you going to tell your father?"

"I'll think of something…anyway, what I'll do is, I'll leave as late as I can tomorrow, drive over here and we'll have a bite to eat. We'll pick Annie up in Ballycrag and we'll head off for Carrigroe."

"I don't know."

"I'll call here tomorrow, anyway. I'll go on my own if you're not coming."

Annie sat between Owen and Fergal, the delivery van bumping along the road.

"There's one good thing about these roads," Fergal said, spinning the wheel this way and that in an effort to avoid disaster from crater-like potholes, "no self-respecting guard is going to risk his bicycle on them."

"He doesn't have to," Owen massaged the part of his head that kept striking against the roof with every jolt, "all he has to do is lie on the floor of the barracks and listen for the banging and rattling of the van. He could climb up on the roof then and look for the cloud of dust."

"You're getting too soft in your old age, my boy…" Fergal nudged Annie "…it's time you had a touch of the hard life for a while. Why don't you come to the Aran Islands with me this summer?"

"No!"

"Ah come on! This is the umpteenth time you've gone back on your promise. We were supposed to go the summer after we qualified, remember. You were the one…"

"I can't go this summer."

"Why not?"

"I just can't."

"Afraid to…is that it?" Fergal nudged Annie again. "Afraid the Germans will invade Ballycrag while you're gone and ravish the…?"

"No…shut up! Concentrate on the driving."

Annie went into the ladies room to re-do her makeup and stayed in the dancehall with the rest of the girls who were waiting while the majority of the men went first to the pub to slake their thirst and fortify their courage. Owen nursed a bottle of stout while Fergal quickly drank two pints of porter.

Annie danced almost every dance. Owen moved self-consciously and awkwardly on the floor, dancing only the slow-waltzes with her. The quicksteps and old-time waltzes she danced with Fergal, whose energy and sense of rhythm made it easy for her to move in time with the music. She was aware of Owen's less than happy glances as she whirled around the dance floor with Fergal.

It was approaching eleven o'clock, with daylight still lingering, when Owen bought minerals and they took them outside to avail of the cool air. Fergal joined them about ten minutes later with a girl he introduced as Peggy. She had attended the Convent Secondary

School, finishing there when Annie had completed her first year and they were soon chatting amiably together.

They paused to listen now as the conversation between Owen and Fergal cut across them.

"Come on, Owen!"

"I'm not going."

"Ah, man! You'll come back with a new zest for life…and love". Fergal rolled his eyes at Annie.

"I told you…I'm not going."

"Come on, Owen…you're giving up on the chance of a lifetime…the chance to hear the language of your fathers flowing crystalline as a mountain stream from the mouths of the islandmen."

"Words, Fergal. Words!"

"Ah man! Don't you want you to walk the steep and stony paths of Inish Meáin, with Inish Oirr on the one side and Inish Mór on the other, and feel the uplift in your soul and the powerful stirring of your imagination?"

"No!"

"Or face the raw power of the Atlantic in a currach…a pair of hand-blistering oars and faith in the Almighty your only hope of reaching safe harbour? Well?"

Owen lowered his head for a moment and then raised it to look across at Annie, uncertainty in his eyes.

"Why don't you go with him, Owen? It will do you good to get away for a while."

"There you are!" Fergal said. "Listen to Annie now."

"I don't know."

"Ah…come on!"

"I…" Owen hesitated, and again Annie nodded "…when would we go."

"Ten days from now. It's all set."

Owen was quiet on the journey back to Ballycrag.

"I don't know why I agreed to go to the Aran Islands with Fergal," he said as he walked Annie to the gate of the cottage.

"You'll have a lovely time. It will be a good break from all the teaching."

"The summer will be over by the time I come home. You could be going off to the teachers' training college, or the Civil Service, shortly after that. We won't…"

Annie reached up and touched his cheek: "It will be good for you to go."

"Yes…well…I'd better not keep Fergal waiting any longer…he has to get home…and we both have to teach tomorrow."

"You mean today…it's already Monday."

"I'll come over after school this evening."

"Don't…you'll be very tired. You'll need an early night. Wait until Tuesday…it's all right for me, I'll be able to sleep on. Thank God, the exams are over."

Owen kissed her and shuffled off to join Fergal in the van.

5

Moments before Owen Dara called to the cottage on the Tuesday evening, Paddy Luhan returned from having worked all day on the estate at Fernmount. He had worked there on and off for the past four years, earning the extra money needed for Annie's fees at the convent. Seven miles to the north of Ballycrag and about the same distance from the town, the extensive dairy farm was divided into tillage and pasture with rolling parkland.

"They're lookin' for a girl to help out at Fernmount for a few weeks," Paddy said as he sat down to the food Annie had prepared for him, "Miss Hargrove, the housekeeper, asked me if I knew anyone. I told her you might be interested. She said the work is yours if you want it."

"Oh!" Annie had only once been to Fernmount House when she was about nine years old. Her father had taken her with him on the carrier of his bicycle. She remembered thinking that the gate-lodge, just inside the big iron gates, was the house and had been surprised when her father had continued cycling along the tree-lined avenue until they had reached the open space in front of the house itself.

The first thing she had noticed was the big, shiny motor car and then her eyes had taken in the columned entrance porch, the sweep of the rising limestone steps and the large pair of urns either side of the doorway. It was a mansion, straight out of one of the fairytales her mother had told her. Later on, when she had begun reading novels, whenever a genteel country residence featured in the story, an image of Fernmount always entered her mind.

"What kind of work would I be doing?"

"Whatever a girl does around the house, I suppose. Cleanin' and polishin' an' things like that."

"What about the work here?"

"We'd manage…it's only for a couple of weeks, anyhow."

The previous summer she had helped her father with the cutting of the turf and the saving of the hay, and she had still been able to spend time with Owen, almost anytime he called, something she could not have done if she had had to work for someone else. This summer would be different, with Owen going off to the Aran Islands.

"How much would I get?"

"Twenty five shillin's a week."

"Twenty five shillings! When could I start working there?"

"You could start tomorrow if you like, or the next day. I told Miss Hargrove I'd let her know in the mornin'."

"Are you sure you can manage?"

"I can manage."

"You can tell Miss Hargrove that I'll be there on Thursday morning."

"I'll hardly see you at all now before I go away," Owen nudged at a tuft of grass with the toe of his shoe. "I won't even be here for your birthday. Maybe I should tell Fergal I'll go with him some other time."

"Ah, don't…you can't disappoint him like that."

"I thought that we would be spending a bit more time together before I went to the Aran Islands…but now, you're going off to work and…"

"It's only for a couple of weeks."

"I know…but we've hardly had any time alone together for the last six months."

"That's the way we agreed that it would be," Annie said defensively, remembering the circumstances under which the agreement had been made.

An acute troubling of her conscience had followed the night of the ceilí at the end of the previous summer. She had been able to push her guilty feeling away when she and Owen were together, but afterwards, the guilt had always returned and had begun to trouble her even more. Worst of all, she had no longer been able to receive

Holy Communion. She had finally gathered her courage and had gone to confession, burning with shame as she struggled to explain to Fr. Hayes the nature of her transgressions.

"How old are you child?"

"Seventeen, father"

"And how old is he?"

"Twenty six, father."

"Do your parents approve of this man?"

"There's only my father...he likes Owen Da..." Annie checked herself just in time: she had nearly said *Owen Dara*. She held her breath, the momentary silence of the priest unnerving her.

"Do you intend to marry this man?"

Relief swept over her. Fr. Hayes had said "this man" and not referred to "the master" or "Owen Dara."

"I...I don't know, father."

"Has he asked you to marry him?"

"No...but I think he would like to get married."

"Do you love him?"

"I...I'm not sure, father."

The priest was silent again for a moment.

"You are still attending The Convent Secondary School?"

Annie's heart lurched: surely the priest couldn't have recognized her? She had barely spoken above a whisper and she had kept her head bowed and had stayed leaning back into the darkness of the confession box all the time. Her voice trembled: "Yes, father."

"My child...," the priest sighed, "...you and the...this young man...are in danger of engaging in intimacy that belongs only in the holy sacrament of matrimony. You must understand that this is a very grave matter."

"Yes father."

"Until such time as both of you may decide either to marry or to go your separate ways you must stop meeting with this man...or at least meet with him less often. Is that clear?"

"Yes, father."

"Whenever you do meet with him, make sure that there will always be someone present or close by."

"I will, father."

Feeling as though she had been relieved of a nightmare, Annie sang to herself as she cycled home and only when she was climbing the hill at Ballycrag did she remember that Owen would be waiting for her at the cottage. She would have to tell him about her confession but it would be all right. He would understand.

Owen had remained silent while she had told him of the priest's judgement of the gravity of the matter and of the instructions he had given her. Only when she had gone back to the beginning of her confession and had begun to relate the questions that Fr. Hayes had asked her and the answers she had given him, had Owen reacted. He had jumped up from his chair and had stood over her, his eyes blazing: "You gave him my age...*and my name*!"

"Only your Christian name...and anyway, he asked me."

"He asked you *my name*?"

"No...not exactly...it's just that I..."

"You told him without being asked...Oh God!"

She had begun to cry then and that had silenced Owen. He had paced up and down the flagstones stopping only when Annie had asked: "What are we going to do?"

"What can we do now...except do as the priest says...and hope that I still have a job to go to?"

He had left the cottage shortly afterwards and she had been left feeling that she had done something terribly wrong. She had cried herself to sleep that night and on several nights in the weeks following, when he had neither sent word nor tried to contact her.

She had avoided staying with Elizabeth and had not left her room at Aunt Nora's any evening, pretending that she needed to study long and hard for the Leaving Certificate. She had gone home to Ballycrag every weekend and when her father had observed that he hadn't seen Owen around for a while she had told him that the schoolmaster was giving her the opportunity to study on her own without interruption. Her father had nodded his head and had said no more. Annie had felt that he had not believed her.

When Owen knocked on the cottage door on a Saturday night, a few weeks later, her father had let him in, welcoming him as though nothing had happened.

"I was just thinking I'd call over to see a neighbour," Paddy Luhan had said, almost the moment that Owen had crossed the threshold, "and now that you're here, I'll be off straight away."

Annie had jumped up from her seat by the fire, not answering Owen's choked: "Hello, Annie."

Within seconds her father was closing the cottage door behind him.

Owen took a few steps towards her and stopped: "I had to come and see you...I haven't been able to sleep or eat..."

Annie sat down, turning away from him, looking into the fire.

"...I didn't know what to do or where to go." Owen came forward and stood behind her chair: "I love you Annie...I..."

She rose quickly from the chair and moved away from him to the other side of the hearth.

"Please, Annie..."

She *had* been relieved to see him, but she had been angry too, angry and hurt. In the beginning she had refused to listen while he tried to explain why he had acted in the way he had had, but in the end she had given in. Before her father had come back she had promised to meet with him the following Saturday. He had put her arms around her then and held her for a little while.

When they did meet, Owen had reluctantly agreed that they would only see each other two or three times a month, until the exams were over. In return she had promised that, after that time, they would discuss what the future might hold for them.

"We also agreed that we would talk about us...when the exams were over," Owen reminded her now.

"I know," Annie said, "but it's only a few days since the exams finished. I've hardly had time to draw breath."

"Why can't we talk now?"

"My head is tired after weeks of studying and I don't want to think or talk about anything serious just now…can't we just wait until you come back from the Aran Islands? It's only for a few weeks."

After Owen had left, Annie sat alone on the back wall. Her father would probably think that she was being foolish, or unreasonable, or ungrateful if she broke off with Owen, but it wasn't at all like that. It was hard to explain, but something inside her had changed since the night he had walked away and left her without her knowing if she would ever see or hear from him again.

She went back to the kitchen. She would be meeting with Owen one more time before he went to the Aran Islands. After that it would be five or six weeks before she saw him again. She would leave things as they were until then.

6

Annie arrived early on the Thursday morning at Fernmount. The elderly Miss Hargrove, tall and spare, dressed almost completely in black, studied her closely before conducting her to a small but comfortably furnished room off the end of the long, high-ceilinged hallway.

"Please take a seat."

The housekeeper indicated one of a pair of armchairs facing an ornate walnut desk and seated herself behind it.

"Before we begin I would like to ask you a few questions."

Annie was taken aback. Her father had said that the work was hers if she wanted it but now it appeared that she was about to be interviewed.

"How old are you?"

"Seventeen."

"And you have just finished at the Convent Secondary School?"

"Yes, ma'am."

"I would prefer it if you called me Miss Hargrove." The housekeeper shifted slightly in her seat: "Now...the work here will entail a little of everything, polishing, cleaning, and helping out in the kitchen. You are prepared for all that?"

"Yes."

"You will take your instructions from me only...or Mrs. Ashby."

Annie felt uncomfortable. The housekeeper kept her eyes fixed on her, eyes that seemed to want to see inside her head; eyes that appeared to Annie to have no light in them.

"Now...I have to ask you one or two questions of a more personal nature...if you don't mind?"

"No."

"Is there a young man in your life?"

The question startled Annie, but after a moment's hesitation she answered: "Yes."

"How long have you and he been...been together."

"About a year."

Miss Hargrove seemed to ponder this fact, her unblinking eyes still directed at Annie: "You and he are serious about each other?"

Annie paused fractionally before answering.

"Yes."

"Good..." Miss Hargrove seemed to brighten a little "...that's everything." She stood up: "I will now show you around the house."

"The drawing-room."

Through a large bay window, Annie could see lawns sloping downwards, with stone steps leading from one level to the next. Where the trees broke either side at the end, sunlight glinted on the waters of a distant lake. Within the room itself, the high ornate ceiling and the large gilt mirror over the white marble fireplace reminded her of the convent, but there was nowhere in the convent that exuded such an atmosphere of ease and comfort.

Passing from drawing room to dining-room, from study to breakfast-room, Annie had never before seen anything like the furniture, paintings, silver and china that appeared to be everywhere. Some things, she thought, must be extraordinarily rare and the prospect of being in the house for a few weeks, surrounded by such beautiful furnishings, excited her.

"The library."

Miss Hargrove indicated a door they had passed by on their way from the drawing room, the only room they had not entered: "Don't go in there unless you are asked to do something or your presence is required."

"Yes, Miss Hargrove."

"Before I take you downstairs to the kitchen I will introduce you to Mrs. Ashby."

They had reached the foot of the staircase leading to the upper storeys. Annie followed the housekeeper up the curving stairs to the landing and along the corridor of the first floor, passing large dark portraits and pictures of fox hunting and steeplechasing.

"Wait here a moment."

Miss Hargrove tapped lightly on a door near the end of the corridor and entered without waiting for a reply. Annie could hear the murmur of voices from within as she waited.

The housekeeper reappeared after a few minutes: "Come inside, Annie."

Sarah Ashby, her back to Annie, was seated at a dressing-table, putting on a necklace.

"This is Annie Luhan." The housekeeper kept her hand on the doorknob.

Sarah turned to look at Annie, studying her, a lock from her short wavy brown hair, contrasting strongly with the pale oval of her face and the green of her eyes. A smile barely touched her lips as she looked wordlessly at Annie.

She might have been quite beautiful at one time, Annie thought, was still beautiful in a way, but there was something in her face that took away the softness from her looks. When she finally spoke, the tone of her voice surprised Annie. It sounded like a young girl's, slightly high-pitched, but very clear: "Miss Hargrove has explained your duties to you?"

"Yes, ma'am."

"Very good. See that you carry them out diligently and with care."

"Yes, ma'am."

Sarah turned back to the dressing-table mirror.

Before she passed from the room Annie caught sight of the lake, clearly visible now through the bedroom window and thought how beautiful it all was. Out in the corridor Miss Hargrove introduced her to Bridget O'Meara, the housemaid, who nodded without speaking.

Downstairs in the basement, in what seemed to Annie to be a cavernous kitchen, the cook, Mary Conroy, was busy at the huge range. She barely acknowledged Annie, but dark-haired Janey Lonergan, the kitchen maid, small and thin, with a sharp, pale face and eyes that seemed always to be focused elsewhere, greeted her warmly. A year or two older than Annie, Janey's sleeping quarters and those of Bridget O'Meara were beside each other in garret rooms at the top of the house. Mary Conroy lived with her herdsman husband in the gate-lodge.

Annie's work was mainly dusting and polishing under the regular supervision of Miss Hargrove who moved constantly throughout the house and seemed to confer often with Sarah Ashby.

Janey spent all of her time in the kitchen and her only opportunity to speak to Annie came whenever Annie returned there and they had a moment alone together.

"Mr. Ashby is gone off on one of his trips to Dublin. He don't go much anymore, except now and again. He…" Janey broke off as Miss Hargrove came into view, resuming as soon as the housekeeper was out of earshot again: "He only goes away when his back's not at him…gets terrible trouble from his back, he does."

"Miss Hargrove pointed out photographs of Derek Ashby when she was showing me around," Annie said.

"There's only him…they has no more children He was at school in England. He's in the army now…goin' off to fight in the war. He's…"once again Janey broke off, this time to attend to Mrs. Conroy "…I'll tell you 'bout him again."

The brief snatches of conversation carried on throughout the day and Janey asked questions about the Convent Secondary School, the nuns, Annie's family and about Annie herself: "Are you courtin'?"

Annie paused only briefly: "Well, I am going with someone. What about you?"

"Oh…" Janey tossed her head "…sometimes I am…an' sometimes I'm not. Sometimes, 'tisn't worth the bother."

Annie laughed and changed the conversation asking what Bridget O'Meara was like.

"She don't say nothin' to no one. Keeps to herself an' only speaks when you ask her somethin'. When it suits her, she won't say nothin' atall."

Leaving Fernmount on her way home that evening, Annie retrieved her bicycle from the coach-house, wondering if the motor car under a tarpaulin cover was the same one that she had seen when she was a child. With no one else about, she stood in front of the house, admiring it. Looking upwards, she thought she saw a movement behind the curtains of one of the upper windows and quickly lowered her eyes. Glancing up again, this time she was sure that someone had hastily drawn back from the window.

She wheeled her bicycle past the house, uncomfortable with the knowledge that she was being watched.

She was surprised to see Owen waiting for her near the entrance gates. They were not supposed to see each other until Saturday night.

"I had a letter from my mother this morning," he said, before she had reached him. "My brother is arriving home tomorrow. My mother wants me home for the weekend."

"I didn't know your brother had been away."

"It's not my brother at home…it's my brother Hugh…the one out on the Foreign Missions. He hasn't been well. They're sending him back to Ireland for a while. I had to come this evening…I won't be here on Saturday."

"That's all right…you have to be there to meet your brother."

"I wouldn't mind if it was any other time…if you didn't have to go to work in that house maybe you could have come with me."

On the way home Annie kept the conversation centred on Fernmount, describing the furnishings, re-telling little inconsequential things that Janey had told her and making observations about the house in general.

Paddy Luhan greeted Owen with his usual pleasure when they reached the cottage. While Annie prepared a meal for the three of them, Paddy engaged the schoolmaster in conversation, paying close attention to whatever Owen had to say. Annie was very aware of the respect her father had for the schoolmaster and the thought that she might be telling him, when Owen came back from the Aran Islands, that it was over between them, troubled her yet again.

She glanced at Owen covertly now, at the earnest expression on his face as he talked with her father.

"So, how much *are* the bog workers gettin'?" Paddy was asking.

"Ninepence ha'penny an hour...that's for a forty eight hour week...with a shilling an hour for overtime. They're trying to get a shilling an hour flat rate."

"That's not bad money all the same...the war must be good for someone."

"Well...with no coal coming into the country..."

He's so serious about everything, she thought. If only he was a little less so, maybe things would be different. It was a pity he couldn't be a bit more like Fergal.

She had met Fergal by chance on more than one occasion in the town over the last few months and each time he had lifted her spirits and made her laugh. He had a brightness about him that was catching and he always seemed to be happy in himself. He was the same age as Owen, but somehow he seemed younger. She turned away to the kitchen dresser, reaching for three of the best plates that were on the top shelf.

"I never went to the Aran Islands," Paddy said as Annie joined them at the table and they began eating. "When I was younger I always wanted to go but then I got married. I hear that the islandmen are a hardy race, tough and wiry...great men for the fishing and for bein' able to grow things on ground that no one else could. It must be a hard life all the same."

"They seem to manage well enough," Owen said.

"Is it true they can row one o' them currachs out into the sea, draggin' a cow or a horse on a rope...?"

Annie listened to the conversation, aware that Owen was finding it hard to concentrate. Anytime she looked across at him, his eyes were fixed on her, the expression in them like that of someone who found himself lost and did not quite know where to go from there. She felt a twinge of guilt, but there was nothing she could do about it. She could not help feeling as she did.

"That was grand, Annie." Paddy Luhan stood up: "I won't bother with the cup of tea...I'm off now to see Peter Melody...he needs a hand with the fixin' of a cart wheel. I'll have the tea over there."

Annie began clearing away the dishes in the silence that followed her father's departure, while Owen stood uncertainly, running his fingers inside the collar of his shirt.

"Did your mother say anything about your going away?" Annie asked, breaking the silence.

"No…well, only that I might have offered to help out around the farm a bit."

"Hasn't your brother enough workmen around to do the work?"

"He has…but you know my mother." Owen had relaxed a little: "Here…I'll take that!"

He joined Annie at the hearth, lifting the heavy iron kettle from the hook suspended over the turf-fire and poured the boiling water into a basin. Annie added a small amount of cold water from a bucket.

"I'll leave these to steep for a while," she said, putting the soiled dishes and other pieces into the basin and sprinkling them with a handful of soap powder.

As she reached behind her to undo the strings of her apron, Owen put his arms around her and drew her to him, pressing against her breasts. Her body tensed and she pulled away from him: "We should wait until you come back."

"I'm going away next Wednesday, Annie…all I'm doing is saying goodbye." The lost look she had noticed earlier was back in his eyes: "We won't be seeing each other again for ages."

"It's not all that long, Owen…it's only for a few weeks."

"I know we said we would wait to talk, but couldn't we just…?"

"Don't, Owen. I can't go into it now. I'm very tired." Annie re-tied her apron strings: "I'd better start washing the ware now instead of waiting until later…I have to get myself ready for work in the morning as well."

Annie stood at the gate, watching Owen's back, as he wheeled his bicycle up the hill. She turned away before he reached the top and walked slowly along the path to the cottage, pausing briefly in the silence of the kitchen, her eyes scanning the emptiness. Entering her bedroom, she lay on her bed, staring at the ceiling, before turning on her stomach and burying her face in the pillow.

7

Mid-morning on the following day, Annie and Janey were alone in the kitchen.

"Mr. Ashby came home last night..." Janey was on her knees, black-leading the range "...his back was killin' him again."

She stood up, rubbing the base of her spine with her gloved hand: "I could do with a rub of Sloan's Liniment or somethin' meself. 'Twas straight to his bed for him. He has to take some sort of medicine to make him sleep. Sleeps like the dead he does until he wakes up." She knelt down again: "Fell off his horse he did...nearly killed he was."

Annie looked up from the silver candelabrum she was polishing: "When?"

"Years ago. He had to give up his business...a solicitor he is. He don't do anything around the place. Spends his time walkin' around or stuck in the library with his books an' pictures. He leaves everythin' to Mrs. Ashby...her an' Miss Hargrove."

Janey rested back on her heels and turned her head to look over at Annie: "She ran away one time."

"Who did?"

"Mrs. Ashby. Ran off with another man an' took the baby an' all with her."

"She ran off with another *man*?"

"Yeh...Johnny...Johnny Power that works in the dairy...he told me."

Janey rose from her knees and bending down gave the area she had been working on a final buff with a soft cloth: "Now, that's that." She turned back to Annie: " It all happened years an' years ago...Johnny got the story from Tom Rogan who used to work here...he's dead now. Anyway, she came back again but me man followed her." Janey walked over and leant her elbows on the small pine table at which Annie was working, drawing back almost immediately: "Lord! The smell of that polish is awful...I hate cleanin' silver...I'd sooner scrub pots."

"I don't mind it." Annie resumed polishing: "So, he followed her."

"He only came when Mr Ashby wasn't here." Janey lifted her apron and blew her nose: "Mr Ashby might never have found out only for the day when..."

She stopped dead at the sound of steps on the stairway to the kitchen and immediately ran to the sink, running the tap. Sarah Ashby entered the kitchen: "Annie, I want you upstairs. I have some work for you to do."

Annie followed her, her heart pounding. She was relieved when Sarah gave her, her instructions and left her alone to carry on with the work.

At lunchtime, Annie was about to seat herself at the kitchen table next to Bridget to begin eating when Janey caught her by the arm and whispered: "Hold on a minute."

"Miss Hargrove..." Janey inclined her head in the direction of the housekeeper, who was having a low-toned conversation with Mary Conroy "...'tis a lovely day an' me an' Annie would like to take our food outside."

"You should be eating up and not dawdling. You have work to do, girl."

"Aw! *Please*, Miss Hargrove?"

The housekeeper waved an impatient hand: "All right, but don't be too long,"

Janey scurried out into the yard and Annie followed her at a more measured pace as Janey led the way to the orchard. They settled themselves under the shade of an apple tree.

"'Tis grand here..." Janey spoke between bites "...I'm nearly boiled all day in the kitchen...an' anyway you couldn't be talkin' with everyone around the place."

Janey ate quickly while Annie ate more leisurely, enjoying her food and the sight of butterflies, wings flickering, sweeping hither and thither among the tall grasses. In a far corner, lost to view among the fruit trees, the *swish swish* of the cutting blade of a scythe, wielded by one of the farm workers, was barely audible in the quiet.

Her food eaten, Janey stood up, gave her apron a flick, and leaning sideways peered through the orchard gate into the yard. Satisfied that there was no sign of anyone near, she sat down again, picking at her teeth: "My heart nearly stopped when her ladyship walked into the kitchen this mornin'."

"I know."

"Thank God, she never heard me. She couldn't have said anythin' anyway...I was only tellin' the truth."

"Truth or not, I don't think she would have liked hearing herself being talked about like that."

Janey made a face: "She couldn't a been any more put out than she must have been the day Mr. Ashby caught her an' me man."

"The man she...?"

"Yeh him...Baba..." Janey scratched her head "Baba somethin'...I can't remember her name. Baba was a maid here at the time, workin' upstairs an' she was just comin' out on the landin' when she spotted himself..."

"Who? Mr. Ashby?"

"Ah no! The man Mrs Ashby ran off with. She spotted him goin' into Mrs Ashby's bedroom an' after a good while when there was nothin' happenin' she crept along the corridor only noticin' then that the bedroom door was open a bit. She nearly died when she took a peep inside an'...the Lord save us...there was me man on top of her ladyship in the bed."

"My God!"

"Baba was makin' for the stairs when she heard Mr Ashby comin' up...supposed to be gone away for the whole day, he was, but he came back early. Into Mr. Ashby's room she ran an' stayed in there, not a breath comin' out a her, listenin' with all her ears, waitin' for somethin' to happen but all she heard was them talkin' but not a word they were sayin'. She was afraid then that Mr. Ashby would come in on top of her so she thought to get out a there as quick as possible. Just as she was goin' out the door me man came out of Mrs. Ashby's bedroom like a shot an' walked straight into her putting the heart crossways in her an' no wonder. She didn't stay long at Fernmount after that…went off to work somewhere else."

"What about the man?"

"What about him?"

"Did he come back again?"

"I don't know…I don't think so." Janey jumped up: "We better go back before Miss Hargrove comes after us."

Annie went back to polishing the silverware, returning the items to the dining-room as they were finished and bringing back others with her to the kitchen for cleaning. Many of the pieces she did not have a name for and could only guess at their use. She wished that she was not so ignorant of such things and thought how wonderful it must be to be rich: to have a beautiful, big house and servants and everything you could ever need.

Her thoughts turned to Janey's story about Mrs. Ashby and she wondered if it could really be true. Something probably did happen, but if it had happened the way Janey said it had, surely it would still be affecting their lives. From what she could see everything was perfect at Fernmount, although, there *was* something about Mrs Ashby…

"Annie!" Miss Hargrove broke in on her thoughts "when you have finished those entrée dishes return them to the dining-room and leave the rest for now…the windows in the library need cleaning."

A stepladder and cleaning materials were waiting for her when she accompanied the housekeeper to the library.

"This is a good time to do these. Mr. Ashby is out walking."

The housekeeper stayed watching her for a while: "Take care not to splash any of the volumes…" she indicated the mass of books from ceiling to floor in the open bookcases "…I'll be back presently."

Annie worked quickly and had completed her task before the housekeeper returned. The array of books surrounding her, some beautifully bound and some with worn spines, excited her and she had to resist the temptation to take one or two of them out and flick through the pages. Instead she turned her attention to a large volume lying on a leather-topped circular table in the centre of the room. *Art & Architecture* she read, nervously opening the heavy volume at random, fearing the return of Miss Hargrove at any moment. She was absorbed in an engraving of Greek temple statuary when a movement caught her eye: the tall figure of a man was turning away from the open library doorway, only his back visible to her. Annie closed the book, the blood rushing to her cheeks, knowing in an instant that Edward Ashby had been observing her from the dim light of the hallway.

8

Miss Hargrove had already left on her bicycle for the town when Annie arrived on Saturday morning.

"There's some work for you to do upstairs...Bridget knows what's to be done...Miss Hargrove left her the instructions," Mary Conroy told her the moment she came into the kitchen. "And you're not to make any noise...Mrs. Ashby isn't feelin' well."

"Where's Janey?"

"She's out in the dairy...never mind about her...go on up now to Bridget."

On her way through the hallway Annie stopped in front of a painting she had been admiring from the moment she had arrived at Fernmount but had not had the opportunity to really look at. The full-length portrait was that of a smiling young woman, leaning against a wooden fence. Behind her, apple blossoms glowed softly in hazy sunlight, the light reflecting off her long flowing white dress that was gathered in at the waist. A lock of golden hair peeped out from under the brim of her wide straw hat.

"She's beautiful, isn't she?"

Annie turned quickly away from the painting, feeling the rush of blood to her cheeks. Edward Ashby was further down the hallway standing in the library doorway.

"She *is* beautiful," he repeated and came slowly towards her.

Annie moved to the side as he stood in front of the painting.

"Well? Don't you think she's beautiful?"

"Yes."

"You know," he looked from the painting to Annie, "you are not too unlike her in looks."

Annie blushed all the more and smiled up at him. The previous afternoon, after she had caught her first glimpse of him outside the library door, she had passed him in the hallway on her way to the dining-room, noticing the stiff, upright way he had of carrying himself. She had only looked up at him for the briefest of instances before they passed each other in silence.

She had passed him again, on her way back to the kitchen. He had said "Good afternoon" then. She had looked directly at him as she returned his greeting and had smiled. He had smiled back at her, his grave face suddenly transformed and she had been really surprised at how handsome he was.

"Allow me to introduce myself," he said now, returning her smile, "I'm Edward Ashby and I believe that I already have the advantage of knowing who you are...you're Annie Luhan?"

"Yes, sir."

"So...what does Miss Annie Luhan do, when she's not in other people's houses admiring paintings?"

"I have just finished doing my Leaving Certificate at the Convent Secondary School."

"Ah! And what do you hope to do, now that you've finished at the convent?"

"I would like to be a teacher...or join the Civil Service."

"Indeed. Well, now, Annie...I'm off for a little walk in God's good fresh air."

Bridget's silence as she worked alongside her, allowed Annie to replay in her mind her encounter with Edward Ashby. He was not all like she had imagined. From what Janey had told her about the family she had expected him to be different, 'though different in what way she wasn't sure - maybe older looking, or less handsome, or cold and withdrawn. He was none of those things and his eyes were wonderful: deep and dark and misted over like someone who was near to tears. Her heart palpitated a little and she sought to distract herself from her thoughts by making an effort to talk to Bridget, a task she found most difficult and in the end she gave up trying.

Downstairs, in the kitchen, she had a few moments alone with Janey: "Mr. Ashby speaks so nicely."

"The likes of him all talks like that."

"He has a lovely smile."

"Easy for him…he don't have nothin' to do nor nothin' to worry about."

"He doesn't look that old…his hair is a little bit grey but it kind of suits him…Mrs. Ashby looks older than him."

"Why wouldn't she? Anyone that goes around most a the day with a face like sour milk is bound to end up lookin' old."

Miss Hargrove called her that afternoon.

"You are to go to Mr. Ashby in the library," she said quite sharply.

"Now?"

"Yes…now!"

Annie wondered what had caused the housekeeper to fall into such a bad humour. A short time earlier, Miss Hargrove had been quite pleasant with her and had praised her for her work.

She had almost passed through the kitchen door when the housekeeper's voice arrested her: "Annie!"

"Yes, Miss Hargrove."

"You are to excuse yourself the moment you have finished and return to the kitchen immediately…you are not to delay."

"Yes, Miss Hargrove."

As Annie entered the library, Edward Ashby was unlocking a mahogany cabinet with long, shallow drawers: "This is really an architect's cabinet for storing plans, but I use it to house my collection of drawings."

He pulled out one of the drawers, removed a large portfolio, and carried it to a rectangular rosewood table: "These particular drawings are not stored in the way they should be…they really ought to be mounted properly…they will be in time. For now, I would like you to help me by checking that the tissue covering them does so properly."

Sitting side by side, they began flattening creases and straightening out curled-up edges in the tissue paper.

"I acquired my first drawings while I was still very young…in Italy. I have been collecting them ever since then," Edward told her "though it was really when I spent my first student holiday in

Switzerland after the last war that my *grand passion* really began." He was silent for a moment: "I made a friend there…an art dealer. He had a wonderful collection…" he paused "…I learned a lot during the weeks I spent with him."

He turned to look at her directly: "You studied history at the convent?"

"Yes."

"Did your study include the Renaissance…the great period of artistic flowering in Europe?"

"Yes…well…only in passing." Annie was nervous, fearing that he would question her on it and find her lacking. "My history teacher, Sr. Catherine, said it was important that we should at least have some knowledge of the influences that created the great works of art to be seen in places like…"she searched her memory "…like the Sistine chapel in Rome or the…the Uffizi Gallery in Florence. In case we ever got the opportunity to travel abroad."

He smiled, the transformation that Annie had observed earlier that day again evident in his face: "Indeed…that was very enlightened of your Sr. Catherine."

"She showed us pictures…and there were some art books in the convent library that we were allowed to look at," Annie blurted out, unsettled under his gaze.

Edward turned back to the drawings: "Most of my collection is from that period…fifteenth and sixteenth century…some are seventeenth. Just a few are later than that."

He began to explain how the pictures were drawn and coloured: with pen; brown, grey and grey-blue washes; black, red and white chalk; and black lead. He talked about the images before them: scenes from the bible; episodes from classical mythology; glimpses of privileged and ordinary living: of palatial courtyards, shepherds in the fields, men on horseback. Depictions of the naked body, male and female, he spoke about as easily as he did about any of the other drawings.

"Look, Annie" he held a drawing of a nude young girl aloft "see how beautiful, how graceful she is…how naturally her body blends with the flowers and rocks and the stream, and yet, she stands out, manifesting the greatest and most exquisite example of all creation." Annie's embarrassment kept her silent and she was grateful that Edward did not look to her for comment.

"And see, Annie," Edward continued, "see the compassion in her eyes and in the incline of her head inviting us to surrender all that we are…all our desires, our hopes and dreams to her."

Edward seemed to become totally absorbed in the study of the drawing then and while she waited for him to break the silence Annie began to think that her embarrassment was really out of place and not at all necessary.

"You know, Annie," Edward turned to look at her now, "beauty is what makes this world bearable…makes it possible for us to go on living and hoping even in our darkest moments. Perhaps it is what heaven is like: a place of unimaginable sensory delight that stays with us for all eternity. We search for it here, in a sunset or in the dawn rising or in a blue sky over a golden meadow…and we search for it in others. We want to reach out and grasp it…to draw it into the depths of our being…to fill our souls. We hold it for a moment, but then it slips away, and we are left empty and bereft. The great artist captures that fleeting moment on his canvas and holds it for all to see." He looked again at the drawing: "The human body is beautiful Annie, not only in what it reveals but in the great mystery of life that it conceals."

Sr. Catherine had told them of the great artists: Michelangelo, Titian, Raphael, Leonardo da Vinci, and the names had rolled on Annie's tongue and fired her imagination with visions of life in fifteenth century Venice, Florence and Rome. Now, as Edward told her of other artists who had drawn the pictures before them: Raimondi, Passarotti, Zuccaro, the names sounded even more beautiful to her as he spoke them.

As he continued to talk it seemed to Annie that his knowledge had no limit and his way of imparting it, clearly and simply, in his soft, easy voice, made her feel as though she wanted to remain forever just sitting beside him and listening to him.

"There are a number of drawings in the cabinet which are

particularly special that I will show you another time," Edward said as they reached the end of their task. He picked up the last one from the table: the perfectly drawn head of a young man, studying it closely.

"This one is later...eighteenth century...black chalk and pastel...quite beautiful...it owes a lot to Raphael. Look Annie! See the expression on his face...in his eyes."

Annie leaned closer. The young man's head, with his uncombed curly hair, was angled slightly back, looking upwards.

Edward spoke, almost in a whisper: "The soul of an angel pleading through human eyes."

By the time she returned to the kitchen, it was almost time for her to go home. Miss Hargrove, grudgingly it seemed to Annie, counted out the twelve shillings and sixpence due to her for her three days work.

"I will see you here on Monday morning."

The housekeeper left Annie wondering if she had offended her in some way, but when she thought about it, she decided that Miss Hargrove's bad humour had nothing to with her at all.

Janey caught up with her as she was about to cycle away from Fernmount.

"I have every second Sunday off...I've no work tomorrow...I was thinkin' that maybe I could meet you for a bit."

"Where? Here?"

"Ah no, Annie. Somewhere towards your house."

"Well...I..." Annie hadn't planned to do anything on the Sunday. She had thought that after she had gone to Mass and had cooked her father's dinner that she would take it easy and catch up with a few things, but she didn't like to refuse Janey: "Where would we meet?"

"You know the bridge you pass on the way here...'tis about two miles from here?"

"Yes."

"Could you meet me there at three o'clock?"

9

The leaves sparkled in the sunlight that had re-appeared moments after the rain had stopped and despite the freshness in the air the rain had brought with it, Annie could still smell the wet dust that had been matted into the surface of the road.

She cycled along slowly, not having slept well the previous night, the restlessness she had felt all evening, staying with her, even when her eyes were closing in sleep.

Janey was already waiting at the bridge, leaning on the parapet, throwing pebbles into the stream, pausing every so often to look towards a bend on the road, in the opposite direction from which Annie was approaching.

"I couldn't have walked no more," she said, the moment Annie reached her. She massaged her foot through the leather of her shoe: "I have a sore toe…maybe we could sit here on the bridge for a while."

After they had settled themselves as comfortably as possible Janey asked: "How long'll you be at Fernmount?"

"I don't know…Miss Hargrove told my father that it would only be for a couple of weeks."

"I don't know why you was brought here…'tisn't that anyone minds or anything…maybe 'tis because I heard talk that Derek Ashby might be comin' home."

"Oh! When?"

"It could be any day…'tis more'n a year since he was home last…there's always extra things to be done when he's comin' home."

"What is he like?"

"He looks more like his father than his mother…he don't get on too well with Mr. Ashby."

"Oh!"

"The mother really spoils him…gives him anything he wants…her an' Miss Hargrove. God! These stones are goin' right through me." She got down off the bridge, brushing the back of her skirt: "You have to keep your eyes open when he's around." She hauled herself back up: "There was a maid here when I came…Nora Ryan. She told me that one night Derek got into her room an' jumped on her in the bed but she got hold of her shoe an' gave him a belt with it…an' that was the end a that. What time is it?"

"It's about ten or a quarter past three."

"Lord", Janey sighed, "time goes very slow sometimes." She lowered her voice: "I'll tell you somethin' else though…somethin' a lot worse…somethin' that happened a long time ago…" she was almost whispering now, "…somethin' 'bout Mr. Ashby."

"Mr Ashby?"

Janey nodded: "There was this girl that came to work here…she was from up the country somewhere. By all accounts Mr. Ashby was soft on her…s'posed to be very soft. Anyway, as soon as Mrs. Ashby found out, the girl was gone."

"I don't know why people talk so much, about…about other people's talk," Annie said, getting down off the bridge.

"Oh, well…" Janey fixed her cardigan "…'twas worse than that…there was talk that she was in trouble as well."

Annie turned to face her: "That she was going to have a baby?"

"Yeh."

"That's a terrible thing to say when it's only gossip."

"Well," Janey tossed her head, "the only thing was…there was talk as well that the baby might a been a bakery man's from the town that used to bring special bread to Mrs Ashby. Whichever way it was…"

"You shouldn't be listening to all that gossip…or repeating it either." Annie sat back on the bridge: "It's not…"

Janey grabbed her arm: "Shh! shh!"

"What?"

"Shh! I thought I heard somethin'."

Annie listened, hearing only the noise of the rushing stream beneath them, and the intermittent notes of birds rising above it.

Janey released her hold on Annie's arm: "'Tis nothin'. Anyway, they sent her off to the nuns an' after she had the baby she had to give it up to 'em." Janey shook her head: "It must be awful to have to give a baby away…shhh! Someone *is* comin'!"

The sound of voices drifted towards them and then, the noise of heavy boots on the road.

"Oh Lord!" Janey looked this way and that, brushing at her hair with her hand and fixing her skirt as two figures, carrying heavy green Local Defence Force overcoats, came round the bend below the bridge.

"Mickey…and Seán Brennan," Janey spoke out of the side of her mouth.

"Mickey who?"

"Mickey O'Brien…he's over from Garrybeg…works on the farm at Fernmount"

The girls waited in silence as Mickey, the taller of the two, quickened his pace, while his companion hung back.

"Well, Janey?" Mickey threw his heavy coat across the bridge and stood in front of Janey, his eyes on Annie.

"Well what?" Janey said, blushing.

"What brings *you* out on a fine Sunday evenin'?"

"The same as what brings you out." Janey blushed a deeper shade of red and looked towards Seán Brennan who stood a little away from them, his back against the bridge wall; his arms around his heavy coat: "Come up a bit nearer, Seán."

"You're not from around here?" Mickey moved closer to Annie.

"No."

"Where are you from?"

"She's from Ballycrag…" Janey answered for her, jumping off the bridge and pushing herself between Annie and Mickey "…an' she don't like nosy people."

Mickey grabbed a handful of her hair and gave it a tug.

"Owww!"

Janey twisted in pain, real or affected, but managed to lean into Mickey's chest. Annie eased herself off the bridge and walked past Mickey to where Seán Brennan was standing, still holding on to his big green coat.

"Were you training with the LDF today?" she asked him.

He blushed scarlet: "Only for a while…the rain got too heavy. We…we saw a fox when we were comin' across the fields."

"Oh?"

"If we could a killed him we could a got five shillin's."

"Five shillings?"

"Yeh. The guards are payin' five shillin's for every fox that's killed. But we would a had to bring the fox to the guards barracks…or his head…an' cut out a bit of his tongue while the guard was there."

"Uggh!"

Mickey O'Brien released Janey and moved up behind Annie, catching her by the shoulder: "Would you like to go for a bit of a walk?"

She turned quickly, brushing away his hand: "No! I would not."

He stood in her way as she made to walk past him, grinning into her face: "Where's your hurry? I don't see a fire anywhere?"

She ignored the remark, forcing her way past him, and walked back to where her bicycle lay against the bridge.

"I'm going home…I'll see you tomorrow, Janey."

Janey made no effort to detain her: "All right."

"I could walk a bit of the way with you…" Mickey tried again with Annie "…it'll shorten the journey for you."

Annie made no reply.

"I'm not standin' around here all day," Janey announced and began walking away in the direction of Fernmount.

"I'll go with you." Seán moved after her.

"Well?" Mickey turned again to Annie.

Annie did not look at him as she put her foot on the pedal of her bicycle and cycled quickly away.

Mickey made as if to run after her and then stopped. Grabbing his heavy coat off the bridge he shouted after Janey and Seán: "Hould your horses!" and hurried after them.

Annie felt better after she had washed and changed her clothes. She had cycled back to Ballycrag faster than she normally would have done in the warmth of the sun that had grown stronger during the afternoon, her annoyance with Janey driving her forward. Janey had used her meeting with her as an excuse to be at the bridge when Mickey O'Brien came along and all Annie had had for her efforts was a few minutes listening to Janey's scandalous gossip.

She took an oil sheet from the trunk in the kitchen and a rug from her bedroom - the rug her mother always brought to the seaside with them when Annie was little. Crossing the yard, she climbed the stone wall and spread them at the meadow's edge, under the shade of the beech tree that cast its shadow at both sides of the wall. She lay on her side, resting her head in the crook of her arm and began to read the book she had brought with her

She read just a few pages before putting it down. A little more than a year had elapsed since she'd first read *Jane Eyre* and it was really all too fresh in her mind. She should have remembered to borrow some books in the library in the town, using Aunt Nora's card.

The humps and hollows in the rug were a miniature mountain range of muted colours as she looked sideways across it, the uncut grass of the meadow beyond, a dense forest of beige and yellow-green. *Maybe the grasshoppers and ladybirds and all the tiny insects inside it are watching me.* She smiled at the thought. *Maybe they're wondering what kind of giant creature has come to lurk outside their territory…*

A butterfly flickered in her direct line of vision, folding its wings as it landed. Holding her breath, she watched the orange, black, and blue-tipped fragile wings rise and fall as it balanced on a hump in the rug.

She sat up when it fluttered away, a little splash of floating colour against the grey of the stone wall, her eyes following the flickering wings as they swept down and up, and down again, on its journey over the meadow.

Clasping her arms around her knees, she rested her cheek against them, the dark eyes of Edward Ashby looming in her consciousness: *He would have shared the moment of the butterfly with me…marvelled at its beauty…talked about the colour and delicacy of its design.* She closed her eyes: *He would have smiled at me and I would have smiled back at him. He would have reached out his hand…*

She opened her eyes, as the air cooled about her, and raised her head. The sun was losing its warmth and light in the dark mass of a drifting cloud. A breeze ran silently up through the meadow, ruffling the tall grasses, chilling her as it passed over.

It was gone just as quickly as it had arrived and the air warmed again, the sun re-appearing in all its fullness. She stood up, gathering the oil sheet and the rug in her arms. This time, she walked slowly along the length of the wall and opened the gate into the yard.

"That Mickey O'Brien is a brat!"

Janey slammed an empty pot down on the draining board.

Annie had just returned to the kitchen. All morning, she had been with Bridget and a local woman who had come in especially to help with the laundering of the bed linen. She greeted Janey's outburst with silence now, her mind pre-occupied. Moments before, she had been pegging out sheets when Miss Hargrove had approached her: "Leave those to Bridget, Annie. I want to speak to you. Go into the kitchen and wait. I'll be along presently."

The housekeeper's tone was the same as it had been on the Saturday, and again Annie wondered if she had offended in some way.

Janey banged a second pot against the draining board and this time Annie reacted: "What's wrong, Janey?"

"Nothin'…'tis…'tis just that…that…"

Janey withdrew her hands from the soapy water in the sink and lifted her apron to her eyes.

Annie moved over beside her, placing an arm around her shoulders: "Janey…what's wrong?"

Janey turned, wriggling out from under Annie's arm her small, pale face streaked with tears, and leant back against the sink: "I couldn't sleep nor nothin' last night."

"Why, Janey?"

"After you was gone yesterday an' we were walkin' along, first Mickey asks me all sorts of questions about you but I told him nothin' an' then after a while he tells Seán to go on ahead an' we would catch up with him." She wiped her eyes with the corner of her apron: "Everythin' was goin' grand…we were courtin' a bit. And then we got as far as Lowry's cross an' there was Lily Markham…her father works on the farm as well. There she was, standin' with her bicycle all brazen an' smilin' an' makin' wind across her face with her big ugly hand."

The tears welled up again and Janey dabbed at her eyes: "Mickey goes up to her an' well Lily he sez an' she gives a big sigh an' sez ooooh I'm flagged out from the heat I wish there was someone to carry me home on the carrier of my bicycle. So…Mickey turns around and sez did you hear that, Janey, there's a lady in distress an' I have to help her out. An' the next thing I'm standin' there in the road lookin' after the two a them and the bicycle waltzin' over an' back across the road with the weight of the big lump of her an' she laughin' an' screechin' like a stuck pig."

Annie resisted the temptation to smile: "And he didn't come back?"

"No…an' I would a had to go back on my own, except Seán was waitin' for me a bit up the road."

"Sean's a nice lad, a much nicer lad than Mickey O'Brien."

Janey sniffed.

"He likes you as well."

Janey sniffed again.

"I'd say he likes you a lot."

"D'you think so?"

"I do. As soon as you left yesterday didn't he go with you straight away?"

"Oh! That's right." Janey gave her eyes another wipe with her apron and turned back to the sink: "He was here this mornin' too."

"Who? Seán?"

"No! Mickey O'Brien…he was lookin' for you."

"For *me*?"

"He had some old excuse, only Miss Hargrove was here an' she told him never to come near the house again."

Annie didn't like hearing about Mickey O'Brien at all and was about to tell Janey so when Miss Hargrove entered the kitchen: "Would you come with me, please, Annie."

Miss Hargrove faced Annie across the room in which she had interviewed her on the morning of her arrival at Fernmount.

"When you were asked to come here, it was because Mrs Ashby and I felt that we needed an extra pair of hands to prepare the house for the arrival of…well, that does not concern you. What *does* concern you is the fact that there is not as much work to be done as…"

Miss Hargrove stopped speaking as the ringing of the doorbell echoed through the hall.

"One moment!"

The housekeeper left the room and walked along the hallway to the front door. After a brief pause, Annie heard her footsteps returning, and passing hurriedly by. She waited for what seemed a long time before she heard the approaching voices of Miss Hargrove and Mrs. Ashby.

The housekeeper entered the room alone: "Well, Annie…oh, do sit down."

Annie sat in the same chair that she had sat on during her interview, but this time, the housekeeper stood beside the desk, one hand resting on the edge: "Now…what I was about to tell you, before we were interrupted, was that you were brought here to help prepare the house for the homecoming of Mrs. Ashby's son, Derek, and that, until a moment ago, it seemed that he would not be coming home at all. Well…" Miss Hargrove's smile took Annie by surprise "…we have just received a telegram confirming that he will be arriving on Thursday. We will be having a dinner party on Friday night in his honour and we expect that it will end quite late. Some of our guests are likely to remain here until Saturday. We would like you to stay overnight on Friday."

"Yes, Miss Hargrove."

"Good! That's settled then. You may return to the kitchen now. Mrs. Ashby is already there, informing the others of her good news. I will be along presently to give you your instructions."

Annie made her way downstairs, certain that the housekeeper had been about to tell her that she was no longer needed at Fernmount, but had changed her mind. For a moment she had thought that it might have had something to do with Mickey O'Brien but of course it hadn't. It would have been ridiculous anyway if it had had.

The idea too, that Derek's homecoming had been in doubt was only an excuse: Miss Hargrove had known all along that he was coming for sure. She couldn't understand it. She hadn't done anything. The housekeeper had gone from praising her work one day, to not wanting her in the house at all the next. It was all a bit strange - and disappointing as well. It now looked certain that she would be gone from Fernmount by Saturday. She would never see Edward Ashby again after that.

It was not until Wednesday morning that Annie had the opportunity to speak with Edward and only then because Sarah Ashby had gone to town to see after some last minute items. Since the arrival of the telegram on the Monday, Sarah had been here, there and everywhere, requesting that certain things be done one minute, changing her mind the next. Annie found herself running backwards and forwards about the house with hardly a moment to spare.

She had met Edward a few times, but only in passing, when he had come in from his walks. He had barely smiled at her, his face showing no trace of the forthcoming pleasure evident in Sarah, Miss Hargrove and even in Janey.

"You are being kept busy, Annie?" he asked now, as he entered the library, moving up close to where she was on her knees polishing the base of a rosewood lectern. She paused to look up at him and smiled, bending to her task again to hide her blush.

"My son is lucky to have such preparations being made for his homecoming, even though his visit is going to be such a short one. He has to leave again on Saturday…did you know that?"

She looked up at him again: "No."

"Yes, indeed…but then, were it not for the influence of one or two well-placed friends in the Armed Forces, he would not have been allowed home at all. We must be grateful for that."

He was silent then and Annie felt uncomfortable, wishing that he had not caught her in such an ungainly position. She worked as quickly as possible to finish her task.

"This war will cut short many lives, Annie…" Edward said as she stood up "…many young lives."

His shoulders drooped as he walked over to one of the open bookshelves and removed one of the books: "Have you read *Wuthering Heights*?" he asked, without turning around.

"Yes."

"And *Jane Eyre*?"

"Yes…I began re-reading it again last Sunday," she added, immediately regretting that she had said it.

He was smiling now as he turned to face her: "Did you, indeed?"

He began talking about the Brontë sisters then and about other authors and novels she had read, and again she felt that she could go on listening to him forever.

Before Miss Hargrove came into the library, looking for her, he talked to her about the teacher's training college, the civil service and about her mother: "What a shame…such an untimely death. Life can be very harsh, very cruel."

His eyes looked sad then.

"A letter came for you today," her father said, handing it to her the moment she arrived at the cottage that evening.

"Oh."

After studying the envelope briefly, she took the letter into her bedroom and put it in a drawer.

"I think it might be from Owen," Paddy said, when she returned to the kitchen.

"Yes, it is."

He looked at her questioningly.

"I'll read it later," she said and busied herself preparing supper,

Annie lay awake, unable to settle down. Maybe it was a mistake to have gone to bed when she did. She wouldn't have gone so early but for her father and his interest in Owen's letter.

She had been thinking about washing her hair when he had asked: "Well…how's Owen gettin' on?"

"I…I haven't read his letter yet." She had stretched, feigning tiredness: "I'm going to bed shortly…I'll read it then."

She had taken it out when she had undressed and had put it back again, deciding to leave it until the morning. She had dozed off for a while, but a noise from the kitchen or something had woken her up. Since then, she had tossed and turned, unable to shake off the memory of Edward Ashby's sad eyes.

She imagined herself comforting him now, holding him close. Desire warmed her body and she willed it away, feeling guilty and ashamed. She must try not to think about him and try to sleep. Anyway, it would soon be morning. He would be at Fernmount when she got there.

11

Late on the following afternoon, an hour or more after Miss Hargrove had announced his arrival, Annie had her first sight of Derek Ashby. She was at work in a corner of the kitchen when his hurried footsteps were heard on the stairs and he came bounding in, the housekeeper in close pursuit and went directly to Mary Conroy to greet her.

The moment he entered, Janey drew a short breath, a blush rising in her pale cheeks. She moved quickly to stand beside Annie.

"Don't he look handsome?" she whispered.

Annie had to admit that the tall, lean figure looked striking in his military uniform. He had travelled in civilian clothes, but had changed almost immediately at the request of his mother. Neatly cropped dark hair topped an angular face and when he glanced in her direction, she could see the resemblance to his father across the forehead and around the eyes; eyes that opened wide at first, then narrowed as he looked at her.

She kept her head turned away as Miss Hargrove took him by the arm and ushered him out of the kitchen. She was sorry for Janey, whom he had not acknowledged, but then, he had not had the opportunity to do so since Miss Hargrove had all but pushed him out of the kitchen.

Annie did not see him again until the next morning. She was cycling along the drive on her way to her work when he stepped out from behind one of the sycamore trees and stood directly in her path. She braked hard and came to a wobbling halt. He reached out and grabbed the handlebars: "There should be a warning against *speeding lady bicyclists* posted at Fernmount."

Annie was taken aback at the deliberate way he had stepped in front of her and the disadvantage he had placed her at. She hid her upset by letting go of her bicycle and brushing her hands against the front of her dress.

"You're Annie if I'm not mistaken and my information from Miss Hargrove is accurate?"

The accent was crisp, without any of Edward's softness. Annie did not reply and he gave a short laugh: "I can see you do not believe in conversing with strangers without a proper introduction."

Annie took hold of the handlebars, taking the bicycle from him. She tried to move past, but he put a restraining hand back on the handlebars: "Obviously, I had better introduce myself." He stepped away and snapped to attention: "Derek Ashby, soon to be defender of King and Country, at your service."

He stood, ramrod straight, staring past Annie. He remained perfectly still, moving only his eyes to look sideways at her, forcing a reluctant smile from her: "That's better…permission to stand at ease?"

In spite of herself, Annie couldn't help broadening her smile.

He relaxed his body: "So, Annie, you're over from Ballycrag."

"Yes…but I must get to work now."

His eyes narrowed in the way they had done when he had looked at her the previous afternoon: "Your work can wait a moment or two, don't you think?"

Annie's smile began to fade: "I really must get to work."

"Well then, I won't detain you any longer"…there was an edge to his voice now "…but do allow me to assist you."

He held the handlebars, the front wheel between his legs: "Your trusty steed is ready for mounting."

Annie put a foot on the pedal and removed it again.

"Please let go. I can manage well enough on my own."

"Are you quite sure? This is a skittish animal. A temperamental animal too from what I can see."

Annie had stopped smiling: "Let me pass, please."

"You may pass on condition that when I look for refreshment, later in the morning, that you will be the one to serve me."

"I have to go now."

"No you don't…not until I have your word that you will do as I say."

Annie began to feel a little helpless.

"Well, do I have your word?"

"Please, I must get to work."

She was angry now and pushed at the bicycle but he resisted: "A mettlesome animal too, by Jove!"

He let go of the handlebars and Annie brushed past him, walking a few yards, her cheeks burning, before getting up on her bicycle.

"Don't forget!"

The sound of his laughter grated on her and she was still angry when she walked into the kitchen.

As she helped prepare vegetables for dinner she wondered how there could be such a difference between father and son. They resembled each other in looks but the similarity ended there: Edward's presence warmed her, while Derek made her feel guarded and ill at ease.

Later, just as she had decided that the matter of her having to serve Derek Ashby had been forgotten about, Miss Hargrove told her to prepare a tray and to take it to the drawing room.

"Could someone else do it, please Miss Hargrove?"

"No, Annie." The housekeeper looked at her searchingly for a moment: "The tray is for two people, Mrs. Ashby and Mr. Derek."

Annie was relieved and after she had served them in silence, Mrs. Ashby dismissed her with a wave of her hand but not before Derek had treated her to a sly, triumphant smile as she retreated from the room.

He came into the kitchen as the afternoon wore on and exchanged laughing conversation with Miss Hargrove. Annie turned her back and was relieved, once again, when one of the extra women brought in to help out for the evening called out: "Miss Hargrove says to come out right away, sir. Major Bindon and his wife and Miss Isabel are comin' up the drive in a hackney cab."

Annie forgot about Derek in the excitement and tension that began to build around the house as more guests followed. Preparations in the kitchen and dining-room were nearing completion and she was glad now that she was there and had a part to play in the occasion. Despite rationing and scarcity, it seemed to her that a sumptuous feast was being prepared and would be served in a resplendent setting.

A pair of tall, ornate silver five-branch candelabra, their wax candles ready for lighting, stood close to either end of the dining table. In the middle, a large silver centerpiece, in the form of a stag, standing antlered and stately beside a rocky outcrop, supported glass dishes for the petit fours; and beautifully arranged flowers, rising above other gleaming silverware and gilded and royal blue dinnerware, added colour and a festive air to the otherwise sombre room.

The gossip in the kitchen, among the women brought in to help, added to the occasion and Annie began to feel as though each guest was no longer a stranger but an acquaintance about whom she was learning more and more.

The middle-aged, unmarried Welby sisters, Agatha and Rose, who were staying overnight at Fernmount with their niece, Aurora Dalby, were, according to Kitty Kirby "very nice, but a bit strange."

"They talks to the plants an' trees…an' sings to them as well, they say."

"Lord save us! What about the niece?"

"Over from England she is. Sent over by the sister to get her out of the clutches of some married fella she was dotin' on…goes mopin' around the house all day, she does, like one that's half-dead."

"Faith then, she didn't look like no one half-dead when the parson handed her down outa the trap…all smiles she was an' he blushin' all over his face."

The Rev. Andrew Stone, a shy, gentle man, all the more bashful since the death of his wife, two years before, had arrived on his bicycle shortly before Aurora and her aunts. They had rolled up the avenue in a trap, the pony lathered in sweat from the two-hour journey. The petrol shortage made no difference to them as neither could drive and their dear-departed brother's motor car lay mummified under a covering of sheets and layers of dust in the coach house of their home.

As she passed to and from the kitchen to the dining-room, Annie stole more and more glances at those seated around the table, her interest increased by the gossiping and the information available in the kitchen.

"Who's the big man with the loud voice?"

"Oh him! He's Mr Deignan, the solicitor."

Alphonsus Deignan, heavy jowled, big-bellied, with a booming good-natured voice, had been able to travel by car having waived his fees on a case in return for petrol without questioning its source. He was comfortable with the thought that he was more than a match for any guard that might dare to stop him and query the need for what might be deemed an unnecessary journey.

"And the small little woman?"

"That's his wife."

"Lord!"

Bridget Deignan, a petite, mousy woman seemed to Annie to be perpetually silent. The only time she had heard her speak was when she had asked for the sauceboat to be passed to her; and then her voice had barely risen above that of a whisper.

Neilus Ryan, Edward's doctor, because of his position, was also able to bring his car. A small, gruff-mannered man, he and his wife Helena arrived at the same time as Barney Roche.

"The doctor's wife's a lot taller than him."

"That's 'cause she has such long legs…a dancer she was." Delia Reilly seemed to know more about the guests than anyone else.

"A dancer?"

"A dancin' girl that does be in the music-halls in London. He met her when he was on his holidays there. Love at first sight they say…on his part anyhow."

Biddy Hannigan shook her head: "A dancer! Wouldn't you think he could a done better for hisself?"

"He's happy enough…they has two lovely little girls. But sure…" the unmarried Delia's ample breasts rose in unison with her wistful smile "…when love comes knockin' tisn't always the right thing to do to lock the door. There might never be another knock."

Barney Roche, the only other guest that would stay overnight at Fernmount, had arrived on horseback. The stocky, good-humoured Barney, his ruddy face always ready to break out in a grin, was still a bachelor at forty five and likely to remain so by all accounts.

"Too fond a the fox huntin'," Delia confided. "And gives the hounds the run of the house, I heard tell from Nellie O' Brien. He asked the same Nellie in for tea one evenin'. She nearly passed away from the smell but she was still goin' to drink a sup o' tea not wantin' to be bad mannered. The cups, the butter, the sugar, the tea and a loaf of bread were all sittin' on the table. They could have been sittin' there for weeks Nellie said. 'Twas all right when the kettle was boilin' but when Barney started to take a cut of bread from wan end of the loaf didn't a mouse poke his head out from a hole in the other end. Nellie ran away outa the house as fast as she could. She wouldn't go inside it ever again…not for love or money."

"Hasn't he no servant girl or no one?"

"After the sister died…she wouldn't let no woman in the house while she was alive…there were a good few that came, but none of 'em stayed too long."

"Why so?"

"He couldn't keep his hands off any of 'em."

"What was wrong with that? He could a been a good match for any girl."

"He could. But by all accounts it was his mother's dyin' wish that he'd never marry no one except she was of the same persuasion as the Roches. And he wouldn't go against his mother. But that didn't stop him tryin' to get them into his bed…but there was never goin' to be a weddin' ring."

"Maybe the major's daughter would take a fancy to him."

The retired Major Bindon had procured a hackney cab and had paid well for the privilege of having the driver remain to take them home after dinner. His "plain as a pikestaff" daughter, Isabel, it appeared had "high hopes" concerning Derek Ashby, notions that were judged by those in the kitchen to be doomed to failure.

Entering and leaving the dining-room, serving courses or removing dishes, Annie felt part of an exotic and exalted world. As the dinner progressed and the wine from Edward's cellar began to take effect on the diners, her head swirled from the rising volume of conversation and laughter.

There were moments of solemn faces and hushed voices as the progress of the war was discussed but these were short-lived. Sarah Ashby forbade any grim intrusion into the pleasure of the evening and refused to consider what possible dangers lay in store for Derek on his return to his unit in England.

In the kitchen, flushed faces and tiring feet and hands, reduced the animated conversation of earlier in the evening to quiet comment, but Annie was still buoyed up and still deriving pleasure from the occasion

Sarah Ashby had embarrassed her momentarily, when she had chided her - unnecessarily Annie had thought - for a lack of concentration and she had felt her face go crimson as Helena Ryan told her: "You're pretty enough to be a film star."

Edward Ashby had smiled at her any time she had caught his eye, but she had avoided looking directly at Derek, conscious that he was watching her all the time.

As the meal drew to a close, Miss Hargrove, who had moved constantly between kitchen and dining-room, announced that as soon as everything was restored to order that they could all gather in the hallway outside the drawing room.

"What will happen?" Annie asked Kitty Kirby.

"Oh" Kitty tossed her head "a bit of la-di-dah music an' singin' 'till the drink warms them up an' one or two a them forgets about the airs and graces. There'll be a bit of sport then."

12

After a slow start, more or less as Kitty Kirby had predicted, Helena Ryan took possession of the piano stool and launched into a medley of popular songs, remembered from her time in the music-halls. A hush descended, but only for a moment: Barney Roche gave a whoop and a jump and went over to the piano to lend willing support in a pleasant baritone. The mousy Mrs. Deignan's serious face brightened and she happily joined in, in a strong voice that belied her tiny frame. Major Bindon, without altering his sober expression, hummed along under his breath, and the Rev Andrew Stone blushed to the roots of his hair as his tapping foot accidentally tapped the foot of Aurora Dalby.

The revelry was well under way when Annie joined those gathered in the hallway and, bit by bit, edged closer to the doorway, her eyes seeking out Edward Ashby. Her heart missed a beat when she saw him, leaning back against the marble fireplace, sipping from the glass in his hand. He turned his head, glancing towards the doorway. His eyes held hers and he smiled, barely lifting his glass.

Annie returned his smile, clasping her hands to her breast, in an effort to still the trembling in her body. She stood, oblivious to those around her, until he turned his head away again. She pushed her way back into the hallway then, and leant against the wall, all else receding from her consciousness except Edward's smiling face.

It seemed to her that only seconds had elapsed before Derek Ashby was beside her, grasping her hand and pulling her inside the doorway. It happened so quickly, that she had no time to think about resisting him.

In the drawing room, he leant close to her and asked, almost in her ear: "Do you sing?"

She jerked her head away at the same time as Miss Hargrove came quickly towards them and took her by the arm: "Come with me."

Out in the hallway, the housekeeper steered her towards the staircase: "I want you to go upstairs, Annie, and turn down the covers and plump the pillows in the guest bedrooms. Close any open windows."

"Yes, Miss Hargrove."

The housekeeper stood looking after her as Annie climbed the stairs, her cheeks burning.

"Oh…Annie!"

Annie turned on the stairs.

"Yes, Miss Hargrove."

"When you have finished you may go down to the kitchen and have some tea and then go to bed. I want you to be fully alert in the morning."

"Yes, Miss Hargrove."

Having finished her task, Annie was disconsolately collecting the small overnight bag containing her nightdress and some toiletries from the bottom of one of the cupboards in the kitchen when Janey rushed into the kitchen: "Annie, would you come out a that. There's great sport goin' on. Barney Roche is singin' with Miss Agatha an'…"

"I can't go. I have to go to bed."

"Lord! Why?"

"Miss Hargrove told me to."

"She couldn't have meant you to go this minute?"

"No…she said I could have tea first."

"Ah, Lord…sit down so an' I'll have it made in two shakes of a lamb's tail."

Annie sat at the kitchen table, placing her overnight bag on the floor beside her chair. The water in the large copper kettle, sitting on top of the big cast iron range, was still hot and was boiling again almost immediately as Janey took a tea caddy from a cupboard.

"What are you doing, Janey?" Miss Hargrove came into the kitchen and walked directly to her, taking the tea caddy from her: "I have told you before…you are not to make tea without permission. It is too scarce a commodity at the present moment and must be used sparingly."

"But I…"

"Run along now and join the others."

Annie rose from her chair, pretending not to notice the faces that Janey was making as she passed by: "Janey was only…"

"Sit down, Annie…I will make the tea."

Annie sat in silence while the housekeeper rinsed a teapot with water from the kettle, before adding a careful measure of tea with the caddy spoon and returning the caddy to the cupboard.

"You did well today, Annie…" the housekeeper had her back to Annie as she poured boiling water into the teapot "…Mrs Ashby is very pleased…with everybody." She covered the teapot with a cosy and brought it to the table: "Leave it to draw for a moment or two before…" she paused as Janey ran into the kitchen "…what is it now, Janey?"

"Mrs. Ashby wants you in the drawing room, Miss Hargrove."

The housekeeper began moving towards the door: "If I am not back before you have had your tea, Annie, you are to go to bed directly. I will be calling on you very early in the morning. And Janey…"

"Yes, Miss Hargrove."

"…you may stay with Annie if you like until she has finished and then go back and join the others for a little while."

"Yes, Miss Hargrove," Janey said sweetly and promptly stuck her tongue out at the housekeeper's departing back. She took a cup from the draining board and brought it to the table: "She's a right old hake."

"Did she say anything to you about an early start in the morning?"

"No…nor to no one else as far as I know." Janey pulled a chair up beside Annie: "You wouldn't know what does be in her head half the time. Anyway, you might as well have your tea considerin' 'tis such a…" Janey grasped the teapot handle and raised it aloft, screwing up her face and attempting to mimic the housekeeper "…*a scarce commodity.*"

Annie's response was laughter and they were both laughing when Derek Ashby's voice issued from the doorway: "So, this is where you are, Annie."

He came forward, glass in hand, and sat on the table beside her. Annie stood up immediately, bumping against Janey. Scalding liquid from the teapot Janey was still holding aloft splashed across the back of her hand and she drew a sharp intake of breath as the pain hit her. She held her hand in front of her, her body trembling.

Derek slid off the table and grasped her arm: "Janey! Turn on the tap."

Annie allowed him to steer her towards the sink and to thrust her hand under the streaming tap. She gasped in pain as the cold water hit the scalded spot and her body sagged against him. Derek drew her close but she pulled away immediately: "I'm alright."

Janey looked as though she was about to cry: "I'll get Dr. Ryan."

"There is no need for that" Derek's tone was deprecating. "I can get something to dress it with from the medicine cupboard."

"But Dr. Ryan is a doctor an'…"

"Take Annie to the table and sit her down."

Derek foraged in the medicine cupboard and after a moment or two returned to the table. Annie reluctantly allowed him to sprinkle some powder on her hand. He covered the scalded section with a piece of lint and deftly applied a bandage: "There!"

He held on to the fingers of her injured hand until she forcibly withdrew them.

"You can have your tea now, Annie," Janey said, reaching for the teapot.

Derek put a restraining hand on her arm: "I will look after it. You go off now and join the fun!"

"But Miss Hargrove said I…"

"But…but…but…" Derek placed his hand against Janey's back and gave her a push"…off you go now."

As Janey, head down, walked out of the kitchen Anne tried once again to stand up from her chair. Derek, his hand on her shoulder, prevented her: "Have your tea." He picked up the cup: "This is not clean. We can't have that."

Annie sat with her head bowed, cradling her hand, as he fumbled at the kitchen dresser and did not lift it even when he placed a full teacup in front of her and asked: "Sugar?"

"Thank you."

"Milk?"

She nodded and raised her head, not looking at him, as he stirred in the milk.

"Drink up now."

He stood sideways to her, sipping from his glass while she drank the contents much too quickly.

"I have to go to bed now."

Bending down, she reached for her overnight bag. Derek's hand brushed against her hair and she dropped the bag, bumping her head against the table as she straightened immediately. She threw out her arm to ward him off but he had moved quickly away from her, his eyes on the doorway. Annie turned in her chair and saw the figure of Edward Ashby enter the kitchen.

"Annie scalded her hand...I put a dressing on it," Derek said, as Edward walked slowly towards them. "Janey spilt some hot tea on her."

"Let me see, Annie."

Annie proffered the bandaged hand and Edward held it gently: "How is it? Is it very painful?"

"It's just a little sore."

"Maybe we should have Dr. Ryan have a look at it?"

"It's all right."

Edward turned to Derek: "Don't you think you should be with our guests?"

Derek made as if to say something, but changed his mind and walked out of the kitchen.

Edward was concerned: "Are you sure you are all right?"

"Yes...I..."

He placed his hand against her forehead: "A glass of water...or milk perhaps would not go astray, I think. Wait a moment."

Annie sat still while Edward found a glass and filled it.

"Here! Drink this now."

Annie drank until the glass was empty: "I must go to bed." She remembered her nightdress and bent down to pick up her bag.

"Let me help you."

Edward took her bag and Annie sagged against him as he walked with her to the kitchen door, almost colliding with Miss Hargrove.

"Annie's feeling a little unwell…she burned her hand. I believe Janey spilt some hot tea on it," Edward said, releasing her elbow. "It appears to be alright…she's on her way to bed now."

The housekeeper looked from one to the other, shaking her head: "I'll see her to her room."

"One moment!" Edward held out Annie's bag. The housekeeper did not look at him as she took it.

Annie felt as though she was dreaming as she followed Miss Hargrove upstairs to the smallest of the family bedrooms on the first floor, vaguely conscious that she was finding it difficult to keep her balance

The housekeeper opened the bedroom door and handed her the overnight bag: "Go to bed directly, Annie. You have an early start in the morning." The housekeeper paused a moment before closing the door quietly and walking away.

Inside the room, the bag slipped from Annie's hand and she tripped over it, the bed preventing her from falling over. She held on to the bed-clothes for a moment, thinking that she ought to draw the curtains against the dimming midsummer light, but the thought left her as she released her hold and twisted her body so that she could sit on the side of the bed. She took off her shoes and stockings, finding it difficult to stay upright as she dragged her dress over her head. She rolled onto the bed then, lying on her back, not bothering to draw the bedclothes around her.

13

Warmth brushed against Annie's cheeks and caressed her forehead. Her eyelids fluttered briefly and were still again. The warmth encircled her breasts, slowly drifting downwards, going round and round and round, until it came to rest between her thighs.

Her legs rose in the air and her slip touched against her hips, rippling against her belly, pausing at her breasts. Her body rolled from side to side, the slip passing over her, falling across her face, the silky cloth creeping into her mouth, stifling her. Weight pressed against her, starving her lungs.

The slip left her mouth, her gasping intake of air cut short by a slavering pressure that covered her lips, stifling her once more, until the weight lifted from her and she could breathe again.

She was restful a moment, vaguely aware of the brush of her knickers, sliding over her hips, plucking at her calves and passing over her feet. The spreading of her legs disturbed her then and the weight returned, thrusting again and again against her body, awakening a sliver of pain somewhere deep inside her. A doleful cry distracted her for an instant and the weight crushed against her once more.

She thought she cried out - a cry that merged with another cry somewhere above her. The weight was no more then and she was drawn into the peace of dark, relieving nothingness.

She was dreaming. Her body was moving, dragging, lifting. She wanted it to stop, to rest, but it would not.

She was resting in a soft place now, trying to shut out the noise of voices around her. She heard her name being called but she did not answer. Her arm was grasped in a hard grip, hurting her, and she was dragged from the softness, her body jarring as it struck a hard place, her eyes opening to a blurred image of Sarah Ashby, standing over her: "Get up and get dressed and leave this house instantly."

Her clothes were thrown on top of her and she struggled to her feet, her clothes falling around her onto the floor. She held herself upright for a moment trying to focus her eyes, falling sideways against the softness she had been taken from a moment before, the dreamy lightness in her head lifting for a moment: *Edward Ashby's bed! The softness is his bed!*

She saw him then, standing across from her, dressed in a robe of bright shimmering colours.

"Why…?" She could not ask the question that formed in her mind, the words too heavy on her tongue, the dreamy lightness filling her head again.

"Come with me."

Miss Hargrove's voice was beside her now: "Come with me, Annie. I have all your things". The housekeeper took her by the arm and she tried to resist, giving in as the voice of Sarah Ashby screamed inside her head: "Get out! Get out of my house!"

The housekeeper led her along the landing and into another room.

"You must get dressed."

Miss Hargrove placed Annie's dress over her head and shoulders and pulled it down.

"Now…your shoes."

She bent down and lifted each of Annie's feet in turn, placing them in the shoes and tied the laces.

Miss Hargrove stood up: "That will do for now. Your stockings and the rest of your things are in your bag. You can put them on later. I have also put your week's payment in the bag. You understand, of course, that your employment here is terminated."

Miss Hargrove helped her down the stairs, along the hall and out through the main door. Annie was surprised to see her bicycle already by the front steps.

The housekeeper held the bicycle steady as Annie tried to sit comfortably on the saddle, but she was hurting: "I...I have to walk."

Miss Hargrove remained standing on the steps until Annie passed out of sight round a curve of the drive.

The early morning sun hurt her eyes and only the support of her bicycle kept her from falling. She felt sore. She stopped and looked at the bandage on her hand. The soreness in her body must be underneath the bandage. She wanted to lie down and rest but not here. Her bedroom was at home in the cottage. She must keep moving.

"What are you doing home so early?"

Her father stopped short on his way to the lavatory outside. He came close to her and looked at her, his eyes worried

"Are you sick?"

"I'm...tired."

"God Almighty, how could they send anyone home like that? Did you get no sleep last night or what?"

Annie's body began to fold. Her father grabbed her and held her up.

"For God's sake, Annie, what's wrong?"

Annie rubbed her bandaged hand across her forehead, trying to clear her mind: "Mrs. Ashby told me...go home."

"What happened to your hand?"

"Burn. I...I...went upstairs. Mr. Ashby's bed...I had to go...home."

Paddy stared open-mouthed at his daughter: "His bed! You were...! Here...sit down."

He helped her into one of the armchairs, turning death-pale as Annie's dress and her slip caught an edge of the chair and rode above her hips, exposing the flesh of her inner thighs: "Oh! Jesus!"

Paddy clasped his head in his hands and reeled back as though physically assaulted.

Annie made a small sound in her throat.

"Oh, Jesus!" Paddy tried to fix her dress, averting his eyes. He reached under her armpits, lifting her from the chair: "I'll take you into bed."

He stood by the bedside staring down at Annie, his heart thudding in his chest, his body shaking. He waited until she was breathing easily in deep sleep before he went to his bedroom and took his good clothes from the wardrobe.

14

Carefully propping his bicycle against a sturdy shrub, Paddy Luhan removed the bicycle clips from his trousers ends, and straightening his suit, walked up the steps and into the hallway at Fernmount.

"Miss Hargrove!"

Crossing the hall to the dining-room the housekeeper turned her head and stopped short, her eyes narrowing as Paddy came up close to her, his grip tightening on the bicycle clips in his trousers pocket: "I want to see Mr Ashby?"

The housekeeper moved back a step: "Why?"

"I want to know what happened to Annie?"

The housekeeper moved back another step: "Have you not asked her?"

"She's not in a fit state to be asked about anything."

"Where is she now?"

"At home in her bed, asleep."

The housekeeper's eyes flickered: "Go home, then…let *her* tell you what happened when she's awake."

Paddy removed his hand from his pocket: "I want to see Mr Ashby."

"Mr Ashby is having breakfast at the moment with his family and guests and he cannot…" she stopped as Paddy began walking past her. She moved quickly to stand in front of him, grasping his arm: "Wait! I will speak to Mr Ashby."

Paddy shook off her arm: "Get him out here…get him out. Now!"

The housekeeper opened her mouth, closed it and opened it again: "Come with me…*please!*"

Paddy turned away from the window as Edward Ashby reached behind him and slowly pushed the library door closed.

"Please…" Edward raised his hand and gestured at one of two leather armchairs at either side of a rosewood table.

"What happened to Annie last night?"

Edward lowered his hand and awkwardly moved to one side, supporting his back against a shelf of books.

"I gather from Miss Hargrove that Annie has already given you a version of…"

"Annie's hardly able to talk."

Edward grimaced in pain as he straightened himself against the bookshelves: "I don't know…what she's told you…but…" Edward's voice was uneven"…the fact is…Miss Hargrove alerted my wife early this morning to the fact that Annie was missing from her bed and…and after a search of the house found your daughter in my room. How she…"

"She wasn't only in your room…" Paddy came forward and stood close to Edward "…she was in your *bed*."

"Look here…" Edward averted his eyes "…I don't know why she was there…or how…"

"She was…interfered with."

Edward shook his head: "All I can tell you is that, for whatever reason, your daughter…"

Paddy reached out suddenly and grasped Edwards's lapels, dragging him away from the bookshelves, twisting him around, wrenching his back.

"Ahhhh!"

Edward's cry of pain reached Derek Ashby in the hallway, interrupting his low-toned conversation with Miss Hargrove and brought him crashing through the library door. Paddy, his back to the door, released Edward and half-turned his head, as Derek, without altering his stride, shouldered him away with all the force his momentum carried with it. Paddy staggered sideways, losing his balance, and tried to prevent himself from falling by grabbing at the edge of an occasional table. The delicately–made table crashed to the floor, with Paddy sprawled on top of it, the vase that had stood on it smashing to pieces.

Miss Hargrove, following closely on Derek's heels, moved quickly to stand beside Derek and placed a restraining arm on him as he stood over Paddy.

"That's enough!" Edward stepped forward, wincing from the effort, as Paddy rose shakily to his feet, breathing hard, blood from a gash on his chin already staining the collar of his white shirt.

Edward looked from Derek to Miss Hargrove: "Leave us…now!"

"Before you make any rash judgement…" Edward sat on the edge of the seat of one of the two armchairs and faced Paddy, sitting opposite him in the other "…you should know that recently one of the farm hands has been skulking about the house, asking after Annie and…"

"Who?" The heavy fall had tempered Paddy's anger and he had given in to Edward's repeated request that he sit down.

"I believe a young man called O'Brien. Miss Hargrove has had to order him away with strict instructions not to come here again."

"Are you sayin' that *he* had something to do with what happened to Annie last night?"

"No. What I am trying to explain is that whatever you think may have happened to your daughter…and how exactly it happened…or why she found herself in my room…"

"She was in your bed!"

"Look! It has been suggested to me that she may have taken wine or…"

"She doesn't drink!"

Edward averted his eyes from the sight of the blood on Paddy's chin: "Well, it appears she could have done so last night and…and allowed someone to…allowed something to happen…as a consequence of which…"

"Are you sayin'…that Annie was…that some fella…that afterwards she crawled into your bed." Paddy stood up, his body trembling: "Jesus, Mary and Holy St. Joseph! are you sayin' that she did it to try and lay the blame on you?"

Edward flinched: "No! No! I'm not saying anything of the kind. All I'm doing is simply stating the situation as Miss Hargrove has advised me."

Paddy leant back, his hands on the arm rests, his breath coming in short shallow bursts: "You…you expect me…to believe that…that all this happened…and you knew nothin' about it?"

"I…I have medicine I take to help me sleep. When I do fall asleep nothing wakes me."

"You woke this mornin'."

"Not without the efforts of my wife. Look! However it appears to you, I cannot give you any other explanation than the one I've just given you."

Paddy sat back in the armchair staring into space for a moment: "There were people here last night."

"You mean our guests?"

"Yes…and your son was here."

Edward struggled upright from his chair: "I would advise you to be very careful about pointing the finger at anyone…or making accusations that have no foundation in fact."

Paddy looked deep into Edward's eyes: "What about this…this O'Brien?"

"I really don't know anything about him…nor am I saying…"

"Who knows him?"

"The herdsman…and I believe Janey, the kitchen maid."

"I want to see her!"

"I don't think…"

Paddy rose from the chair: "I'll go down to the kitchen myself."

"Wait!" Edward moved away from the armchair with difficulty: "I'll have her sent up here…and please sit down."

Only minutes elapsed before there was a knock on the library door and Janey entered. She stood just inside the door, picking at her apron, her eyes darting from Edward to Paddy and to the table, its leg broken, lying on its side on the floor, pieces of the broken vase scattered around it.

Edward had remained standing after his return from the hallway where he had straight away met with Miss Hargrove and had requested Janey's presence. The housekeeper had hesitated: "Are you sure that you…?"

"Have her sent to the library…at once!"

He gestured to Janey now: "Come closer…Mr Luhan has some questions for you."

Janey came forward and stood facing Paddy, her mouth falling open at the sight of the blood around his chin and on his collar.

"You know a fella called O'Brien?"

Janey turned bright red: "Mickey O'Brien?"

"Does Annie know him?"

"She…she only met him the once…last Sunday…she only stayed a minute…she didn't talk to him atall."

"Was he here last night?"

"No."

"Are you sure?"

"He couldn't a been…him and Seán Brennan are gone off trainin' with the LDF since yesterday evenin'. They won't be back until tomorrow."

"Were you with Annie last night?"

Janey looked behind her at Edward Ashby, confusion in her eyes.

"It's all right, Janey, just answer Mr Luhan," Edward said.

Janey turned back to Paddy: "Was it before she went to bed?"

"Yes."

"I was…only Miss Hargrove sent her off to bed early."

"Did she have anything to drink before she went to bed?"

"She had the tea in the kitchen…I didn't mean for the tea to burn her…"

"Did she drink wine or anythin' else last night?"

"Lord no!"

"And she was all right goin' off to bed?"

"She…"

Edward interrupted: "I myself happened to be in the kitchen when Miss Hargrove conducted Annie upstairs to her room. She appeared to be a little tired…that was all as far as I was aware."

Paddy was silent, while Janey stood uneasily, moving from one foot to the other.

"I think, perhaps, that you have no need to question Janey further," Edward said.

Paddy shook his head. He waited until the door closed behind Janey: "What are you goin' to do about Annie?"

"I'm afraid there's little we can do. We can make enquiries but…"

"I'm goin' to go to the guards."

"You must do whatever you see fit…but what do you think the guards will be able to do?"

"They can find out what happened to Annie."

"And if they don't?"

Paddy was silent again.

Edward did not look directly at Paddy: "I think you may find that the best thing to do, difficult as it may be for you, is to let the matter rest for everyone's sake…especially for your daughter's sake."

Paddy walked slowly out of the library. He left the door open behind him as he passed through into the hallway.

Annie was still asleep when he returned to the cottage. He went to his room and changed his shirt, bundling up the blood-stained one and shoving it under his bed. In the kitchen, he gingerly wiped his chin and neck with a wet cloth before going back to Annie's room.

At the touch of his hand on her shoulder she jumped up, clutching the bedclothes to her.

"It's all right, Annie. It's all right!"

Annie stared him, her expression blank: "What happened to your face, daddy?"

"It's nothin'. I have to go out for a while, Annie…will you be all right?"

"I'm very tired."

"Are you hungry? Will I get you somethin'?"

"I'm thirsty, daddy."

Paddy brought her a glass of water. Annie sat up, drinking it greedily.

"How are you feelin' now, Annie?"

"I'm very tired."

Annie settled herself down again, her eyelids already beginning to close.

"I won't be too long, Annie," Paddy said. "Are you sure you'll be all right?"

Annie was already asleep.

15

Paddy kept his head down, his hand covering his chin, while he sat in the doctor's waiting room at Kilcrone. An hour or more passed before he was seated in the surgery.

Dr Ryan swabbed the cut: "There was no need for you to come and see me with this."

Paddy was silent.

"Now…there we are. Don't go at it for a few days…it'll heal itself."

Paddy made no move to get up.

"There's no more to be done," the doctor said curtly.

"I want you to see Annie."

"What?"

"My daughter, Annie…somethin' happened to her last night."…

"What are you talking about?"

Paddy struggled to explain the events of the previous night and morning as Dr Ryan listened uncomprehendingly and impatiently, until Paddy mentioned Fernmount.

"What exactly are you trying to say? Would you start again and tell me the story straight…and stop beating about the bush."

This time, the doctor paid full attention to what Paddy was saying. At the end he said: "She's all right at the moment then…I mean, she's not showing any great signs of injury or anything like that, is she?"

"No…well…no…but somethin' was done to her last night."

"But you don't know that for sure?"

"That's why I want you to come and see Annie."

Dr Ryan did not reply immediately.

"Tell me…" he said after a moment or two "…ah…is your daughter company-keeping?"

Paddy was slow to answer: "There's a young man…a teacher…he

helps her with her studyin'…he's away in the Aran Islands."

"How long since he went there?"

"A couple of weeks ago…are you goin' to come and see Annie?"

"There is no need for me to go and see her…it's not an emergency…she can come and see me here from Monday on if she wants to. Now…I have a lot of patients to attend to."

Annie could not understand why she was in bed and that there was only silence all around. The music from the drawing room at Fernmount was still in her head. The room felt strange and for a moment she thought that it was morning and that she ought to be getting up to go downstairs to Miss Hargrove.

Her head cleared a little when she sat up and she realized that she was in her own bed. Maybe she should be getting up to go to work at Fernmount…or maybe to go to school. Her hand hurt and she withdrew it from beneath the covers. She had burned it…no, Janey had. She had had to go to bed then.

She was thirsty…and hungry. She must get something to eat.

The kitchen was strange too.

"Daddy!" she called "daddy!"

She looked at the clock on the wall, puzzling over the time. *A quarter to three…it couldn't be the morning!*

She drank thirstily from the bucket near the kitchen dresser. The bread knife slipped from her hand two or three times as she cut a slice from the loaf. She had cut it too thickly and put too much butter on it. She ate only half the slice and drank the milk she had poured from the jug. The feeling of drifting in a haze of calming drowsiness began to leave her and she wondered why everything seemed so unreal, so out of joint and why her body felt so different.

She went back to her bedroom and looked at herself in the mirror. A white-faced, bedraggled-haired stranger with wide luminous eyes stared back at her and she turned away immediately. Something was terribly wrong.

She walked back into the kitchen.

"Daddy!" she called again, "daddy!"

Something stirred in her mind then and she began to cry.

Paddy walked up and down outside the guards' barracks in Kilcrone until one of the guards came out and slowly ambled towards the gates: "Are you wantin' something?"

"I…no…I was just waitin' for someone."

"Ah!"

"What time is it now?"

"It must be after three o'clock."

"'Tis later than I thought…no use waitin' any longer."

Annie was still asleep when Paddy came home. He milked the cow and threw out a bit of feed for the hens, not bothering to check for eggs. He was too tired.

He looked in on Annie again before he set potatoes to boil. He'd make pandy when the potatoes were ready and make sure she ate some of it at least.

Annie handed her father the plate. She had barely picked at the food.

"Thanks, daddy."

"You didn't eat much." Paddy sat on the edge of her bed.

"I'm not really hungry."

"Is there anything you want to tell me about…about last night, Annie?"

Annie drew herself up, resting her back against the bedhead. She did not reply.

"Anythin' at all, Annie?"

Annie just picked at the quilt.

"What happened before you went to bed?"

"I was listening to the music and the singing but I had to go upstairs to fix the beds. Miss Hargrove said I was to go to bed myself then…but I could have tea first.

"And did you have the tea?"

"Yes."

"Nothin' else?"

"No…only the tea Derek Ashby gave me…and the milk Mr Ashby got for me…that was after I burned my hand." Annie withdrew the bandaged hand from beneath the bedclothes: "Derek bandaged it for me."

"Derek Ashby?"

"Yes...Janey wanted Dr Ryan to do it, but..."

"Dr Ryan was *there* last night?"

"Yes."

Paddy stood up, his hands shaking: "I'll take the plate out."

In the kitchen he dropped the plate in a basin and turning to the table gripped the edge hard.

"Daddy!" Annie called from the bedroom. "Could I have another glass of water please?"

"I'll..." Paddy swallowed hard "...I'll bring it in...in a minute."

"Are you gettin' up for a while?" Paddy took the empty glass from Annie.

"No...I...what time is it?"

Paddy went to the doorway and looked at the clock in the kitchen: "It's near half seven."

"I might get up for a while later on. Are you going somewhere?"

"No...I...I'm goin' to get ready for mass in the mornin' an' then maybe I'll listen to the wireless for a while before I go to bed."

"I forgot tomorrow is Sunday...are you all right, daddy?"

"I..."Paddy's voice shook "...Annie, they said...they said that you went to Mr Ashby's bed yourself..."

"Who said?"

"Mr Ashby...Miss Hargrove...they said that maybe someone had...well Mr Ashby said that it could look like you were tryin' to blame him for...for whatever happened."

"Mr Ashby said that!"

"Well he...oh, Annie!" Paddy went to her as she burst into tears, but she turned away from him and he stood helplessly by.

"I don't know...what happened." Annie's tears had begun to subside.

"I know...I know."

Annie turned to look at him.

"When did you speak to Mr Ashby?"

"This mornin'…I went there after you came home."

"Oh! And that was all he said?"

"Yes…and only that he was asleep all the time an' didn't know anythin' at all."

Annie just stared at her father.

"Maybe the best thing is to try an' put it all behind us now," Paddy said "an' get on as best we can."

He moved to the bedroom door: "You…you don't have to go to mass in the mornin' if you're not feelin' right."

Annie turned her head away, waiting until the bedroom door closed quietly behind her father.

As the shadows in the kitchen began to dissipate Annie raked the embers in the hearth and added kindling. A few turns of the bellows fanned the flames and she put on the hard, black sods of turf, turning the wheel again. By the time she had brought in extra water from the well the fire was strong enough to boil water. As quietly as possible she drew the tin bath out from beneath its place under the stairs to the loft and brought it into her room.

Lying in his bed, watching the dawn lighten the night sky through his window, Paddy heard the noise of the fire being stoked in the hearth and then, the sound of the tin bath dragging on the flagstones. He thought to get up and to go to Annie, to help her prepare her bath, but instead he lay there, the rage and the feeling of helplessness that had kept him awake all night turning in his gut again.

He sat up clasping his stomach in his arms, rocking backwards and forwards, stopping when he became conscious of the creaking and rattling of the iron bed.

He lifted his head, staring sightlessly at the wall opposite, until he blinked his eyes and they focussed on the photograph of Annie's mother on the dressing table. His body quietened and he began to cry, softly at first and then just as hard and as desolately as he had cried in the long nights after she had died.

Annie was up and dressed by the time Paddy was ready for mass.

"I might be a bit late gettin' home…but not too late…you'll be all right?" he said as he was leaving.

"I will."

He paused in the doorway of the cottage, looking up at the sky: "'Tis just as well you're not comin'…that rain that's startin' is goin' to pour out of the heavens. You could be soaked in it."

Before mass had ended, Paddy made his way round to the sacristy, waiting until he heard the bustle of the congregation beginning to leave the church before knocking on the sacristy door. An altar boy answered his tentative knock.

"Wait a minute!"

The boy disappeared back inside and returned after a short delay: "You're to come in."

The parish priest, Fr. Hayes, was removing his vestments: "Paddy! How are you?"

"I'm all right, father."

The priest looked at him keenly for a moment: "Sit down, Paddy. I won't be long."

Fr. Hayes finished removing the vestments and hung them in a large pitch pine cupboard: "All right boys! You can all go home now."

The priest waited until the altar boys had left and drew up a chair: "Well, Paddy, how are you…and your daughter? She's at the Convent Secondary School now, isn't she?"

"She is…she did her Leaving Cert a few weeks ago." Paddy rubbed his hand across his forehead: "'Tis Annie I came to see you about, father."

"Ah!" concern showed on the priest's face.

"Well, father…" Paddy faltered, his body sagging a little in the chair.

Fr. Hayes's concern deepened: "Nothing wrong I hope? She's not in any trouble now, is she?"

Paddy straightened: "No, no! It's just that…well, I was thinkin' that…well Annie was sayin' that it would be a nice thing to have a mass said for her mother an' I was thinkin' that it would please Annie if I got you to say it."

The priest looked puzzled: "That's what you wanted to see me about?"

"Yes, father."

"Nothing else?"

"No." Paddy stood up and reached into his pocket: "Will this be enough, father?" He handed the priest a half crown.

"That'll be grand, Paddy."

At the door of the sacristy, Fr Hayes cleared his throat: "If there's anything, anything at all that ever troubles you, you'll come and see me."

"I will, father."

Fr Hayes stared thoughtfully after the departing figure of Paddy, before looking down at the coin in his hand. Shaking his head, he shoved it into his soutane.

"Would you think of going to see Dr Ryan…tomorrow, maybe?"

Annie pushed her dinner plate aside and looked across the kitchen table at her father: "No."

"It could do no harm to go an' see him."

Annie stood and picked up her dinner plate and began scraping the leftovers into a pot for the hens: "No."

"Well…maybe we could go and see your Aunt Nora then. We could cycle into town this evenin' if you like?"

"No."

"You'll want to talk to…"

"Please, daddy…I'm all right now."

16

Owen Dara was surprised when his brother called.

"I just took a chance that you might be home from the Aran Islands," his brother said as he followed Owen along the hall to the kitchen.

"I only got back about an hour ago…how's mammy?"

"She's fine." His brother threw his cap on the kitchen table and drew up a chair: "Hugh's already talking about going back to Africa. He seems to be feeling much better."

"That's good." Owen sat opposite him: "What brought you to Kilcrone?"

His brother reached forward and picked up his cap: "Well…" he cleared his throat "…there's been a lot of talk goin' around."

"Talk? What talk?"

"Talk that wouldn't be doin' *you* any good."

"What do you mean?"

"Well…that girl that you brought to see my mother…"

"You mean, Annie?"

"Yes, her…well…as far as we can make out it she was workin' over at Fernmount House for a while…around the time you went off to the Aran Islands…"

"I know that."

"Yes…well, it seems that she caused a lot of trouble there."

"Trouble? What do you mean?"

"Well…there was some kind of a do on there one night and it seems she got herself drunk…and she gave one of the workmen…or maybe someone else…his way…you know what I mean."

The blood drained from Owen's face.

"Anyway, the father was over creatin' blue murder. It seems that she was tryin' to blame…"

Owen jumped up from his chair. His brother followed him out of the kitchen to the shed where Owen kept his bicycle: "Wait now! Don't be in such a hurry to be doin' anything foolish."

Owen pushed past him and his brother followed him to the front gates: "You'd be better off stayin' away from *her*."

Owen left his brother standing there and cycled away.

Annie held her breath, her back against the kitchen wall. Owen had already knocked and banged several times, rattling the latch, calling her name. Only moments before he had arrived, her father had gone out into the fields and she had bolted the door behind him.

She crouched down beneath the kitchen window and lifted a tiny corner of the curtain. Her heart lurched as the material of his coat passed in front of her eyes. He was on his way round the back of the cottage! Thank God, she had drawn the curtain in her bedroom. Her stomach heaved, bile rising inside her. Why couldn't he just go away and leave her alone? Why did he have to come back *now*? If only...

She thought she heard the sound of his footsteps passing back by the window and held her breath again, waiting and praying that he would take his bicycle and go. Fearfully, she lifted the corner of the curtain once more. His bicycle was still outside the front gate and he was nowhere to be seen. He was not going to go away! He was going to wait!

She tiptoed to her bedroom, switching on the light, and leaned back against the wall, her arms clasped around her stomach. The past weeks had been one long nightmare and even yet, there was still no end to it. If only Owen had waited one more day.

The moment her father came back she would have to tell him that there was no way that she could see Owen. Her father would think it unfair, maybe, but there was nothing she could do. What could she say to Owen? How could she even begin to explain to him all that had happened while he was away?

She had gone to stay with her aunt on the Tuesday following that night in Fernmount, but had left again after only two days. She couldn't bear to stay any longer. Aunt Nora had followed her back to the cottage, and a fearful row had taken place between her father and her aunt. Annie would have run away, except that there was nowhere to run to. Aunt Nora couldn't - no, *wouldn't* - believe that nobody knew what had really taken place, nor who had been responsible. She had even gone so far as to suggest that Annie wasn't telling the whole truth and she had accused Annie's father of being a fool and a coward. She had left the cottage vowing never to speak to her brother again.

Annie had remained at home after that, not going out unless it was absolutely necessary, cycling all the way into town on Sundays to go to mass, kneeling at the back of the church and leaving quickly the moment mass had ended.

She had clung to the hope that Edward Ashby would come to see her; that he would call without warning and foolishly, she had made sure that she had presented herself well every day. She had even thought about going to see him at Fernmount until her father had returned one evening, having dressed up and gone out earlier in the day, telling her that he had had to go and see someone. She had thought that it might have been the parish priest because he had asked her if she would think about going to see Fr Hayes but she had refused.

"All I'm sayin' is that it might be a good thing for you just to talk to him."

"I'm not going."

"But, Annie…"

"Please! Daddy, don't ask me anymore."

When her father had returned that evening, he had been very quiet in himself. Just before she had gone to bed he had said out of the blue: "When people like them don't want anyone to know, no one will ever find out. They have their ways of keepin' it to themselves…and they always will. There's no gettin' around them. They'll look after their own…the rest of us don't count."

She had said nothing in reply. She had accepted the fact that her father had been back to Fernmount, and that what he had said, had been his way of telling her that he had got nowhere. She had made up her mind then not to go there, and she had cried herself to sleep just as she had done on so many nights.

She had put off going to the doctor when the morning sickness had persisted until her father had lost patience: "You'll just have to go and see the doctor, Annie." She had waited to go back for the result of her test on a day when her father had left the cottage early.

After the doctor had told her about the baby, he had continued to talk for a while. She had tried to concentrate on what he was telling her until he had said: "Your parish priest, Fr. Hayes, is not without experience in these matters. He can advise you on a course of action that would be best for all concerned. " She had lost concentration after that and had only wanted to get home as quickly as possible.

Cycling back to Ballycrag, she had not returned a single greeting from those she had passed by on the road, but had averted her eyes, feeling that the change in her life was already obvious to anyone who might know her or care to look closely at her.

Her Leaving Certificate results had arrived that same day, together with a letter from Mother Paul congratulating her on having achieved the best marks ever of any of the students at the convent, and on having brought honour to the school. She had been saddened by her father's efforts to show pleasure and pride over her achievement and she had been unable to bring herself to tell him about the baby.

After breakfast the next day she had told him that she needed to go to town to buy some things. She had gone directly to Aunt Nora and after only a short visit she had left her distraught aunt crying into her apron. She had walked around the town for a long time, and then, not knowing who else to turn to, she had called to the convent to see Mother Paul. She might not have gone to see her at all if the nun had not written in her letter:...*come and see me any afternoon and together we can discuss the many avenues for further success that are now open to you.*

She had followed her father out into the fields when she'd come home and only then had she told him about the baby and about the arrangement that Mother Paul was sure that she would be able to make for her.

Her father had only nodded his head when she had finished telling him everything and had said quietly: "Go on home so, Annie. I'll follow you on in a while."

Everything was arranged now. She would be leaving Ballycrag in the morning and going to live in the midlands with Mother Paul's widowed and childless sister. "Nobody there need know the story, Annie. Your husband could have been killed in the war, or had an accident or something," the nun had said.

She slid down the bedroom wall now, still clasping her stomach, feeling weak inside. If only Owen had waited one more day, she would not now be going through this awful situation.

It was a terrible way for her to leave him: to leave without saying anything – not even goodbye. She couldn't help it. She just couldn't face him. She just didn't have the strength left to deal with any more upset.

She crawled on her hands and knees to the chest of drawers and took an old handkerchief from the already open bottom drawer and wiped away the tears that had begun to roll down her cheeks. She saw the postcards and letters then – the postcards and letters Owen had sent from the Aran Islands- the postcards and the letters that she had placed unread in a corner of the drawer.

During the times she had thought about him, she had wondered if everything would have worked out differently if her feelings for him had not changed. She thought about it again now, and the answer to herself was still the same: maybe - but only if she hadn't gone to work at Fernmount.

Almost from the very moment that she had stepped inside the house, she had suddenly wanted more from her life, more than the future had offered. And then there was Edward Ashby. Maybe what had happened had been a punishment, a chastisement, for having wanted too much and for having entertained wrongful thoughts and desires.

Taking a deep breath she closed the drawer. She rose slowly to her feet and walked to the side of her bed. Bending down, she withdrew the suitcase that her father had bought only the day before and began packing the things she had laid out on the bed. When she had finished, she sat back on the bed and waited.

Paddy Luhan paused outside the gate to the yard watching Owen Dara's back and his hunched shoulders as he sat on the wall staring into the distance.

Owen came instantly alert at the sound of the gate squeaking on its rusty hinges and swinging his legs back over the wall he strode over to Paddy: "Where's Annie?"

Paddy held on to the gate with both hands.

"She can't see you now."

"Why?"

Paddy studied Owen's face: "She might be asleep."

"Is she all right?"

Paddy did not reply as he pushed the gate forward and came into the yard, closing and bolting the gate behind him. Owen followed him across the yard and around the gable end of the cottage, waiting while Paddy tried the latch a few times.

"Annie!" Paddy called. "Annie!"

At the sound of the bolt being drawn back Owen moved close to Paddy's shoulder.

"Wait here a minute." Paddy pressed on the latch and opened the door, just enough to slip through, closing the door behind him. It was the first time that Owen had been left standing outside the door since he'd begun calling to the cottage.

The door opened again and Owen stepped forward, but Paddy held it open only a foot or so wide, blocking him.

"She can't see you now."

"Why not?"

"She…it's better that you go away."

"Can't I just see her for a minute?"

"No."

"I have to see her!"

"You can't see her."

"For God's sake, can't you tell me what's wrong?"

"You'll have to go now."

"I want to see Annie!"

"You can't see her now…go on home."

"I have to see her!" Owen pushed at the door, but Paddy held it firm.

"I told you…you can't see her now…go on home."

"What about tomorrow? I'll come back tomorrow then."

"If that's what you want."

Owen heard the bolt slide into place after Paddy had closed the door in his face.

The following morning Annie stood, one foot on the running board of the motor car Mother Paul had sent to take her to the train station. The driver, a newly appointed curate from the town, a cousin of Mother Paul's, had already put the leather suitcase into the car. Packed in it were some of her clothes and a few little pieces her mother had brought with her on the day she had married Paddy Luhan.

"We have to leave now. We don't want to miss your train."

The curate had stood at a discreet distance, but now he moved close to Annie and placed his hand on her elbow: "I'm sorry, but we really must leave now."

"Wait!"

"Please, Miss Luhan, we have to leave now or you'll miss the train."

The curate stood aside as Paddy took Annie's arm and ushered her into the car: "I'll come and visit you" he said, closing the car door as gently as he could.

Annie kept her head twisted, looking back, until the car passed over the crest of the hill and she could see her father no more.

The curate entered the compartment in the train with her, storing her suitcase in the rack overhead. He put out his hand: "Goodbye, Miss Luhan. I wish you a safe and pleasant journey."

Annie did not take his hand. Her head was turned to the side, her eyes staring blindly through the carriage window.

He stood for a moment, looking down at her. He reached forward and touched her shoulder lightly: "Goodbye, Miss Luhan."

The hissing of steam, the noise of shunting trains, the clamour of people and the overall pall of grey that hung over the interior of the train station, were all part of the nightmare of her going. She was dimly aware of the shrill whistle of the guard and the slow, rumbling motion of the train as it eased its way out of the station. In the confined space of the iron and stone building, the *whoosh, whoosh, whoosh* of the steam belching out from the engine seemed to pass through her whole body like a recurring shiver.

She was barely aware of the hustle and bustle; of the movement of people in and out of the carriage; of the numerous stops at way stations; of the piercing whistles, the grinding of brakes and the laboured breathing of the engine as it struggled to build up speed. Other occupants attempted to engage her in conversation or offered food and drink but she closed them off by silence or a weary shake of her head. Some looked with concern and sympathy on her pale face and her slumped almost inert figure.

She turned her head into her shoulder as the tears rolled down her cheeks. She would have the baby. It would be hers and she would look after it.

The Father

1

Bullock Harbour
Dublin, Ireland
Late Summer 2001

On the day of the centenary celebrations at Lisbeg National School, less than three months ago now, I rose early and instead of going to breakfast, I left my hotel and walked out into the early morning sunlight. A rain shower had only lately passed over and had left the cultivated greenery of the hotel grounds, and the wild foliage of the hedgerows outside its confines, bathed in the sweet-smelling freshness of summer's bounty. Under different circumstances, it was a balm that would have lightened the anguish and the anger that had festered and boiled within me all through the night. I had felt the nausea of revulsion for the man who had shattered my mother's life - the man who was my father - and for those who had colluded with him in his crime. And they had used me, her child, to finally break her resolve to stand up to them.

After I had returned from my walk and had eaten breakfast my first thought was to go upstairs, pack my bag and leave – leave and not look back. Before I reached my room my resolve had weakened when I thought of the young girl, my mother, who had left her home all those years ago her choice to stay or go not hers to make. I had that choice and yet I was going too; only I was running away; running away voluntarily, running from the same past that had taken my mother's right to choose and was now taking mine. I could not allow that to happen.

I lay down on my bed then and while the returning rain tapped a sonorous rhythm against the bedroom windows I drifted into sleep, waking an hour or more later on when a startled hotel maid entered to make up the room. After I had showered I went down to the residents lounge and relaxed until it was time for me to leave for the school.

I had a clear memory of how the school had looked in my time there and I was neither touched by nostalgia for the past, nor taken by surprise, at the changes that had taken place after so many years. The shell of the original building remained but the big windows, set high in the walls, had been removed and had been replaced by an increased number of smaller ones that no longer hid the world outside from the view of young enquiring eyes. The two large schoolrooms had been divided into three and were brightly decorated with artwork from the children. The iron–framed pine desks, with their hard plank seats, had given way to more appealing individual tables and chairs. A durable, colourful carpet covered the boarded floor and the nostril tingling odour of dust, mixed with chalk, no longer hung in the air. A corridor had been added to the side, leading off to a relatively new extension that housed a recreation room, toilets and offices.

The school garden, where once spring and early summer vegetables grew, was just a sprinkling of shrubs rising out of concrete. The sycamore I had climbed on the day I had "run away" was gone, a play shelter in its stead. Close by, a water tower stood as tall as the absent sycamore.

The sun broke through moments before the parish priest was due to begin the open-air mass that marked the start of the celebrations. During the ritual I stood well back behind the rows of chairs, feeling like an intruder. The moment the mass ended, tea, coffee, sandwiches and cakes were served and as the buzz of conversation swelled around me I wandered off to the playing field. It was there that Mikey caught up with me.

"Sorry I'm late…the traffic out of Dublin was much heavier than I had bargained for…Laura is taking it easy back in the hotel."

His voice was enthusiastic, his eyes alight. I was glad to see him. He and his family, especially his mother, had been among the few who had been kind to, and accepting of my mother and me. After we had exchanged pleasantries I thought about suggesting that we shorten our visit to the school and go somewhere else but Mikey had other ideas. He dragged me off to meet the parish priest, the teachers and some old friends of his, two or three of whom he assured me had been in the same class as me. I remembered none of them. An hour or so later I steered him back to the quiet of the playing field.

"So…what is this *news* you have for me?"

"What?"

He frowned for a brief moment and then laughed: "Oh! You're talking about the note I left at your hotel."

"Yes…"I fished in my pocket and held it up, "…the note that read*s*: *By the way, I have some news that should interest you…*"

"Well…remember that day we met in London…"

It was the previous year. I had just finished viewing a sale of Old Master drawings and paintings at Sotheby's and, on a whim, had wandered into another saleroom that held a collection of antiquities.

I was idly examining an Etruscan bronze when I became aware of being studied. I raised my eyes and looked across at the man who offered a tight smile in return. There was something vaguely familiar about him: the sense of energy, the lock of grey hair falling down on his forehead, and the eyes - the bright, appraising eyes.

"Do I know you?"

"Maybe." He moved closer: "The name's Sullivan…Michael Sullivan."

The accent was American but there was a softness to it: an Irish softness. I was quite thrown for a moment. It was such a long time ago. I was trying to imagine dark hair and glasses and a much slighter framc.

"Mikey?" I ventured.

The eyes that had not changed in half a century lit up: "It *is* you! I knew it."

Over lunch, he told me that he had flown out of Shannon the day before and had attended a meeting in the offices of London associates of the law firm he was a senior partner in, in Philadelphia. He was using his free hours of that morning to visit Sotheby's and pursue his interest in antiquities that had begun a long time ago after he had eventually discovered that the "rocks like curled-up snails" that he had found in the quarry when he was a boy were ammonites.

"I went from fossils to antiquities to the relics of ancient art. At one time I thought I would become a palaeontologist...or an archaeologist

He had won a scholarship to University College Dublin and after graduating he had gone to the United States, working at various jobs. Three years on, he had begun studying at night and had obtained a primary law degree, after which he had taken out American citizenship and had married Laura Kilbride, the daughter of a second-generation Irish-American building contractor. His father-in-law had made it possible for him to attend Yale, where Mikey had distinguished himself and had been able to pick and choose from the eminent law firms that had been anxious to recruit him.

"We have three children and, wouldn't you know, all boys. Two of them are lawyers and the third, the youngest is in real estate...what about you?"

"I had a wife...no children. It's a long story." I veered away from that topic: "Tell me about Billy...and Tommy...either of them follow you to the United States?"

"Billy did...lives in Florida...Key West. Has a tidy little offshore fishing business. His wife is English."

"And Tommy?"

"Tommy's a priest."

"A priest?"

"He's in Brazil...been there a long time. It was a couple of years after he joined the priesthood that the folks sold up." His face clouded over: "My father had become ill...cancer...it's the reason they moved into town. My mother nursed him all through his illness. She only lasted a few years herself after he died."

"God, I'm sorry!"

"Yeah...I know. They're the main reason I started coming home each year...to visit their graves...felt guilty in a way that we had all left them…but hey!" he brightened up again, "that's enough about the Sullivan family. What about you…your mother?"

I told him of my mother's marriage to a director of the bank she had worked in for many years, in the year that I had taken my A-levels before going on to Cambridge to read history. I did not tell him that in the same year, while waiting to go up to Cambridge, that I had found temporary work with an insurance company, in St. James's Square, off Piccadilly, and that I had rented a bedsitter in West Kensington, a move which my mother was against but which I argued was simply my need for independence. I could not explain to her then, not even to myself, why it was that her imminent marriage had filled me with an intense feeling of revulsion for the very idea of sharing family life with a man who was not my real father; or why it was that I could not wait to get away from London quickly enough when I had finished at university.

"After Cambridge I drifted a bit," I told Mikey now, "hitch-hiked around Europe…lived in Paris for a while."

"You were really livin' it up!"

"No…not exactly…I just couldn't settle."

"So…you came back to London?"

"No…I moved on to Italy and…"

"You really were enjoying the good life."

"Well…anyway…my step-father came and persuaded me to go home. Asked me what I wanted to do with my life. I told him, I thought that I could be happy working in an art gallery…only then I had something like the Louvre in Paris, or the Uffizi in Florence in mind. He arranged a job for me in a gallery in Bond Street that was owned by one of his clients…and I went from there. With my mother's help and that of my step-father's I eventually opened my own gallery in the Midlands for a number of years before returning to open my present gallery in London."

Before Mikey left to catch his flight to Boston, we exchanged phone numbers and e-mail addresses.

"I can't wait to tell Laura. She's going to be bowled over. You've got to visit us. The next time I'm in London, I'm coming to visit *you*."

In the weeks following our chance meeting I was deluged with e-mails from Mikey, with photographs of his children, his wife. Sometimes he either forgot, or ignored the time difference, and phoned me at two or three o'clock in the morning. Slowly, persistently, he whittled away at the protective wall I had forged around myself over the years and I began to share with him many of the things that had been locked away inside me that I would not, or could not, share with anyone else.

I even talked to him about my marriage to Anthea, but I did not tell him everything. I still carried a sense of shame then, but not anymore.

2

I first met Anthea, the daughter of a wealthy Scottish landowner, in a small country hotel in the North of Scotland in January 1979. She was home from London on a weeklong visit to her parents. She was twenty four years old then and I was thirty five.

I had been at the sale of the contents of a country estate, conducted by local auctioneers. The recently deceased owner, a widow in her nineties, had only one surviving blood-relation, living in Australia, who had instructed that the estate and house contents be sold and the resulting monies forwarded to her.

My gallery in the Midlands had been established by this time and I had developed a coterie of *runners* and *door-knockers*: freelance dealers who held no premises, but sold to the trade and knocked at doors, hoping to gain entry and buy something of value, usually at a low price. For a commission, they would often advise the owners of established antiques shops or galleries of a potentially lucrative item of fine art or of a painting, that they themselves were unable to purchase or unwilling to risk their money on.

One *runner* in particular, Arthur Jolly, had an instinctive "feel" for good paintings and drawings but he neither had the confidence nor the cash to gamble on it. His gambling was done on horses. My dealings with him had proved very rewarding, so I was quite disappointed when he advised me that he was moving to Scotland, promising to keep in contact.

I had not heard from him for quite some time, when he phoned to tell me of the sale of the estate and house contents in Scotland close to where he now lived.

"As far as I can tell, for some reason or other, it has been advertised only locally. There are some very interesting paintings in the house."

"You've seen them."

"Yes. The auctioneer is not exactly a friend, but I got to know him quite well over the past year. I can arrange a private view for you at any time before the auction. I think, though, that you should come at least three or four days before the sale…in case you need to do some research."

It was just a few weeks after Christmas and business was slow. There was likely to be more profit in closing the gallery for a week and taking off on a potentially lucrative buying trip.

I arrived two days before the official viewing day. The hotel I booked into - a converted manor - I remember as being mostly freezing cold on the nights I stayed there. It did not bother me: the opportunity to be able to view privately a house contents that appeared to have remained untouched for over a hundred years more than compensated for any discomfort I might have felt.

It was snowing heavily outside and the light inside the house was poor on the day I did my first viewing. I had the impression then, that apart from the works of a few notable, nineteenth century British painters, the pictures in the main were well-executed late sixteenth or early seventeenth century copies of Renaissance and Old Master paintings. A few of these pictures appeared to have the possibility of being better than they appeared at first sight and it was these I concentrated on. I would take a chance and hopefully would not have to gamble too much. I returned again, on the following day for another look, trying to ensure as far as I could that the lots I had listed the day before were worth the bids I intended to make for them.

I was about to leave when I found myself in a kind of study off one of the bedrooms that for some reason I had missed the day before, perhaps assuming that it was a bathroom. It was here that I discovered a painting that sent a tingle of excitement through me and kept me awake that night and the night preceding the auction.

There were heavy snowfalls on the official viewing day, restricting travel and reducing the numbers that attended. The day of the auction showed an equally poor attendance. As the sale progressed, I bought all the lots I had earmarked for less than I had intended to pay. Now, as the one painting I really desired came up, I tried to hide my nervousness.

"Lot two hundred and forty three...*Cattle and Sheep in a Landscape*...by Thomas Sidney Cooper." The auctioneer, a red-faced, dour looking man, more at home selling cattle and who treated every lot as unfeelingly as he might have pots and pans, bent his head towards the clerk and asked in a hoarse whisper: "Is it signed?"

The clerk nodded: "It's on your sheet."

"Oh, right!" The auctioneer looked down at the description in front of him: "Signed by the artist...and there are two other pictures in this lot...three altogether."

One of the "two other pictures" was just a stained, tinted engraving of a sentimental Victorian domestic scene and worth only pennies. The other, the one I desperately wanted, was a wonderfully vibrant panel, painted by the Frenchman, Eugene Boudin, of a beach scene at Trouville.

The panel was dark, covered with grime, the signature and date visible after the application of my thumb and a little spittle, while the auctioneer's clerk, who had accompanied me around the house while I viewed the contents, had left me on my own for a moment. It would require only surface cleaning to restore it to its former glory. Happily, I thought, whoever catalogued the sale had thrown it in with the Cooper, obviously not considering it worth offering as a separate lot.

Smaller canvasses by Cooper had averaged around five hundred to fifteen hundred pounds in the London salerooms during the previous seventy seven, seventy eight season but his larger and earlier canvases, such as this one was, had made as much as six thousand pounds. This was a particularly fine example of his early work and could be sold in my gallery for perhaps seven thousand pounds but not more. I had that cushion against the Boudin. How much more I was willing to pay under the hammer I did not want to consider.

I wanted the Boudin. I wanted it for the particular sensory response it evoked in me, but I also had a wealthy client, an avid and discerning collector, who would pay well to own it. I would have it barely surfaced cleaned and have the pleasure of holding it in my possession, until the dictates of business demanded that I let it go.

"Who'll give me an opening bid of three hundred pounds for this lot?"

The auctioneer's eyes covered the room and after a pause he said briskly: "Right, then, I'll take an opening bid of one hundred."

A hand went up.

"I have one hundred pounds…and five…and ten…" The bidding was slow all the way up to five hundred pounds.

From my vantage point, standing at the back, I could see everyone in the room. I had scanned as many faces as possible during the course of the auction and had been relieved not to recognise anybody. I knew a number of the more prominent picture dealers by sight and not one seemed to be there. The bad weather and the poor advertising were working well in my favour. There were some local dealers present, but pictures were obviously not their main interest.

"I have five hundred pounds…any more?" I was about to raise my hand when the opening bidder came in again. "I have five twenty…five forty…five sixty…five eighty…six hundred…" the bidding was speeding up, "…six fifty…seven hundred…seven fifty…"

I raised my hand at *nine hundred and fifty.*

"One thousand pounds!"

For a moment it seemed that the lot was mine. The original bidder had given up at eight hundred and what appeared to be the last bid of nine hundred and fifty before I had raised my hand had come from one of the local dealers.

"I have one thousand…going once…"

"Eleven hundred!"

A woman's low, but clear voice, pierced the quiet that had descended on the room. This seemed to be an area where anything selling over one thousand pounds was considered not only high but even "a mad price". I had heard the whispers and bent my head against the curious looks when I had paid that much for a pair of views of Venice by John Callow and close to that amount for a number of other paintings. Now, even that price had been exceeded and might even increase.

"I have eleven hundred pounds...do I have twelve hundred?"

The auctioneer looked expectantly down the room at me. I nodded – a slight, but perceptible nod of the head.

"I have twelve hundred pounds!" His voice was triumphant.

Once again a pause and a rustling as people turned or strained to look back at me. I bent my head again, hoping for the fall of the hammer.

"Thirteen hundred pounds!" The woman's voice again. I looked up quickly and nodded at the auctioneer.

"Fourteen hundred! I have fourteen hundred from the gentleman standing at the back."

"Fifteen hundred!" The woman wasn't giving up.

"Sixteen hundred!"

"Seventeen hundred!" The woman again.

This time I made a circle in the air with my finger. The auctioneer understood the signal: *Round it off at two thousand!*" an old trick of the trade, jumping the bidding suddenly forward in order to startle the under bidder and perhaps throw him or her into confusion.

"I have two thousand pounds!"

For the first time the woman turned round, removing the Burberry hat she had been wearing. I caught a quick flash of fair hair before I looked away to my right as though I too was seeking out the person who was either rash or crazy or both.

"Two thousand I have...going once...twice..."

"Two thousand five hundred!" The woman's voice, the same tenor as before, even and controlled, stilled the murmuring, the shifting and the rustling.

It was I who was startled now. The woman was playing the game. Knew exactly what she was at. I raised my hand - and had to raise it again and again.

Applause followed the fall of the auctioneer's hammer at five thousand pounds. I left the room immediately and went directly to a small study at the end of the main hallway, where two of the auctioneer's staff were taking payment for lots already bought. I did not want anything to happen to the paintings, especially the Boudin.

It took more than an hour, before I held the Boudin in my hands. My cheque for close on fifteen thousand pounds, for all my purchases, had been accepted, but not before my *runner* friend, Arthur, had convinced the auctioneer of my *bona fide*. Arthur had a van into which we packed the Cooper and other paintings. He would make the journey to the Midlands and my gallery as soon as the weather permitted. The Boudin, the Callows and two other small canvasses I locked in the boot of my own car and having paid Arthur a reasonable fee I returned to my hotel and an eagerly awaited meal.

I had my car parked where I could clearly observe it under the light of the lanterns that reflected brightly off the snow in the forecourt, directly outside the dining-room window. I would remove the paintings to my hotel room after a long slow dinner. Mid-way through a main course of deliciously tender roast beef a woman walked into the dining-room, scanned it briefly and then walked directly to my table: "You could have had the Cooper for three thousand, you know, if you had not tried to be so clever." Her tone was not upbraiding, her voice soft, throaty.

Her fair hair framed a smiling oval face with startling blue eyes. "Don't disturb yourself", she added as I began to stand up, "you don't mind if I join you, do you? You're not expecting company or anything?"

"Please do," I indicated the chair opposite. I was taken quite off guard. She had come on purpose. A dealer perhaps, certainly connected to the trade in some way, I thought.

She removed her bulky coat and slung it over the back of the chair. She was tall, well-proportioned, very attractive. Beautiful, in fact.

"Are you in the trade?" I asked, as she made herself comfortable. She reached out across the table: "What are you celebrating with?" and picked up the bottle of wine, I had ordered, studying the label.

"Would you like to try a glass?"

"That would be nice."

I signalled the waiter: "Another glass, please."

I waited until she had taken a sip: "You haven't answered my question?"

"I like this…" she cradled the glass in her hands, "…no, I'm not in the trade. I run a trendy boutique in London with a friend." She accentuated trendy, for no apparent reason.

"Well, then..?"

"Well, then", she mimicked, "since we are now almost acquainted let's introduce ourselves. She proffered her hand: "Anthea Mc Cleod."

"Seán Luhan."

"You're Irish?"

"Yes…and you? You have a Scottish surname without a Scottish accent."

She laughed: "My mother's English. My father's ancestors are here for generations. My accent is a combination of my mother's and my father's…mostly my mother's."

"It's delightful…but you *are* going to great lengths to avoid direct questions."

"Not really," she laughed again, "I'm just enjoying a glass of wine in the midst of a highland winter…and unless you've lost your appetite, your food will not be fit for eating in another moment or two."

I picked up my knife and fork: "Have you eaten?"

"Yes."

"So…?"

"So, am I here by accident or by design?" She inclined her head: "Curiosity really…simple curiosity."

She had read about the sale in the local paper, had noted the presence of the Cooper and had decided to buy it for her father as a birthday present.

"I was hoping to persuade him to hang it in the dining-room instead of a vicious and horrid Snyders picture of a stag being torn asunder by hounds that I have hated since the day I was born. I think it's ugly and gruesome… but now," she looked at me over the rim of her wine glass, "having failed in my mission, I wanted to meet the smart dealer who is obviously not from these parts."

"But you behaved as an experienced dealer might have behaved."

"That's because I had a friend in London who was in the business and I attended quite a number of sales with him. He taught me all the tricks of the trade."

"Did you say *was*?"

"He moved lock stock and barrel, to New York. Anyway, I had a maximum price of three thousand for the Cooper. I simply ran you on the bids. It wasn't really the Cooper you wanted, was it? It was one or both of the two pictures that were sold with it?"

"Yes."

"I hadn't bothered to look at them during the view. I had no interest in the sale except in buying the painting for my father."

She did not ask and I did not tell her about the Boudin, there and then. I told her later on while we talked and shared a second bottle of wine until I remembered that I had to transfer the paintings from the boot of my car to my room, a task she insisted on helping me with.

After I had given the Boudin painting a cursory wipe with a damp towel from the bathroom, I proudly detailed the qualities with which I believed the artist had imbued the panel. She had listened respectfully and attentively as I rambled on and on and then, in a moment, she cupped my face in her hands and kissed me.

She stayed with me that night. I had become overwhelmed with sexual desire long before we had reached the hotel bedroom and the joining of our naked bodies, in fulfilment of that desire, was the most heady, most requiting encounter I had ever before experienced in my life.

I was to experience it again and again in the year before our marriage, and for the following eight or nine months, right up to the time she walked out on me for reasons I could never have envisaged - not in my wildest imaginings.

3

During our conversation on the day of our chance meeting, I had told Mikey Sullivan that, despite all appearances, I was becoming more and more disenchanted with life in London.

"Sometimes I think of moving on...of starting a new life elsewhere."

"Why don't you? There must be lots of great places in Europe for you to choose from...what with all the knowledge and experience you have of the place."

"Yes...but it's not Europe I think about, it's Ireland. The West of Ireland, as a matter of fact...somewhere like Ballycrag."

Mikey raised his eyebrows: "Ballycrag! You're kiddin' me?"

"No, I'm not."

"But you weren't exactly there for a lifetime...and I seem to remember that you and your mother didn't have a very good..." Mikey checked himself. "You were only a kid then. It couldn't have made that strong an impression on you."

"I think it did." I deliberately ignored his allusion to the circumstances that had led to our having to leave Ballycrag. "I have good memories of that time locked away somewhere deep inside me. And I did live in the country before we moved to Ballycrag."

I had said *like Ballycrag* and I had meant just that, not Ballycrag itself. I did have *good* memories of it, but I had other memories too, memories that were not so good. I did not think it necessary to tell that to Mikey.

"Why don't you think about going back, then?"

"I have thought about it...but then, life gets in the way again and I forget about it until the next time."

"You know," Mikey said seriously, "I still have contact with the old place. I'll keep my ear to the ground. If something comes up in the way of a property, I'll keep you posted."

I had forgotten all about that part of our conversation until that moment at the school when he told me: "Well…there's an old country house that could be coming on the market shortly that I thought might interest you. It's been neglected and needs some work…some modernising, I guess…but I believe that it's basically in good shape. If you're still of a mind to move back here, maybe you should take a look at it."

"Oh!" I had hoped for something altogether different: the chance to see an interesting painting maybe, but certainly not this. Mikey was quick to pick up on my reaction

"So…you've not given any more thought to moving over here then?"

I couldn't tell him that coming to live anywhere in the area was the furthest thought from my mind at that moment: "No…no…it's not that…it's just that I had forgotten about our conversation in London."

"Well, anyway, it's only seven or eight miles past the place where you used to live," Mikey went on. "The house stands on about ten or eleven acres. It was much larger estate when I was a boy, even during the time you were living in Ballycrag…Fernmount it's called."

"Fernmount!"

He looked puzzled at my evident surprise, only it wasn't surprise it was shock: "Don't tell me you know about the place already."

"No. No." Much as I regarded Mikey, and despite our growing friendship, there were some things I was not ready to tell him and perhaps never would. "I probably heard the name when I was here as a child."

"Oh…well if you want, you can see the place before you go back to London. I know the lawyer, Niamh Trenton, who's handling the affairs of the owner…met her when I was here on holiday about five or six years ago. There was some kind of get-together for lawyers in the hotel Laura and me were staying in. We just got talking to Niamh and struck up a friendship. Call to see her anytime I'm back."

"I'm not sure if I'll have enough time. There are one or two things I want to do before I leave on Tuesday morning."

"It's up to you, but if you do want to take a look you can talk to

Niamh this evening…we're having dinner at her place tonight and you're invited."

As I began the drive to Fernmount the next morning I could think of little else except Niamh Trenton and the night before. From the moment she had turned to greet me, after she had hugged Mikey and Laura affectionately, she had transformed my visit to Ireland from one of disappointment to one of renewed hope and expectation.

I had been instantly reminded of Renoir's portrait of the young Julie Manet in the Marmottan in Paris, but unlike that portrait, there was no hint of sadness in Niamh: there was only a sense of unrestrained pleasure and joy with the world. The warmth of her welcome was reflected in her hazel eyes and in the oval of her face under her golden-brown hair. It was like an invisible veil that hovered over her lips and mouth. The hand she extended clasped mine just long enough to give me the feeling that I already belonged in some small way in the brightness that was hers.

"Michael has already told me quite a lot about you, all interesting, all favourable."

I laughed, easily and comfortably. I laughed again and again during the evening and felt more alive than I had done in years.

Mikey's wife, Laura, whom I had met for the first time outside the gate to Niamh's home, was not at all what I had expected. She was a little taller than him, and had a calm, settled air about her. *Quiet* is how I would have described her in a word, but she was neither dull nor lacking in a sense of humour. Perhaps she needed to have that kind of personality in order to have a successful relationship with Mikey.

"Have you decided yet when Fernmount is coming on the market?" Mikey asked Niamh, as the evening drew to a close.

"Not yet…but why are you asking? You had no interest in it a week ago when I mentioned it to you."

"I still don't…but maybe Seánie does."

She turned to me: "Are you thinking of moving over here?"

"Well…yes…I could be…" At intervals during dinner I had

allowed my thoughts to wander into the realm of possibility of meeting with Niamh again; of building up a relationship with her; of ending the long period of living alone with past rememberings that were of no comfort to me; of ceasing to exist in a present that was often arid and joyless. Showing interest in Fernmount, and going through the motions of furthering that interest was simply a way to keep in contact with her: "Mikey said that you could arrange for me to see the property before I go back to London."

"I can do that. I should tell you, 'though, that it needs a lot of renovation…a lot of money will have to be spent on it…but it would be a beautiful property when it's finished. It stands on eleven acres."

"You should take a look…" Mikey said "…get some idea of what the market is like."

"Yes." I turned to Niamh: "Is it possible to see it in the morning as Mikey suggested?"

"I don't see why not…but I can't give you any specific details regarding price or anything like that…not yet anyway…in a week or two, maybe. An estate agent has still to be appointed…and there is no certainty that the old lady who owns it will agree to sell it, 'though I don't see that she has any other option."

"The old lady?" I tried to sound only mildly curious.

"She's in a nursing home in Dublin. From what I gather, it doesn't seem likely that she'll be returning to the house again. She's quite frail. Physically she's not in good shape, but mentally she's as bright as a button."

She volunteered no name and I did not inquire. Instead I asked: "Does she not have family to look after her or take her in?"

"None that I know of…her husband died a long time ago. They had a son. He was killed during the Second World War. Her family has been clients of ours for generations. We're the nearest she has to family. For the last ten years she won't deal with anyone except me" While I was digesting this information she continued: "I can't be at Fernmount in the morning but I will arrange for the caretaker to be there to meet you. I'll try phoning him now…what would be a good time for you?"

I waited with Mikey at the gate of Niamh's house to say my goodbyes to him and his wife. They were leaving on an early flight the following morning. While we waited for Laura and Niamh to finish the conversation they were having in the doorway, Mikey lowered his voice: "She's unattached, you know"

"Niamh?"

"Who else?" he grinned and then, seriously: "She's one lovely lady."

"Yes…she is."

"Her husband was an architect…died just a year or so into their marriage…they had no kids."

"Oh!"

"She's not without suitors and admirers…" he grinned again "…I guess the right guy hasn't come along…not yet anyway."

"She's…ah…somewhat younger than me."

"So…is that a problem?"

"No…no…I…I was just making an observation."

"Sure…" he nodded his head slowly in mock-seriousness, and then, as Laura and Niamh joined us "…we're coming back around the end of September…we'll expect to meet you here. If not, I'm coming over to London to get you."

I laughed: "It looks like I'll have to make it my business to be here then."

After Mikey and Laura had left, I turned to Niamh:

"I was wondering…would you'd like to have dinner with me…tomorrow night…before I go back to London?"

She inclined her head: "Tomorrow night?"

"Yes."

"Well…I…"

"It will be my last night here…I have to fly back on Tuesday." I was pressing her to meet with me. It was a long, long time since I had done that to any woman.

Niamh smiled: "Dinner would be very nice."

Driving back to my hotel, tree and bush and fern seemed to fuse together in a misty aura as the headlights pierced the thickening drizzle. A *soft* night, I thought. A *grand* night. The old memories came back then – the memories that only ever seemed to return whenever I dared to entertain the hope of finding a measure of happiness again in my life.

This time it was different: I did not have to fight them. I felt strong enough to remember - to remember without having to endure the usual sinking, desolate feeling and the sense of hopelessness.

4

Anthea and I were married almost a year to the day I met her. It was an extravagant occasion, for which her father was almost wholly responsible. Not only did he provide a lavish celebration, he also saw to it that we had a fashionable house in London to return to after our honeymoon in the Caribbean.

The year leading up to the wedding was an exceptional year for me on all fronts. I had opened a gallery in London, following the successful and extremely profitable sale not only of the Boudin painting, but also of the other paintings I had bought at the sale in Scotland, each one proving to be better than the other. Somebody had collected the paintings with a most discerning eye, most likely on a *Grand Tour* in the eighteenth century.

I had moved my gallery to London, much less for business reasons than for the closeness it brought to the physical presence of Anthea. Any time spent apart from her was unbearable and I believed that her entry into my life had been responsible for the success I began quickly to build on. She was my lover, my lucky charm and my introduction to a whirlwind of social life I had not experienced before. She belonged to a wide circle of what seemed to me to be the offspring of very wealthy and indulgent families. I had not a moment to relax, to think, or to be in any way concerned about where I was going, or whether or not marriage was the right thing.

Anthea introduced new clients to my gallery, some of whom were acquainted with her family and others who were part of the affluent circle to which she belonged. The boutique that she ran in partnership with her long-time friend, Jennifer Elengorn, was not only *trendy* but exclusive. Many of the husbands or boyfriends of the women, who shopped there, were also brought to the gallery. Sales and requests for works by specific painters rose dizzily. I began to get the feeling that I was destined for unparalleled business success and that I had well and truly come of age in all aspects of my life.

The only dents in an otherwise perfect existence were my mother's reaction when I told her that we were to be married; and the encroachment of Anthea's business partner on our lives.

While I had been made to feel most welcome by Anthea's parents, especially by her father, my mother was quite reserved with Anthea from the beginning; a reserve that only slightly lessened as time went on. On the day, some five or six months into our relationship, that I told her of our intended marriage I was quite disappointed by her reaction.

"But you hardly know her?"

"It feels like I've known her forever."

"Yes…but don't you think you should take more time to get to know her better? Marriage is a very serious step."

"I know that."

"It's not something to be rushed into. You have to take time to get to know each other…how you feel about things that are important."

"We have talked about the things that are important to both of us and we are in agreement on so many issues that it hardly seems possible."

"That may be so now, when things are going well…it's when things go wrong or difficulties emerge in the future that differences show and…"

"If you're worried about us having a child and how it will be brought up there's no need. Anthea's going to take instruction in the Catholic religion and…"

"I'm not talking about religion…not that it's not important…it's just that I think you should take more time to really get to know her before you rush into marriage."

"Anthea's a good person. I know we'll be able to work things out together…I'm sure of that…I thought you liked her?"

"I have nothing against her…and it's not a question of me liking her or not it's…"

"I thought you'd be happy for me"

"I am glad to see you happy.

While Anthea displayed an unerring flair for beautiful garments, Jennifer Elengorn it was who ran and controlled the financial side of things. When Anthea went abroad on buying expeditions, it became clear from the outset that it was Jennifer who would travel with her and not me. From the first time that Anthea had introduced me to her I had not felt any kind of approval coming from Jennifer. In fact, I had felt only the opposite and, as time elapsed, even after our marriage, I detected an ever-present iciness in Jennifer's attitude towards me. Any time I had reason, or no reason at all to call into the boutique to see Anthea, I was made to feel quite unwelcome by Jennifer.

On the first few occasions I broached the subject, Anthea laughed away my complaints: "That's just Jennifer being Jennifer." Later on she fobbed me off with: "Jennifer believes only in business. She has no time for any kind of interruptions." When I was really annoyed, she circled my waist with her arms and pressed the side of her face into my chest, the scent of her and the taste of her hair in my mouth, melting whatever annoyance I might have felt, as she told me: "Anything or anybody that's a distraction upsets her, so you can't blame her for seeing *you* as a prime distraction."

When we were settled in, in our new home, our quiet and languid evenings were frequently disturbed by phone calls from Jennifer, often quite long, which Anthea sometimes ended in anger or near to tears. Anytime I suggested to her that perhaps an end to the partnership was what was needed, she would grow quiet and mutter something to the effect that she had tried, but that always it had resumed again. I could not understand her. She was capable and would have had my backing or unquestionably that of her father's, to open her own business, but whenever I made this suggestion she would become glum or even strained for a while.

On one occasion she turned her gloomy mood quickly around by fixing me with a wicked smile and proposing that my concerns or bother would evaporate if I would consider taking both herself and Jennifer to bed.

"She's quite attractive you know and really a wild seductress underneath that icy exterior, as you call it."

After I had protested my aversion to such a suggestion she seduced me in such a way that I was left too sated and too replete to have even the slightest inclination to be bothered by Jennifer or anything else.

One Friday afternoon, with the prospect of a satisfying weekend with Anthea looming, I had a call from my client who had bought the Boudin. I hadn't heard from him for over six months. He lived in a manor in Worcestershire.

"Could you come to the house this evening…stay the weekend?"

"Well, actually my wife and I had planned to…"

"Please! I have to see you…alone!"

I was concerned now.

"What's wrong?"

"I'll tell you when you get here. You *will* come?"

I told him that I would phone back within the hour.

Anthea was not upset when I called her at the boutique.

"You should go. He's an important client"

"He's talking about my spending the weekend there."

"It's only the weekend."

"I know but…"

"I'll try and live without you," she laughed. "I'll find something to keep me occupied while you are away in the country."

I arrived quite late at my client's home, even though I had not delayed after leaving the gallery, but had made a brief stop at our house to gather a few necessities and throw them into an overnight bag, before setting out on the hundred-odd mile journey to Worcestershire.

He himself answered the door to me. There was, it appeared, nobody else in the house - not his wife, his son, or daughter, and not a single member of his staff was in evidence anywhere, not then or by the time I left.

His hand trembled, as he took mine. I was quite startled at his appearance. His eyes seemed to have shrunk way back into their sockets. He was unshaven, a day or two of hair growth on his face, like dirt against his sickly-white skin. He was wearing a business suit that looked as though he had been sleeping in it, the peak of one end of his shirt collar sticking out over the jacket.

I followed him along the hallway to his study.

"You'll have a drink first."

Without waiting for a reply he shakily poured two whiskeys from a decanter that stood on an occasional table close to the window, while I glanced around the normally immaculate room, with its fine Chippendale desk and equally fine bookcases and other items of furniture. Papers were scattered on the Persian carpet, the remnants of hastily prepared food lying on a butler's tray, a sock totally out of place on the open flap of a secretaire. He handed me the whiskey: "Have a seat." He indicated one of the leather armchairs in front of the fireplace. He remained standing and drank deeply from his own glass. I waited for him to open the conversation, to tell me what it was he needed to discuss with such urgency.

He sat on the edge of the other armchair: "I need cash…and I need it fast."

He told me the reason why. His wife had introduced him to a Portuguese businessman, with whom she had become acquainted at the home of an old school-friend. The Portuguese had been to dinner at my client's home on a number of occasions in the months following. He was personable, talked big, and appeared to have the trappings that suggested wealth and success in business. My client, with reluctance, but with the encouragement of his wife, had invested an amount of money in a business venture with the man and the return had been fast and quite profitable. He had invested again, this time heavily, his wife asserting that she had gone to the trouble of ascertaining that her new-found friend was trustworthy and above board. He had accepted his wife's recommendation and had borrowed a large sum to fund his part in the scheme.

"I won't bore you with the details, nor with a defence of how I could have placed myself in a position to be so completely hoodwinked, but the situation is, the money I invested is somewhere in Brazil in the dirty hands of that bastard of a con-man and so is my wife."

I just looked at him, open-mouthed, while he stood up and took my glass, refilling it and his own.

He laughed, a bitter laugh: "My wife had the help and collusion of her old school-friend who allowed herself to be duped into believing my wife when she spun her a story about living with me in a hell that she was unable to extricate herself from. My children are with the school-friend at the moment. She's looking after them until something can be sorted out. She's trying to salve her conscience in some way. It's a bit late for that." He emptied his glass in a long gulp: "In the meantime, I have a hefty commitment to meet with my bank. Time has run out and so have my so-called friends at the bank and elsewhere. If I don't deposit a great lump of cash in my account within the next few days…" He broke off and for a moment I thought he was going to ask me for money: "Look! Here's the situation. Have you someone…anyone…on your books that would buy the Boudin and some other paintings from my collection, without screwing me altogether…someone that would come up with the cash straight away?"

"Well…"

"I know I should have come to you earlier…" he poured himself another drink "…and I know that I'll have to take less than their value for quick sale and for cash. It will be up to you just how much I can get."

"Have you tried any other galleries? I'm sure…"

"I don't trust anyone else, at this moment. No one except you."

I hesitated. I hated being in the position he had just put me in. It was not only the temptation that his situation offered: it was because I had known him for so long; and, more than that, he had proved himself a fair and discerning client and had played an important role in the building up of my business.

He did not wait for my answer: "I expect you to charge a reasonable commission of course, but you'll have to work fast. That's why I asked you up for the weekend. I want you to go through all the paintings and do a running total of what you would expect them to quickly sell for. I also expected that you would begin making calls to your clients or whoever, tomorrow afternoon or evening…on Sunday even, if necessary."

I tried again: "Is there no other way, or someone else that…?"

"No!" He raised his voice for a moment: "Good God man, if you only knew what…" He stopped abruptly, his voice almost pleading: "Will you do it?"

I did not have to, nor did I want to, stay any longer than the Saturday evening. I knew his collection. I had remembered every picture of note that he had in his house, in the way any good picture dealer would have remembered. Several of them I had sold to him, the prices of which I already knew in my head. Others in his collection I asked him about. A few I told him were not worthwhile offering for sale at that particular time; perhaps later when the vagaries of taste changed to include them. By late afternoon on the Saturday, I had placed sufficient of his paintings to bring some kind of relief to him. Others I would dispose of with difficulty in the ensuing weeks, a difficulty that emerged because of the turn my own life took later on that Saturday night.

I had phoned Anthea earlier in the morning. Jennifer had answered and had been quite civil to me for a change.

"Everything all right?" Anthea asked when the phone had been passed to her.

"So far…I'll tell you about it when I get back."

"Don't rush. Do whatever it is you are doing and don't fret yourself. It is to *work* that you have been invited, I presume?" She was giggling now.

"Actually", I could not join in Anthea's good humour, "I'm doing something I really have no heart for."

"Well, so long as your heart remains in the right place. Whatever you do, enjoy the weekend."

"I'll try."

I did not tell her that I hoped to be home that night. My

intention was to surprise her. I succeeded in my aim, but not in the way I could ever have had expected.

5

On my way to Fernmount, I felt a quickening in my pulse the moment I began the ascent of the hill at Ballycrag. As the car rounded the final bend and crested the hill, I was holding my breath, not knowing what to expect or how I would feel after all the years.

The little narrow, winding road still ran downhill between ash and sycamore and hawthorn that rose high from banks of fern and briar. It still lost itself in the distance among hedgerows heavy with the rich growth of summer, only now it cut through a much smaller canvas than I had remembered; and there were gaps in the landscape - disappointing gaps.

There was nothing where our cottage had stood; nothing but a lumpy patch overgrown with tangled grasses, weeds and brambles. It had been tumbled, and what remained of it had been drawn back into the folds of nature. The piers and gates outside Mikey's old home were gone too, replaced by a cattle grid. The dry-stone wall that once wore the appealing colours of mosses and ivy and straying blackberry bushes, and the trees that formed a canopy over them, had all been removed. A low, painted fence gave an uninterrupted view of the home that was barely recognisable now in its coat of pristine blue and white.

I wondered for a moment what Mikey must have thought when he had seen it; wondered if he too had felt the same disappointment. I drove on then, the rain that had been sporadically mingling with the light of the sun on the windscreen, ceasing altogether as I approached the river.

My memory of it, on the one occasion I had gone to it with the Sullivans, was of a great, gaping cavern with soft, grey walls and a dull flowing centre, carving its way through banks of green, fringed with tall, thatch-coloured reeds. Now, with the tide at the full, it was a wide ribbon of sparkling life, merging with the land. Beyond the far bank, cattle and sheep were grazing against a backdrop of distant hills that I had not remembered seeing with my child's eyes.

I stopped the car for a while and thought about the Sullivan brothers and of my time with them - a time that now seemed to have belonged to a different world in a different universe, where the innocence of childhood had been allowed to run its course; and I thought of the schoolmaster whose life had been shattered in part by the finding of a sock that had been left in haste on the riverbank.

Away from Ballycrag, the road wound its way through little stone-walled fields, spattered with ancient, crinkled rocks until it climbed upwards towards the sun and brought me to the top of a hill and a view of a more fertile landscape. It was from here that I saw Fernmount for the first time.

And it was from here too that I saw, through a break in the trees surrounding the house, the mirror-gleam of the lake.

The heavy wrought-iron gates at the entrance to the winding, leafy avenue were open wide in expectation of my arrival. Emerging from the car into the sunlight I stood in front of the house and had an immediate eerie sense that I was there to fulfill a destiny that had been pre-determined a long time ago. The creaking of the heavy front door interrupted the sensation as the caretaker came out of the shadow of the hallway and stood at the top of the steps. With eyes half-closed, he silently took my measure before he spoke: "A fine day!"

"Yes, it is."

I began walking up the steps: "I've come to look at the house."

The house that had seemed the embodiment of dreams to my mother, when she had first entered there, was tired and neglected. Curtains and chair coverings were worn and faded with just a few good pieces of furniture still remaining, the rest obviously removed or sold and replaced with pieces that lent nothing to either the rooms they occupied or the spaces they filled. Incongruous shades replaced chandeliers and, in the hallway, a naked bulb hung in place of a lantern. A large, modern, Italian plaster-framed mirror, over the white marble fireplace in the drawing room – the fireplace that Edward Ashby, glass in hand, had leaned back against on the night when my mother's searching eyes had locked with his - spoke of defeat and of surrender to necessity. Remnants of books lay discarded in the library, the architect's cabinet that I remembered from my mother's journal, still standing there, the drawers empty.

The dining-room that had been resplendent with the gleam of candlelit silverware and porcelain for the homecoming dinner for Derek Ashby was dull and uninviting; with just a large Victorian mahogany sideboard and a dumb-waiter the only items that blended in, in some measure, with the faded reds of the Turkey carpet that covered the floor. The disproportionately small, modern dining-table looked lost in the centre of the room; and odd chairs filled spaces where a serving table or a wine cooler might have stood. The walls were bare. And bare too were the walls around the curve of the thread–bare staircase and along the dimly-lit landing of the first floor.

I stopped short outside the door of the first of the bedrooms - this, or any of the other bedrooms I would enter, could be the room in which my mother had been violated or where, in the early hours of the morning, she had been viciously torn from her sleep and humiliated. For a moment it seemed that just by being there that I was in some way betraying her, maybe even betraying myself. I could leave now, I thought, call Niamh Trenton and tell her I was not interested in this house - this *mausoleum*. But then, to do so would be a refusal to face what was, in reality, part of the history of my beginning. I would not run. I would stay and carry on, walk amidst the ghosts of the past, face them and, perhaps, lay them to rest. I would look upon the house for what it was: a run-down abode that might be brought to life again.

Only one of the bedrooms was furnished in its entirety and looked as it might have done fifty years ago, but even that too, like the other rooms, looked abandoned, the lifeless air of absence almost tangible. Another bedroom, containing an unmade single bed and a man's clothes scattered here and there, had the odour of recent habitation – the caretaker's most likely. In other bedrooms, a wardrobe, or dressing table or spring and mattress, or just bed ends and irons were the only testament that these rooms had once been used to provide rest for tired minds and bodies.

On the top floor, small items of blue and white-painted pine – a chest of drawers, a lop-sided crutch mirror, a washstand – gave colour and a sense of warmth to the place. The thought crossed my mind that the servants' quarters exuded some sense of the vitality of the lives that had occupied them, while the rooms of their masters indicated lives that had simply stagnated.

"There's a stairs behind that door over there that leads into the attic…if you want to look up there."

The caretaker's voice startled me. He had made no sound coming up behind me. He had left me to look around on my own and had then disappeared. I followed his lean, weathered body up the stairs to another, narrower door.

"Here…you'll need this…" he handed me a torch, "…I'll be down in the kitchen when you're finished. Be careful…there's a hole or two in the floor."

The air in the attic rooms was dry and dust-laden, the floors littered with countless dead flies. I walked carefully, where loose and missing boards held the threat of a twisted ankle, or of a foot disappearing through the floor into a room below.

Only one room held my attention. Beside a wooden, lidded chest I recognised the shape of a large picture frame under the covering that lay over it. I carefully lifted away part of the covering, revealing a gilt frame, the gesso already crumbled at the corners. Removing the covering completely I stood back, shining the torch directly onto the canvas, wondering why the portrait of the young Edwardian woman in a long flowing dress and wide–brimmed straw hat seemed vaguely familiar, and then, I knew: my mother had written of it in her journal. She had described how Edward Ashby had spoken to her for the first time as she gazed at the painting when it hung in the hallway downstairs.

I replaced the covering on the painting and went hurriedly down the stairs, the slap of my shoes against the tiles in the hallway, alerting the caretaker.

He came out of a doorway opposite the dining-room: "The kitchen's down this way."

"I'll take a walk outside first, if you don't mind?" I handed him back the torch.

"Whatever you want."

"How do I get to the lake from here?"

"Just go through the arch into the yard. Opposite the stables there's a side gate into the garden…walk through the garden…there's an opening in the wall…the gate is gone. After you cross the field there's a path through the trees…it's a bit overgrown." He turned away.

"Just one other thing…" I waited until he was facing me again "…who owns this house?"

He paused before answering, his half-closed eyes seeming to close even further: "Mrs Ashby."

"That would be Sarah Ashby?" I had to be absolutely sure.

"Yes."

Over the lake, a patchwork of clouds moved slowly across a blue sky. At the shore, water rippled gently, and somewhere hidden from view, a mallard called out a warning. Further along, a fringe of corn-coloured reeds swayed against silver birches, and water hens gathered around the blackened carcass of an almost submerged tree. Across the lake, the gorse-yellowed, sloping hills were rich-green and lazy, with sheep grazing, and here and there a cottage rested cosily in a defile.

It was beautiful; beautiful and tranquil; and I had an immediate sense of having arrived at a place that I had unconsciously yearned for.

The uplift of the moment was tempered by the thought that, just a short walk from here, with bird song and bird call, wind whisper and water rustle the only sounds breaking the quiet, that my journey into life had begun in circumstances that were so unworthy of this golden place.

I turned away, only to turn back again at the call of a male mallard, the *weeb, weeb, weeb* clear and distinct in the stillness. The silken–green head appeared just below me, the orange webbed feet, treading water beneath the gliding body, visible in the light that pierced the shallows at the lake's edge. It raised its head and regarded me with an imperious eye, the white collar over the purplish breast, like that of some exalted cleric.

The breeze picked up suddenly and rushed in among the treetops, a muted ocean-sound interspersed with the quickening calls of birds. In the wake of the strengthening breeze, the clouds thickened over the lake and darkened in colour, signalling imminent rain.

On my way back to the house I thought on the circumstances that had brought me to Fernmount: a chance meeting in London with Mikey Sullivan; an invitation to a school celebration; an emotional response to a woman I had only met for the first time the night before. It was as if I had been steered to a road of many twists and bends that I was obliged to follow, to a destination I had no knowledge of. Had I now walked around the last bend on that road and was Fernmount the destination?

I had a cursory look at the kitchen area downstairs before I left and as I drove down the winding avenue I felt a desire forming in my consciousness; a desire that prompted a short-lived surge of elation; a desire to return here and build a foundation on which the remainder of my life would rest.

I followed a different route on the journey back to my hotel, the road passing by the little barn church that had featured so prominently in our lives while we lived at Ballycrag. I drove past, stopping the car about a mile further on before returning to it.

The little church was empty, a taped version of Gounod's Ave Maria played on a violin, filling the silence, inviting reverence. The interior had not been changed except for the removal of the altar rails, the heavy brass altar gates, and the threatening, cavernous confession box. It was a humble place and I liked it straight away. It did not have stained glass windows but low sills that looked out on the trees enfolding it. The altar and the tabernacle surround were of carved, painted wood, plain and simple. Simple too were the wooden beams supporting the roof and the wood panelling of the walls. High above the altar a painted scroll bore the legend: *Come to me all you who labour and are overburdened and I will give you rest.*

The practise of my faith had wavered during my late teens, had all but ceased during my time at Cambridge and had come to an abrupt end following my parting with Anthea. Since that time I had struggled to regain it and had entered churches much less to pray than to view paintings that were important, not just to the history of art, but were, in the hands of the Masters, the incarnation of the struggle of the human spirit to find a spiritual home.

Over dinner in my hotel, later that evening, I told Niamh Trenton that I could be interested in Fernmount.

"Good…I'll call you or e-mail you as soon as Mrs Ashby agrees to the sale of the property and an estate agent has been appointed. It may take some time before she comes to a decision."

"That will be fine." I was glad to have an excuse to stay in touch with her. Meeting with her was a perfect antidote to the tensions of the day. Everything about her - her laughter, her voice, the way she inclined her head when I was being mock-serious, the expressive movement of her hands, her eyes, her hair - were a continuous source of pleasure. The hours in her company seemed all too brief.

She kissed me, a light kiss on the cheek, in the doorway of her home after she had thanked me for "a lovely evening."

I lowered the window and waved as I drove slowly away. Standing in the open doorway, she waved back and smiled. I carried the memory of her smile until I fell asleep and carried it again with me on the flight home the following morning.

6

When I had set out on my journey to Ireland to attend the school celebrations I could not have conceived of the new set of emotions I would return with to London just a few days later. I was preoccupied in equal measure with the feelings my meeting with Niamh had stirred and with the sentiments that my visit to Fernmount had evoked. From the moment I had met Niamh I had not felt the rush of desire and need that had led me into short-lived relationships in the years following the end of my marriage – it was simply a comfortable and exhilarating feeling of finding someone that had made me feel whole again. And yet I was fearful: fearful and uncertain for the future of a relationship that did not even exist except in hopeful expectation. Was the experience of the past forever skulking in the shadows, waiting to blight the promise of the future? And what if Niamh entertained no such thoughts?

I was disturbed too; disturbed by the thought that I had been in the house where my father had been; that I had, perhaps, walked in his footsteps from room to room and out through the garden to the lake, breathing the same air, hearing the same sounds. Had he even known that I had been born, I wondered, or had he walked away without a single thought for our welfare, our future?

And what of my mother? Was even my entertaining of the thought of buying Fernmount an affront to her; a selfish disregard for her feelings? I would have to tell her; tell her at least something, if not all, of what had unfolded while I was in Ireland.

I phoned her before leaving my apartment in Canary Wharf to ensure that she would be home and not out walking as was her wont, especially during summer afternoons. For once I drove, uncomplaining, through the afternoon city traffic, unconsciously comparing the turbulence that was London to the tranquillity that was the West of Ireland, my thoughts drifting back to the beginning of our lives in the city.

We had lived in a bed-sit in Fulham for a short time before coming to lodge with a Mrs Ryan, a widow, in Highgate. She had some business interests and my mother had worked as a kind of secretary to her which had given her flexible hours and enabled her to be at home while I attended primary school. When she began taking evening classes, Mrs Ryan took care of me. A year or so, after she had finished her studies, she went to work for the bank with which she would have a long and successful career.

Whenever she had had an evening out it was Mrs Ryan who again looked after me and I remember those occasions as being the result of days or even of weeks of Mrs Ryan's pressing of my mother to accept some invitation or other: "You should go, Annie. You don't go out enough."

Quite often, a rueful smile was the only reply and Mrs Ryan would emit a deep sigh.

There were the times when the phone rang in the evenings and Mrs Ryan answered and either called out: "Annie, for you," or laid down the receiver and came to where my mother was, speaking so low that I could not hear. More often than not my mother would shake her head and Mrs Ryan would sigh again.

On some evenings when the doorbell shrilled, consternation would result and was only resolved when my mother either ran upstairs or eventually opened the hall door. Whenever I escaped the clutches of Mrs Ryan or boldly satisfied my curiosity, which I was forbidden to do, it was nearly always a man who stood on the doorstep.

By the time I had started secondary school my mother had rented a house in Muswell Hill where we lived until she married my stepfather.

Our move to Muswell Hill brought us closer to Highgate Wood, where I had spent happy hours playing and watching the grey squirrels among the oaks and the hornbeams, after school and at weekends. Within easy reach were Parliament Hill Fields, the open areas of parklands in the South East corner of Hampstead Heath, and the Heath itself. As I grew older, these were vast and rambling alternatives to the loss of the Irish countryside I had longed for during my early years in London, a longing that was now rising and receding and rising again.

I stopped the car at Parliament Hills Fields and made my way to the top of Parliament Hill. I sat for a while on the same time-worn seat that I had sat on in my late teens and at various times as I grew older, most often when life was either confusing or weighed heavily on me. From there, the highest point in London, I could look down over the sprawling mass of the city that was noiseless and still and, for a while, feel detached from people and from the busy-ness and complications and uncertainties of living.

My mother's Edwardian home, set on the edge of Hampstead Heath, was only a short drive away.

"So, did you have a good trip to Dublin?"

We were in her drawing-groom, my mother seated on the Art Nouveau settee she had always said was uncomfortable but since it matched the period of the house she had kept it. I stood, leaning against a cabinet.

"I wasn't in Dublin…I was in the West of Ireland."

"Oh?"

"I went to the centenary celebrations of Lisbeg National School…with Mikey Sullivan."

"You were with Mikey?"

I had told her about Mikey a few days after I had met him in Sotheby's. She had been saddened at the news of the deaths of Joe and Mollie. It was some time later on that she had said: "At least, I know now why I failed to get in touch with Mollie.

"Mikey arranged the invitation to the school," I said now. "That's how I knew about it."

"You never told me you were going?"

"No…I…"

"Was the school anything like you remembered?"

I told her about the changes that been made, about the event itself and then I said: "I was invited to dinner by a friend of Mikey and Laura…from the town."

"From the town?"

"Well…she lives there. Her name's Trenton…Niamh Trenton."

"Trenton? I don't remember any Trentons in the town."

"She's a solicitor…conveyance mainly. In fact, Mikey brought up the subject of a house that could be for sale in the area…he thought I might be interested in it…so…"

"Are you thinking of moving to Ireland?"

"I just happened to mention it to Mikey last year…a sort of throwaway remark, but Mikey took it seriously. I said I'd have a look at it before I came home."

"And did you?"

"Yes…well…the thing is…it's Fernmount House."

She just sat there.

"I had said I'd go to see it…before I really understood where I was going. I didn't…"

I stopped speaking as she got up and walked to a side table and began re-arranging framed photographs, her back to me. I waited, not knowing what to say. After a long pause, she spoke very quietly: "Who lives in Fernmount, now?"

"Nobody…there's just a caretaker. Well…Sarah Ashby was living alone there until she had to go to a nursing home in Dublin. They don't think she'll ever come back. Niamh Trenton is her solicitor. She believes the house will have to be sold. Sarah Ashby has no family. All she…"

My voice trailed off. I was about to break the awkward silence that followed when she said: "Did you read any of the journals…the diaries and things I gave you?"

"Yes…well…I took a few with me to Ireland"

"Did you read any of those that centred around the…the time that I first left Ballycrag?"

"Yes."

"So you know…you know what happened…why I left?"

"Yes."

After another pause she turned to face me: "I was very young then...very immature when I wrote them...it was the only way I knew how to try and cope with what was happening in my life at that time. Maybe there are things I left out...I don't know." She looked away: "I couldn't bring myself to read them over the years. Perhaps it wasn't the thing to do, to give them to you. If you hadn't taken them that day, I don't think that I would ever have given them to you...I probably would have destroyed them. I didn't even know if you would ever read them." She turned her eyes to me again, her voice softening: "When I look back, it's like looking at someone else...someone entirely different. I was so...so naive...so trusting. The day I left Ballycrag I think that I still believed that your father would come looking for us...take us both off somewhere. Where, I had no idea, only that it would be someplace where we could all be together."

I did not want to ask, but the words just tumbled out: "Have you always known, then, who my father was?"

She shook her head: "For a time I believed I knew. It was just a...a kind of wishful thinking. I was seventeen years old. I had no idea of the world...before I had the chance to grow up a little my life was turned upside down."

She walked back to the settee and sat down again: "I wished so often over the years that I could have told you about your father. There were times when I even thought about making up some kind of story...to give you something worthwhile to hang on to...something to help you as you grew older...to help you through the difficult times."

Remorse seeped through me then for my ingratitude for all the years she had given up to attend to my needs and demands during my teens and the years after, when deep down, I blamed her for my not having a father. I thought of the summers, when I had stayed with her and my stepfather while I was at Cambridge, and of my coming home drunk, or staying out all night, while she lay sleepless; of my churlishness and stubbornness; of my disappearing abroad after I had graduated, when she had no idea where I had gone; and of the time, when I had contacted her, penniless, with no idea of where I was going or what I wanted to do. She had sent my stepfather to bring me home and had defended me then, and during the days of disappointment and frustration, until I finally made an effort to get my life in order.

I wanted to tell her now of my regret, of the guilt I felt, but I could not find the words: "Everybody experiences difficulties in their lives," I said, lamely.

"Maybe so…but for you…from the very beginning it was always going to be that much harder…your marriage…that was a very difficult time. When Anthea came on the scene I was fearful that you were being carried away just as I had been all those years ago. I wanted to try and explain it to you…but you were much older and much more attuned to the world than I had been…and yet…the similarity to the way you were being drawn into a different life made me afraid. I wanted to warn you to try and look beyond the trappings and the outward show…to prevent you from making a mistake."

"There was nothing you could have done. I…I had to find out for myself. And my life is good now."

"Anyway", she gave a little sigh, "it's just that you're being in Fernmount brings back memories…"she smiled, ruefully"…the house seemed immense back then…and very beautiful."

I relaxed a little: "It is a big house…a fine house really…it's just that it has been neglected. It needs a lot of work…it could still be made to look beautiful, 'though…and the lake is wonderful."

"And…do you think you could be interested in buying it?"

"I don't know. I don't even know if it is going to be sold or not.

"Well, if it comes up for sale…?"

"I'll probably have another look at it…and I'd like to meet Niamh Trenton again."

She began to rise: "I think I would like a cup of tea."

7

My interest in business had waned in recent times but now, as I waited in hope for Niamh to call, I seemed to have found a new energy and an increased appetite for work. In moments of quiet, I sometimes wondered whether or not I was deluding myself with regard to Fernmount House and simply embarking on a charade in order to further my chances of developing a relationship with Niamh. I dismissed the thought and busied myself even more. When she did call, ten days later, I could barely conceal the pleasure that the sound of her voice gave me.

She came directly to the point: "I had to be very gentle with Mrs Ashby, and not appear to be pressing her. It must be a very difficult decision for her to make, giving up her home and the memories it must hold for her over a lifetime."

"Yes," I said.

"Anyway, I left her to consider the options and told her that I would visit her again in a week or so."

"That's fine."

"I'll be in touch as soon as I have any further news."

After she had hung up I felt disappointed at not having prolonged the call; of not having attempted to engage her in light conversation and maybe developed some measure of empathy between us. I almost called her straight back with some trumped-up excuse but I could not think of anything convincing enough to explain my reason for doing so.

Doubt and uncertainty set in then and was only quelled when I thought of the possibility of seeing her again.

I was aware of the boom in Ireland and the staggering prices that were being paid for residential properties there, but this was London and I had become familiar with what seemed to others as excessive values being placed on houses. I had the advantage of the currency differential and had had a particularly successful decade behind me, enhanced by the acquisition of a number of Chinese and Russian clients, with resources that appeared to be unlimited; and by the generosity of my late stepfather. The financial aspect was not a consideration; it was more a need for a sense of fulfilment in my life. I had everything and I had nothing. I was going forward, comfortably armed materially, but emotionally I was impoverished. I was not designed or created for single life or for the prospect of living out my days surrounded by luxurious trappings with no intimate to share with. I was incomplete. My life was empty.

Niamh's call came after two weeks.

"Mrs Ashby has agreed to sell Fernmount."

"Oh!"

"It's being advertised in the local and national papers."

"It will be sold by public auction then?"

"No…by private treaty. I can have the estate agents fax the details to you…that is, if you're still interested?"

"Yes…yes I am!"

I was telling the truth. Only a night or two before, I had wrestled yet again with the situation, questioning my motives, my goal, for whatever future I had left and had finally accepted, Niamh apart, that I had found a place that I had unconsciously yearned for.

"I'll have the details sent to you then."

"That would be fine…but what I would really like to do is to take another look at the house first and then call on the estate agents…if that's all right?"

"Of course…when do you think you will come over?"

I caught a late flight to Shannon the following evening. Niamh was waiting for me in the arrivals lounge. My nervousness eased when her eyes lit up the moment she caught sight of me and she waved.

"Welcome back," she said as I reached her.

"It's good to *be* back," I said.

On the way to the hotel our conversation ranged from Mikey and Laura, to Fernmount, to London, to the vagaries of our respective professions, and back again. The content of what was spoken counted for little: all that seemed to matter was the act of sharing words with each other.

Somewhere on the road Niamh broke off in mid-sentence and reached forward to turn up the volume on the car radio: "I love this tune" and began to hum along at first, and then, to sing the words of a song I was not familiar with.

Her spontaneity warmed me. I had lived for years among people who had lost the ability to openly express honest emotion with freedom. It was just another part of her that I found so attractive.

A moment or two later she laughed, turning down the volume: "That song always gets to me…it's such a happy little tune."

The journey to the hotel lasted an hour or so, maybe more, but it only felt like minutes. After I had checked in I invited Niamh to join me in a late snack or coffee or a glass of wine but she declined: "Thank you, but I have to get on home…I have some work to finish for the morning." My disappointment lifted when she added: "What I was thinking was, that I could meet you here tomorrow morning, say around ten thirty, and take you out to Fernmount…that is, if you haven't any other plans."

"That would be great. But won't it interfere with your work…disrupt your day?"

"No…not all. As a matter of fact I have arranged only the one appointment for the morning. I have the rest of the day free for a change."

Niamh had been to Fernmount on a number of occasions and was quite familiar with it. She pottered about the grounds, leaving me to view the house on my own. Her presence nearby, and her involvement in the sale, helped to hasten my viewing of it: my concentration was neither slowed by thoughts of the past, nor by any considerations as to the calibre of those I would be dealing with. I was simply able to look at the place again and confirm to myself that what I hoped to do was right.

"Are you hungry?" Niamh asked as the car moved slowly along the drive away from the house.

"Not particularly…I had a very full breakfast at the hotel."

"Do you want to go and talk with the estate agents now…or would you like to see something of the countryside?"

"I can leave the estate agents until tomorrow. My flight doesn't leave until late in the evening."

"Good! We have time to drive to the coast then. We could have lunch there…if you can last that long?"

"I'm sure I can."

For the first hour or so, we travelled through countryside that matched my childhood memory of what an Irish countryside should look like, and then it began to change. Fields bordered by hedgerows, and low, verdant hills, gave way to more open craggy terrain, criss-crossed by walls that had been built, stone upon laboured stone. Hazel groves appeared and little by little, swelled into dense woods that enveloped the landscape either side of the narrow road until it seemed that we were being intimately embraced in Nature's waywardness.

A few miles on and the hazel woods petered out into a vista of pavement after pavement, and tier upon tier, of boulder-strewn limestone, shimmering silver-white in the sunlight. *A desert of stone* I thought, and even after Niamh had told me of the rare species of plants that grew amidst the fissures of this region that had formed beneath a tropical sea millions of years ago, I could not imagine it other than in its sculptured nakedness that was as beautiful as it was arid and intimidating.

The sea became visible; a shard of frosted glass, wedged between two sloping mountains of towering rock.

"Galway Bay", Niamh said. "You can see right across to the Connemara coastline."

We had lunch at a pub-restaurant, sitting outside in the sun at an

Atlantic-weathered wooden table that looked out on a harbour with a scattering of fishing boats and with gulls that glided effortlessly over the sea, or perched on seaweed-covered rocks that seemed to rise and fall with the movement of the incoming tide.

When it was served, the seafood platter for two that we had ordered was a glistening array of lobster, prawns, crab claws and mussels, interspersed with sliced lemons and green herbs, resting on a bed of crushed ice.

"Look at that! An artist's palette to tempt any palate."

"They knew you were coming," Niamh laughed, lifting her wine glass, "here's to Neptune's bounty."

"I'll drink to that," I said, the moment a surreal glimpse of undreamt-of happiness.

8

"There are times when Sarah Ashby treats me more like a daughter than her solicitor," Niamh said, after two women had just left the table next to us and the younger of the two had turned back: "Mum, you've left your handbag behind."

"Oh, yes?"

"Yes…she gets impatient to be done with any business matters and then settles in for a chat…and the things she tells me."

"All strictly confidential, I suppose…client privilege and all that?"

"No," Niamh laughed. "It's just conversation…and a need to unburden herself at the end of her days, I think. Each time I've been to see her recently she keeps telling me about her early life. She told me…but you don't want to hear about…"

"Yes, I do."

"She's told me a lot about herself and her family…I don't know whether I should really be repeating it or not."

"Other people's lives are always more interesting to hear about…especially when they deflect attention away from ourselves."

"I don't think Sarah sees it that way. It seems as if the story of her life has been going round and round in her head and that she's been waiting for the right time or the right person…"

"Until you came along?"

"I'm probably the only one who has taken the time to listen to her." Niamh was pensive for a moment or two: "She went right back to her teens, to when her father died and left her and her mother penniless…and their estate, Castlemore, on the brink of bankruptcy."

"Not a good start…for her."

"No…her father had gambled everything away apparently. Her mother had to sell off most of their lands and to dispense with servants and labourers…and it still wasn't enough to secure them. It was cousins of her mother's, the Ashby's, who bailed them out…on condition that Sarah would marry their son, Edward."

"She was forced to agree?"

"She wasn't consulted…but she actually adored Edward from the moment she set eyes on him at her father's funeral…and marrying him was what she would have wanted, anyway. What was upsetting for her was when she found out about the arrangement only after their son was born. But what had been even more upsetting for her, before she married Edward at all, was when one of the long-serving maids, who had lost her job at Castlemore, told Sarah that her mother wasn't her natural mother…that Sarah was the daughter of a one-time governess in a neighbouring estate…the result of an affair with Sarah's father."

"And Sarah knew nothing about it?" I queried casually, hiding the impact her revelation had on me. For a moment I empathised with the old lady but then I resented the fact that, at least, Sarah would have had the comfort of knowing her mother's name; of knowing that she was a governess; that Sarah had been born as the result of an affair and not of a shameful violation.

"No…" Niamh's sympathy was tinged with anger "…it was a cruel way for the poor thing to find out about her mother…and coming on the heels of her father's death made it even worse."

I nodded, quelling my rising resentment, thinking that there were even more cruel ways of hiding the truth of someone's parentage.

"The story was that Sarah's mother couldn't have children…she'd had several miscarriages…and when she found out the governess was pregnant she arranged for her to be sent abroad. Shortly after, Sarah's mother let it be known that she, herself, was expecting a baby. Some months later she too went abroad with Sarah's father…on the pretext that her confinement required a more favourable climate. They returned after an appropriate absence with a baby daughter…"

"Sarah?"

Niamh nodded: "And what worried Sarah then was that the truth about her origins would have affected her chances of Edward ever marrying her. She needn't have bothered her head, though…Edward's family would have known the story…it's probably why she was chosen to marry Edward in the first place…someone who they could manipulate if needs be…someone who would be at a social disadvantage."

"What need would they have had to go to such lengths?"

"Because they had an even bigger skeleton in the closet than Sarah's family had at that time."

"Oh?"

"Yes…poor Sarah thought she had what was a *blissful courtship*…her words…" Niamh smiled, a thin smile, "…Edward was *tall, blue-eyed, handsome and very gentle*…her words again…and they had an equally *blissful* honeymoon… she had just turned eighteen. They travelled all over Europe…and what Sarah remembered most was the number of galleries and antiques shops they spent hours in, in Vienna, Florence, Rome and God knows where else, searching for old drawings for Edward's collection. Fernmount was waiting for them when they returned. His family had seen to everything…had even bought him a partnership in a legal practice in the town. There was also a dairy herd on the estate…an experienced herdsman, to see after it."

"She wasn't *too* hard done by," I said, thinking how different my mother's life had been when she was the same age as Sarah Ashby had been at the time of her marriage.

"No…not in that sense…but from the start it began to go wrong for her. The marriage wasn't consummated until well into their honeymoon…when Edward returned very late one night to their chalet in Switzerland…and they were intimate only once or twice after that before they returned to Ireland. From then on it seems the…the intimacy between them grew less and less…and of course, Sarah blamed herself. She thought that she was inadequate in some way…or maybe not pretty enough, even though from the very beginning he told her how beautiful she was…and had continued to do so every…"

"If she was beautiful, I'm sure he meant it," I said, looking directly into her eyes.

"She *was* beautiful…" a faint blush tinted her cheeks "…she showed me a photograph of herself…a close–up taken in Paris on their honeymoon…it was a bit faded but you could still see her beauty. But you should see the clothes! The hat was…"

"A roaring success?"

"What?"

"They were there around the nineteen twenties, weren't they?"

"I suppose so…I don't know…but what has that..?"

"You know…the twenties…the *roaring* twenties…the *bright young things* and all that…the fashions."

"Oh! For goodness sake…are you getting bored with the story?"

"No…I'm not!"

"Well…Edward started going to Dublin on legal business. He'd be away for days at a time on occasion. When they found out she was pregnant he told her that it wouldn't be good for the baby if they were intimate…so he moved into a separate bedroom. A few weeks before her baby was due he came back from Dublin one evening with a friend in tow, a young man…from another law firm…*very handsome, very charming,* Sarah said."

"Are not all solicitors of the same ilk?"

"Oh! Stop! You *are* getting bored."

"No! No…really! It's an interesting story."

"Well anyway…Sarah left them alone after dinner and went upstairs to bed. She lay awake for hours, waiting for him to come to her room to kiss her goodnight…that was the ritual then. Eventually she got up and went to his room. His bed was empty. Further along the landing she saw light coming from the guest room. The door was slightly ajar and she peeked in. Edward was lying on the bed with his friend…they were both naked."

"Oh!"

"It was dreadful for her…I wanted to turn back the clock and find something to clatter her husband with…and the other fellow. Sarah locked herself into her room for two days…only allowed food in for the sake of the baby. She came down to breakfast on the third day. It seems Edward looked like death…began making excuses…talked about being attracted to beauty in any form…*of his desire to possess it…like his drawings,* Sarah said. It was later that morning that Edward had a very bad fall from his horse…"

Niamh broke off: "I must find the ladies' room."

While Niamh was gone, I reflected that, unwittingly, she had given life back to the silent rooms of Fernmount; resurrected ghosts that I had thought to lay to rest. And she had brought back a memory that I would rather not have had at that moment: the memory of the night I had driven back home from Worcestershire having spent the day trying to help my client find a way out of the difficulty he had found himself in.

9

It was after midnight when I drove into London. The physical and mental fatigue I had been feeling began to lift as I drew nearer to our home and the prospect of Anthea's comforting arms.

All the lights in the house were switched on as I turned the car into the driveway. I had expected to see no lights on at all or, at most, one: the light in the upstairs window of our bedroom. I let myself in and closed the hall door quietly.

"Anthea!" I called, not very loudly, not wishing to startle her, "I'm home!"

The expectation I had that she would come running into the hall, to throw her arms around me, did not materialize. I went directly to the kitchen, and then to the living rooms, all the time softly calling Anthea's name. I was not concerned until I noticed items of clothing scattered here and there on the floor and on the couch in the lounge.

I became aware of the sound of music from somewhere above me and went quickly up the staircase, making straight for our bedroom, realizing only then that the music I had been hearing was coming from there. I threw open the bedroom door, a cloying odour reaching my nostrils, a blast from *The Valkyrie* assailing my ears and stood for a moment, devoid of comprehension, taking in the scene before me: standing on our bed, her arms outstretched, a leg either side of the naked body of my wife, was the equally naked figure of Jennifer Elengorn, head thrown back, her breasts thrusting forward, writhing and swaying in the throes of some macabre dance.

"Anthea!" I shouted.

Jennifer froze, and then, jumped to the floor, blocking my way as I rushed forward. I brushed her aside and reached down, grasping Anthea's shoulders, pulling her to me, her slack body like a loose-limbed doll's.

"Anthea!"

"You…came…home." Her eyes were dilated, her speech slurred. "Oh God, Anthea!"

"You should've called…I…"

"Can't leave her alone…" Jennifer's voice was venomous "…not even for a moment."

I turned to her. She was moving towards the door some item of clothing held against her nakedness.

"Have to be in control all the time, don't we?"

I stared blankly at her.

"Of course we do," she hissed.

I let Anthea's body fall back on the bed and stood up: "Get out!"

"Hah!" she sneered, reaching for the doorknob, "his majesty has found his voice. Well, your majesty, it's time you understood…"

"Get out!"

"…you don't *own* her."

I took a step forward: "Get out of my house!"

Jennifer backed through the doorway: "Bastard!" She spat the word and slammed the door shut.

I stood for a moment staring at the closed door before turning back to Anthea. She was breathing heavily now, her eyes closed. The music ceased at that moment and I drew the bedclothes over her. I sat on the edge of the bed then, my body sagging, all energy drained from it.

"I think, maybe, we should get moving," Niamh said, as she sat back at our table: "There's a lot more I want to show you…I shouldn't…" she added, reaching for a stray prawn on the edge of the platter: "I don't think I've eaten so much since I don't know when."

"Good food ignores good intentions…we'll head on if you like…but you haven't told me the aftermath of Edward Ashby's accident…you said he had had a bad fall."

"Very serious, it seems…"she paused to divest the prawn of its shell and to pop it in her mouth, savouring the pink flesh. "Mmm…that was good." She poured glasses of water for both of us: "The doctors thought in the beginning that he would never walk again…he was taken to hospital in Dublin…and a distraught Sarah went with him…she stayed at his parents' house in Rathgar. It was a very stressful time for them all…and only days later their son, Derek, was born. Sarah found out from Edward's mother that they had known all along about Edward's *other side*, as Sarah put it…that they had hoped that his marriage would change all that. She couldn't bear to stay there any longer after that and she went back to Fernmount with the baby…"

While Niamh continued, describing how it was more than a year before Edward returned to Fernmount and months after that before he would be able to walk again, I could not help thinking that my mother had had to leave her home with her unborn baby, while Sarah had been able to return to her home with her baby, despite *her* misfortune.

"Edward's role in the law firm had been maintained in some measure," Niamh said, "his partner in the practice coming regularly to the house to confer with him. Other than that, Edward spent his days with his books and drawings and corresponding with galleries in London and Europe. He became very attached to their baby son Derek and Sarah began to harbour thoughts that their married life could become a normal one in all respects…Lord, when I think about it, Sarah's life was a disaster…and I'm sure you've heard enough of this story."

"No…so, I take it that Sarah's hopes were dashed?"

"Yes, they were."

"What happened?"

"Oh…" Sarah tossed her head "…this time it was to do with the son of a well-got merchant from the town. He'd come to Fernmount to learn about horses…they had a few at the time…and shortly after Edward was caught out…the same carry on as before. Apparently Edward's legal partner prevented a full-blown scandal."

"How did Sarah react to all that?

"She did the only thing she could do at the time…she up and left and took herself and the baby back to Castlemore to her mother…but there was more trouble facing her there." Niamh shook her head:" I don't how she coped with it all. Her mother was facing financial ruin and her health was poor. Sarah persuaded her to sell up and Edward agreed that she could come and live at Fernmount with them, but she died of heart failure only days after the sale was concluded. Sarah was distraught…she didn't want to go back to Edward…but there was nowhere else for her to go." Niamh sighed: "The times she lived in were certainly not in her favour. Redress for a woman…a married woman, especially…was non-existent unless she had family or an influential, independent someone to stand behind her."

"No," I said, remembering my mother's helplessness in the face of the circumstances she had found herself in.

"Being on her own, with nobody to turn to, left her vulnerable to anyone who offered a shoulder to cry on…and of course, as usually happens…there was such a body waiting in the wings…"

"A man?"

"Yes…the man who had bought Castlemore from her mother. He had been abroad for years and had just returned to Ireland. He wasn't taking possession for a few weeks so he allowed Sarah to stay on. However, he came there every day, offering sympathy and understanding…and consolation of a more physical nature in the end."

"She succumbed?"

"Yes…she described herself as being foolish. And then one evening, he began talking about her divorcing Edward, and the two of them getting married. He told her that he would expose Edward…that he would make certain that custody of her son would be given to her. She was even more upset then…and frightened. She returned to Fernmount the next day."

"And that was the end of that?"

"He didn't let her go that easily…he kept on turning up when Edward was away, promising that each time would be his last if she…" Niamh shrugged.

"And she did?"

"She was afraid not to…afraid that he would make trouble. Edward caught them, of course…was probably well aware of what was going on behind his back and had been checking up on the fellow. Edward produced some written evidence which sent the fellow legging it back to Castlemore. Sarah never saw or heard from him again.

"He must have had a wife somewhere...or been involved in something that he didn't want made public," I said.

"Bigamy wasn't that uncommon when somebody had lived abroad for a long time...and information technology wasn't anything like it is now. Whatever it was that Edward had dug up put paid to him...maybe it could have all worked out better in the end for Sarah if she'd left Edward for good."

"So...she was worse off now than before?"

"In a way...but something unexpected happened...it probably saved her from a miserable existence altogether."

"Oh, yes?"

"She found a confidante...or rather the confidante found her...a Miss Hargrove. She arrived on Sarah's doorstep looking for work as a housekeeper. She had good references...and Sarah needed someone to help her out."

"So she got the job?"

"Yes..." Niamh looked at her watch: "We should go...where did I leave my car keys?" She began searching her handbag.

"Here," I said, picking them up from behind a plate of lobster and mussel shells.

"Oh, thanks...I've mislaid my keys so many times that I get almost paranoid as soon as I can't see them."

I left Niamh and waited in line to pay for lunch, thinking that peoples' lives were never quite what they appeared to be on the surface. They were invariably like the finest Gobelin tapestries: beautiful images to be seen on the outside, but when viewed from the inside they were just a mess of indecipherable knots.

As we left the harbour, Niamh said: "The road turns inland for a bit." She waved a hand to our right: "Skirts those trees."

"A grove," I said, half under my breath.

"A groove?"

"No...a grove...a small wood"

"Oh, that!"

"Yes…and only a while ago you were speaking about a Miss Har…*grove*…," I said, looking across at her"…the woman who helped Sarah Ashby to see the wood from the trees, I gather."

"Ahh…" Niamh groaned "…juggling with words."

I waited a moment: "Did she really make such a difference in the old lady's life?" I hoped that my question would encourage Niamh to disclose more.

"Well…she certainly helped Sarah to cope with the mess her life was in…and she adored Derek, apparently. She didn't have much time for Edward, though."

"That wouldn't be altogether surprising," I said.

"No…she respected his position but that's as far as it went. Only a few months after her arrival at Fernmount, Edward's father died and his mother sold up and came to live with them."

"Not the most ideal arrangement for Sarah, I should imagine?"

"Not really…her mother-in-law lived with them for two years before she became quite ill and was confined to a nursing home for a short time where she died. Before she passed away she told Sarah that huge sums had been spent providing for Edward's future…and in keeping his good name intact…on more than one occasion."

"The old lady has really confided in you, hasn't she?"

"Well…yes…I suppose…the last thing she talked about was her son Derek…about sending him to boarding school in Dublin when he was only seven years old."

"That was very young to be sent away from home?"

"Well, apparently it was common practice among his peers at the time."

"Common practice or no it was still too young."

"Sarah herself was desolate…torn between wanting to keep him at home with her and at the same time wanting to do what was best for him. Miss Hargrove was very much against it…she was capable of tutoring him herself…and now," she said lightly "you'll be seeing the sea again any minute."

The winding road turned seaward and began rising as it reached the coast and continued snaking upwards until it levelled out above steep cliffs.

"We'll hop out here," Niamh said as she parked the car beneath an overhang of jagged rocks "there's something special I want you to see."

We held hands to steady each other on our way to the cliffs' edge, skipping over crevices in the limestone and avoiding loose boulders.

"Look!" She pointed out to sea: "The Aran Islands."

A flash of recognition of the islands' name struck me while I covered my eyes from the light of the sun, glinting off the sweep of the Atlantic below me, in an effort to focus on the hazy-blue humps rising out of the ocean.

"You should go there…especially to Inish Meáin."

"I should?" I asked, remembering in an instant where I had recognised them from: the schoolmaster, Owen Dara, had gone on holiday to them all those years ago.

Her eyes were serious: "Oh yes! There's something special about them. It's…it's like suddenly finding yourself in a place that existed somewhere in your memory, a place that you had belonged to in another life. It's like…like…" she bent her head and laughed, a light, shy laugh "…maybe it's just me…but I think they're magical."

A mile or so further on, the road ran downhill and away from the sea for a time before it turned shoreward again.

"There's a beach at the end of this track" Niamh said, after we had left the road and the car bumped along between dunes covered in thick, swaying grasses with patches of sea holly at the edges. "It's wild and beautiful."

The strand was an elongated arc of sand the colour of deep gold that made the white crests of the waves seem even whiter and gave the green of their curved underbellies the hue of polished emeralds as they pounded the shore.

In a moment, Niamh had removed her shoes and socks and was running bare-footed on the sand, waving her arms, her cries of sheer delight almost lost in the thunderous roar of the approaching sea. When I caught up with her, she was lying full-stretch in a cradle of sand among the dunes, shaded from the sting of the on-shore breeze.

She opened her eyes and smiled up at me: "I'm listening to the heart-beat of the sea" and closed her eyes again.

Yielding to an impulse that seemed as natural as the surroundings that enclosed us, I knelt beside her, and kissed her, a short kiss. I raised my head, looking into her eyes. The sparkle in them had dimmed to a mistiness that might have stretched back to the beginning of time. I kissed her again, and her hands crept over my shoulders and pressed against the back of my neck.

Niamh did not have time to linger at my hotel when we arrived back after our day out.

"Coffee is fine...I have some work to catch up with."

"I'll see the estate agent in the morning," I said, as I walked with her to her car, after what seemed like only a few minutes, and then: "Do you think you'll have time for lunch tomorrow?"

"I'll make time," she said, smiling.

"Good...I really enjoyed today."

"I'm glad."

I held the car door open and just before she sat in I kissed her again.

I stood in the car park staring in the direction that Niamh's car had taken, long after she had driven away. Our day together had been more than I could have wished for and the feeling of pleasurable warmth stayed with me until Niamh's conversation over lunch, and the remembrance of Anthea that she had brought back, returned. I felt the cooling onset of self-doubt and uncertainty and a more sombre mood descended on me.

In an instant, Anthea had changed from being as familiar to me as my own heart, to a stranger I had never known and would never know. I was fearful of losing again; of enduring once more the anger, the despair, the rejection, the betrayal. During the pain and bitterness and sadness of disentangling our lives, I had felt trapped like the badger in the burning place on the heath that I had remembered from childhood. I too had run blindingly hither and thither, facing an end I did not want to face; that I could not avoid; an end that would come, it seemed then, only with the stilling of my last breath.

I went back into the hotel and walked slowly up the staircase to my room, thinking of the philosopher of old who had turned his back on love because the pain was too great. I shrugged the thought away. I would forge ahead and let results ensue whatever way they would.

10

The asking price for Fernmount seemed not unreasonable, but I did not make an offer there and then. I would wait until I had a building engineer do a survey.

"I could help you with that," Niamh said, when I told her over lunch. "I know a very good engineer...expensive but very thorough...knows his job. I could put you in touch with him if you like."

"That would be good."

"I'll have him phone you this afternoon."

On the way to the airport that evening I told her: "The engineer said that he would have the survey completed in ten days."

"If he said that, then you will definitely have it in ten days."

I was back again in Fernmount in less than two weeks to discuss the engineer's report with him. Overall it was a positive one, confirming that the house was structurally in good shape, but that, bringing it up to standard would require a lot of work and that much would depend on the kind of restoration and the changes that I envisaged incorporating. I had expected as much and was satisfied to proceed.

When I called on the estate agents I was informed that "a good deal of interest" had been shown in the property and that offers had already been made, the most recent offer quite close to the asking price.

I left their offices and walked about the town for a time, thinking over the situation. After a cup of coffee I returned and gave them my offer. It was just above the asking price, an asking price that could easily have been much higher, except for the restoration that needed doing and which would require painstaking, skilled craftsmen to do it properly. I had the advantage of having the contacts in London who would provide me with the personnel to do just that.

The man I was dealing with only raised an eyebrow slightly when I added: "The offer stands firm for twenty four hours only. After that I will either be paying you the appropriate deposit…subject to contract, of course…or I will be withdrawing the offer and looking elsewhere."

It was a calculated gamble, the kind of gamble I had taken quite often in my business when I had no desire to wait around while somebody, somewhere, wondered if an offer could be used to extract more money either from me, or from another interested party.

Niamh called me on my mobile in less than an hour: "You don't waste any time."

I laughed.

"You're staying on until your offer is accepted or rejected?"

"Yes…I've booked a late flight for tomorrow evening."

"It means I won't be able to meet you for dinner tonight…I'll have to go to Dublin this evening."

"Oh!"

"I have to meet with Sarah Ashby in the morning. She's too old to make a decision on her own. She needs reassuring…personal contact. I will not, in any way, be trying to influence her decision. I'll just be there for her."

"I understand."

Niamh's schedule was thrown into disarray by her having to meet with Sarah Ashby at such short notice but she did arrive back in time to have coffee at the airport with me the following evening before I flew back to London.

Just before I entered the departure lounge, I said: "I'm sorry we didn't have the opportunity to spend more time together."

Niamh smiled: "If we'd had, I might not be saying goodbye to the probable new owner of Fernmount. I might not even be seeing him ever again."

"You would! If…if he was welcome, that is."

Niamh's eyes danced a little and she inclined her head: "What do *you* think?"

I drew her to me: "I think he might be welcome after all."

A few days after contracts between my solicitor and Niamh's office had been exchanged I was back again, this time in the company of an architect I had brought with me from London. There remained only a search of the title to be carried out by my solicitor and the signing of the contracts and Fernmount House would be mine.

Niamh accompanied me to Fernmount with the architect and remained while I discussed with him the work to be carried out and the alterations that I intended to make. After he had left we walked to the lake.

"It's so beautiful here," I said, "so peaceful."

Niamh smiled and I reached out, taking her hand.

"What do you really think of Fernmount...I mean the house itself?" I asked her.

"I love old houses...always did..." she answered, gently withdrawing her hand "...Andrew didn't...he thought they were too bogged down in the architecture of the past...he had dreams of becoming another Gaudi or a Frank Lloyd Wright."

She was remembering her dead husband, young and vibrant as he must have been, sharing his dreams with her for their future together. Would I have the chance to make new dreams for her to share with me, I wondered?

"I love it here," she said then, her hand finding mine in a reassuring clasp.

The lake was calm as we walked by its edge, weaving through tangled undergrowth and gnarled trees that spread their roots into the water, forming little wooden grottos, darkened and worn. Now and then a noisy water hen, wings flapping, sent ripples gently rolling to the shore and regal swans, unruffled and disdainful, glided silently in the midst of squabbling mallards.

The remnants of a wooden seat, overgrown with grasses and wild things, became visible as we entered a clearing. Further in, a hut, its timber frame covered in ivies and mosses, was set back under the spreading branches of a pine tree.

"The setting for a fairytale," Niamh said, clasping her hands in delight, "Little Red Riding Hood...or Goldilocks and..."

"There were no wolves or bears in Ireland..."

"Yes, there were..." Niamh playfully tapped my arm "...a long time ago...well, maybe no bears. And anyway, fairytales can have whatever creatures they like in them."

"Unicorns and dragons and..."

"Princes!"

"And princesses!"

"And knights!

"And knightesses!"

"Knightesses?" Niamh's laughter soared to the treetops.

"Well...witches!"

"Wizards!"

"Magicians!"

Niamh shook her head: "Same thing as wizards."

"No, they're not."

"Wizards and magicians have the same powers. They can both..."

"I should know better than to argue with a lawyer...especially when hunger is beginning to get the better of me...let's find a place to eat."

Hand in hand, we scampered back along the path, like laughing children hurrying home to the promise of supper.

The restaurant Niamh guided me to, had a traditional reed thatch, uneven walls whitewashed inside and out, and exposed rafters with old kitchen items and old tools hanging from them.

"Quaint," I said.

"There's nothing quaint about the menu...and the seafood is particularly good."

"I love seafood."

"I gathered that...that day we had lunch by the coast. Which reminds me...the morning I went to see Sarah Ashby...the morning when the estate agents called her with your offer on Fernmount...she cajoled me into spending an hour with her after we had finished our business. I really was anxious to get away...I wanted to reach the airport on time to wish you a safe flight...and of course

I had to listen to more of the family's trials and tribulations."

My immediate thought was to steer clear of the subject, but I wondered now if Sarah had mentioned my mother during any of her story-telling.

"But you enjoyed it?" I asked.

"Enjoyable is not how I would describe it."

"More difficulties…more trauma?"

"You're asking me to tell you?"

"If you want to…and other…"

"I know…other peoples' lives are more interesting…but we'll order first."

After we had done so – steak for Niamh and sea bass for me – Niamh told me that after Derek had been sent to school in Dublin, life had settled down at Fernmount for a number of years, the relationship between Edward and Sarah one of peaceful co-existence but nothing more, with Sarah believing that Edward's *straying*, as she called it, had ended and had been confined to young men of striking good looks. Her belief was to be shattered after a *very pretty* young woman came to Fernmount, to work as a housemaid.

"Shortly after her arrival," Niamh said, "the housekeeper, Miss Hargrove, was warning Sarah that the girl was *sweet* on Edward and that he was encouraging her. Sarah didn't believe that Edward's interest in her would involve anything more serious…she waited until it was too late. The girl got pregnant and this time, whatever the pressure was that was brought to bear on the family, Edward was obliged to sell his interest in the legal practice. Sarah was determined then to try and protect Derek from any further scandal and when he was old enough she sent him to boarding school in England."

"That must have been hard on her." I said.

"Yes, it was…but she wanted him away from his father as much as possible…and she found some bit of relief and distraction in his coming and going from school. She really looked forward to the holidays…they were her best times."

After we had begun eating Niamh told me that during those years, Edward still made trips to Dublin, a few to London. Sarah no longer cared about what he did or where he went. Derek's coming and goings were all that she lived for and he seemed to be developing in a way that pleased her. Her earlier fears for him began to recede and though she knew that Edward loved his son, she never allowed Derek to travel any great distance alone with his father.

"Not until Derek was fifteen years old…a sensitive age in a boy's life, I gather?" Niamh looked enquiringly across the dinner table.

"Well…the hormones certainly tend to go on the rampage…girls become the most awesome creatures…and the emotional and amorous responses lie somewhere between those of the gormless and those with a close link to an ape-like ancestry."

"Hmm!" Niamh eyes twinkled." It doesn't seem to go much beyond that for a lot of men, I'm sorry to say."

I laughed at that.

"Present company excluded, of course…," she added, "…but to finish the story…"

"Don't forget to finish your steak…my bass was delicious."

"This steak is too…"she chewed on the last pieces "…mmm…it was just the way I like it." She lifted her napkin dabbing the corners of her mouth: "So…Derek had been invited to Dublin to spend a night or two at the home of a school friend and, for once, Sarah allowed him to travel with Edward…he was off to look at some drawings, I think. After Edward had booked into his hotel, Derek went by cab to the home of his friend only to discover that the boy had been taken seriously ill just a short time before and had been rushed to hospital. Derek was sent back that evening to the hotel. He went directly upstairs to tell his father and had just entered the corridor that led to his father's room when he was confronted by the sight of his father and a young man…*passionately embracing*, Sarah said, in the doorway."

"That would have been very difficult for him to get his head round…I don't know how a fifteen year-old boy would have reacted then…or now, even, for that matter."

"He ran away from the hotel…his father hadn't noticed him…and he wandered all night alone in the city. He returned home by train the next morning in a dreadful state. Sarah tried to explain to him about his father but he wouldn't stay to hear what she had to say…just ran out of the house and into the woods. Miss Hargrove followed him and finally caught up with him. Derek barely spoke to his mother for a long time afterwards. He didn't speak to his father at all. He…"

"Would you like dessert?" I interrupted, as the girl who had served us began clearing our dinner plates.

"I could be tempted," Niamh smiled. "Let's see the menu."

The girl waited patiently as Niamh studied what was offered.

"Are you having dessert?"

"No," I said. "Coffee is fine for me."

"Good…it makes it easier for me to resist…two coffees, then," she said, handing the menu back to the girl.

"I was just thinking that Derek Ashby must have been quite disturbed…quite unsettled by his father's behaviour" I said, as I stirred sugar into my coffee.

"It had quite an effect on him, I gather…and it became evident some months after his sixteenth birthday."

"Something happened?"

"The Ashby's had a letter from Derek's headmaster…the father of a girl in the nearby village had accused Derek of…of some *impropriety* towards her, according to Sarah. Apparently, Derek avoided expulsion by the skin of his teeth…and then, when he was home on holidays the following summer, and the summer after, there were some incidents in Fernmount…*quite worrying*, was all Sarah said…I didn't press her on the issue.'

"Quite worrying could mean anything," I said, the thought hitting me then – the thought that *anything* could have included my mother.

"It didn't matter in the end…the moment he finished school he enlisted in the army…world war two was raging. He was killed only months later…he was just eighteen."

On the way home, Niamh said: "It's ironic, you know."

"What is?"

"Sarah Ashby's story…I think she came more or less to the end of it with the death of her son…and on the same day that she sold the family home."

"It does seem ironic alright."

"The end of a life...the end of a family line...well, almost," Niamh continued to muse "...and the end of a story...no more to tell."

No more to tell for Niamh, I thought, but Sarah hadn't told her the whole story; hadn't answered all the questions that needed answering.

11

How quickly life can change direction, I thought, on the flight back to London. I had gone back to Ireland the first time with a vague sense of hope that I could come to terms with the not knowing who my father was and to face the shadows that had been cast on the lives of my mother and me during the short time we had lived in Ballycrag. Only a matter of weeks had elapsed since then and I had been back to Ireland again and again, only now there was nothing vague about my purpose: I was within days of taking possession of the house wherein I had been conceived and the young life of my mother altered in such an unimaginable way. And I had met with a beautiful woman who had brought a resurgence of promise and hope for the future back into my life. Despite this transformation, the moment the plane touched down at Heathrow, I had a sudden feeling of apprehension. The emotion was fleeting and was replaced by optimism for what was yet to come.

Just days before the deadline for the closing of the sale of Fernmount a phone call from Niamh brought back the apprehension, only stronger: "Sarah Ashby wants to meet with you."

"Oh! Why?"

"I think she just wants to take a look at the man who is taking over her home…to reassure herself that it is going to be in good hands."

"Could you not have assured her of that yourself?"

Niamh Laughed: "Of course…but I already vouched for you credentials…your being a respectable gallery owner in London, with your mother as your only living relative as far as I knew…and, oh yes, I might have said that your mother had been in banking."

I was quite taken aback at Niamh's mentioning of my mother to Sarah Ashby. I had not told Niamh anything about the events of fifty years ago. When she had asked about my family I had told her: "I never knew my father...he was out of our lives before I was born. My mother married my stepfather, a director of the bank she had worked in for years...when I was in my teens." I had also told her that I had rushed into marriage a long time ago; that it had been a mistake and had lasted only a few months; and that I had had no contact with Anthea for a very long time. I had quickly turned the conversation to something else then.

Her words shook me now and I said without thinking: "Can't we close the sale without my having to see her?"

"I'm sure we can...but it might be a courteous and understanding thing to do to accede to the old woman's request."

I hesitated: "Let me think about it. I'll call you."

Niamh was undoubtedly puzzled by my reaction, maybe even disappointed in me, but I could not help that. She could not have known the turmoil in my mind that her seemingly simple and relatively unimportant request had stirred.

What was the real reason behind Sarah Ashby wanting to meet with me, I wondered, except perhaps that she had somehow made the connection between me and the girl, my mother, that she had thrown out of her home all those years ago. Would confirmation of this mean that she would withdraw from the sale of Fernmount? Would the ensuing explanation to Niamh of the reason for her action change Niamh's perception of me, affect our growing relationship in some way?

While I had been keeping my mother informed of what had been happening, I realized now that I had spent most of the time talking about Niamh and had shown no real consideration for the affect that my buying of Fernmount might be having on her. I had given no thought to the painful memories that might have been awakened; or to the feeling, maybe, that she was being betrayed all over again.

"I didn't expect to see you today," my mother said as I followed her to the kitchen. "Would you like some tea...coffee?"

"No, thank you...I came up because I'm not sure what to make of a request from Sarah Ashby."

"Oh?"

"Niamh phoned me earlier to tell me that Sarah wants to see me...I mean, everything is in order...there's nothing more to be done...there's just her signing of the contract. The closing date for the completion of the sale is only a few days away...and now this."

"Did you not ask why she wants to see you?"

"Niamh doesn't know...she thinks that the old lady just wants to see what the new owner is like before she signs."

"But you don't think that's the reason?"

"I don't know."

"Did you not ask your own solicitor?"

"No...I came straight here after Niamh phoned."

My mother frowned: "It can't be anything of importance. Your own solicitor would have been informed if it was."

"I never thought of that."

"So...you think that, maybe, she has made the connection between you and me...that if she has that it will affect the sale in some way?"

"I...I suppose so."

"I doubt that. She must be very old by now...she probably doesn't even remember me. It might simply be an old woman's curiosity...I wouldn't think you have anything to worry about.

I felt at ease for a moment and then I remembered the other thought that had been running through my mind: "How do you really feel about my buying Fernmount?"

She paused before answering: "It just seems so extraordinary. So...so strange in a way. When I went there all those years ago...it was like walking into another world...and now..."

"Does the thought of my buying it upset you in any way?"

"No...it just brings back memories...if anything it gives me a sense of...of redress...of vindication in a kind of way."

"What should I do about Sarah Ashby?"

Again, she paused: "I don't think it would do any harm to go and see her...but it's entirely up to you."

I called Niamh later that evening.

"As soon as you set up the meeting with Mrs Ashby, I'll fly directly to Dublin...spend a night there, maybe. Thursday next would be a good day for me...the day before the closing date."

"Thursday will be fine...any day would have suited...all I have to do is phone the nursing home and tell them when you'll be there. I expect her to be ready to finalise the sale the moment after you've seen her...sign the contract and all that."

"You'll be in Dublin on Friday, then?"

"Yes...but I'm actually going up on Wednesday...I've a few things to do. I could collect you at the airport."

"That would be great..." I hesitated "...and what hotel would you recommend?"

"The one I usually stay in...the food is good. I'm not sure about the seafood, though."

"Could you book me in there?"

"I could...what accommodation would you require?"

"I...well...would you...would you consider...sharing?"

There was silence for a moment and I held my breath.

"Sharing?"

"Yes."

"With whom?"

"With the purchaser of Fernmount."

"Oh, him! Yes...I would."

She must have heard the breath leaving my body and laughed.

12

After my arrival at the airport, Niamh drove directly to our meeting with Sarah Ashby. Our journey through the city was slow and Niamh showed her exasperation as the heavy traffic came to a halt on more than one occasion.

"It seems to get worse and worse, each time I come to Dublin now. I don't know how people living here put up with it. I know I…"

"The tail-back of the tiger?" I ventured, not at all put out by the situation, happy just to be with her.

"The what?"

"You know…the Celtic tiger."

"Oh! *That* tiger…there are times I wish that it had never been born."

"The country seems to be thriving on it…by the way…has Mrs Ashby said anything more to you about why she wants to see me?"

"No…and the more I think about it, the more I think that she's just adding a little bit of extra drama or something…or whatever…to the last big event in her life. She *is* very old you know…you will have to be extra patient with her."

"I'll try to remember that…but nothing happened that was in any way different from your usual sessions with her?"

"Nothing…nothing that I can think of…except…the last time I was with her she asked me to show her your photograph again."

"What photograph?"

"The one Michael Sullivan took of you and me together the night you came to dinner." She was blushing now.

"You never told me you had it. Where did…?"

"Michael sent it to me."

"And you said nothing about it…how did Sarah Ashby know you…?"

"I just happened to have it with me when she asked to see me after she had agreed to the sale of Fernmount." She was quite embarrassed now.

"And you just showed it to her?" I asked, covering the instant thought that had occurred to me, that perhaps it was the photograph that had been the source of Sarah Ashby's interest in my personal details and not just my name,

"Well…no. She asked me how long it might take to sell the house and I told her not too long, maybe…then I said I already had a query from somebody…"

"From me?"

"Yes…I didn't say who you were…or anything about you…not then. It's just that I…I only had the photograph a day or two. I thought it was a very good photograph. I…I just decided to show it to her…I don't know why. If you open the pocket in front of you…there's a brown envelope…it's in that. I hope you're not offended or annoyed? I mean, I wouldn't…"

"No…no," I assured her, taking out the envelope and extracting the photograph. It showed Niamh and me in smiling conversation, our faces angled towards the camera. It was a close-up and had been enlarged.

"It *is* a good photograph…of you certainly," I said. "I'm not so sure about me."

"I look terrible. It's you who looks…"

"You look…beautiful."

She laughed then, and I asked her: "Did you get all your business done yesterday?"

"No…as soon as I leave you with Sarah Ashby, I'll be off to an appointment…for which I'll probably be late."

"Oh, sorry…that's my fault."

"It won't matter if I'm a little late. I'm not sure how long my business will take…it could be quite a long meeting. You can call me as soon as you're ready…I'll know better then. At least you'll be able to enjoy the sea air while you're waiting."

Thoughts of Sarah Ashby receded for the moment as the memory of our first day by the sea brought the warmth of anticipation rolling over me.

The sun was high in a near-cloudless sky by the time we reached our destination. The nursing home overlooked a small harbour and, out in the bay, white sails were making slow progress in a light wind. Fishermen cast their lines from the quay wall and the quiet was broken now and then by the sharp cry of a gull.

The sister in charge conducted us upstairs and out onto a veranda.

"Your visitors are here, Mrs Ashby."

The small, hunched figure seated at a white painted metal table, shaded from the sun by the overhang of the roof, her back to us, turned her head slightly in our direction and barely lifted a hand in acknowledgement.

"I will be in my office if you need me."

The sister left us as Niamh walked round the table and faced Sarah Ashby: "How are you, Sarah? It's a beautiful morning, isn't it? I have Mr Luhan with me."

"I'm well, thank you, Niamh." Her voice was reedy, but clear.

Niamh nodded towards me and as I moved to stand beside her, made the introduction: "Mr Luhan…Mrs Ashby."

I waited for her to extend a hand and when she did not I said: "How do you do, Mrs Ashby?"

She studied me intently for a moment "How do you do, Mr Luhan?" She looked back to Niamh: "I would like to speak to Mr Luhan alone, Niamh."

"Certainly, Sarah."

Niamh smiled as she passed me: "Call me when you've finished."

Sarah waited until the door closed behind Niamh: "Please sit down."

The metal legs of the chair scraped against the floor as I settled in the chair opposite her.

"You came over from London?"

"Yes."

"You have an art gallery there?"

"Yes, I do."

"Paintings?"

"Yes."

After a moment's silence she asked: "You will have work done on Fernmount...restore it to what it once was?"

"Yes...I hope to."

"It was wonderful when I first came to live there," she smiled, a tiny smile "I was charmed by the house...everything about it. We had dinner parties and picnics by the lake...the lake is wonderful, don't you think?"

"It is, Mrs Ashby."

"Yes...those were wonderful days..." she sighed wistfully. "It all changed so...so quickly and then...then Edward, my husband, had an accident...just before my son, Derek, was born." She paused: "You were educated in England, Mr Luhan?"

"Yes."

"My son was at boarding school in England. He joined the army from there...he was just eighteen. The war was on, you know." She turned her head to the side, looking out over the bay: "War is a dreadful thing...and Derek was so young. They sent him to the front. He never came home again."

"I'm sorry," I said.

In the brief silence that followed I studied her. Wispy, white hair, brushed away from her forehead and her temples, came together in a little bun under a tortoiseshell comb at the back of her head. The parchment-like cheeks, stretched over high cheekbones, had a faint blush of applied colour, and pink lipstick matched the pink of the high-collared blouse cradling her chin. A white linen jacket, bunched over her shoulders, accentuated the physical deterioration ageing had brought with it.

"Yes..."she resumed, her head still turned to the side "...before he was sent to the front he was allowed a brief visit home. He looked so handsome in his uniform...I was so happy."

She lapsed into silence again for a moment, before turning to me: "We had a dinner party for him...a number of guests. It was a wonderful occasion...and Derek was so full of life. When...when the evening had ended and all but Miss Hargrove, my housekeeper, had retired for the night I spent some time alone with him…the last time that we had together on our own." She paused, withdrawing a small handkerchief from the sleeve of her blouse and dabbed at the corners of her eyes: "You know, Mr Luhan, I always seemed to be saying goodbye to him…from the time he was a child." She tucked the handkerchief back into her sleeve: "His life wasn't easy…his father was not…not what a father should have been. It did not help Derek. He was always trying to be manly and larger than life. He brought a lot of trouble on himself."

I could feel the burn of resentment beginning to grow inside me.

"When I left Derek and went to bed that night it seemed as though I had just closed my eyes when Miss Hargrove shook me awake to tell me that…that the young girl we had brought in to help…she was staying overnight…was missing from her bed. We…we found her in my husband's room."

"Why are you telling me this, Mrs Ashby? Why did you ask me to come here?"

"I asked you because…because there are some things I feel I must tell you."

"Yes…but…"

"I will explain, Mr Luhan…please bear with me."

I made no reply and she continued: "The only thought I had then was to have the girl out of my house…"she looked away, "…I was so terribly upset. I had been through it all before…there had been other incidents…I could not face any more." She turned her head back to look at me: "When the girl's father arrived later that morning there was quite an upset but Edward was able to settle the matter. It appeared that Miss Hargrove had discovered that the girl had left her room in the early hours…to meet with one of the farm workers…that she had mistakenly returned to Edward's room…to his bed. I did not question anything. All I wanted was to be free of the situation…to have it go away. Some time afterwards I learned from Miss Hargrove that the girl's father had been back to see Edward again…that the whole affair was finally at an end."

"Mrs Ashby," I tried to keep my voice even, "*the girl*...the girl you're referring to...who was she?"

She paused a fraction: "Annie...Annie Luhan."

"Annie Luhan is my mother's name, Mrs Ashby."

"Yes...she was a beautiful young girl...very beautiful...but please...please bear with me, Mr Luhan."

But for Niamh's admonition to be 'extra patient with her' I would have insisted that she get straight to the point of what my visit was all about.

"It was weeks later that Dr. Ryan, our family doctor, informed us one evening over dinner that Annie was pregnant...that she had left the area. I did not dwell on the matter...my only concern was for my son. And then...then the dreadful news came that Derek was missing in action...presumed dead."

She turned her head to the side, plucking at something on the sleeve of her jacket: "Edward began rising very early...sometimes at four or five o'clock in the morning...wandering about the house...going for long walks by the lake or through the woods. Other times he spent night and day locked in the library with his books and his drawings. On several occasions Dr Ryan had to be called to persuade him to at least leave it long enough to eat something."

She faced me again: "One morning...two or three months after the news about Derek...he left the house. No one noticed his going...it was Miss Hargrove who missed him. He was found later that evening. He had collapsed while crossing a stream in the woods...his mouth and nose had been covered by just a few inches of water and he had smothered."

She began fiddling with the tortoiseshell comb, bending her head to reach it: "I was so angry...he had brought so much grief into our lives and had simply left it all behind...had left me to pick up whatever pieces were left."

I might have felt sympathetic towards this frail old lady, but I could not forget the part she had played in our lives, especially my mother's.

"I burned every photograph of him," her head was still bent

"…and his papers and letters from museums and galleries from all over Europe. I would have destroyed his drawings too, but for Miss Hargrove. I saw them as part of all that had deprived us of a life together."

She stopped fiddling with the comb and patted her hair, lifting her head to look at me again: "I never knew what went on inside his head…but he hurt others…he hurt me…he hurt Derek." Her eyes seemed to look beyond me now: "Derek felt that he had to prove himself…not just in the way any young man feels that he has to…he had to prove that he was not like his father. He…he had to have conquests. I don't think he could accept being spurned by any woman. He…" She paused, her eyes fixed on me now: "You're so like him…the same eyes…the same…"

"Like who, Mrs Ashby?"

"Like…like your father

I rose from my chair: "Who was my father, Mrs Ashby?"

There was a long pause before she turned to look up at me: "My husband was your father. My husband…Edward Ashby."

I walked to the rail that surrounded the veranda. The breeze coming in from the sea, warmed from the sun, fanned across my face and unconsciously I loosened my tie, removed it and opened the buttons of my shirt.

I don't know how long I stood there but not a word passed between us during that time. We might have been familiar friends that were comfortable enough in each other's presence not to feel threatened by, or fearful of silence.

When I returned to the table Sarah Ashby was sitting with her head resting against her shoulder, her hands in her lap. She looked tired and worn, like an old discarded shoe caught in the light of an evening sun. I might have left her then, but I had to know the whole truth.

"Mrs Ashby, what happened that night in Fernmount?"

She straightened herself with effort and laid her small, curled-in hands on the table: "Miss Hargrove was aware how…how Edward and Derek and the other men were observing Annie all evening. She gave Annie tea with some of Edward's sleeping draught in it and sent her to bed early…"

"Why?"

"She believed that if Annie fell into a deep sleep that it would safeguard her in some way. It was very wrong…very misguided." She drew her tiny hands from the table and down into her lap. "She meant no harm to your mother…she never, ever trusted Edward. After he had said his goodnight she checked his room a short time later…he was not there. She…she found him in Annie's bedroom. By then, the sleeping draught he had taken, had begun to take its full effect on him…she had to use all her strength to help him back to his room. She changed the bedclothes on your mother's bed believing, perhaps, that your mother might not even realize what had happened to her when she woke the following morning. Miss Hargrove came downstairs then and behaved as though nothing had happened."

"And nobody saw or…heard anything?"

"No…the party was still going on. Later that night, unable to sleep, she worried that if there was any trouble that Derek might be blamed. She rose from her bed and half-dragged, half-carried your mother to Edward's room and put her in the bed beside him, knowing that he would remain asleep because of the sleeping draught. She even gathered her clothes and laid them on the floor by his bed. She…"

"You knew all this…and you made not the slightest effort to try to…to…redress the situation?"

"I only found out after Miss Hargrove died…it was too late then."

"Did you not think that…?"

"It was all too late…and she had never meant to hurt Annie. After she died I found a personal record that she had kept among her things…it was from this that I learned the truth of what happened to your mother that night at Fernmount…"she paused, "…and I found out that Miss Hargrove was my natural mother, Mr Luhan."

"Your mother?"

"She was forced to give me up when I was born. She…she had sworn never to try to contact me or lay claim to being my mother while she lived."

"She never said anything?"

"She carried guilt and shame with her all her life…and she was afraid…afraid that I might have rejected her. She had waited until mother's death to come to Fernmount. She was very protective of me and of Derek from the moment she came to us."

She placed one small hand back on the table this time, as though balancing her tired body.

"That morning after Annie had gone away Miss Hargrove came back up to Edward's room and brought me to my room. I could feel her body trembling as she helped to settle on my bed. I did not know then that she was deeply regretting her actions; regretting that she had not allowed matters to take their own course…that she had begun to fully realize what she herself had done…that she had no recourse but to continue with the deception. It…it…" she was really wilting now and her voice was weakening "…it was a little later in the morning…before Annie's father came to Fernmount that she told me the story about the farm labourer. I believed her. She had already given Edward the same story…to use to defend himself. She had saved him…but only because of me…*and* Derek. And because of what she herself had done."

She looked away then and I stood up, drawing back my chair.

"Edward never meant to hurt anyone…" she was still turned away from me "…he…he just couldn't help himself. He was obsessed with anybody or anything beautiful. He…he tried to possess it…like his drawings. He…he tried to explain it to me in the beginning…tried to make me understand."

"I should leave now, Mrs. Ashby."

A few moments passed before she turned to me: "The house needs a lot of attention…and the garden." She smiled, a thin, regretful smile: "I loved my garden. Without my garden, I don't know how I should have carried on…especially after…after Miss Hargrove passed away." Her smile faded: "I could not keep it up eventually. It became too much for me…and I couldn't find the help anymore." Her eyes seemed to close now: "Would you please ask Niamh to come and see me tomorrow…to finalize everything?"

"Yes."

"What are left of the furnishings in the house are yours…and Edward's drawings. They are stored in a chest in the attic." Again a wistful smile touched her thin lips: "They meant so much to Edward."

"Thank you."

"You will come and visit me again?"

My thoughts were already deep in a shadowy landscape.

"Goodbye, Mrs Ashby."

Epilogue

It is quiet here by the harbour that lies just below the nursing home. I have been here since leaving Sarah Ashby. After I had arrived, I had waited a few moments, breathing in the tangy air, willing the slow beat of the sea to roll over me; and then, I had called Niamh.

"I'm sorry," she had said, her voice guarded and just above a whisper. "I won't be finished for another couple of hours…maybe more."

"That's alright…I'll be fine…" I had tried to make my tone light, "…I can enjoy the sea at my leisure…build a sandcastle."

That is what I have been doing all summer long, I thought, after I had pressed the *off* button on the phone: *I have been building a castle of sand to which I have pinned all my hopes and dreams; and now, in the blink of an eye, it will melt into the sea leaving behind only a memory of what might have been.*

That was hours ago and while I have been waiting for Niamh, it is as if all of my life's recollections have passed before me, surging and receding in my mind like the waves along this shore and all the other shores wherever the seas caress or pound the boundary of the crumbling land. The deep's unending song is no longer a soothing chant but a lament for the passing of a dream.

Before setting out for Heathrow Airport and my flight to Dublin this morning, I took a short walk by the Thames. The sun, sparkling off the calm waters, was in perfect harmony with the optimism I was feeling for the day. Any doubts I had had that my meeting with Sarah Ashby would be anything other than just polite conversation were cast aside. Foremost in my mind was the thought that Niamh would be waiting to meet me when I arrived at Dublin Airport. That optimism has changed to fearful uncertainty now and all the misgivings and mistrusts that I had thought that I had laid to rest have returned.

Any moment of hopeful expectation that rises in me is quickly overtaken by the bleakness of the reality of how I was conceived in the house that is meant to be the foundation on which I had thought to build a new and better life. The belief I had had that I could, in some way, vindicate my mother's life and the lives of all that were ravaged within its walls has faded: I see only spectres from the past that are mine to exorcize; and I don't know if I am equal to the task.

The embers of faith that still faintly glow within me will only flame into life if whatever trust Niamh has already placed in me will remain after I have told her of Sarah Ashby's revelations. How can I disclose the truth to her, without her believing that I used her simply as a means to add to what little I already knew? And what doubts will enter her mind when she wonders about how much of my father lies within me? Will she wonder too about my marriage to Anthea and what really happened?

The truth about my father has neither brought the relief nor the closure I had once believed it would. At this moment, all I can think of him is of someone who indulged unbridled passion with no thought of the consequences for those he used to satisfy his unworthy appetites. At the end, Sarah Ashby had said *he was obsessed with anybody or anything beautiful. He...he tried to possess it...like his drawings. He...tried to explain it to me in the beginning...tried to make me understand."*

What was it that he had tried to make her understand? That his life had been governed by instincts that he had struggled against, and failed to control? That, in immersing himself in what he saw as art of the highest form, that he had sought to rise above the pain and isolation that his way of life had imposed on him? Had he believed that he had found a comforting, maybe even a spiritual, realm that had enabled him to find solace or excuse for a life that was completely out of step with what was acceptable; or was his obsession with his drawings, whatever their artistic or uplifting merit, nothing more than a means of escape from taking responsibility for his actions?

An image of my mother, young and beautiful, her dreams swirling around her still intact, looms before me. What do I tell her: that the man who had told her that *beauty is what makes this world bearable…makes it possible for us to go on living and hoping even in our darkest moments* had been the man who had brought ugliness and pain into her life and had left her dreams in tatters?

To keep silent may be a kindness, or a further betrayal of her trust. My father had taken the promise of her life from her while giving life to me. Am I, the fruit of his transgression, destined to strive to redeem him in some way? Is that why I was led by some devious trick of fate to Fernmount? Has fate also decreed that whenever I am presented with the elusive opportunity for happiness that it has to be torn from my grasp in some unworthy or undeserved fashion?

Fearful anticipation strikes me now at the thought of Niamh's imminent arrival. I want to believe that she will understand why I did not tell her the whole story, or at least what I knew of the story, the moment she began to relate what Sarah Ashby had told her. Will her trust in me be irreparably broken if she cannot accept that neither I nor my mother knew the truth about the circumstances of my conception?

Whatever the outcome, there is no turning back: I have to keep faith with what I had hoped for; yearned for. The road into the future will not be without its twists and turns; will still broaden and narrow; will lead me to the highways of certainty and the byways of doubt; but it will be going forward; and I will keep trust.

Acknowledgements

My thanks to my son, Angus, for his preparation of all aspects of the manuscript for publishing. My thanks also to Annette Treacy for her insightful comments and suggestions; and to my daughter Shelley for her proof-reading of the manuscript.

My grateful thanks to Kathleen Campbell for being my inspiration and support throughout.

www.ingramcontent.com/pod-product-compliance
Lightning Source LLC
Chambersburg PA
CBHW031059260626
47172CB00001B/126